The Star of Morcyth

The Star of Morcyth

Book Five
The Morcyth Saga

Brian S. Pratt

The Star of Morcyth
Book Five of The Morcyth Saga
Copyright 2005, 2010 by Brian S. Pratt

For information concerning books written by Brian S. Pratt, or where to obtain them in either paperback or eBook formats, visit the author's official website at:

www.briansprattbooks.com

ISBN-13: 978-0983338406

Books by Brian S. Pratt:

The Morcyth Saga

The Unsuspecting Mage
Fires of Prophecy
Warrior Priest of Dmon-Li
Trail of the Gods
The Star of Morcyth
Shades of the Past
The Mists of Sorrow*
***(Conclusion of The Morcyth Saga)**

Travail of The Dark Mage
Sequel to The Morcyth Saga

Light in the Barren Lands
Book 2 *Forthcoming 2011*

The Broken Key

#1- Shepherd's Quest
#2-Hunter of the Hoard
#3-Quest's End

Qyaendri Adventures

Ring of the Or'tux

Dungeon Crawler Adventures

Underground
Portals

Non-fiction Works

Help! I don't Want to Live Here Anymore

For all my readers, whose enthusiasm has kept me going. Two in particular I would like to mention. Joey from California, the first to express an interest, and Bjorn from Germany, whose suggestions and emails kept the fires of creativity alive.
Thank you all.

Chapter One

"I'm close enough!" states James with finality. Had he known this was part of the deal he never would have agreed to it.

"You've got to see it for yourself or it isn't binding," Rylin says from across the room.

"I can see just fine from where I'm at, thank you."

"No you can't," Rylin says with impatience. "There can be no doubt. Now get over here."

Reluctantly moving closer, he says, "If I would have known I was going to have to do this I never would've agreed."

"We didn't realize you didn't know," says Rylin. "I don't like it any better than you do, but custom is custom. We thought you knew and by the time everything got underway, it was too late to change."

Moving closer, he stops halfway across the room. "Closer," prompts Rylin and he slowly moves until he's near.

"Will this do?" he asks, voice a little raspy.

"Yes," replies Rylin. "You're not looking," he accuses him.

Turning his eyes, he looks at Rylin and watches.

"There," says Rylin. "Did you see it?"

Red faced, James stammers, "Yes."

"Alright then," he says. "Get out of here."

With great relief, James turns and rushes for the door, glad to be out of there.

Opening the door, he hurries out and shuts it behind him. Blood rushing to his face, he looks over at Miko who's one of a hundred people staring at him expectantly. He's got a mischievous grin on his face, earlier he got to listen to James as he bemoaned this particular duty he was to perform for his friend Rylin.

The crowd grows silent as the door shuts and every eye is upon him. Clearing his throat, he says loud enough for everyone to hear, "The marriage has been consummated." A cheer rises up from the crowd and the musicians waiting nearby begin a lively tune.

Shortly after returning from his expedition to Saragon, a messenger arrived with an invitation to the wedding between Rylin and Sheila. Rylin asked him to be the best man at the ceremony since he more than any other had helped this union to be. Of course he gladly accepted.

The ceremony was to be held in Trademeet where Sheila's family ran their family business. He took Miko, Jiron and Fifer with him, everyone else remained at The Ranch. The festivities lasted a week, at the end of which was the wedding and this particular duty the best man was to perform. Of course he didn't actually find out about his duty until the third day into it and by that time it was too late for him to back out.

It was the quaint little custom of their religion that someone had to witness the consummation of the marriage in order for it to be binding in the eyes of the people. That job traditionally fell to the best man.

Shawna approaches him and asks, "Will you be staying long after the feast tonight?" The feast was the final activity in the week long celebration of her daughter's wedding. The week long celebration wasn't a week long party, that aspect only started on the sixth day. Up to then, it's smaller things only the family and close friends attend.

"Maybe," he replies. "I'm waiting for the return of Jiron and Fifer. When they show up I'll be heading back home."

"You were right," she says to him. "He does love her more than anything and I'm thankful you made me come to see it. I just wish her father had lived to see this."

"So do I," he replies.

"But enough talk, there's a wedding to celebrate," she says. "Go find a beautiful girl and dance."

"I may just do that," he tells her.

"You'll have to excuse me," she says as she moves away to talk with a richly dressed gentleman. He's another wealthy trader who's been a long time friend of hers.

He looks around for Miko but he's disappeared in the crowd. On the far side of the courtyard are tables set up with all manner of food, including tarts. James is afraid that they may not have enough for the ravenous appetite of Miko. Sure enough, he sees Miko coming toward him with another berry filled tart in hand.

"Isn't that your seventh?" he asks as he draws near.

"Maybe," he replies, wiping his mouth off on his sleeve. "Haven't been keeping track." Smiling, he then shoves the rest of it in.

James just gives him a grin and shakes his head.

Just then Darria, a daughter of one of the trading houses here in Trademeet comes over and takes Miko by the arm. Dragging him over to the dance floor, she soon has him in line to begin the next dance set.

Miko has begun to realize that since the Fire prematurely aged him and made him a man, that the girls are beginning to take notice of him. At first he hadn't known what to do and every time one came to him, he would get all nervous and shy away. But ever since coming to the wedding, his attitudes are certainly changing.

When before the thought of going out onto the dance floor terrified him, now he joins in with glee. Darria has had the most to do with it. Ever since laying her eyes on Miko, she's marked him for her own. James figures that if they were to live here in Trademeet, Miko would be lost and soon married. But since they're not staying more than another day or two at the most, he doesn't have much to worry about.

He crosses over to where the food tables are set out and helps himself to the fare. The roast goose is especially good and he takes an extra helping as well as a variety of others. Turning back to the dancers, he finds Miko out there moving gracefully with a smile on his face. Yes, he's definitely coming into his own.

If only Meliana were here. The girl whom he met when he was in the city of Corillian has been on his mind lately. He would give anything to be able to see her again, perhaps one day he can make the trip back down to see her.

Occasionally others would come and see if he cared to dance, and once in a while he accepted. He did actually enjoy the dancing here, he prefers the structure of it over the types which were common back home in California.

Hanging out at the edge of the crowd as is his want, he continues eating while watching the people and eventually hears a round of applause beginning as Rylin and Sheila emerge from their home. He's dressed very fine and she wears a startling dress worth more than some common laborers make in a year.

With her hand resting on his arm, they make their way to the dance floor. James walks over and reaches the edge of the dance floor just as the musicians begin to play. Dancing by themselves, Rylin and Sheila move gracefully to the music, the people around them talking quietly amongst themselves while they watch.

Miko comes to stand next to him and he looks to see if Darria is with him. When she isn't, he asks, "Where's your girlfriend?"

"Talking with some friends, I think," he replies. "They sure do make a good looking couple don't they?"

"Yes they do," James replies.

As the musicians bring the music to a stop, Rylin and Sheila end the dance facing each other and then give each other a kiss to the cheering of the surrounding crowd. Breaking off the embrace, Rylin turns to the crowd and holds up his hand for quiet.

Once the crowd has quieted, he says, "I thank you all for joining us in this most happiest of times." The crowd erupts in cheers again briefly before quieting back down. "My lovely wife Sheila and I would like to express our appreciation for our best man James, who's stood by us through this entire ordeal." Another round of applause, though not as energetic as the previous one breaks out and a few snickers as well. It's been the running joke of the celebration about how James reacted when he learned of having to witness the consummation of the marriage. He had the misfortune of having it witnessed by many and has been the butt of many off colored jokes since. "There's plenty of food and drink. Enjoy!"

Signaling the musicians to begin, he takes Sheila's hand as they begin another round of dancing. This time, other couples join them.

James moves again to the side of the festivities since crowds make him nervous. He's never been one who liked being around a lot of people. Taking his position on the fringe, he watches the dancers, including Miko whom Darria has dragged again to the dance floor.

As he enjoys the music and watches the dancers, he takes notice of two scruffy looking individuals moving along the outer edge of the crowd. Moving to intercept them, he makes his way through the crowd.

"Thought you guys would never make it back," he says.

"You worry too much," replies Jiron. Fifer just grins at him.

"Did you get them?" he asks.

Jiron pats a bulge in his tunic and gives him a nod. "We got plenty," he says.

"I couldn't believe how many there were," exclaims Fifer. "I mean, you and Jiron told me, but I didn't really believe. But then when we went into that cave, my god! There must be thousands more waiting to be harvested."

When the messenger arrived with the news of Rylin and Sheila's impending wedding, he decided this would be a good time to collect more of the gems from the cave in the Merchant's Pass. Taking Jiron and Fifer with him, he sent them up the river shortly after arriving to try and find the entrance to the cave where the gems lay. Jiron was sure he could locate it, so he and Fifer went to search for it while he attended the festivities.

Jiron had taken several of the gems when they last passed through and had them appraised by Alexander back in Trendle. He told them that the gems were of good quality and highly sought after, especially by gem cutters. He informed them of one down in Bearn who would pay an honest price for the rough gems. James then secreted them in his stash in his room at The Ranch to await Delia's caravan. If she were to sell them, it would draw less attention to him and his activities than if he did it himself.

Roland was glad to see the gems, their immediate problem for coins had been solved. If they made routine expeditions to gather more, then they would never again have to worry about money.

"You guys get cleaned up," he tells them, "you're pretty ripe."

"Was planning to," replies Jiron. "Just wanted to let you know we're back."

"Better hurry, the feast is going to start in a couple hours," he says.

"Will do," Jiron says as they begin heading away from the celebration and to the room he and Fifer are sharing while they're in town. Shawna had agreed to put up James and Miko, but told him the other two would need to find an inn in town.

When the music stops, Miko hurries over to him and asks, "Was that Jiron and Fifer?"

Nodding, he answers, "Yeah."

With a slightly disappointed look, he says, "Then we'll be returning in the morning?"

"That's right," James tells him. "Go dance with her while you can."

"You know it!" exclaims Miko as he makes a beeline for Darria. Shortly they're back on the dance floor.

James sees Shawna standing off to one side talking with another of her trader peers and makes his way over to her. When she sees him coming, she says a few more words to her friend before disengaging and moving to meet him.

"Jiron and Fifer showed up so we'll be leaving first thing in the morning," he informs her.

"I understand," she says. "We're all glad you were able to make it."

"I wouldn't have missed it for anything," he assures her. Unsure if whether or not it would be a breach of protocol, he extends his hand and asks, "Would you care to dance?"

A smile begins to spread across her face as she replies, "Yes, I would like that."

As the musicians bring the current song to a close, he escorts her out to the dance floor. Rylin and Sheila see them coming and make room for them. Taking their places, all stand ready as the musicians begin another moderately quick song and the dancing commences.

The rest of the evening goes by quickly. The feast, the last in a long line of feasts they've attended throughout the celebration, is by far the grandest. Speeches are made and the festivities last far into the night. Before the feast actually begins, Fifer and Jiron make their appearance. Freshly cleaned, each is wearing a new outfit bought just for this occasion. Jiron is much more pleased with this attire than he had been with the one he wore back in Corillian at the ball celebrating Nate's return to his family.

Throughout the night, Miko dances primarily with Darria though another girl somehow manages to get him out of her clutches briefly. By the end of the night, everyone is tired. The couple for whom this is for has long since retired, Rylin saying he was tired but no one believed him. Especially when he flashed them all a grin as he and his bride leave the hall.

James finally disengages Miko from his admirers and takes him up to their room on the second floor. "Made quite an impression didn't you?" he asks.

Miko gives him a grin and replies, "They have nice girls here in Trademeet."

"That they do," he agrees.

Back in their room, they get undressed and are soon asleep in bed.

The morning dawns a little grey, and with the summer now over, there's a bit of a chill in the air. James is the first to awaken and gets dressed quickly. "Wake up!" he hollers over to Miko who groans as he opens his eyes. "No sleeping in today, we have a long way to go."

Sitting up, Miko tries to come awake as another large yawn escapes him. "Do we have to leave so early?" he asks, swinging his legs over to the floor.

"Yes," replies James. "I would like to make it home before tomorrow night."

"Couldn't we leave later and get there the next day?"

"No. Now get up," insists James.

With another pitiful groan, he gets up and commences to put his clothes on. "It's cold!" he complains when his bare feet hit the stone floor.

James just gives him an annoyed look. Strapping on his slug belt, he then puts his shirt on, effectively covering it. Never again will he be caught ill prepared should something go wrong.

Waiting impatiently for Miko to finish getting ready, he moves over to the window and looks out over the city. From their room, you can see across Trademeet to the Silver Mountains. Clouds blanket the sky and he hopes rain will not be in their immediate future.

Turning around, he finds Miko slipping his boots on. "Ready?" he asks.

He slips on the last boot and stands up, "I suppose so."

"Good," he says. "Let's go."

Leaving their room, they head down the hallway to the stairs and take them down to ground level. The smell of the morning's breakfast greets them before they even arrive at the dining hall.

Rylin and Sheila haven't come down yet and he hates to leave without saying goodbye. Shawna is there and waves them over to sit with her. "They probably won't be down until later," she tells them. "Newlyweds."

"I understand," he assures her. One of the servants brings over a plate of food for both he and Miko.

"Just tell them we wish them all the best and sorry to have missed them," he says.

"I will," she replies.

The breakfast is a hearty one of eggs, ham and bread. James gets a large glass of milk, freshly milked this morning and tasting quite a bit different than the pasteurized milk he's used to getting back home. When they found out he liked milk, they made sure to always have some on hand. Fresh of course, he doesn't care for chunks in his.

Once they're done eating, he makes his goodbyes to Shawna, leaving her with a slight kiss on the cheek.

"Come back when you can," she tells them.

"We will," he replies. "And if your travels bring you near Trendle, be sure to stop by."

"I promise," she says.

Miko is finishing his second plate of food when James stands up. "Let's go," he says to him. Grabbing two slices of the bread he makes a ham and egg sandwich to eat as they go. "Bye ma'am," he says to Shawna as they leave the kitchen.

After stopping by the estate's stables to get their horses, they ride through town to the inn where Jiron and Fifer are staying. They find them finishing their meal. All are soon mounted and heading through the streets to the western gate.

They'll follow that road until they reach the crossroads an hour or two out of town where they will turn north toward the town of Villigun. A none too exciting town, mainly an agricultural center for the region. Shortly after that is where they will enter the Forest of Kelewan. Within its borders will be where they will stay for the night. After that it'll be one more full day's ride and then home.

Thankfully, the rain withholds its presence through the first day and they make it all the way to the Forest without any delays or problems. All in all it's been a rather pleasant journey.

James isn't very talkative during the ride, his mind mulling over what he learned in Saragon when he and Jiron went back there. The old man's riddle continues playing in his mind:

When the Fire shines Bright,
And the Star walks the Land.
Time for the Lost,
Will soon be at Hand.

At the foot of the King,
Bathe in his Cup.
Pull his Beard,
To make him sit Up.

Seven to Nine,
Six to Four.
Spit in the wind,
And open the door.

The first two lines make the most sense, an obvious referral to the Fire of Dmon-Li and the Star of Morcyth. After that it gets a little confusing. He's also worried about Igor's fate. The strange little creature that saved him during his time in that other land, reality, or it could've just been a dream. If it had been real, did he survive? He may never know.

The girl Aleya they hooked up with after Saragon, Jiron and she seem to be getting serious as well. She's currently back at The Ranch. Jiron offered her to come with him, but when she found out Roland was teaching people to read, she opted to stay there and learn. That had hurt his feelings but not much he could do about it.

Actually, the class of just a few students has grown as news circulated through the community. Now he not only has all of the irregulars, Jorry and Uther have joined as well as many of the sons and daughters of the farmers in the area. Roland has set the limit for his class at twenty, charging two coppers a week for those not affiliated with The Ranch.

James at first argued with him about charging, but his reasoning was this: if they're willing to pay then they'll be willing to learn. He didn't want a bunch of deadbeats hanging around just so they'll be out of their parent's way for awhile. Remembering the layabouts in his classes back home that were there simply because they had to be, he understands the logic.

Once they've moved past Villigun and enter the Kelewan Forest, he's surprised at how much his anxiety level rises. The memories of those first few fateful days upon this world still haunt him. Although this time he's in the company of friends and has little to worry about from a pack of wolves. His magic could take care of them readily enough.

As they're setting up camp, Miko removes his crossbow from the pack mule and goes in search of dinner. By the time they have a fire going, he's returned with two large rabbits. In no time at all, they're skinned and roasting over the fire.

A light drizzle begins by the time they're ready to call it a night. Fortunately they've managed to find a tall tree with wide limbs under which they can take shelter. Only a very little water works its way down to where they are, the majority runs off the outer limbs leaving them dry.

The drizzle continues on through the night and is still present when they get underway the next morning. From what the locals tell him, this sort of weather is common for this time of year. When winter comes in full force, it gets rather cold and a foot of snow from a single storm isn't unheard of.

As they make their way through the forest, the canopy of leaves which covers the road keeps the worst of it off of them. The road is fairly straight and they make good time. With only a brief stop for lunch before continuing on, they ride fast and are pretty sure they're close to Trendle when daylight begins to fade.

A shadow disengages itself from the treeline ahead of them and when they draw near can see that it's Yern.

"What are you doing here?" James asks.

"Waiting for your return," he says.

"Why?" he asks. "Nothing wrong is there?"

"Don't know for sure," he replies. "It's just that Ceryn has us posted along the roads from Trademeet looking for you. He would like you to meet him at his cabin." He holds up his hand to forestall any further questions and then adds, "He didn't tell us why, just said it was important for you to go there, alone, before you return to The Ranch."

"Alone?" he asks.

Nodding, Yern says "Alone."

James glances to Jiron who only shrugs. "Don't look at me," he says.

"Could you be in some kind of trouble?" Miko asks. "Lord Colerain maybe?"

Worried, James replies, "I don't know." To the others he says, "When we get to Ceryn's cabin, you continue on to The Ranch and I'll be there later."

"As you wish," Jiron says.

It isn't very far before they come to where Ceryn's cabin lies, sitting off the road a little ways. Two horses are tied out front, neither of them are Ceryn's. "Looks like he's got company" states Jiron.

"Looks that way," replies James. Turning his horse toward the cabin, he says, "You all go on home. I'll be along directly."

"Good luck," Miko says as he and the others continue on toward Trendle and The Ranch.

He sees a light coming from the front window as he rides up. Securing his horse to the front post next to the others, he starts walking to the door when it opens and Ceryn steps out.

"Greetings James," he says, a smile on his face.

The fact that he's smiling puts him at ease as he replies, "You too, Ceryn." Extending his hand he gives him a firm handshake. "What did you need to see me about?"

"Come inside and we'll explain," he says as he leads him into his cabin.

"We?" James asks as he follows Ceryn in. A smile breaks across his face when he sees Perrilin sitting in a chair against one of the walls, his instrument propped up beside him. "Perrilin!" he exclaims as he comes over to greet him.

Coming to his feet, the bard asks, "Been a while hasn't it?"

Giving him a hearty handshake as well, James nods then takes the seat across from him and asks, "What brings you around here?"

"Actually, that's a rather interesting story…" he begins as the door to the bedroom creaks as it starts to open.

James' attention is drawn to it. Suddenly, the door swings wide and a young man steps out. His lower jaw quivers, eyes are opened wide. "J...James?" he stammers.

Jumping to his feet, James replies in utter astonishment, "Dave?"

Chapter Two

"Oh James," he cries out and comes forward, tears streaming down his face.

James takes him in his arms, concerned for his friend as wracking sobs come from him. "Here, here, it's alright," he says in a soothing manner. He glances back to Perrilin.

"I found him in the Empire," he explains. "I was playing that song of yours and he came forward. Thought there was something odd about the way he was acting so I investigated. It was hard to piece things together, he doesn't speak the common tongue at all and only a smattering of the Empire's. But the fact he didn't speak any language I knew well, plus his reaction to the song all made me realize something was odd. Then it hit me that he might have come from where you did."

Taking his friend over to one of the chairs by the table, he sets him down and then takes the seat next to him. "Are you okay?" he asks.

Dave's face comes up, tear tracks down both cheeks as he asks, "What?"

Then it hits him, Dave was still talking in English and he had asked the question in the common tongue. Having been so immersed in the language of this world for the past month or so, he has to consciously work at getting the correct English pronunciation out. "Are you okay?" he asks again, this time in English.

Dave nods his head, "I am now."

"What happened?" he asks. "How did you get here?"

"After you went through the door for the interview, I sat there and waited for you," he explains. "I must have waited there for an hour before I started getting impatient. I got up and went over to the door to listen to what was going on inside but couldn't hear anything."

"I knocked on the door and when I didn't receive any answer I opened it. You could believe my surprise when all that I saw on the other side was an empty office with no other way out."

"An office?" asks James. "Didn't you make it to this world when you went through the door?"

Shaking his head, he says, "That came later. I got worried and called your name. I knew you hadn't come back out through the waiting room so I didn't know what to think. Then the stories of the missing people came to mind and I hurried down to the lobby where I called 911."

"The police showed up quickly and cordoned off the entire area. When I told them what happened, they didn't believe me. They searched the office and didn't find any trace that anyone had ever been in there. They did find traces of you and me in the waiting room."

"They took me down to the police station and questioned me extensively. What they were asking me began to make me think they thought I had something to do with your disappearance. After what must've been hours, my mom and dad finally were allowed to take me home."

"Outside the police station, the reporters began their inquisition as my dad took me to the car. My mom said a brief statement about how she was just glad I was okay before getting into the car with us. When we got home, your grandparents were waiting for us in the driveway."

James sat back at that. He knew they would've had a bad reaction about his disappearance and now he's going to hear about it.

"Your grandfather asked me what happened while your grandmother cried. I sure felt sorry for them and told them all I knew, which really wasn't very much. My parents invited them in and while I went to bed, they stayed up all night talking. The police stopped by sometime in the night and asked my parents more questions. Sometime before I woke up, your grandparents left for home."

"I wish I could tell them I'm okay," James says sadly.

"I know," replies Dave. "They really care about you. Anyway, I stayed home all day Sunday, didn't leave my room. I was hoping you would call or the police would find you since they knew where you had last been, but nothing. When the news hit about you and that I was the last one to have seen you, Seth's dad shows up at our place, demanding that I tell him where his boy is."

"He grew angry and almost came to blows with my dad. In a fit of rage, he finally left, but not before giving me a look saying 'this isn't over'. That's when my dad turned and saw me there. He gave me a look, a look that cast doubts about whether he believed me or if I hadn't told everything. What more could I say?"

Ceryn comes over with two cups of ale and sets them in front of the two friends then returns to his seat. Neither he nor Perrilin are able to understand what's being said.

Taking the offered cup, Dave takes a drink then continues. "Seth's dad was seen driving slowly past our house a couple of times that afternoon but thankfully never stopped. My dad was worried about what he might do. He suggested that I stay home from school on Monday but I didn't want to just stay at home and dwell on things. I actually thought going to school would take my mind off things. How wrong I was."

"I no sooner got to school the next day when other students, kids I've grown up with come to me and begin accusing me of being the killer. Can you believe that? Me? A couple friends of Seth from the football team dragged me in the boy's bathroom and beat the crap out of me, at which time I was sent home. I was suspended for fighting!"

"A group of reporters were waiting for me outside my home when I got back. They flew at me like a pack of vultures and started asking me the most outlandish questions. Like, 'Why did I kill my best friend?' and 'How does it feel to know everyone thinks I'm a killer?' stuff like that. I tried to bull my way through but they were blocking my way. Finally my dad showed up from work and shoved them aside. After we were inside and the door was shut, I went straight to my room and closed the door."

"My life was beginning to spiral down into the gutter. Not only do I have the worry of what happened to you, but now everyone thinks I'm guilty. Even my parents were no longer as supportive as they had been. Of course in my state of mind I may have imagined that, but I knew I had to find out what happened to you. And the only place to do that was back where I last saw you."

"So later that night I sneaked out and wearing that hat from Bakersfield that was always too big for me, I was able to sneak to the bus stop before anyone recognized me. I took the bus downtown and made it to the building on Commercial. A cop was stationed in the lobby. I waited until he was distracted by another person then hurried over to the elevator and got in. The door closed before he had a chance to see me. I got off on the twenty third floor and went down to room 2334."

"The doorway was covered in that yellow police tape. I didn't really expect to find anything there, after all the police had gone through with a fine tooth comb and they didn't come up with anything. But I knew I had to do this. Removing the tape, I opened the door and stepped within."

"That's when I was hit from behind and fell to the floor. I turned and saw Seth's dad standing there. 'I thought you might come back here. The killer always returns to the scene of the crime,' he said. I then told him, 'I did not kill anyone!' But he didn't believe me."

"He came at me and I scooted away, knocking over a table in my attempt to escape. He kept yelling at me to tell him what happened to Seth and the others all the while trying to reach me. I scrambled away, finally got back to my feet."

"I saw the blow coming and tried to block it but it connected with my jaw and actually knocked me back off my feet. I crashed into the wall and fell onto one of those small tables that were there and knocked it over. Books and magazines went flying. I felt a static shock from something before he grabbed me and threw me across the room."

"Hurt and praying nothing was broken, I got back up and looked into the eyes of a madman as he approached me. I had to get out of there, all thoughts about finding out what happened to you gone. I was now simply worried about my own survival. He was between me and the door to the hallway outside. I tried to make it around him but he caught me and after a quick two blows to my stomach, threw me again across the room where I crashed through a door and hit the floor."

"Groaning, I twisted to look at him coming and the shock of what I saw, after all I've been through must've been too much and I passed out."

"What did you see?" James asks.

"When I came to, I was lying in a clearing. Standing over me was this little creature, it had a weird hat and some kind of vest or something. It frightened me and I got up and ran away through the trees. I could hear it calling to me but I wasn't paying any attention to what it was saying. The enormity of what I was experiencing was overwhelming."

"At first I thought I was hallucinating, and then after awhile thought maybe this was the afterlife, though it sure wasn't any afterlife I'd ever heard about." He takes the cup in his hand and takes several more drinks.

James can see he's looking to him for a response, but he's not sure what kind to give him. That creature was definitely Igor, of that can be no doubt. But why doesn't Dave have an understanding of the language like he did? Could it have been because he ran away from Igor? Hard to say for sure.

"I experienced the same thing when I went through the door to the interview," he tells him. "The creature you met is an agent of a god in this world, he's really not all that bad." After taking a drink himself, he asks, "Then what happened?"

"What happened?" parrots Dave. "I ran and ran and ran hoping to find a way home. I eventually came to the edge of the forest and saw several people riding horses, as well as one man leading a team of horses pulling a covered wagon. Running out of the forest, I yelled to them and flagged them down." A haunted look comes over him as his voice softens, "I thought they would help me. I was wrong." Tears begin welling up in his eyes and a sob begins to escape him.

"They weren't interested in helping me," he says, eyes looking toward the floor. "When I came close to them, they began talking to me in a language I never heard before. I tried to tell them I was an American and that I spoke English, but they didn't understand."

James can see his emotions getting the better of him and says, "It's okay, you don't have to tell me anymore."

"I need to," he says as a tear runs down his cheek. "I was later to find out they were slavers, on a raid to take people so they could sell them at a slave market."

"When one of them dismounted and drew a wicked looking knife, I knew I was in trouble and tried to get out of there. I turned and ran but was soon overtaken. I fought with them, but they overpowered me. They tied my hands behind my back and with their knives, cut my clothes off of me. Stripped naked, they hauled me up into the back of the wagon. Two other people were there, one was a young girl. I..." Overcome with emotion, he stops his narrative.

James lays a hand on his shoulder and says, "I understand. I've run across these slavers before and I know the kind of people they are. You needn't tell me anymore than you feel you must."

Dave brings his eyes up off the floor and gazes into his friend's as a smile comes to him. "That first night was the worse. The things they did to that poor girl..." a shiver runs through him. "Anyway, we traveled for days. I gradually began to be able to understand basic commands. They captured several more, and when they had ten of us tied and naked in the back of the wagon, they made for the slave market."

"We traveled for days and that covered wagon got extremely hot while the sun was beating down upon it. When we at last came to the slave market, we were separated and ushered into pens. I was there for three days before it became my turn up on the slave block."

"My first master was none too pleased to discover I didn't speak the language and beat me often. Within days, he sold me to another who treated me even worse. I longed to die, just to end the humiliation and agony which had become my life. But I simply couldn't bring myself to do it."

Lifting up his tunic, he shows James the patchwork of scars, the result of being beaten and tortured by his former owners. From neck to waist, he can see where his friend had been cut, burned and who knows what. Dave twists and he can see his back is even worse. "I'm sorry," is all he can think to say at the horror his friend must have endured.

Replacing his tunic, he continues, "Finally I was sold to an inn and worked there until I heard him play 'Home on the Range'. I couldn't believe what I was hearing at first. Then something came over me and I had to reach him, to see if he was real. In the back of my mind I knew I would be facing a beating, but I couldn't stop myself. I rushed through the crowd and made for the stage where he was playing. But I didn't make it. They stopped me before I could reach him and dragged me out of there. I was beat to within an inch of my life."

"As I lay there in my pen later that evening, pain throbbing in every part of my body, Perrilin came to me. You know the rest."

Tears in his own eyes, James comes forward to give his friend a hug. "You're safe now." Glancing back to Perrilin, he says, "Thank you for bringing him here."

"I take it you know him then?" asks Perrilin.

"All my life, he's my best friend," replies James.

"How did he come to be here?" Ceryn asks.

"I'll tell you sometime, but right now I just want to get him back to The Ranch," he says. "You're both welcome to come too."

Perrilin shakes his head and says, "I can't. As much as I would like to find out more about this, I have an engagement that can't be put off any longer."

"I'll come by in a few days," Ceryn tells him.

Getting up, he brings Dave to his feet as well and says, "Thank you both again." Leading Dave outside he says, "Let's go." He hears the other two get up and follow them outside.

Indicating one of the other horses, Perrilin says, "Your friend can have this one."

"Thanks," James says. Helping Dave onto the horse, he then mounts his own.

As they ride back to The Ranch, James glances over to his friend. Glad to have him with him again, yet saddened by all that's happened to him. He may never know the extent of the pain he went through, and he's not really sure he wants to.

After getting back onto the main road to Trendle, Dave breaks the silence and asks, "How have you been?"

"Not too bad," James replies. "I have a place and some friends here. I'm sure you'll fit in just fine."

"I want to go home," he says sadly.

"I know, I'd like to as well, but I'm afraid we're stuck here," he says. Feelings of guilt assail him as they reach the outskirts of Trendle. Where his friend has had the worse sort of experiences since coming to this world, he's actually thrived. He comes to the conclusion he'll put off telling him about his magical ability until it's absolutely necessary. Not sure how he'll react to that.

"This is the town of Trendle," he tells Dave as they pass through. "Not much more than a farming community, but it's a nice place to live. The people are good, if a bit stand offish at first. You'll like it here."

Dave looks around but makes no comment.

After leaving Trendle, they soon come to the lane leading to The Ranch. Devin has the duty of guarding the entrance today. When he sees James coming, he takes his horn and blows a single note.

James pauses upon reaching him and asks, "What was that for?"

"They wanted to know when you showed up," he replies with a smile.

When he glances to Dave, James says, "This is my friend Dave. He doesn't speak the language yet."

Devin gives Dave a nod who nods in return.

Getting the horses moving again, they make their way down the lane to the house. Indicating the construction going on, James says, "I'm having a new house built as well as a few other buildings."

"Doing well then?" Dave asks.

Sighing, James replies, "Yes, actually." Almost everyone has come out to see what's going on, they're all anxious to find out what went on over at Ceryn's.

A quiet muttering can be heard as they approach, many casting glances to Dave riding beside him. As he comes close, James says, "This is Dave, a friend from where I come from." At that, he can see several of them react in surprise, the ones who know the full tale of his past. "He doesn't speak the language yet, but I want each of you to treat him well."

To Caleb, Illan says, "Take their horses."

"Yes, sir," he replies and steps up to take their reins as they dismount.

"Ezra has dinner ready for you," Roland tells him. "When you have a minute, we need to go over a few things." As James gives him a questioning look, he adds, "Nothing pressing."

"Okay," he says and then to Dave he asks, "Hungry?"

"You bet," he replies.

Leading him through the front door, James takes him through to the kitchen where Ezra has two plates set out, each overflowing with food. Someone must've forewarned her about Dave, maybe saw them coming down the lane from the road.

As he sits down to eat, he can hear Illan from the other room telling everyone to go about their business and to leave him alone with his friend. Miko, Jiron and Roland join him at the table. After a brief round of introductions, he gives them a brief rundown of what Dave told him.

James can feel the awkwardness in the room and realizes the dynamics of his group have just changed with the introduction of an important person from his past. None, even Dave, are sure of how to act or what to do. But he hopes that will change over time.

To Roland he asks, "What's going on?"

"Delia returned with the money from the sale of those knives you made," he begins. "Got twelve hundred golds for the lot. She also dropped off another sack of crystals, it's out in your workshop. Surprised you didn't pass her on your way through Trendle, she just left."

"I gave her some of those gems Fifer and I collected," adds Jiron. "She's going to try and find that gem cutter Alexander mentioned next time she's in Bearn."

"It looks like our money problems are over," Roland says happily.

To Jiron he asks, "Where's Aleya?"

"She and Errin are out hunting," he explains. "They've become rather good friends and have appointed themselves the hunters of the group. Makes sense as they're the best with bows we have."

"She's picking up her letters pretty quickly too," adds Roland.

"How is the class going?" James asks him.

"Most are doing well," he says. "I've started them off with basic letters and we'll progress from there."

Nodding, James continues eating as he mulls over the information they are giving him. From the front room, he hears Tersa begin a song as the evening gathering commences. Finishing his meal, he says to Dave, "Every evening, we have a get together in the front room where people sing songs or tell stories. Let's join them."

Looking slightly out of place, Dave hesitantly says, "Okay."

They get up and make their way to the front room where James sees his favorite chair vacant as well as another someone placed next to it for Dave. Taking their seats, they settle back as Tersa finishes her song.

After a song by Jace about a farmer and his cow, Jorry and Uther begin another of their improbable tales. James does his best to translate for his friend while they relate the events of a journey to save a merchant's daughter from a band of slavers.

During a lull, he relates Dave's tale one last time to those gathered so they will better understand what's going on with him. As well as to squash any wild rumors which may be in the making.

By the end of the evening, Dave has begun to visibly relax. The stories and songs, though in a language he's unable to comprehend, helps to bring him into the group. When at last it's time for it to end, James offers to share his bed with his friend. When they're in his bedroom alone and the door closes, Dave turns to James and says, "I'm glad I found you."

Sitting on the edge of the bed as he begins pulling off his boots, James replies, "Me too. I'm really sorry you went through what you did."

"Hey," interjects Dave, "you didn't do the things that were done to me, and I don't want you to feel blame. It's not your fault."

James just continues getting undressed in silence. Then both he and Dave crawl under the covers and they spend the next hour talking of home, the things they miss the most, that sort of thing. Eventually, sleep comes and takes them away.

Chapter Three

AAAAHHHHHHH!!!!!

A cry in the night startles James out of a dead sleep. Dave is thrashing around in the bed next to him caught up in some nightmare. He turns to him and shakes him vigorously as he says, "Wake up!"

The door to his room bursts open as Jiron rushes in wearing nothing but his nightclothes with both knives drawn and ready.

Dave sits up and lets out another scream as he snaps awake. "He's just having a nightmare," James says to the crowd who's gathered at his door. "Go back to bed."

"Thought someone was dying in here," comments Jiron as he leaves the room, shutting the door behind him.

Dave's eyes dart around for several moments as if he's not aware of where he is. Slowly, his breathing begins calming down and his eyes settle on James. "You okay?" James asks.

"Yeah," he says, voice quavering. James can still feel him shaking from whatever nightmare he just experienced. "Thought I was somewhere else for a minute."

"Where?" James inquires.

Turning his eyes to James, he says very quietly, "I don't know. It's fading."

"That's the way with some dreams," says his friend. "Just try to go back to sleep."

"I'll try," replies Dave.

What happened to him in the Empire must've really screwed him up. Worry about his friend keeps James from falling asleep for awhile, but eventually he makes it.

The next morning, he wakes up before Dave and gets dressed quietly so as not to wake him. Going to the kitchen, Ezra prepares a plate of food and sets it before him on the table.

From where she's cleaning up at the washbasin, she asks, "How is your friend?"

"Alright, I guess," he says. "Did he disturb you last night?"

"I think he disturbed everyone last night," she replies.

"Sorry about that," he apologizes. "He went through a bad time in the Empire."

"I understand," she says.

He eats in silence and when he's through tells her that he'll be out in his workshop should anyone need him.

Once out the back door, he sees where Illan has the recruits doing morning exercises as they begin their daily drill. Glad he's not one of them, he walks across to his workshop and goes inside.

The sack of crystals Delia brought is sitting atop his workbench. He checks and finds them similar to the ones she brought before. Next he goes over and makes sure the receiver crystal isn't aglow. A glow would indicate someone or something has disturbed the hiding place of the Fire. He'd hate to think what that would mean. Satisfied it has remained undisturbed, he goes back to the problem of what he learned in Saragon.

If the old man's family hasn't unraveled the mystery in the centuries it's been in their keeping, what hope do I have?

Knock! Knock!

"Come in!" he hollers.

The door opens and Dave walks in. "Good morning!" James says cheerfully.

"You too," he replies. The cheerfulness that he once knew in his friend is nowhere to be found. The harshness of his recent past has subdued his spirit measurably.

"What are you doing?" he asks as he comes over to the workbench. Looking around, he takes in the sack of crystals on the floor next to him and the other things James has in his workshop. Reaching down, he picks up one of the crystals out of the sack and takes a look at it.

"Just some thinking," James replies.

"You always did do a lot of that back home," he says.

James considers what to tell his friend about his life here, what he's up to and what he can do with magic. "True," he says. "I want to show you something."

Putting the crystal back in the sack he asks, "What?" Turning to look at James he sees him holding out his hand, palm up. Suddenly, a glowing orb appears, springing to life upon his hand. "Whoa!" Dave exclaims as he leans closer to look. "How did you do that?"

James cancels the orb and it disappears. "Remember that ad I showed you in the lunch room?"

"Yeah," he replies.

"Remember how it said 'Magic! Real Magic! Ever wanted to learn?'?" he asks. "Since coming here, I've been able to do magic. I even brought Rocky to life."

"Rocky?" questions Dave, not entirely understanding what he's talking about.

"Sure," he says. "That stone construct you always used to use during our role playing games."

"Oh, right," he says. "How do you do it?"

"Just concentrate, think what I want to do, and it happens," explains James. "That's the basics though it is a little more complicated than that."

"Can anyone do it?" he asks. "Could I?"

"Maybe, I don't know," he says. "Most of the people of this world can't. You need a calm mind and concentration, I don't know if you'll be able to right now in the state you're in."

Holding out his hand, Dave concentrates on forming something similar to the glowing orb he saw James make. After several moments, nothing happens. Lowering his arm, he gazes to him with a frustrated look. "Can't do it."

"Maybe once you're life has quieted down you'll make it happen," encourages James. He can see his friend's disappointment at not being able to summon the orb.

"Maybe," he says. "What else can you do?"

"A lot," he replies. "Whatever I can imagine, provided I have enough power to do it, I can."

For the next several hours, they sit and talk about this world, magic, and some of James' experiences since coming here. He doesn't mention the Fire or some of the other stranger occurrences he's encountered, like spirits of dead priests and headless torsos.

After lunch, he takes Dave back to the workshop where they spend the rest of the afternoon just being together and talking of old times. It seems that reminiscing about the past brings him a better mood, or maybe it's just being away from the others.

That night during the evening gathering, Dave seems a little more animated, as if his old self is once more trying to assert itself. A smile actually comes to him during one of Tersa's songs.

Seeing his friend come alive more and more gives James encouragement that the devastation wrought upon him by his time as a slave may not be irreversible. On their way to bed after the evening winds down, he actually hears his friend humming one of Tersa's songs to himself. He goes to sleep feeling much better about things than he had the night before.

Get out!

A cry startles him out of a sound sleep in the middle of the night. Then another scream followed by the sound of a scuffle. Thinking they're under attack, he grabs his slug belt and races out the bedroom door.

In the light of a candle held by Roland, he sees Jiron on top of someone outside of Tersa's door. One of his knives is held to the throat of the man on the floor. As he comes closer, he sees it's his friend Dave.

"What happened here?" he demands as the others in the house come to see what the commotion is. Illan and Fifer both have their swords in hand believing an attack was in progress.

Everyone starts talking at once. "Quiet!" he shouts, cutting through the noise. Everyone becomes quiet as they look at him. Turning to Jiron he asks, "What happened?"

"Your friend here was about to accost my sister!" he says with vehemence.

"I didn't do anything James," exclaims Dave. "I swear!" He may not have understood what Jiron had said, but the accusation in his voice was unmistakable.

From the doorway to her room, Tersa says, "He came in here and grabbed me!"

He sees the pleading in Dave's eyes and the anger and promise of violence in Jiron's.

"I'm sure this is all a misunderstanding?" he says.

"Misunderstanding?" shouts Jiron. "I aught to kill him right now!"

"I went to the bathroom and got mixed up in the dark," pleads Dave. "I got lost and went into the wrong room!" He looks to James, imploring him to believe him.

"Get off him Jiron," he says.

When Jiron hesitates, he adds, "Now please."

With hate in his eyes, he gets up off the frightened Dave. The knife in his hand remains out and threatening.

"Dave, get back to our room," James tells him.

Scrambling to his feet fast, Dave moves quickly to James' room and they hear the door shut.

Every eye is upon him. "He simply went into the wrong room is all," he tells them. "I've known him a very long time and I assure you, he isn't like that."

Jiron comes close to him and says, "Just keep him away from my sister. I held back because he was your friend, I won't a second time." After meeting his eyes for a second in defiance, he turns and moves into Tersa's room and then shuts the door.

"Everyone back to bed," Illan announces to the rest. "Nothing more to see." As the others begin moving back to bed, he comes over to James and asks quietly, "Was it a mistake?"

"It has to be," James says defensively. "Dave isn't like that."

"A mistake it may have been, but whatever trust he had with everyone in this house is now gone," he says. "If another 'mistake' occurs, I believe Jiron will make good his threat."

"So do I," he says. "I better go see how Dave is doing." Turning around, he makes his way back to his room.

Inside, he finds Dave sitting on the bed facing the door. "You have to believe me James, it was an accident."

"I do," he replies shutting the door behind him. "But no one else here does. You'll need to step carefully for awhile and rebuild their trust."

"Why don't we just leave here, the two of us?" Dave asks.

"I can't," he says. "I've been through too many things with these people to suddenly turn my back on them. They're all good, solid friends, you've just gotten off to a bad start. But once they get to know you better, they'll come to see what kind of man you are."

"Thanks for saving me back there," he says with a slight smile.

"You're welcome," James replies. "Just don't make that mistake again."

"Rest assured, I won't," states Dave.

"Now let's go back to sleep."

Lying back on the bed, he listens to Dave as he slowly succumbs to sleep. He's worried about his friend. This was not a very auspicious beginning and the others are not going to be too trusting of him for awhile. The worries churning in his mind at last quiet down and he's able to fall asleep.

The following morning at breakfast, those still there when he and Dave come to the kitchen give Dave cold stares and hardly talk at all. Most excuse themselves as soon as he and Dave sit down.

Ezra fills their plates and Dave's is decidedly lacking in the better portions of the food. He may have missed that little nuance, but James certainly picked up on it. After last night, it's only what he expected. He's actually surprised that Ezra didn't demand he go out and eat with the recruits. Probably would've if he hadn't been friend to the master of the house.

The morning goes pretty much the same. Wherever Dave goes, the others either pointedly ignore him or slight him in some small way. James feels bad for his friend, but knows only time will heal this rift between his friend and the others.

A little before noon, two notes are blown by the sentry down at the road and every one rushes out to see what's going on. James and Illan are standing outside the front door as a rider comes toward the house.

"He's wearing the King's colors," Illan says. "Which means he's on official business."

"What in the world would bring him here?" asks Jiron.

"I don't know," Illan replies.

The man is wearing the coat of arms of the King of Cardri. James recognizes it from his time in Cardri earlier when he met with the Archive Custodian, Ellinwyrd. The appearance of the herald can only be bad news.

As the herald reins up before them, he dismounts, turns to them and says, "I bear a message from King Colbern, King of Cardri for the mage known as James. Would one of you be he?"

Stepping forward, James says, "I am."

Removing a rolled scroll bearing the wax seal of Cardri, he extends it to him. "I am to await your response."

Taking the scroll, he cracks the seal and reads it:

To the Mage known as James:

You are forthwith summoned to appear before the Royal Court with all due speed.

His Royal Majesty,

King Colbern Cardri

He shows the letter to Illan and then asks the herald, "Why am I to appear before the Royal Court?"

"That was not told to me sir," the herald replies. "I am simply to await your reply and then return to the King."

"Give us a moment," he says. The herald nods his head.

Indicating they should go back into the house, James moves inside and the others follow. "What do you make of it?" he asks.

Handing the letter back to him, Illan replies, "I don't know. Maybe your reputation has at last reached the King and he wants to see you for himself."

"Maybe. But what should I tell him?" he asks, gesturing to the herald waiting outside.

"You have to go," he tells him. "You cannot ignore the summons of the King, no matter what. Not if you wish to reside in his kingdom."

"He's right," adds Roland. "A local noble here and there is one thing to antagonize. But it wouldn't be wise to put the king of the land against you, as surely would happen should you ignore his summons."

"So I have to go all the way to Cardri?" he asks.

"Yes, you have no choice," Illan states.

"There's always a choice," he says as he returns back to where the herald is waiting.

The herald sees him coming and says, "And what is your reply?"

"You may inform his majesty that I will leave first thing in the morning for Cardri," he tells him.

"Very well," he says. "I shall so inform his majesty." Mounting his horse, he turns it around and rides down the lane back to the road.

James watches as he reaches the end and turns onto the main road. Glancing at Jiron, he says, "Not only do I have the bother of people coming here to gawk at me, but now I have to travel for days for the King to."

"This may prove beneficial to you," he replies.

"In what way?" James inquires.

"Ellinwyrd, the Royal Archivist in Cardri you mentioned before, may be able to help you with what you discovered in Saragon," he explains.

Nodding, he says, "You may be right." To Illan he says, "I'd like you and Fifer to accompany me to Cardri. I'll also bring along Miko, Jiron and Dave."

At the mention of Dave, Jiron gets a dark look. The thought of traveling with him brings back the anger from the night before.

Seeing his reaction, James turns to him and asks quietly so only he may hear, "Would you rather me leave him here?"

Realizing that would be even worse he shakes his head. "No," he says, "best to bring him along."

"You know, he really isn't a bad person," James assures him. "I'm sure last night was just as he said, he simply went into the wrong room. He probably got confused being in a strange house in the dark."

"Maybe," Jiron says, though the tone of his voice tells he doesn't believe that. His eyes dart to the door and he sees Dave standing there. Turning around, he stalks away from the house.

James can hear Illan mumble under his breath, "This is going to be a fun trip." Shaking his head, he knows that if they just give Dave a chance, they'll come to find out he's not nearly as bad as they think. They've just gotten off on the wrong foot.

He returns to the house and takes Dave out through the kitchen where he picks up a couple of towels. Leading them through the back door, he leads him out to his bathing pool.

"What are we doing?" Dave asks as they approach the water.

"Taking a bath, why?" asks James.

"Out here?" he asks.

"Sure," replies James. "Not much privacy around here." When he sees Dave hesitating, he adds, "Everyone knows to avoid this area when someone's here. Don't worry, no one will disturb us."

"Okay," agrees Dave hesitantly. As he gets undressed, James can again see the patchwork of scars and mutilations across his body. No part of him seems to have escaped the wrath of whoever owned him.

As they settle into the water, James is greeted by the coldness. Taking baths here certainly cannot continue much longer. He glances over to the construction site of his new house. The outside is practically complete and the inside is coming along nicely as well. Soon he'll be able to have a hot bath.

During the time they spend in the pool, they talk about inconsequential things. James learns a little more about Dave's time in the Empire, but nothing of any real relevance. He in turn, tells of some of his exploits.

By the time lunch is ready, he's ready to get out. Drying themselves off with the towels, they get dressed again and head back to the house.

The rest of the afternoon is taken up with preparations for their trip to Cardri. James is annoyed at having to make the trip, but at the same time is looking forward to seeing Ellinwyrd again. Maybe as Jiron suggested, he could help in figuring out the enigmatic riddle he came across in Saragon.

The riddle continues playing through his mind,

When the Fire shines Bright
And the Star walks the Land.

Time for the Lost
Will soon be at Hand.

Time for the Lost. What could that mean? Suddenly, a memory comes to him, something he hasn't thought about for quite some time. It was during the time when Igor had taken him to Disneyland in that dream, vision, whatever it was. He had bent over and picked up a wallet. But it was what he said about it that stops him in his tracks:

> *"Sad when something gets lost," he tells James. "When you lose something, you always hope an honest person will find it and work to get it back to you. All too often though, you never see it again. Such is life."*

Could there be a connection? Something to do with Igor is lost? Or with Morcyth? His mind churns over the idea. Other visitations by Igor have had ulterior meanings, why not that one. He always thought that particular one had to do with Disneyland being a focal point. But maybe it was to do with returning something that was lost.

A shiver runs down his spine as he suddenly comes to the realization of what this could all be pertaining to. The Star of Morcyth! *Of course! That makes perfect sense.* Taking out the medallion bearing the symbol of the Star, he holds it up and looks upon it. *Could that be why I'm here? To find the lost Star of Morcyth? Then that could mean the second and third stanzas of the riddle could be directions to lead him to it.*

He hears Ezra call them for dinner and he practically skips on his way to the dinner table. Excited, he takes his seat and the meal commences.

"What's got you all happy?" asks Miko from where he's filling his plate with boiled tubers.

"Oh, nothing," he says. But the grin on his face belies his statement. He would like nothing more than to talk about it, but too many here don't know the whole story and it wouldn't be wise to mention it in front of them.

"Sean said the new house will be ready in a couple weeks," Roland says. "Maybe when you come back, you'll be able to move in."

"That would be nice," states James.

"If he's done in time, we'll be sure to get your stuff transferred over," Roland assures him.

"Thank you," replies James.

Dave sits quietly to the right of James as he eats his dinner. The attitudes of the others have begun to mellow, some beginning to realize that he could have actually stumbled into the wrong room as he says. That James vouches for him gives credence to his story as well.

None come right out and really talk to him, and James is worried for his friend. He wants him to become a part of his life here and over time, he's sure he will.

The evening's gathering goes by quickly and they soon head to their respective beds. When he and Dave are lying in the dark, Dave asks, "Where is this Cardri?"

"It's several days away, out on the coast," he tells him. "The king has a large castle, just like the ones I've always wanted to see. Was able to see it up close a month or so ago." Turning to his friend, he says, "I'm sure you'll like it."

"I'm sure I will," he says. "Thanks for being a friend, James."

"Always," he assures him.

"No matter what?" he asks, hope in his voice.

"No matter what. Now get some sleep," James says as he turns over to go to sleep.

Chapter Four

The following morning, those heading to Cardri with James rose early and met in the kitchen. Illan is leaving Yern in charge of the recruits' training in his absence. The last time he left Miko in charge, he won't be making that mistake again. He's no good at maintaining discipline or getting them to do what they're supposed to. When Illan had returned from The Merchant's Pass, the schedule of training he left with him had barely been done. Yern on the other hand, is a whole lot more apt to get done what needs to be done.

Everyone turns out to see them off, even those whose duty is to patrol through the outlying trees. James mounts his horse and turns to face Roland. "Seems I'm off again," he says with a grin.

"That's why Ezra and I are here," he replies. "To look after things."

"Everyone's ready," Illan announces.

James glances back at those mounted behind him. Miko and Jiron ride next to him and Dave is just behind. He looks sullen at having to be in that position, but makes no fuss. "Let's go," he says as he gets his horse moving.

"You be careful," Tersa hollers to her brother from her position by the front of the house.

Jiron turns and waves to her as he gives her a reassuring smile. Next to her stands Aleya. Things have cooled off between them since his return from Trademeet, he's not sure why.

Errin has the watch at the end of the lane today and she comes to attention as they ride by. James gives her a nod in passing and then turns onto the road heading south. Four long days lie ahead of them before they reach the walls of Cardri.

He can't help but be a little overwhelmed at being summoned by the king. From what he's heard of the man, the king is a just and kind ruler whom the entire populace of Cardri adores.

The grey sky above prevents the sun from warming the morning chill from the air. Fall is in full swing, the colors of the trees bright and cheery as the leaves begin turning orange, red and yellow. A gust of breeze now and then sends a flurry of leaves scattering across the road.

The evening of the second day, they find themselves an hour south of Bearn. Passing through made James a little leery as it's the home of Lord Colerain and the man has had it in for him almost since his coming to this world. For some reason, he has the idea that James stole something from him. Of course James has not, but he's had two attempts made on him.

It wasn't very long ago when he made the last attempt. He actually had the temerity to send men out to The Ranch to abduct him. It would've worked except Miko recognized one of the captors which led them to Bearn. And Bearn led them to Lord Colerain. After Illan and the others rescued him, he told Lord Colerain that if he again moved against him that he would come back to Bearn and raze his house to the ground and destroy everything of his that he could find. So far, it seemed the man had heeded the warning. James is usually a patient man and has the philosophy of live and let live but Lord Colerain has pushed him beyond that.

As the sun begins to set, a cluster of buildings begins to appear ahead of them, just another of the small areas set up to cater to travelers. Most of the ones they've passed the last two days only had an inn, a chandler's shop, and little else. This one is no different.

No sign on the inn, but the fact that it is an inn is unmistakable. "Shall we stop here for the night?" James asks Illan.

Nodding, he replies, "I doubt if we'll find another before dark."

"Alright." Dismounting, he and Illan go inside to see about rooms while the others stay with the horses.

Inside they find a man bearing a tray of drinks over to a table. He pauses when he sees them enter and says, "Just a moment and I'll be with you."

"No problem," responds James.

After setting the mugs of ale on the table before two customers, he makes his way back to where they're waiting. "My name is Jared, welcome to the Restful Traveler. Can I help you sirs?" he asks.

"Need three rooms and stalls for six horses," replies James.

Nodding, the man says, "It'll be three coppers a room, meals are extra. And another copper for each of the stalls."

"Very well," replies James and he removes the required number of coins from his pouch and hands them to the man. Walking with Jared over to the counter, he accepts three keys from him for the rooms.

"The stalls for the horses are around back," he tells them.

"Thank you," says James and then he and Illan return outside to the others.

Leading their horses around to the back, they get them situated in their stalls before returning to the inn. They then go upstairs and put their things in their rooms before heading down to the common room for dinner.

During the course of eating dinner, a commotion near the entrance of the inn draws their attention.

"I said not to come around here again!" Jared the innkeeper says sternly.

James looks over and sees a young woman, obviously very poor and looking destitute turn around and leave. When their serving girl comes near, he asks her what that was about.

"Oh, she comes by here from time to time, looking for a handout," she explains. "My father used to give her food but then she started coming every night and annoying the customers. That's when he put a stop to it. Poor girl, I feel sorry for her but what can you do?"

"Thank you," he says.

"You're welcome," the girl replies as she moves along to help another customer.

"Kind of feel sorry for people like that don't you?" asks James to no one in particular.

"Some," agrees Fifer.

Before the end of the meal, an itinerant musician sets up in one corner of the common room and places a bowl on the floor before him for any donations the patrons would care to give. Most musicians of this world have no paying patrons and just go from tavern to tavern looking for a place to play. If the proprietor has no one to provide music already, he'll let the musician set up and play for tips, often supplying his dinner if he plays well.

They sit back after the meal and listen as he plays. Not nearly Perrilin's standard, but who is? Still, he does play well and the songs he sings are on key. During one intermission, James goes over and puts a silver in his bowl.

Sitting back down, he notices Dave is gone. "Where did Dave go?"

"Who cares?" says Jiron. His feelings for Dave have hardly become better over the last couple days. While Dave has done nothing further to antagonize anyone, if anything he's been trying hard to get along, he still has yet to allay Jiron's feeling of distrust.

"Jiron, stop that," Illan says disapprovingly. To James he adds, "He said he was tired and was going up to sleep."

A big yawn escaping him, James says, "I may go on up too." Then the musician begins playing a song James has heard before, one he especially likes. Sitting back down, he looks to Illan and says with a smile, "Maybe after one more song."

Illan laughs and James sits back as the musician makes his way through the piece. It's a whimsical song about a layabout who winds up mistakenly courting his benefactor's daughter. Rather a long song, but from the reaction of the other patrons there, more than just James like it.

When the song ends, he gets up and stretches. "Definitely off to bed now," he says amidst another big yawn. "See you all tomorrow."

"Good night James," Illan says. The others bid him good night as well.

Heading up to his room, he finds Dave asleep in bed just as Illan had said. Getting undressed quietly so as not to awaken his friend, he slips into his own bed and relaxes as he begins drifting off to sleep.

The following morning when they're in the common room having a quick bite to eat before heading out, everyone seems to be mellowing toward Dave. Jiron still has an edge, but it's beginning to soften somewhat as he gets to know him a little bit better. It's unlikely he'll ever have total trust in him, but as time goes on, James hopes he will.

They finish their morning meal quickly and are soon on the road. As they pass by the last of the buildings James sees someone standing against the wall of the last building, staring at their party. It's the woman who the night before the innkeeper told to leave his place. When she notices him looking at her, she turns and runs away. Not looking back, she goes around the corner behind the building and is soon out of sight.

Odd, he muses to himself. Dismissing it as the vagaries of humanity, he returns his attention to the road ahead. Dave beside him begins whistling a tune from their world and he soon joins in.

The next two days fly by fast. By the end of the fourth day, the walls of Cardri come into sight. When the view first appears before them, James can hear a gasp from his friend Dave. Turning toward him, he sees the awe in his eyes. "Told you it was impressive," he tells his friend.

"I know," he replies softly. "But I never expected this."

The scene before them is one of breathtaking beauty. Far away on the horizon, the sun lies low near the ocean, its light a dazzling display of sparkles upon the water. Ships of every size are either at anchor at one of the many docks lining the shoreline or upon the water under sail. The walls of the castle itself gleam in the light and the city surrounding it sprawls for miles in every direction.

To Illan, James says, "There's an inn called the Silver Bells located within the second wall. I know the proprietress and it would be a good place to stay while we're here."

Shrugging, he says, "One place is as good as another."

A branch of the Kelewan River flows to the east around the city before emptying into the sea. Just as they are about to ride onto the bridge spanning the river, Fifer points off to the east and exclaims, "Illan!"

In an area adjacent to the river, sits a large encampment of tents. The pennant flying from the largest of the tents bears the Empire's insignia. "What are they doing here?" James asks.

"I don't know," replies Illan as he glances at him, a worried expression upon his face.

"Can't have anything to do with me could it?" asks James.

"I wouldn't think so," he says. "Best to give them a wide berth. No sense looking for trouble."

"I agree," replies James. To the rest he adds, "While we're in town, keep your ears open for what they may be doing here."

"You got it," replies Miko.

Just knowing they're over there gives James a bad feeling. What could they be here for?

The evening crowd moving through the gates into the city is not very busy and they soon reach the gates. After a few brief questions by the guards on duty, they're waved on through. Somewhat familiar with the layout of Cardri, James takes the lead and they work through the city to the gates in the second wall.

As they approach, the guards have them pause. "What business do you have here in Cardri?" one of them asks.

"I have an audience with the king," replies James. "Plan to stay at the Silver Bells while I'm here."

Nodding, the guard steps back and waves them on through. Passing to the other side, he gets his bearings and turns down the street in the direction of the Silver Bells. He's not exactly sure he went the right way and when he sees the three silver bells hanging in front of the inn, he breathes an internal sigh of relief.

He brings them to a stop when they reach the front and then dismounts. "You stay here, I'll be right back," he tells the others. While he moves to the front door, they dismount.

Opening the door, he enters the inn and it's just as he remembers it. Clean and opulent, expensive too if he remembers correctly. Off to one side, he sees Miss Gilena berating one of her workers over some infraction the poor man made.

"...think they grow on trees?" she asks the miserable looking man. "Next time be more careful or I'll take it out of your pay. Understand?"

"Yes ma'am," he says dejectedly.

"Now go about your work," she tells him. He then turns and leaves, carrying a bundle of tablecloths. Turning, she sees James approaching and breaks into a broad, warm smile. "Well bless my soul," she says, coming toward him. "I didn't think to see you again so soon."

"I have business here and am in need of three rooms," he tells her.

When she reaches him, she wraps her arms around him and proceeds to give him a big hug. Disengaging himself from her embrace, he steps back a moment and asks, "Has Perrilin been by lately?"

Shaking her head, she says, "No. Most likely up to no good again. I swear that man can't keep himself out of trouble." She begins walking over to the counter where she keeps the room keys.

James takes out the golds she'll need for the rooms and has them ready before she produces the keys for the rooms.

"You remember eh?" she asks with a smile. Taking the golds, she gives him the keys.

"I would be hard pressed to forget my last experience in your fine establishment," he says.

Laughing, she replies, "True. So, what brings you to Cardri?"

"The king sent a summons for me to appear before him," he replies.

"Why?" she asks, the smile fading from her eyes. "Nothing wrong is there?"

Shrugging, he says, "I don't know. I was simply told to present myself before the Royal Court."

"I hope it goes well," she says, a worried expression now upon her face.

"Me too," he agrees. "Be back in a bit," he tells her as he turns to rejoin his friends out front.

"Good to see you again," she says.

"You too," he replies just before exiting through the door.

Out front, the others turn toward him as he leaves the inn. "We'll take the horses around back and get them settled in," he announces. "In the morning, I'll go up to the castle to find out what's going on." Taking the reins of his horse, he leads them around to the stables.

Back by the stables, Gunther the stableboy shows them which stalls will be theirs. Once the horses are secured within their stalls, he gets pails of grain ready for each and then starts currying them.

James and the others make their way to the inn and enter through the back door. Taking the stairs, they head up to their rooms where they get settled in before going downstairs for dinner.

Miko is somewhat put out about having to share a room with Jiron. He would rather be sharing one with James, but his friend Dave has that honor. "I don't see why he has to always get to be with James," he complains to Jiron.

Turning to him, Jiron explains, "They've known each other a long time, far longer than any of us have known him. Besides, he still doesn't speak the language very well though he is doing better."

"I can't believe you're actually defending him," states Miko.

Getting a slightly angry look on his face, Jiron says, "I'm not defending him, merely answering your question. I don't like him."

"Neither do I," admits Miko. "I try to get along with him for James' sake."

"I know," he says.

Knock! Knock!

"Come in," hollers Jiron. James opens the door, his friend Dave is standing in the hall behind him.

"We're heading down for something to eat," he tells them. "You guys want to join us?"

"Sure," says Miko as he heads for the door.

"Be down in a minute," replies Jiron.

"Alright," says James as he steps aside to allow Miko to pass into the hall. "See you in a bit."

Illan and Fifer have just come out of their room and they all go downstairs where they find a table large enough for all of them. Several minutes later, Jiron joins them.

They order their food and are soon enjoying a meal of spiced ham, bread and assorted vegetables. A group of four musicians take the stage and before long the room is filled with rollicking music.

James sits back and enjoys himself, listening to the musicians and watching them play their instruments. From all around him, the buzz of conversation is subdued as they all wish to hear and enjoy the music of the musicians. From out of the buzz, one comment is overheard from a man sitting just behind him.

"…hear the Empire's ambassador is seen going to the castle regularly the last few days."

"I heard that too," the other man at the table says.

Turning around, James asks them, "Did you just say there's an ambassador from the Empire here?"

Somewhat taken aback at his interrupting their conversation, one man says, "It isn't polite listening in on other people's conversation."

"How rude," the other man says with an annoyed expression.

"Sorry," apologizes James and turns back to his own table.

He feels a tap on his shoulder and turns to find one of the men looking at him. "But yes, there is an ambassador from the Empire here, has been for a little over a week."

"That's right," says his friend, nodding in agreement. "Why he's here isn't known though, but the popular rumor is that they want us to join their fight with Madoc."

His friend laughs at that, "Like that would ever happen."

"Thank you," replies James.

The man nods his head and then resumes his conversation with his friend, this time keeping their voices slightly softer to avoid being overheard again.

Leaning close to Illan, he asks, "Did you hear that?"

"Yes I did," he says. "If you figure the time it took the herald to reach The Ranch and how long it took us to get here, then we could assume he was dispatched shortly after the Ambassador's arrival."

"What could that mean?" asks James.

"Not sure," he replies, "but you'll find out soon enough tomorrow."

"I suppose," states James. Out of the corner of his eye, he sees Dave give out with a big yawn.

"Tired?" he asks his friend.

Nodding, Dave says, "I think I'll head up and go to sleep."

Handing him the key, he says, "Alright, I probably won't be up for a couple of hours."

"Don't worry about me," replies Dave. "I'll be dead to the world in a short while."

As Dave leaves, Jiron watches him go with some delight. "I thought I'd take Fifer and we would tour the bars tonight and see what we could find out."

"Not a bad idea," agrees James. "See if you can discover any more rumors regarding the Ambassador's visit."

"Will do," states Jiron. Getting up, he glances to Fifer and says, "Ready to go?"

"Always," he says.

They move away from the table and head out the door.

Illan, Miko and James remain at the table late into the evening enjoying the music. Once he starts yawing, James gets up and heads to his room where he hears Dave's snores coming from within before he even opens the door.

Getting undressed in the dark, he slips into the other bed and quickly falls asleep.

Jiron and Fifer leave the Silver Bells and head to the outer section of the city. There they'll find the more disreputable establishments where rumors flow more readily. Never staying very long in any one place, they have a few drinks while listening to the conversations around them. Once in awhile asking a few discreet, innocent questions before moving to the next.

By the fifth such dive, they have accumulated rumors ranging from an attempt to kidnap/assassinate the king to an arranged marriage between one of the king's daughters and a noble within the Empire. All of which seems rather implausible. The most improbable story yet is how the Empire is here to open a slave market within Cardri where they can sell the slaves taken in their war with Madoc. How that one started, no one seems to know and few believe. One man said, 'It'll be a cold day in hell before that ever happens'.

They wander outside the outer walls and plan to hit some of the seediest places yet. The first one they enter must have been standing a very long time. The walls are slightly slanted and most of the windows are boarded up. The odor and density of the smoke within makes it hard to breathe.

Moving to the bar, they order a couple drinks and set about drinking as they take in the clientele. Most are what Jiron would call sewer rats, little more than drunkards and layabouts. The fact that they're even in a place like this tells him all he needs to know.

One man sitting at a table near them, who only has one hand, catches Jiron glancing in his direction. That is all the excuse he needs. Getting up from his chair, he moves toward him and says, "I don't like the way you're staring at me!"

The other patrons perk up at that. "No trouble tonight, Lonn," says the barkeep from where he stands behind the bar.

"I'm not looking for trouble, mister," Jiron says to him. "I apologize if I've bothered you in any way. I assure you it was not my intention."

"You think I don't know what you're thinking about ol' Lonn?" the man asks, anger beginning to build in voice. "Poor ol' Lonn. One handed he is and good for nothin'!"

Jiron can smell the liquor on his breath. He'd like nothing better than to put Lonn on the floor, but he doesn't want to do anything that could come back to James. "I'm not thinking anything like that," he says, trying to diffuse the situation. "Here," he says as he produces a coin out of his pouch, "let me buy you a drink."

"I ain't no drunk!" he says, now enraged. Using his one good hand, he takes a swing at Jiron's jaw.

Easily anticipating what Lonn was going to do, he blocks the attack and follows through with a punch to the jaw. The blow snaps his head backward and Lonn stumbles into a table with three men. He smashes the table, tossing the men's drinks onto the floor, one which spills across one of the men's shirt in the process.

"Get them!" the man cries as he and his two buddies launch themselves at Jiron and Fifer.

Fifer flashes a grin to Jiron as he moves to meet the oncoming men. Both he and Jiron are veterans of the fight clubs back in the City of Light and readily wade into the men. The first man approaching Fifer soon finds himself lying on the floor several feet away, blood running out of his nose from where Fifer had connected with a roundhouse.

Jiron joins the fray as he deflects an uppercut from one individual while striking out with his foot at another. Fists and feet flying, he and Fifer mow them down quickly and it's over before it even begins.

Standing back to back, they look around at the men lying on the floor groaning. When no others move to join the fray, they relax and return to the bar to finish their drinks.

"Sorry about that," replies Jiron to the barkeep behind the counter.

"That Lonn's a hothead alright," he says. "You boys sure know how to handle yourselves."

"Thanks," says Fifer with a grin.

"Would you be interested in making a little extra money on the side?" the barkeep asks.

Shrugging, Jiron replies, "Maybe, what do you have in mind?"

"There's this group of individuals who are looking for someone to fight their champion," he says. "They would pay pretty well, whether you win or lose."

"What kind of fight?" asks Jiron, interested. "Fists or weapons?"

"If you fight with weapons, you get more," he says. "But you can choose either way."

Jiron looks to Fifer who's wearing a grin. "When would this take place? I'm not sure how long we'll be here," he tells him.

"Tomorrow night," he says. "Would you boys be interested?"

"Possibly," says Jiron. "Where would the fight take place?"

Gesturing behind him, he says, "Out back. There's a small lot behind us that's fairly clear. We've held fights like these out there from time to time."

Nodding, Jiron says, "How much?"

"Weapons, you get a gold," he says. "Just fists, two silvers."

"Win or lose?" he asks.

"Win or lose," the barkeep replies.

Nodding, Jiron says, "Alright, I'll do it."

"Great!" the barkeep says excitedly. "Just two hours after sundown tomorrow night."

"I'll be here," he says. Then glancing to Fifer, he nods his head to the door as he begins making his way out of the inn. Fifer downs his drink and moves to follow. Lonn and the others are just now beginning to get up off the floor.

After they leave, Lonn gets up and moves over to the barkeep who slides a silver across the counter to him. "Thanks," he says.

Picking up the coin, Lonn grins and says, "Anytime."

Chapter Five

The following morning when they all meet down in the common room for breakfast, Jiron and Fifer tell them of the rumors they discovered the night before. They do not tell of what transpired at the inn or the fight later in the evening. Jiron told Fifer to keep quiet about that, he didn't think James would like it, much less approve.

"There was no mention of you from anyone we talked to," Fifer tells him. "Most of the rumors were really quite farfetched. I don't think anyone really knows what they're doing here."

"Miko," James says after mulling over what they said for a few minutes, "you're good on the streets. See if you can find out what's going on."

"Will do," he says, glad to be of help.

"What are you planning to do about going to see the king?" Illan asks.

Before James has a chance to reply, Jiron breaks in and says, "About that. The Royal Court convenes in the afternoon, we did find out that much."

"Afternoon?" muses James. "Good, maybe I'll be able to track down Ellinwyrd and see if he knows anything before I go."

"How are you going to do that?" asks Jiron.

"Go to the gates to the castle area and request an audience," he explains. "Last time I was here he said I could stop by anytime."

"Want us to come with you?" asks Illan.

Shaking his head, he says, "No, I don't think that will be necessary. I doubt if anything's about to happen here."

"Very well," states Illan. "One of us will always be here in case you need help."

"Don't worry," James assures him.

After breakfast is over, Miko excuses himself and leaves the inn as he goes to ferret out information on the streets.

Dave gets up and says, "I think I'll just stay here at the inn in case you need me."

"Good idea," says Jiron and their eyes meet. Jiron still carries a resentment toward him that manifests itself every once in awhile.

Frowning, Dave turns and heads back up to his room.

"I wish you would take it easy on him," James says to Jiron after Dave has left.

"I'll try," replies Jiron though from the tone of his voice he isn't planning on trying too hard.

"You have the letter the herald gave you?" Illan asks.

Patting the pouch at his waist, he says, "Right here."

"Good, you'll probably need it to get in to see the Royal Court," Illan advises.

"That's what I figured." Getting up, he says his goodbyes. Waving a farewell to Miss Gilena, he heads for the door and is soon out on the street. Moving toward the gates to the castle area, he goes down several blocks and notices Miko standing with a bunch of older youths near the side of a building. In his hands is a bag of tarts which he is sharing with the others. James just chuckles at that. *That's one way to get the locals to open up to you.* What amazes him is how he got them so fast.

The gates to the castle area are well guarded and when he approaches, one of the guards comes forward and asks him his business.

"I would like to talk to Ellinwyrd, the Archive Custodian," he tells the guard.

"Does he know you're coming?" the guard asks.

Shaking his head, he explains, "No. I arrived into town last night and he told me that if I was ever in the area to stop by."

The guard looks him up and down, as if he's trying to assess the validity of what he just said. Motioning for one of the junior guards to come over, he asks James, "What's your name and business with him?"

"My name is James," he says. "I came through some time ago and he was nice enough to help me with a bit of research. My business I will explain to him."

Looking to the junior guard, the first guard says, "Go tell the Archive Custodian that James is here and would like to speak with him."

"Yes, sir," the guard replies, then moves through the gates and is soon out of sight.

The first guard stands there near James while they wait. He has him move to the side to allow people to pass through from one side to the other. None of the people passing through look even vaguely familiar to him. Which isn't very surprising since he didn't spend all that much time in this area last time he was here.

The one person he's hoping to see or maybe even get to talk to is the Princess Alliende. Her smile she flashed him when he passed through the last time sent a thrill through him.

Ten minutes after the guard left, he returns with one of the palace pages. To the lead guard he says, "Ellinwyrd said to allow him to enter."

Nodding, the guard turns to James and says, "This page will take you in to see him."

"Thank you," James tells them as the page begins moving back into the castle area. From what he can remember, they follow along the same path as he was taken the last time. When they reach the courtyard with the four tiered fountain, beside which he had previously seen the princess, a feeling of disappointment comes over him when she isn't present. He sighs.

The page ahead of him pauses and then turns back to him, "You alright sir?"

"What?" asks James. "Oh, yeah I'm fine."

Giving a quick nod, the page turns and resumes his trek to the Archives. Coming to the familiar building, the page leads him up the steps and opens the door. Allowing James to enter first, he then closes the door behind them and quickly moves past him to lead the way down the corridor.

Coming to the double wooden doors with Ellinwyrd's symbol engraved upon its surface, the page stops and knocks upon the door. From within an 'Enter' can be heard and the page opens the door. Standing aside, he motions for James to precede him into the room.

The room on the other side of the door hasn't changed all that much, still containing disorganized piles of books and scrolls lying about the floor and tables. The state of the room bothers him, being a lover of books as he is.

"Thank you Michael," Ellinwyrd says from his seat across the room.

Michael gives him a brief bow, then a nod to James before leaving the room and shutting the door.

Making his way across the room to where Ellinwyrd sits, he takes extra precaution not to step on and damage any of the books or scrolls lying across the floor.

"James!" Ellinwyrd says as he gets up from his chair. "What an unexpected pleasure!"

Coming to the table, James extends his hand which Ellinwyrd takes and gives a firm shake. "Good to see you again too," he tells him.

Ellinwyrd indicates a seat across from him which James moves over to and sits down. Taking his seat as well, Ellinwyrd says, "I'm so glad you decided to stop by and see me."

"It's not only for the pleasure of your company that I stopped by," he tells him.

"I know," he replies.

"You do?" asks James, surprised.

"Yes. You were summoned by the king to appear before the Royal Court," states Ellinwyrd.

"That's right," agrees James. "Do you know why?"

"Didn't the summons explain that?" he asks, perplexed.

Shaking his head, James says, "No, it didn't." Removing the letter the herald had given him from his pouch, he hands it across the table to Ellinwyrd.

Taking the letter, he reads the brief missive before returning it to him. "Highly unorthodox," he says. "Custom states you are to be given the reason for the summons."

"Does it have anything to do with the Ambassador from the Empire being here in Cardri?" asks James.

Eyes widening, Ellinwyrd asks in return, "What makes you say that?"

"Well, a lot's happened since last we met," he explains. "By the way, why did you have me deliver that book to Ollinearn?"

Smiling, he says, "I was hoping that by being a courier for me, it might've helped smooth things out with local garrisons, things like that."

"It did and I thank you," he says. "But what about that Ambassador?"

"He showed up about two weeks ago," he explains. "I wasn't privy to all that was said, but word has a way of getting around."

"And?" prompts James when Ellinwyrd had grown quiet.

"And from what I gathered, it seems he's here to ask the king for aid in capturing someone," he says, eyeing James questioningly. "It seems this individual has killed scores of people in the Empire and they want him badly."

James slumps in his chair, his demeanor all Ellinwyrd needs to tell him that James believes the individual in question to be himself. "Why don't you tell me what happened," he suggests.

"It started with the fall of the City of Light," he begins. "My companion Miko had been captured and…" He goes on to relate in brief detail some of the events which the Empire could want him for, leaving out the more sensitive parts like the Fire and other things.

When he draws to a close, Ellinwyrd says, "I can see why they want you."

"Yes," he admits. "But I never initiated any of it!"

"Don't see how that will matter one way or another," he tells him. "One sovereign nation has made a request of another for justice. Unless you're able to refute their charges, I don't see what else the Royal Court can do but accede to their request."

"How can you say that!" accuses James.

"I don't believe you're guilty of anything more than defending yourself against hostile forces bent on your destruction," he says. "But my opinions will have little weight in these matters." He looks at James as he sits there, mulling over what he just told him.

"What can I do?" he asks him.

"Appear before the court," he says. "If you don't, any decision made will go against you by default. The only way out is to go forward."

"Great," says James in irritation.

After a moment's silence, Ellinwyrd asks, "Did Ollinearn help you?"

"What?" asks James, coming out of his reverie.

"Ollinearn over in the City of Light, did he aid you in your quest?" he repeats.

Nodding, he explains about the last high priest, the disappearance and how the last high priest was born in Saragon.

"Did you go to Saragon?" asks Ellinwyrd.

"Yes," replies James, nodding. "As a matter of fact I did."

"What did you find out?" he asks.

"I think a long time ago, someone planted a prophecy or riddle or something like that with one family," he explains. "There may have been more but we didn't have time to hunt for them. It went like this…

When the Fire shines Bright,
And the Star walks the Land.
Time for the Lost,
Will soon be at Hand.

At the foot of the King,
Bathe in his Cup.
Pull his Beard,
To make him sit Up.

Seven to Nine,
Six to Four.
Spit in the wind,
And open the door.

When he's done, he sits back and waits for Ellinwyrd's response. "Doesn't make much sense does it?" he asks after Ellinwyrd remains quiet for a few minutes.

"No, it doesn't," he replies. "Some of it I understand. The star must mean the Star of Morcyth, not the medallion you're carrying, but the real one."

"Oh?" he asks.

"Since your last visit, I've been doing research about Morcyth and I've come up with several items of note."

"Such as?" prompts James.

"The Star of Morcyth is the focal point of the god on this world," he says. "Through it, the old writing says, many wonderful things were accomplished by the priests of Morcyth. Just what, isn't mentioned."

"Now the fire which is mentioned, I saw mentioned in the same text as the one which told of the Star. Dmon-Li, the god who obliterated Morcyth's priesthood also has a focal point in this world, that being the Fire. Through it, terrible things happened. It seems that whoever is in possession of one of these focal points is able to have tremendous power. The text doesn't say where any of these are, most likely they're in the possession of the high priest of each order."

"Interesting," states James. Nothing new here, just reinforcing what he already knew.

"The next stanza doesn't seem to make much sense," says Ellinwyrd with a smile. "I mean who's going to bathe in a cup at the king's feet and then pull his beard?"

"I know," says James.

Suddenly, what sounds like a church bell begins tolling. "What's that?"

"It signals that the Royal Court will be meeting shortly," he replies.

Coming to his feet, James says, "I better go then."

"Surely you don't plan to present yourself before the Royal Court looking like that are you?" Ellinwyrd asks.

Looking down at himself, he realizes what he means. His travel worn clothes would be ill suited for such an occasion. "What should I do?"

Getting up, Ellinwyrd says, "Follow me." Moving to the door of his sanctum, he opens it and passes through with James right behind.

"Where are we going?" he asks.

"To get you suitable attire," is the reply.

Following Ellinwyrd, he moves along the hallway and ascends up a flight of stairs to the next level. Upon reaching the second floor, they move down the hallway and come to a halt before the third door on the right. Removing a key from his robe, he opens the door and enters.

A lone window gives the room some light and James can see this is some kind of storage room. Several chests and dressers are placed about the room as well as two wardrobes.

Ellinwyrd goes over to a table and lights the candle to give them more light, then walks over to one of the wardrobes. "It's amazing what accumulates over the years," he says as he opens the door.

Within are five sets of clothes hanging from hangers. All are of good quality and two look to be about James' size. One is green and the other is a dark brown color. "Take your pick," he says as he moves back to give him some room. "These were left by various apprentices I've had over the years."

James removes the dark brown set and says, "I like this one."

"That will do nicely," he says. "We'll go down the hall to a room where you can dress without worrying about getting dust all over them."

Blowing the candle out, he replaces it back on the table and then leads James out of the room and down the hall. Two doors down, he pauses in front of the door as he says, "You can use this one to change."

Nodding, James opens the door and enters. The room on the other side has but a single bed and dresser, a plain room all things considered. Laying the clothes on the bed, he commences changing. As he's putting on the new set, he debates whether to wear his slug belt or not. *They can always have me remove it if it's a problem.* Securing it around his waist, he then slips the jerking over his head and secures the outer belt around his middle. The jerking effectively hides his slug belt and hopefully no one will even notice.

Once he's finished, he bundles his old clothes together and leaves the room. Outside, Ellinwyrd nods when he sees him, "That will do nicely. You can keep them, they've been here for years and I doubt if the original owner will be coming back for them."

"Thank you," he replies in appreciation. These are much better than the ones he had to wear back in Corillian. Thank goodness revealing tights are not the current fashion here in Cardri.

Ellinwyrd takes his old bundle of clothes from him and says, "I'll have these returned to your inn if you like?"

"Yes, that would be fine," he says. "I'm staying at the Silver Bells."

"Ah, Miss Gilena's fine establishment," he says, nodding. "I'll have them sent over there right away."

"Thank you," he says.

Returning to Ellinwyrd's sanctum, he pulls on the rope chord to summon a page. When Michael arrives, he tells him to escort James to the Royal Court.

"Follow me sir," he says as he leads the way out of the Archives.

Once out the main doors and back onto the street, Michael leads James over to the castle. James smiles when he realizes it's to the castle they'll be going. Despite his trepidation at appearing before the Royal Court, the thought of being inside a castle makes him smile.

Taking him to the gates Michael doesn't even hesitate as he passes through. James follows close as he gazes at the way the castle was put together. There are many similarities between this one and the one he had the pleasure to experience in Lythylla during his time with Lord Pytherian.

Once past the gates, they enter the main courtyard of the castle and the page turns slightly to the right as he makes for an entryway on the far side. The hallway on the other side of the entryway leads deep into the castle. James notices several portcullises in the ceiling above which could be dropped to block the entrance in the event of an attack.

A hundred feet down, another corridor intersects with the one they're in and the page turns down it to the right. Ahead of them, the corridor opens up onto a large room with many seats and couches. Half of the available seats are filled by other's who are probably waiting their turn to appear before the Royal Court.

Guards are positioned around the room, a dozen in all. Four stand before an impressive set of double doors which must be the entrance to the Court. An officious looking man sees them enter and moves to intercept them.

The man glances to Michael who says, "Ellinwyrd asked me to escort this gentleman here."

"Indeed?" he asks, now turning his attention to James. "And what business do you have here?"

Reaching into his pouch, he withdraws the summons and hands it to him.

Taking the letter, the man opens it and begins reading. After only a second, his eyes flick to James, really looks at him for the first time and then hands the letter back. "I shall let them know you've arrived," he says. "You may wait here until they're ready for you."

"Very well," replies James.

The man then turns and proceeds over to the double doors and passes through. James catches a brief glimpse of the room on the other side. A short hallway which opens up on a large audience hall, crowded with spectators. Before he can get a better look, the door shuts.

Glancing around the room, he finds a vacant chair over against the wall across from the doors and makes his way over. Sitting down, he leans back comfortably and takes in the people waiting in the room with him.

Several look like local business men while others appear to be of a higher social standing. One gentleman in particular is dressed in clothes of obvious superior quality and has what can only be called an 'uppity' attitude. James wonders what such a man is doing here.

"Excuse me?" a voice next to him brings him out of his reverie.

A man of low standing judging by the state of his clothes is standing next to him. "Yes?" he says.

"Wonder how long they'll be in there?" the man asks.

Shrugging, James replies, "I don't know. Probably as long as they want."

"True," agrees the man. He has a beat up hat in his hands which he is nervously fidgeting with.

"Nervous?" James asks.

"What?" the man asks, seeming to have spaced out for a moment. Coming back to the moment, he says, "A little."

James wishes the man would just go bother someone else, he has way too much on his mind.

Just then, the doors to the audience chamber open and the officious looking man appears. "Farmer Tibbins?" he states loudly.

The man next to James suddenly drops his hat and his face turns pale. "H…here," he stammers, voice cracking.

"The Royal Court is ready for you," the man tells him.

Bending over to pick up his hat, James can see his hands are visibly shaking. "Relax," he says quietly to farmer Tibbins.

The hat again in his hands, he glances at James and then makes his way to the double doors. After he's passed through, the doors once more close shut.

One by one, the people who were there ahead of him are summoned through the double doors, none of which come back out. James figures there must be another exit for those with whom the Court is finished.

Most of the people are not nearly as nervous as farmer Tibbins had been, perhaps they're simply petitioners for one thing or another. He sits there and wonders just what that farmer had done which would warrant such a reaction of nervousness. He may never know.

Over an hour after he initially arrived, the doors open up and the officious looking man announces, "The mage known as James."

Getting up, he approaches the double doors. He can hear gasps from some of those who heard what the man had just said. Every eye in the room is on him as he makes his way across the room to the double doors.

As he reaches them, the officious man turns and leads him into the room. The double doors shut behind him with a resounding thud.

Chapter Six

"You're full of it!" the boy says to Miko.

"Am not!" he asserts. "There are lizards bigger than all of us here put together way down south."

Miko has accumulated quite a gathering of the local youths around himself. At first when he left the inn, he wasn't sure just how to find out what James wants to learn. How he used to do it is no longer an option seeing as he's more a man than boy now.

His first stop had been to a bakery where he bought a bag of tarts. To him, tarts are the best tasting delight he's ever experienced. Shortly after the bakery, he was standing by a chandler's shop when a youth walked by. For some reason he held out a tart and offered it to him.

At first the lad eyed him with suspicion. He completely understands how the lad is feeling, he's been on the other side more times than he can count. Whenever a person offers someone from the street something, there's usually a catch.

He took the tart hesitantly and bit into it. It wasn't long before several more youths showed up and before he knew it, his bag of tarts was empty.

Better than almost anyone else, Miko knew what drove these kids, their needs and wants. Two things above all else were his greatest desires when he was one of them. The first was the finer things of life, such as tarts. As a street kid, you never got such unless you stole them. Any money you acquired had to be spent on more important things like food and at times, protection.

The second thing of paramount importance is diversion, to be taken away from their mundane and harsh existence, if only for a brief time. Tales and experiences, both real and imagined are hungered after by these, the more fantastic the better. So he began to regale them with tales of his experiences with James. He couldn't think of tales any more fantastic than what he's actually lived through thus far. And that's how he came to be talking of rhino-lizards.

In the course of his narration, he notices James passing by but fails to break the mood he's building with these kids by waving hello.

A dozen kids now encircle him as he continues his narration of the swamp. "Not only do you have to be careful not to attract the ferocious rhino-lizards, but you have to watch where you step. You don't want to accidentally put your foot in the water."

"Why not?" asks one girl of about ten who just joined the group.

"Because living within the water are small fish, no bigger than this," he says as he uses his hands to illustrate their size. "With a mouth full of teeth that will rip you to shreds in no time at all!"

"You're lyin'!" one kid exclaims.

"No he's not," another pipes up. "Old Fergus down on Vinet Street has some of them he keeps in a big glass jar. He showed them to me once." Having the attention of his peers, he adds, "He caught a mouse and dropped it in with the fish and they tore the flesh from its bones fast."

"Ooooo," one girl says.

"The fish seemed to like the warmer water down in the Empire," Miko explains. "I doubt if you'll find them anywhere around here."

"Wonder if that Ambassador from the Empire would have any?" one small boy asks.

"Why would he have any?" an older boy says derisively. "That's just dumb!"

"There's an Ambassador from the Empire in town?" Miko asks. He's been waiting for the conversation to turn in this direction.

"You ain't heard?" one boy asks, surprised. "It's all anyone's been able to talk about."

"Just got to town yesterday," he explains. "Wonder why he's here?"

"Hear they got troubles down in the Empire and he's here to ask for help," one boy says.

"That ain't the reason," an older girl says. "I heard it from my brother, who heard it from his master that he's here to arrange a trade agreement."

They begin to argue amongst themselves as each tries to convince the others of the truthfulness of their story and the falsehood of everyone else's.

Miko lets it run for a moment, listening to all the various stories, none of which is anything he hadn't already heard from Fifer and Jiron. Holding up his hands, he says, "Quiet down now."

The kids begin quieting down and one by one turn to look at him. "Now, who would like to earn a couple coppers?" he asks.

A dozen hands fly up into the air as each begins saying they do.

"I want information about the Ambassador, why he's here," he begins.

"What for?" one of the boys hollers from the back of the group.

"My master is a rich merchant," he tells them. "If he is in fact here to negotiate a new trade agreement, it would be to my master's benefit to know." Several heads bob up and down as they begin to see the logic of that.

"So, I would like you all to find out as much as you can and meet me back here later this afternoon," he says. "If any of you can tell me his business here I'll give each of you three coppers and spring for a meal."

"And more tarts?" one small girl with berry stains on her face asks.

"And more tarts too," he assures her with a smile. To the rest, he adds, "But be careful. Those from the Empire tend to deal strongly with spies."

"We'll be careful," one older boy says.

"Okay then, on your way and meet me back here this afternoon before the evening meal."

The kids move away quickly down the street as Miko smiles. *If anyone can find out what's going on here, it's them.* Not willing to leave it just up to them, he plans to do his own investigating.

One of the most prevalent rumors is the trade agreement. That one, more than any of the others, is believed by most. Maybe it's just the most logical, or perhaps there is a basis for it. Asking directions of a local, he soon is heading down to the Merchant's Guild. If there's any truth behind the rumor he's likely to find out there.

The Merchant's Guild building is a large three story complex located within the second wall. He tries to walk through the main entrance but before he even gets close to the door is turned away by the guard stationed there.

Unable to gain entry, he instead works his way around the outside, looking for any other doors which may prove more accommodating. The only other doors he finds are locked from the other side. It seems the only way in is through the main front door which is guarded.

Not willing to give up, he stations himself in an unobtrusive spot across the street in an alley where he can monitor the comings and goings through the front door. A half hour into his vigil, he sees two of the kids whom he sent in search of information wander by and mill around outside the building. Smiling to himself, he realizes they're actually working to find out the information they said they would.

Several minutes later, the kids move off down the street and disappear in the crowd.

He sits there in his place in the alley for awhile longer until he notices two men exiting the Merchant's Guild. A cold shiver runs through him when he realizes one of the men is none other than Lord Colerain. *What is he doing here?*

The man he's with is dressed in fine clothes with a bearing which gives off the aura of authority. They move away from the building and turn to go down the street.

Coming to his feet, Miko edges out of the alley and follows them. He remembers back to their last visit here and the problems Lord Colerain had caused them. At the time, Lord Colerain was staying with a local noble by name of Lord Kindering. The man with whom he's walking could be this Lord Kindering.

He follows them through the crowds, always keeping enough distance between them so as not to be discovered. *Lord Colerain here in Cardri. The Empire's Ambassador here as well. And then James gets summoned to appear before the Royal Court? It can't be just a coincidence!* Something's going on and he intends to find out what.

Keeping them just within sight, he follows them to the gates leading into the castle area and watches in frustration as they pass through. Coming to a halt, he knows there's no way the guards there will allow him through the gates. Positioning himself in an out of the way area, he keeps an eye on the gates in the hopes they reappear.

By the time he needs to return to meet with the street kids, they haven't returned from within the castle area. Getting up, he heads back toward his rendezvous with the kids. On the way he stops by a bakery for a small sack of tarts, enough for each of the kids to have one then continues down the street. When he nears the location, he sees them already there waiting for him.

"Thought you might've forgotten about us," one older boy states.

"Naw," he says, "just got tied up for a moment. What did you find out?"

"Not much," the older boy says. "The word is that they are in fact here for trade negotiations, but that may not be all they're here for."

"Oh?" prompts Miko.

"It seems the delegation which came with the Ambassador also included an Eye," he explains.

"An Eye?" asks Miko. "What's that?"

"Don't know for sure, but that's what they said," the boy replies. "They didn't give any details about what an Eye is, but when they said it you could tell it wasn't good."

"Interesting," says Miko.

"You said you'd pay us!" one younger boy demands.

"Of course," he says as he reaches into his pouch for the promised coins and hands each of them three coppers. "Now, how about that meal I promised too."

"Yeah!" several of them exclaim at the same time.

Smiling, he leads them back a ways to one of the cities open markets where they stop at one of the open eateries which are popular here in Cardri. He buys them each a bowl of stew with a quarter loaf of bread.

While they eat he asks them about Lord Kindering.

"He's bad news," the older boy says.

"Why?" asks Miko.

"He deals with the less than savory factions of the city," another boy says. "Anyone who crosses him often as not ends up dead."

Nodding, Miko thinks that's just the sort of individual Lord Colerain would be associated with. "What else can you tell me about him?"

"He's one of the three Lords of the Merchant's Guild," an older girl says.

"Yeah," adds the older boy, "I think that's why he bears the title Lord. From what I've heard, there's nothing of the nobility in his family."

"So if the Ambassador is here to negotiate a new trade agreement, he would be one of the men involved?" he asks.

"Would think so," the older boy says. "Though don't know for sure."

"Could you find out if there's a connection between this Lord Kindering and the Ambassador?"

"Sure," he says.

He gives the older boy a couple silvers and says, "I'm staying at the Silver Bells. If you find out anything, find me there. If I'm not there, just leave word to meet you back here. We'll meet here tomorrow morning if not before."

"Will do," he says. The kids finish eating and begin to leave. One small girl, the one who had berry filling smeared across her face earlier comes over and gives him a quick hug.

He takes the sack of tarts out of his shirt and hands them to her. "Here you go," he says with a grin.

Taking the sack she flashes him a smile and then runs to catch up with the others.

Sitting back, he feels good about not only successfully finding out information James will want to know, but also about making the lives of these kids a little better if only for a brief time. He finishes his meal and then walks through the streets back to the Silver Bells.

By the time he arrives, it's now late afternoon and the sun is beginning its descent to the horizon. At the inn, he finds Illan sitting in the common room talking with several of the locals. When he sees him approaching, Illan gets up and takes his leave of the men as he meets Miko halfway.

"Was getting worried about you," he tells him.

"Sorry," apologizes Miko. "I was finding out about things."

Nodding, Illan says, "Let's go up to my room where we can talk in private."

As they move to the stairs leading up the second floor, Miko asks, "Where is everyone?"

"James is still at the castle," he explains. "I've had no word about him since he left. Jiron and Fifer left a short time ago, said something about meeting someone. They were rather vague about the whole thing."

Back in the room, Illan shuts the door and Miko fills him in on what the kids had said. At mention of the Eye, he gets a strange look on his face but makes no comment. When Miko tells him about finding Lord Colerain and Lord Kindering at the Merchant's Guild, he gets another odd look.

"It just seems more than coincidence that all these things are coinciding with James being summoned here," he concludes.

"I tend to agree," states Illan.

"What's the Eye?" Miko asks him after a brief quiet.

Sitting back in the chair, Illan considers the question a moment before answering. "The Eye, or rather an Eye of the Emperor, is part of a secret organization within the Empire that seeks out those who jeopardize or challenge the rule of the Emperor."

"But why would one be here?" asks Miko. "James?"

"I don't know, but I don't like it," he says.

"Didn't he say two hours after sunset?" Fifer asks him.

"Yes," replies Jiron as they make their way out to where the fight's going to be.

"Then why are we leaving so early?" he asks. Pointing to the sun which is low to the horizon he continues, "It's going to be several hours before we have to be there."

Giving Fifer an annoyed look, he says, "First of all, I didn't want to be there when James returns to the inn. If he got wind of this he would probably try to get me to call it off. This way, we don't have that problem."

"Secondly, I was hoping we might be able to do a little digging and see if we can find out about who I might be fighting."

"To give you an edge?" suggests Fifer.

"Something like that," agrees Jiron. "Back at the pits, we always had scouts out to find out about newcomers to the pits. Their strengths and weaknesses, that sort of thing. It's amazing how much of an edge one little piece of information can give you."

It isn't hard to locate the inn behind which Jiron agreed to fight tonight. As the barkeep had told them, behind the inn is a sizeable area. Filled with refuse and beggars, its center has been kept relatively clear for the fights that go on here.

"Where should we start?" asks Fifer.

Shrugging, Jiron gestures to the beggars hanging out in the area, "How about with them?"

The first beggar they approach shies away from them as they come near, unwilling to meet their eyes much less talk to them. Looking around, Jiron sees one eyeing them and makes his way toward him. This beggar holds his ground as they approach.

"You hang out here much?" asks Jiron as he stops next to the man.

Nodding, he replies, "Yes."

"I hear there are fights going on here from time to time," he says.

The beggar just stares at him, not responding to what he just said. Producing two coppers, he holds them out and the beggar snatches them away quickly. Looking around, he says, "Occasionally. I hear there will be one tonight." Gesturing around at the many beggars he adds, "That's why so many of us are here."

"Do you know anything about who's fighting?" he asks.

"Maybe," he says. His hand snakes out of his clothing with the palm up.

Fishing out two more coppers, he places them in the beggar's hand.

After his hand is once again within the dirty rags he calls clothes, he says, "Bunch of foreigners have staged fights here with locals the last week or so. They have a champion whom they say no one's been able to beat."

"What is their champion like?" asks Fifer.

"He was big, muscled and fought with two swords," he says. "The last two fights only lasted a few passes before his opponent lay dead on the ground."

Fifer glances to Jiron but he seems unconcerned about what he's hearing. Many tales were told of opponents before they got into the pit with them, most of them were over exaggerated. Those who took rumors to heart tended to be less effective against them.

"I thought they fought with fists at times," Jiron says.

Shaking his head, the beggar says, "No, never saw that. Not for awhile anyway."

Jiron then produces another coin, this time a silver and asks, "Where could a person place a bet on such a fight?"

Hand moving so fast it almost blurs with speed, he snatches the silver out of Jiron's fingers. Indicating a small alley off to the right, he says, "Go down there and knock on the third door to your right. When someone asks who it is, tell them 'It's no one'. That's the password today. Inside you can make your bet."

"Thanks friend," Jiron says as he heads for the indicated alleyway.

"You're not thinking of placing a bet are you?" asks Fifer.

"Of course I am," he says. "I'm not planning on losing."

They enter the alley and find the third door. Pausing only a moment, Jiron knocks upon it.

After a moment, a voice from the other side says, "Who's there?"

"It's no one," Jiron says.

They hear a bar being removed and a lock turning just before the door swings open. An armored man stands there before them, a dimly lit hallway extending from the doorway behind him.

"Put your weapons on the table there," he says, indicating a small table just within the hallway. He shuts the door and secures it again with the bar.

Fifer looks to Jiron who nods his head and they begin removing their weapons and placing them on the table.

Once divested of their weapons, the guard checks them to be sure they haven't 'forgotten' any and then says, "Follow me."

Moving down the hallway, the guard passes two doors before stopping in front of the third. Opening it, he steps aside and allows them to move into the room.

The room is richly furnished, surprising to find such a room here in this part of town. Oil lamps give the room plenty of light and a large desk sits in the middle of the room. A man is bent over the desk, looks like he's going over the books. He looks up as they enter and asks, "What do you gentlemen want?"

"We understand that you take bets on the fights which occur in the courtyard outside," states Jiron.

"Yes, we do," he says leaning back in his chair.

The guard which had let them into the building takes position behind them, hand resting upon the pommel of his sword in the event they were to do something rash.

"I would like to place a bet on the outcome," Jiron tells him. "I understand there's a foreign champion which is to meet a newcomer tonight."

"That's right," he says.

"What are the odds on the newcomer?" he asks as he moves closer to the desk.

"Ten to one," the man replies.

Removing his pouch, Jiron moves closer to the desk and upends it, spilling out its contents.

Seeing the amount of coins the pouch contains, the man's eyes widen slightly. "All of it?" he asks. "You do realize that the champion hasn't been beaten don't you?"

Jiron shrugs.

Then the man's eyes narrow in suspicion. "Why?"

From behind them, a voice says, "It's because he is the challenger."

Turning, they see Lonn entering the room.

"You know him?" the man behind the desk asks.

"You could say that," he says. "They gave me a beating last night."

Laughing, the man behind the desk says, "I see." Taking Jiron's pouch, he upends it on his desk and counts the contents. One of the gems from the cavern under the Merchant's Pass is in among the silver and coppers. Picking it up, the man examines it and asks, "Where did you get this?"

"I found it some time ago," he replies. "It's my hedge against adversity."

Nodding, the man says, "Do you want to include this in with your wager?"

"Yes," replies Jiron.

"Very well," he says. "With the gem you have seventeen golds and five silver. Is that the sum you wish to wager?"

"The gem's worth more than fifteen golds," he objects.

"Maybe so, but that's all I'm appraising it for here and now," the man says.

"Very well," agrees Jiron.

The man takes out a piece of paper and after annotating the amount, signs it before sliding back across the desk to Jiron. "If you win, this piece of paper is worth a hundred and seventy five golds. If you fail to win, you lose," he says.

Taking the paper, he says, "Deal."

"Good luck tonight," the man says.

"Luck's got nothing to do with it," he replies.

To the guard, the man behind the desk says, "Show them out."

"Come on," the guard grunts as he leads them back down the hallway. At the table, he pauses a moment while they collect their weapons and then opens the door for them. Once outside, the door shuts behind them and they hear the bar being placed against the door.

"Still over an hour before the fight," Fifer says.

The sun has just cleared the horizon and the shadows are deepening. "Let's get a small bite to eat," suggests Jiron.

"Alright," agrees Fifer.

They leave the courtyard where in just a short while Jiron will be facing a champion said to have the habit of leaving his opponents dead.

Chapter Seven

The room in which the Royal Court meets is large. Upon a throne across the room from where he enters, James sees a regally dressed man of middle years sitting upon an ornate throne. A simple golden crown sits upon his head. *That must be the King of Cardri.*

In lesser chairs flanking him on either side are six other individuals, three to a side. These must be the other members of the Royal Court. Whether they're here to advise or are part of the ruling body he isn't sure.

The officious man leads him forward to stand before the King. The room is full of onlookers, all but a very few are dressed in garments the cost of which would enable a poor man to live a year. All eyes are upon him as he's led forward.

"Your majesty," the officious man announces once he's come to a stop. "May I present, the mage known as James."

James stands straight and gives the king a deep bow.

"We appreciate you coming with such alacrity to our summons," the King says.

"I would not wish to keep your majesty waiting," he replies.

"Indeed." The King stares at James in silence for a moment, as if he's taking his measure. Behind the king, stands a man in robes. As the silence mounts, James suddenly feels the familiar tingling sensation which heralds another doing magic in the vicinity.

Eyes flicking around the room, they finally settle upon the man standing behind the King. James figures him to be some sort of court magician or wizard. In a world where magic is practiced, it would make sense for a monarch to have one at his side. James refuses to take the bait and keeps his magic still.

"What are you, sir?" the King finally asks.

Startled at the question, James asks, "Your majesty?"

"There have been many strange tales told of a rogue mage traveling our kingdom," he says. After pausing a moment he then adds, "And abroad. Stirring up mischief and if the tales are to be believed, killing at will."

"I have killed no one who has not tried to kill me first," insists James. "I have never initiated any hostilities against anyone."

"So you do admit to the taking of lives?" the king asks.

"Well, yes," admits James. "But only in self defense. I am a peaceful man, wishing only to be left alone." The wizard behind the king whispers something in his ear and James can see the king nod in response to what was said.

"You have been summoned here to answer the charges laid before us," the King explains. He turns his head and nods to the side where a guard stands before a closed door. Opening the door, the guard steps inside briefly before returning with two other people.

James gasps when he sees a person dressed in the garb of the Empire walk through. The other man is similarly dressed.

"This is Ambassador Arkhan of the Empire," the King says as the man comes forward. Ambassador Arkhan looks with hatred at James as he approaches the members of the court. "He has laid charges against you of the gravest sort," continues the King. "Ambassador?"

"Thank you your highness," the ambassador says as he gives the King a deep bow full of flourishes. Standing aright again, he points to James and says, "This villain has killed wantonly within the Empire. He has hurt and degraded one of our most prominent nobles and has completely destroyed an entire island, the act of which ended the lives of thousands of our citizens. We ask that he be given to us to be taken back to the Empire!"

James stares at the man, then turns to look at the King. A snicker can be heard from the group of onlookers and he quickly glances to the source and he's shocked to see Lord Colerain there. The satisfied look upon his face makes James' blood go cold.

"How do you plead to these charges?" the King asks.

Plead? he thinks to himself. *On the face of it, guilty. I did in fact do all those things, but not in the context this Ambassador is stating.* He stands there in indecision while the entire court stares at him. Never good in the spotlight, his anxiety begins mounting and his stress level increases.

Stammering, he says, "Did I destroy an island? Yes, I did." Around the room, those watching the proceedings gasp in surprise. "I and a friend went there to rescue another who had been captured during the Empire's sacking of the City of Light. We were rescuing him from slavery." A murmur can be heard running through the crowd at his words.

"As far as hurting and degrading a prominent noble, that would have to be Lord Cytok." At that the King's eyes widen slightly in surprise. "He took several of our traveling companions captive and was in the process of torturing them. We rescued them as well."

"Enough of his lies!" the ambassador exclaims. "He has confessed the guilt with his own words your highness and we demand justice."

"But your majesty," exhorts James. "None of what I've done has been done in malice or with the intent to hurt anyone. It was the Empire's actions which caused me to do what I did, just to survive!"

"Impertinence!" shouts the Ambassador. "The Empire demands that he be given over to us, now!"

"Demands?" the King says back to the Ambassador with an edge to his voice. "You are in no position to demand anything, Ambassador. We shall not be rushed into judgment on this matter." Turning his attention to where James is standing before him, he asks, "As for you, James. This will not be decided here, today. We must consider all aspects before rendering our judgment. Will you give us your parole not to flee until this matter is settled?"

As James is about to answer, he feels the tingling sensation suddenly spike. The robed man behind the king is staring intently at him. "Yes, your majesty. I shall not leave Cardri until at such time this is resolved."

Glancing to the robed man, the King receives a nod. "Very well, then. You may go, but we strongly caution you against doing anything while we're in judgment which would turn our decision summarily against you."

"Yes, your majesty," replies James. Out of the corner of his eye, he sees the officious man approaching him. "Follow me sir," he says.

James gives the King and his court a bow before turning to follow the man from the room. They leave through a different side door from which they originally entered. A page is waiting for them outside the door and the officious man says, "Take this man back to his inn."

Bobbing his head, the page replies, "Yes sir." To James he says, "This way." As the page leads him out of the castle, James tells him to take him to the Silver Bells. He didn't realize just how long it's been since he first talked to Ellinwyrd until he leaves the castle. He must have been waiting outside the Royal Court for some time for the sun has already gone down and the first stars are beginning to make their appearance.

All the way back, James' mind churns over what happened to him back at the Royal Court. *Why would they let me go on my own recognizance? Maybe that wizard back there had truth-read me? If so, I should try to figure out how he did it. It may come in useful.*

Once past the gates into the middle section of town, the page continues leading him directly to the inn. When they are but three blocks away, James sees a crowd of people congregating near the entrance to an alleyway. "Wonder what's going on over there?" he asks out loud.

The page says, "Maybe they found another body?"

"What?" James asks.

"Earlier today, they found a woman's body mutilated in a different alley near here," he says. "It happens sometimes."

James is slightly unnerved by the callous way in which the page just shrugs off a woman's death. Is that sort of thing so common around here that no one pays any attention to it? "Was she a prostitute?" he asks.

"Most likely," the page replies, "though I'm not entirely sure."

Could be why the reaction, prostitutes are looked down on in most societies so their deaths tend not to be too bothersome. It does sort of go with the trade.

When they reach the inn, the page makes his farewells and returns to the castle. Inside the inn, James finds Miko, Illan and Dave having their evening meal in the common room. Taking a seat at the table, he relates what happened at the Court and the accusations of the Ambassador.

"Seems that since they can't get you by force, they'll try another route," observes Illan.

"Looks that way," he replies. "Have any of you heard about the women killed around here recently?"

They all shake their heads no and he proceeds to fill them in on what he learned. "It's a bad time for this sort of thing to be happening," he says when he's done.

"It's always a bad time when someone dies," states Dave.

"I know, but now with all that's going on up at the castle, I just hope they don't get the idea it's caused by me," he says.

"Do you think they'll decide against you?" his friend asks.

"I hope not Dave," he replies.

"What do you plan to do if they decide to hand you over to the Empire?" Illan asks.

"I'm not going with them, that's for sure," he states with finality. "But I'll worry about that when the time comes."

"If you go against the Royal Court's decision, wouldn't that put them against you too?" Miko asks, worried.

"Who knows?" says James in exasperation.

Illan and Miko then fill him in on what they've learned. Miko was surprised when James didn't react to the fact Lord Colerain was in the city until he explained that he had already seen him in Court.

"Do you think he had a hand in it?" Miko asks. "You being summoned I mean."

Shaking his head, James replies, "I doubt it. He's probably just around to enjoy the situation. By the way, where are Jiron and Fifer?"

"I don't know," Illan replies. "They left out of here several hours ago and weren't too clear as to where they were going."

"I hope they're not getting into any trouble," he says as he digs into his dinner.

The time for the match draws near. Jiron and Fifer begin making their way through the dark streets on their way to the courtyard behind the inn. "Nervous?" Fifer asks.

"Not especially," Jiron replies. Even when fighting in the pits, he never once became nervous or anxious. Some of the others had thought him somewhat odd because of that, but the closest emotion he ever feels at this time would be a sense of expectation.

Other people on the streets are heading in the direction of the courtyard, the word of the impending fight must have spread throughout the poor section. As they reach the inn, they find carriages of obviously wealthy individuals waiting out front. "Seems this goes on a lot around here, they even attract the nobles."

Moving through the alley to the side of the inn, they make their way through the milling crowd. As they approach the courtyard, the press of people becomes thicker and thicker until they have to practically force their way through. Jokingly, Fifer says, "I guess we should've arrived earlier."

"It would seem that way," replies Jiron.

Near the end of the alley, a group of thugs are blocking the entrance to the courtyard. When Jiron tries to move past, one of them says, "Here now, who do you think you are?"

Without even pausing, Jiron strikes out with his fists and the man falls to the ground. His two buddies immediately turn on Jiron and before the others in the crowd even know something is afoot, Jiron drops them too. Stepping over their comatose bodies, he enters the courtyard and passes through the edge of the crowd.

"Needed a warm up," he jokingly tells Fifer. "Glad those guys could oblige." Fifer breaks into a laugh at that.

Passing through the edge of the crowd, they enter the open space in the middle of the courtyard. The barman who arranged this fight stands over to one side with several of his cronies. Upon seeing Jiron, he disengages himself and makes his way over. "Didn't think you were going to show?"

"Sorry about that," replies Jiron. "Was a little bit delayed." Looking around, he asks, "Where's my opponent?"

"They haven't arrived yet," the man replies. "They're known for being fashionably late."

Throughout the crowd are not only the riff raff of the area, but wealthy individuals as well as those in between. To one side a pavilion of sorts has been erected, the fact that it's currently unoccupied leads Jiron to believe it's for the group putting up the other fighter.

The barkeep asks, "So what weapons are you going to choose?"

Jiron pats the knives at his waist.

Looking in disbelief, the barkeep exclaims, "You can't be serious!"

"Very," replies Jiron.

"But you'll not last a minute against their champion!" insists the barkeep.

"I'll be fine," asserts Jiron.

Bystanders begin to notice Jiron and the barkeep together and a buzz begins to circulate through the crowd as he begins to be pointed out as the challenger. Money changes hands as side wagers are placed.

Aside from the crudity of the surroundings, this place isn't much different than the pits he fought in back in the City of Light before it was sacked by the Empire. Few places ever brought a feeling of peace to Jiron like being in the pits. At times that feeling bothered him, like he shouldn't feel that way. Maybe it's because he had made himself there.

From the far side of the crowd, a hushed murmur begins as the spectators begin parting for a procession of several individuals making their way to the fight area. "They're here," states the barkeep.

Five men come walking toward them, four of them obviously being from the Empire. The fifth man, larger than the rest is wearing a hooded cloak which covers his features. As the men approach, the one in the lead says, "We're here. Where is the man to face our champion?"

Jiron steps forward and says, "Right here."

Looking Jiron up and down, he grimaces and says, "I thought you had someone who would be more of a challenge than the last couple."

"He can fight," the barkeep says nervously. "I saw him in action myself."

The man considers it for a moment and then nods his head, "So be it." Saying something in their language to the rest of his group, they make their way over to the pavilion where they prepare.

"Hope you can fight well," the barkeep says nervously.

"Why?" asks Fifer. "What difference would that make to you?"

"If they have another poor fight, it could be bad," he admits.

"Been bringing him a few losers?" Jiron asks.

"You could say that," replies the barkeep. "After the first couple of fights, no one around here is willing to face their champion."

"Just who is their champion?" Fifer asks.

"A very fierce warrior," he answers. "Brought up from somewhere deep within the Empire. Rumor has it he's forced to fight for that man there, but why has never been told."

"Interesting," muses Jiron.

"Looks like they're ready," the barkeep says.

Glancing to the pavilion, Jiron sees the leader of the group and the large hooded man coming toward them. He and the barkeep, with Fifer staying several feet behind proceed to meet them in the center of the cleared area. A hush falls over the crowd as the two fighters meet.

Jiron looks beneath the hood but even with the light of the many torches illuminating the courtyard, he's still unable to make out anything underneath.

The leader says something to his fighter who removes the hooded cloak.

Jiron hears Fifer gasp as the features of the man he's to fight is seen. Tattoos cover most of his exposed skin. Bearing two swords, one longer than the other, Jiron knows exactly who or rather what his opponent is. A Parvati!

Breaking out in a grin Jiron gives the Parvati a friendly nod. A murmur grows through the crowd at his reaction. Never has anyone shown a reaction other than startlement or fear when he removed his hood. Now here's this man, shorter and only bearing knives, giving him a friendly nod.

The expression on the Parvati's leader's face shows his confusion as well. He has always revealed his warrior's features at the last minute to instill fear and doubt in his opponents. But that didn't happen here and he doesn't know why.

If the Parvati has taken any notice of Jiron's nod, he fails to reply. His expression remains placid.

The barkeep steps between them and says, "There's only one rule here. He who lives, wins!"

At that the crowd around them begins to cheer and call out. Raising a red flag high over his head, he continues, "When I let this go, begin the fight."

The barkeep watches as the crowd moves back a little bit further to give the combatants room to fight. When he sees enough room has been cleared he waves the flag in a circle around his head. Just before he drops it, Jiron says to the Parvati, "May your swords drink deep."

Stunned that he would know to say the traditional Parvati greeting, the Parvati stands there motionless when the red flag is dropped. "May your knives drink deep," he says a smile coming to him as he draws his swords.

Jiron draws his knives and the battle begins. The Parvati begins with a few testing maneuvers to see how strong his defenses are. After several passes, he begins the fight in earnest.

When Jiron realized that he faced a Parvati, his first inclination was to produce the necklace and declare himself a Shynti. But what the barkeep said kept running through his mind. *Rumor has it he's forced to fight for that man there.*

Working more on defense than actually trying to do him harm, Jiron easily blocks every strike, deflects every thrust. "Why do you do this?" he asks the Parvati during a series of intermittent probes from the Parvati.

"Do what?" he asks as he launches into a vicious attack which Jiron has a hard time in countering.

"This. Fighting for that man over there," he clarifies. "From the Parvatis I've known, they would never let themselves be used thus." Blocking an attack, he steps back a minute as they both catch their breath.

The crowd has been cheering the interplay of weapons. Over beneath the pavilion, Jiron can see the leader of the Empire's men smiling. He's definitely getting his money's worth.

"I am honor bound to fight for him so long as he doesn't set me against my own people," the Parvati states. Coming at Jiron again, his blades are a veritable blur as they seek to penetrate his defense. But as Jiron is only concentrating on defense, he's unable to find an opening.

"What happens if he should set you against one of your own?" he asks.

"Then I am free and no longer honor bound to obey him," he replies. Stepping backward a moment, he says, "But that is not a very likely possibility."

As the Parvati moves in to continue the attack, Jiron steps back and shouts "Hold!"

Only the fact that what he said was so unexpected did the Parvati pause in his attack. The crowd surrounding them, which had so recently been cheering and screaming at the fighters, have grown quiet at the odd way in which the combatants are acting. Blood should be flowing now, instead they're standing still, facing one another.

Jiron glances over to the men from the Empire as he draws forth the necklace which signifies him as being a Shynti. An honor given only to the most ferocious of fighters, an honor which makes him one of them.

When the necklace comes free of his shirt and the Parvati's eyes rest upon it, he asks in a hushed whisper, "Where did you get that?"

"I was given this by an old Parvati after defeating one of their number during a blood duel in the city of Korazan," he explains.

"You're a Shynti?" he asks, hardly daring to believe what his eyes are telling him.

The leader of the men from the Empire begins to sense things are not going as expected. "What's all this?" he asks as he comes forward. "Fight!" The crowd filling the courtyard begins murmuring as they watch the scene playing out before them.

Ignoring the man, Jiron nods his head and says, "Yes, I am. I have feasted with the Eller Tribe."

"Did you meet a warrior whose name was Qyith?" he asks as a strange look comes over his face.

Nodding, Jiron replies, "He was the War Leader of the Eller Tribe. A nice man all things considered."

"He's my brother," states the Parvati. He suddenly tilts his head back and lets out with a loud, primordial cry.

Reaching their side, the man from the Empire grabs the Parvati's arm just as his cry comes to a close and demands, "Why have you stopped the fight?"

Knocking his hand from his arm, the Parvati rounds on him and says, "I will no longer fight for you."

"What?" exclaims the man. "You are honor bound to fight as I tell you!"

"No more will I fight honorless fights for you," he states with finality. Pointing to Jiron, he says, "He is a Shynti of the Parvati's which makes him one of our people. You put me to fight one of my own so that which was binding is no longer. I am free!"

The crowd, having grown restless when the fight stopped, becomes silent as they watch the growing drama unfold before them. From the pavilion, the rest of the Empire's people come forward to stand with their leader.

"He is no Parvati!" the man cries out in rage. The thought that he's going to lose his champion is almost more than he can stand. "If you do not honor your agreement, then you are an honorless swine!"

Moving so fast as to almost be unseen, the Parvati's sword strikes out, severing the man's head from his shoulders. As the head flies off and bounces on the ground several feet away, the crowd becomes deathly silent as the man's torso stumbles about for a moment before crashing to the ground.

For a moment, the courtyard is silent as a grave, the shock of this unexpected event stunning the onlookers. Then the rest of the men from the

Empire draw their swords as they rush the Parvati to avenge the death of their leader.

Laughing, the Parvati faces them with both swords as he blocks the attack of two men. The crowd suddenly turns into a panicked mob as they race for the exits of the courtyard. None wish to be around with an actual battle going on, not just because they may get hurt, but because they don't want to be around when the city guard arrives.

Deflecting the attack of the two men, the Parvati has left himself open to the thrust of the third. The blade almost strikes his side when its course is deflected by a knife. Out of the corner of his eye, he sees Jiron coming to his aid. Laughing all the more, he cries out, "Come brother, let's send these men to the other side!"

"I'm with you!" Jiron cries out as he follows through with his second knife, narrowly missing the man's stomach.

Suddenly, one of the men facing the Parvati cries out as Fifer's sword takes him through the side. The remaining man facing the Parvati hacks down with all his might. Using his longsword, the Parvati knocks the attacking blade to the side and then follows through with his short sword, sinking it to the hilt between the man's ribs. Wedged in tightly, the sword is pulled from his hands as the man falls to the ground.

Jiron, now fighting the sole remaining man, captures his sword between his knives and kicks out, catching him in the groin. With a groan the man's strength leaves him for but a moment which is all the time Jiron needs. A quick twist of his knives and the sword is wrenched out of the man's hands and sent flying across the courtyard.

Jiron steps back from him just as a longsword strikes out, taking the man's head from his shoulders. Glancing to the side, he sees the Parvati move to where his shortsword is still embedded in the dead man's chest. Placing a foot on the dead man, he draws out his sword. Wiping both swords clean on his opponent's clothes, he turns to see Jiron staring at him.

"Thank you my friend," the Parvati says.

Jiron only nods as Fifer comes to him and says, "We've got to get out of here!"

From around them they can hear the shouts and running of feet as the city guard races into the courtyard. Out of the corner of his eye, he sees the man with which he made the bet on the outcome of the fight. Running over to him, he asks, "Where's my money!"

"What money?" the man asks.

"I won so where's the money you owe me?" he demands.

Giving him a sardonic smile, the man says, "Your winning the bet was contingent on you winning the fight." Nodding to the approaching Parvati, he adds, "He's still alive so you didn't win."

"But..." he begins when Fifer grabs his arm. "We can't stay here!" As Fifer drags him away, the man's laughter follows him.

Suddenly from across the courtyard, men of the city guard begin pouring in from a side alley. "Guards!" cries out Fifer as all three of them bolt for an alleyway on the opposite side of the courtyard.

"Just a second!" he says as he alters his course slightly and heads over to the pavilion.

"What are you doing?" yells Fifer. The guards are coming fast toward them, one of them yells, "Halt! Stay where you are!"

Jiron reaches the pavilion and grabs something off the ground before turning to head for the alleyway where Fifer and the Parvati are waiting for him. With a quick glance back at the approaching guards, he enters the alley. Racing down to the other side, they pray they can prevent being caught.

Chapter Eight

Knock! Knock! Knock!

Startled out of a deep sleep, James sits up in the dark. At first not sure just what awoke him.

Knock! Knock! Knock!

Again the incessant knocking upon his door thunders through the night. Getting out of bed, he notices the knocking hasn't bothered his friend Dave who is still snoring blissfully. Dave always had been a deep sleeper. In a sleepy haze, he makes his way over to the door.

He snaps completely awake when on the other side of the door he finds a squad of the castle guard standing in the hallway. "Are you James?" the officer in charge asks.

"Yes," he replies.

"You're under arrest," he says.

"What?" he exclaims in disbelief. "What for?"

"I wasn't told that," the officer replies. "Now, please come with us."

"Let me at least get dressed first," he says.

The officer glances at him standing there in his small clothes and nods. As James begins closing the door, the officer pushes it back open with his hand and enters. Several of his guards come in as well.

"What's going on," a groggy Dave asks from where he just woke up.

"I'm being arrested!" states James as he begins dressing.

"Arrested?" asks Dave, coming full awake. "Why in the hell are they arresting you?"

"I don't know," he says.

A commotion begins out in the hallway and then he hears Illan's voice say, "James!"

"Illan," he hollers out to him. "They're arresting me!"

"Let me through," he hears him say to the guards blocking his way into the room. One of the guards out in the hallway glances inside and when he receives a nod from his officer, steps aside and allows Illan to come in.

To the officer, he asks, "What's going on here?"

Nodding to James, he replies, "He's being placed under arrest."

"By whose order?" asks Illan.

"By order of the Royal Court," the officer says.

"Why?"

"He won't say or doesn't know," James tells him. Finally dressed, he glances into the worried eyes of Dave and says, "Stay with Illan. I'm sure we'll have this all cleared up in no time."

"Okay," he says.

Escorted out of the room, the guards fall in place around him as they lead him down the hallway. As he leaves the room, he sees a worried and anxious Miko standing in the hall not more than a few feet away.

"James?" he asks, fearfully.

"Don't worry," he assures his friend. "I'm sure this is all a big misunderstanding."

"I hope so," he says as Illan comes out of the room and they watch him being led away. Just as he begins descending the stairs, he hears Miko holler, "Don't eat anything!"

Don't eat anything. That's good advice. On a previous occasion back in Lythylla, he had eaten food laced with a narcotic which rendered his magical abilities useless. He may get hungry, but he really doesn't plan on eating or drinking anything while he's incarcerated. He just may need his magic working.

Outside the inn, their party turns down the street toward the gate leading into the castle area. The streets are filled with soldiers and guards. "What's going on?" James asks his guards.

Unresponsive, they ignore his question as they continue marching on toward the gates. Once past, he's led across the courtyard and through the gates of the castle itself.

The flurry of activity within the castle is even more harried than that which was witnessed outside. Pages are racing through the halls and men-at-arms are stationed everywhere.

Instead of taking him to the Royal Court as he at first expected, they take him through a different set of hallways and finally down a flight of steps into what has to be the castle's dungeon.

At the bottom of the stairs lies a room with several holding cells for prisoners. Currently they're all empty though they look as if they could hold several hundred in a pinch. They move to the first pen and one of the guards opens the cell door. The guard behind James pushes him on the back, indicating for him to enter.

Seeing no benefit to resisting at this time, he acquiesces and walks forward. Turning around to face his guards as they close and lock the door, he sees them about to leave and asks, "Can you at least leave me a torch for light?"

One of the guards gives him a look of contempt and says, "You're supposed to be some fancy mage, why don't you make your own light?" His fellows all begin chuckling and laughing at that.

Shrugging, James says, "Very well." Suddenly, the entire area is filled with a blinding white light as dozens of extremely bright orbs blossom into life throughout the room.

The reaction from the guards is all he could hope for when they turn tale and run out of the room. Chuckling to himself as the last man runs up the stairs leaving him alone, he cancels the spell. The darkness of the holding area lasts but briefly before his normal glowing orb springs to life next to him on the bench. He leans back and tries to get comfortable.

Smiling to himself, he feels under his shirt and rubs the slug belt he had put on when he got dressed to come here. The guards hadn't even realized what it was. Alone in the dark, he ponders why he's here and waits.

After James and his escort of guards goes down the stairs, Illan gestures Miko to follow him into James' room and close the door.

To Dave he asks, "Just what happened?"

Shrugging, he looks up from where he's sitting on the bed and replies, "I don't know. They just came and took him." Dave's command of the language has greatly improved over the last week or so. Being completely immersed in it has helped. Though still not understanding every word and nuance, he's a quick learner.

"What are we to do?" Miko asks.

"You two stay here and I'll try to find out what's going on," he says.

"Okay," replies Miko. Dave just nods his head.

Leaving the room, he heads downstairs and finds Miss Gilena in the common room wearing her night dress and a robe. She's standing near one of the windows looking out upon the street and turns when she hears him coming.

"They took James," he tells her.

"I know, poor boy," she replies sadly.

"Do you know what's going on?" he asks.

Shaking her head, she says, "No. One of my servants woke me up when the guards appeared. They didn't say much other than they were here to take him to the castle for questioning."

Illan looks out the window and sees guards and soldiers moving up and down the street. "I'm going to find out what's going on," he says as he moves for the front door."

"Be careful," she says.

"Not to worry," he says, pausing at the door. Pulling it open, he steps out into the street and begins moving toward the gates to the castle area. If there's any place he'll be able to find out what happened, it would be there.

He doesn't get more than half a block away from the inn before a man wearing the uniform of the city guard sees him and moves to intercept. "There's a curfew in effect," the guard says as he comes close. "You'll have to return to your home."

"But why?" Illan asks. "What happened?"

"Someone's assassinated the adjutant to the Empire's Ambassador," he explains. "His body was found outside the walls of the city in the poor section. The adjutant had been decapitated."

Gasping, Illan's mind begins to whir and things are beginning to click into place. "Do they know who did it?" he asks the guard.

Shaking his head, he replies, "If they do they haven't told us about it yet." Motioning back the way Illan had come, he says, "Curfews in effect until morning, so get off the street."

"Very well," he says as he turns around and heads back to the Silver Bells.

As he comes through the front door, Miss Gilena gives him a worried expression and he says, "There's a curfew and they won't let anyone on the street until morning."

"Did you find out what this is all about?" she asks, coming over to him.

"They said someone from the Empire's Ambassador's party has been killed," he tells her.

"Surely they don't suspect poor James do they?" she asks, concern etching the features of her face.

"I don't know," he tells her. "I'm sure we'll know more in the morning."

"I hope so," she says as she goes back to her place near the window.

Illan turns and heads for the stairs. Returning to the room where the other two wait, he enters and closes the door behind him. "We've got problems," he tells them.

"Like what?" Miko asks.

He briefly explains to them what he learned and his suspicion that the powers that be will think James is the one who killed the adjutant.

"Why would they think that?" Dave asks.

Looking at him like he's an idiot, Illan explains. "Just hours after James finds out the Empire wants him extradited from Cardri for crimes he's allegedly committed in their land, one of the prominent members of their delegation is killed. Think about it."

Nodding, Dave says, "I think I understand."

"What can we do?" Miko asks him.

Sitting on one of the beds, Illan says, "Nothing we can do until morning and the curfew is lifted. After that, we'll see what we can do."

Miko moves to the window of the room and looks out over the city to the silhouette of the castle in the distance. *Hang in there James!*

Holding still and quiet against the alley wall, Jiron, Fifer and the Parvati wait while four members of the city guard march past. Once they've moved further down the street away from the opening of the alley, Fifer whispers to Jiron, "We've got to get off the streets!"

"I know that," he replies with impatience.

Still on the outside of the outer wall, they've been unable to get back into the city. The whole area is swarming with guards and soldiers. It's only been by a miracle that they haven't been discovered yet.

Staying just one step ahead of the patrols, they slowly made their way further from the courtyard where the dead body lies. The Parvati is wearing the hooded cloak that Jiron had grabbed from the pavilion to better hide his features. A tall, extensively tattooed man is hard to miss or forget.

Jiron pokes his head out into the street and finds it devoid of guards at the moment. "Come on," he whispers as they follow him into the street and quickly move to the other side. Staying against the buildings, they hurry down to where he sees another alley entrance, past several more buildings.

Before they have a chance to reach it, light from one of the searching patrols is seen approaching from a side street. Realizing they are not going to have time to make it, he moves to the door of the building next to them and tries to open it.

Finding it locked, he throws his shoulder into it and smashes the door open. The sound of it seems to reverberate through the streets as they rush inside. Closing the door rapidly, Fifer moves to a window and looks out to see if anyone is coming to investigate.

"Anyone?" Jiron asks after a moment.

Shaking his head, Fifer says, "Doesn't look like it. The patrol which was coming into the street went down the other way."

"Good," says Jiron.

The building they find themselves in looks to be some kind of rug maker. Several looms are placed throughout the room with partially completed rugs still attached to them. Massive rolls of string and twine are lying upon shelves along most of the walls.

From above them, they hear a floorboard creak as if someone's walking around. They freeze and listen carefully as another creak sounds a few feet away from the first one. Someone's up there moving around.

Jiron motions for the other two to remain still as he moves to the doorway leading further into the building. The sound of the steps becomes more pronounced as whoever it is begins descending a stairway on the other side of the door.

The Parvati and Fifer move to the side of the room so as not to be readily noticed should the individual come into the room. Jiron positions himself near the door.

The footsteps reach the bottom of the stairs and they hear them coming toward the door to the room in which they're hiding. As the door begins opening, Jiron makes ready and then as the person begins walking into the room, he grabs them from behind.

A knife wielded by the man in Jiron's clutches strikes out at him and he's forced to let go. Fifer and the Parvati move away from the walls, their swords in hand. "We don't want to hurt you," Jiron says to the man.

"What are you doing in my shop?" he asks with fear in his voice as he comes to understand there are three of them.

"We're not thieves or murderers," Jiron tells him. "Drop the knife and I promise we won't hurt you."

After only a moment's hesitation, his knife falls to the floor. Just then, light from a passing search party begins playing upon the window overlooking the street. Jiron nods to Fifer who moves to the window and looks out.

The light gradually increases as the patrol moves toward them along the street. Jiron has his knife against the man's throat to keep him from raising the alarm. When the patrol at last moves past and the light begins to diminish, Fifer glances back to Jiron and nods.

Removing his knife, he says, "My pardon good sir."

"You are the ones they're after!" he says in amazement.

"We don't have time to talk, I'm afraid," Jiron says to him. Motioning him over to one of the looms, he says, "Move over there please."

"What are you going to do to me?" he asks, as he does as Jiron commanded.

"Tie you up, nothing more," he explains. Fifer comes over to supply the gag to keep him quiet and they proceed to tie him with the thread and twine from his own looms. Once the man is secured and not likely to escape, Jiron leads them through the house and to the rear door leading into the alley behind.

A quick glance to make sure the alley is empty and they're through the door, slowly making their way to the end of the alley. "Do you know where you're going?" asks Fifer.

"Not really," he says. "I just want to find some place where we can hole up until James finds us."

"How is he going to find us?" Fifer asks.

Jiron just stares at him a moment before Fifer says, "Oh yeah, right."

The end of the alley opens upon a small area enclosed by the backs of several buildings built against each other. Several sleeping forms are huddled in and around the refuse lying on the ground. Each wall has a doorway, all closed but one.

Jiron steps carefully over a sleeping body as he moves toward the open door. The opening is dark and nothing can be seen on the other side, not even shadows. Moving carefully, he enters through the door with the others following. A knife held in one hand for comfort, he moves deeper into the building.

His right shoulder bumps a wall and when he reaches out with his other hand, encounters another wall on the left. It's not a room but a corridor extending further into the building.

Moving deeper into the building, the sound of the searchers roaming the streets outside begins to diminish. Jiron keeps his right hand against the wall as they walk to hunt for doors. After passing ten feet or so into the building, his hand encounters one.

"Just a second," he whispers to the others behind him as he moves his hand along the door in search of the handle. "I think there's a door here." Upon finding the handle, he turns it and pushes the door open slowly.

The door's hinges protest loudly as he swings it open enough to allow them to enter. Darkness greets him on the other side as he tries to see beyond the door. "Might be a room where we can hole up for awhile," he tells them.

"Doubt if they'll find us here," Fifer says as he follows him through the doorway. Once the Parvati is in, he closes the door to the protestations of the hinges. "Anybody have a light?" Fifer asks.

Nearby in the dark, sparks begin to be seen from where flint is striking and soon, the soft light of a candle blossoms to light. The Parvati stands there, the candle in hand as he looks to his new found companions.

"Good," Jiron says approvingly. The room they find themselves in is dirty and looks as if beggars or other street people have at one time or another called it home. Dirty blankets are strewn around and one corner of the room reeks from where it has been used as a latrine. Rats scurry away from the light.

"What a disgusting room," says Fifer in dismay.

"Disgusting it may be, but at least we're not out there," he says, indicating the streets where the patrols are still searching for them. "Now," he says as he turns his attention back to the Parvati, "just what's your name and why did you have to go and kill that man?"

Setting the candle down on a broken crate that looks to be currently used as a table, he says, "I am Qyrll. I am truly sorry for having brought trouble upon you, but I could not bear the insult which he ascribed to me. Far too long have I endured such by him, honor bound to take the abuse without reprisals. I thank you for my freedom."

"You're welcome," replies Jiron. "I just wish we could have done it without raising the whole city against us."

"I can see why you are called Shynti," Qyrll says. "You are truly a great warrior."

"Thanks," he replies.

"Could you tell me of my homeland?" he says. "It's been many years since I left."

"Seems we have the time," Jiron says as he makes himself comfortable amidst the refuse. "It was your brother whom we first encountered after we…" For several hours Jiron relates his experiences in the Parvati homeland to Qyrll and Fifer as well as learning about this new companion of theirs.

"Hear that train a comin', it's rolling round the bend, I ain't seen sunshine since I don't know when," James's voice echoes in the room with the holding cells. For the past hour he's entertained himself with various songs of his world, the last being an old Johnny Cash song which seemed appropriate for the occasion.

The songs from home have given him comfort, though he's not too concerned about his own safety. He's grown in his ability as a mage and feels confident to take care of himself should that become necessary. As long as the powers that be don't try to hurt or drug him, he'll go along peacefully. The last thing he wants is to antagonize another kingdom against him.

When he gets to the part about shooting a man in Reno, he hears the approach of footsteps coming down the stairs. Bringing the song to a close, he watches the stairwell as a man in the livery of Cardri comes in bearing half a dozen torches, one of which is lit.

The man's eyes widen as he takes in the glowing orb sitting next to James on the bench. He moves along the wall and starts placing the torches in the sconces spaced around the room. After placing a torch into a sconce, he lights it with the one he's carrying before moving to the next.

"What are you doing?" James asks.

"Seems rather obvious," the man retorts as he places his third torch into a sconce.

"Have they finally decided that I deserve some light down here?" he asks.

The man breaks out with a short snicker as he says, "Hardly. Word is that you'll be having visitors shortly. So I'm placing several torches around the room to give them some light."

"Oh," says James.

The last torch the man is putting in a sconce happens to be near James' cell. He approaches warily, eyeing him with trepidation.

"Don't worry," James tells him, "I'll not hurt you."

Not believing him, the man comes closer, all the while keeping an eye on James in case he tries something. When he gets close to the torch sconce, he rushes past the cell and places it in, lights it and then beats a hasty retreat.

"There," says James with an assuring smile, "I didn't bite now did I?"

His job finished, the man moves quickly to the stairs and James is soon alone again. Shaking his head, James gives out with a tired sigh. *Is that the reaction I'm always going to receive? Maybe I will go live on an island or mountaintop somewhere.*

Visitors. Great, just what he wanted. Hopefully when they're here he'll be able to clear himself and he can get out of here. Resting his head against the wall, he tries to resume the song again but can't quite seem to recall it. He hates it when that happens. It's like walking into a room, knowing you're there for a reason, but can't recall why you thought you needed to go there.

Out of the corner of his eye, he catches the glimpse of a slight pulsating coming from the orb sitting next to him. Picking it up, he can detect a slight pulsating as if someone is quickly moving a dimmer switch back and forth. He's never seen it do that before.

The outline of the orb suddenly begins to warp and bend as if the outer edge of it was being molded like clay. Blinking his eyes, he shakes his head and then looks at it again. He suddenly comes to realize it's not the orb, but his vision. The whole room is beginning to turn hazy and move in nauseatingly directions.

What's wrong? Suddenly panicking, he realizes he's slipping into a drugged state. But how?

Ever since the last time he was drugged back in Lythylla, he's been thinking of ways in which to counter it should it ever happen again. He's considered various different ways to both cope and prevent it from happening.

The pulsating of the orb could be in direct response to his drugged state. His mind becoming occluded intermittently prevents the magic from going to the orb, thus the pulsing.

Canceling the orb altogether, he realizes he doesn't have much time. Marshalling all his concentration, he creates a small sphere, no larger than a pea. Firm yet translucent and thus hard to see, he holds it in his hand as he tries to inspect it. Unable to see it clearly and afraid he's about ready to drop it, he slowly and carefully puts it in his pocket.

When he can at last feel it securely inserted in his pant's pocket, he removes his hand and leans his head against the wall of his cell. The last sight he has before he slips into unconsciousness is the burning torch near his cell.

Chapter Nine

Pacing about the room, Illan stops every other time he passes the window and glances at the sky. The dawn isn't very far away. Out on the streets, the soldiers and guards who earlier were combing the streets have all but disappeared. When the sun rises, he plans on making his way to the castle to see about James and what exactly is going on.

Glancing over to the bed, James' friend Dave is fast asleep. How he can sleep while his best friend is in jail escapes him. Miko on the other hand, he's known him to sleep through anything. So the fact that he's asleep on the other bed hardly surprises him.

Not only does he have James to worry about, but Jiron and Fifer still have not returned. That's got him extremely worried but could be the result of the curfew and they're simply unable to return. He may have Miko try to locate them while he heads to the castle. Resuming his pacing, he churns over the events in his mind, and worries about what may be happening to James at this very minute.

When at last the first rays of morning shine on the walls of his room, he immediately moves over to Miko and wakes him up. "It's morning," he says.

Coming quickly awake, he rubs the sleep out of his eyes as he stands up. "Any word from James?" he asks.

Shaking his head, Illan says, "No. Jiron and Fifer are still missing as well. I'm going to head up to the castle to see what I can find out. While I'm gone, see if those kids you are acquainted with can help in locating Jiron and Fifer. I'm not sure what part they may have played in all this, but I'll kill them if they've gone and done anything to exacerbate the situation."

"What should I do with him?" Miko asks, motioning toward the sleeping Dave.

Shrugging, he replies, "Tell him to stay here. We have enough to deal with right now without him making matters worse."

"Alright," he says. "When are you planning on being back?"

"I have no idea. But if you find those recalcitrant members of our group, tell them to stay here at the inn until I get back." Moving to the door, he opens it to leave. As he passes through, Miko's 'Will do', follows him out into the hallway.

Closing the door, he walks quickly down and takes the stairs to the common room below. The room is empty except for one lone early riser. Miss Gilena is nowhere in sight, she must've returned to her bed shortly after he had gone up to his room. Leaving the inn through the front door, he moves onto the street and heads down toward the gates leading to the castle.

The contingent of guards at the gate has doubled since the last time he came by this way. As he draws near the gates, the leader of the group moves to intercept him.

"No one's allowed into the castle area at this time," the guard tells him as he comes to a stop.

"A friend of mine was taken last night and brought here," he explains. "I want to know what happened to him."

The guard eyes him suspiciously, knowing full well who it is Illan is talking about. "Sorry, but orders are, no one enters without expressed permission," he states. "And I'm fairly sure you don't have that do you?"

Shaking his head, he says, "No, I don't."

"Then you can't pass through," the guard says with finality.

Almost ready to turn away, he pauses and then asks, "Can I send word to the Archive Custodian?"

The guard is somewhat taken aback by that. "If you give us a letter, we can see that he receives it," the guard replies.

"I don't have a letter," he explains. "Is there a way you could just tell him that a friend of James is here and would like to talk with him?"

The guard thinks about it for a moment. Shrugging, he says, "Very well," He glances behind him and waves over one of the junior guards. "Find the Archive Custodian and tell him a friend of James would like an audience with him," he tells the guard.

"Yes sir," the guard replies before turning and running through the gates in search of Ellinwyrd.

"He may not be up yet," he says. "It's still quite early."

"I'll wait if it's all the same with you," Illan tells him.

"Suit yourself," replies the guard who then moves back over with his men.

Illan stands there impatiently as he awaits the return of the junior guard. Almost a half hour later, he sees him returning. He waits while the lead guard confers with his man and then watches as he begins moving toward where he's waiting.

"He said that he will meet with you," the guard tells him. "A page is being summoned and will arrive shortly to escort you."

"Thank you," says Illan. A short time later, a boy in the livery of a castle page approaches the gate and Illan moves to follow him into the castle area.

The page leads him through to the building housing the Royal Archives. Going in through the main door, he takes him down to the doors leading into

Ellinwyrd's sanctum. He pauses a moment as he knocks upon the door and when he receives Ellinwyrd's permission to enter, opens the door. Stepping to one side, he allows Illan to precede him into the room.

"Thank you Michael," Ellinwyrd says from where he sits at a table stacked haphazardly with books and scrolls.

Nodding, Michael closes the door.

Coming over to where Ellinwyrd sits, Illan makes his way through the 'obstacle course' as James had called it when he described his visit here. He can see what James meant by this place being a disorganized chaotic mess. It's a wonder that anything can even be found.

Ellinwyrd glances up from a book open before him as he approaches. Indicating a chair across from him, he says, "Please, sit down."

"Thank you for seeing me," Illan says graciously. "I don't know if you're aware of what happened last night, but they came and arrested James."

Closing the book before him, Ellinwyrd nods his head as a sigh escapes him. "I know," he replies.

"Do you know what's going to happen to him?" Illan asks.

"I'm afraid so," he says sadly.

"They're not going to hand him over to the Empire are they?" asks Illan, afraid of the answer.

"Yes, they are," he tells him.

"Why in god's name are they acceding to their request? They have to know he's innocent!"

"Innocence or guilt rarely has much to do with what kingdoms decide," he explains. "First of all, Cardri is not so big that they can afford to antagonize their neighbor to the south. James isn't even a citizen of Cardri in their eyes so to them it's not like they're handing over one of their own."

"Also, when the Ambassador's adjutant was killed, that was just one more strain on an already shaky peace. Giving them James was a way to alleviate that strain."

"You know what the Empire is going to do to him, don't you?" Illan asks. "They'll torture and kill him."

"I know," he replies.

"If they try to give him to the Empire, he's likely to tear down the castle and kill an awful lot of people," Illan tells him. "I've seen him in action."

Shaking his head, Ellinwyrd says, "No, he won't."

"What do you mean?" he asks.

"I mean, there are steps one can take to ensure the safe capture of one who controls the power," he tells him. "I believe it's already begun to be implemented."

"If they try to drug him, he'll resist," he asserts.

"He won't even know it's happening until it's too late," he explains. "There's more than one way to drug a mage. They have torches that when lit, emit a narcotic fume which will render him unable to use his magic." Illan just stares at him in horror. "After that, it's just an easy matter to go in and collect him."

"But we have to do something," he says. "We can't just let them take him."

"From what I've gathered, they'll not be taking him for some time," he says. "They still must conclude the new trade agreement, and that could take another day or two."

Looking at Ellinwyrd, Illan narrows his eyes as he contemplates what he just heard. "A day or two eh?" he breathes as he cocks one eyebrow in question.

Ellinwyrd nods his head. "Our Merchant's Guild is pressing the Royal Court to get good terms with the Empire and the negotiations have at times become heated. But the general consensus is that the Empire's representatives need to finalize the trade agreement for the next five years, and do it soon."

"Alright then," replies Illan as he gets to his feet. "I don't have much time."

Standing up as well, Ellinwyrd reaches into his rumpled tunic and pulls out a scroll bearing his wax seal. Handing it across the table to him, he says, "If you should see James, give him this."

Taking the scroll, Illan asks, "What is it?"

"A number of questions had arisen during our last visit and I think this may answer one," he explains.

Putting it inside his shirt, Illan says, "I'll be sure to."

"Very good," Ellinwyrd replies. Moving over to the decorative pull rope, he summons the page Michael back and has him escort Illan back to the gates.

"I thank you for taking the time to see me," Illan says as he's about to walk out the door.

"Anytime," he says. "And if all this should somehow become resolved, tell James to stop by again."

"I will." Turning to follow Michael he closes the door to Ellinwyrd's sanctum. Back through the castle area and out the gate, he says goodbye to Michael as he heads back to the Silver Bells.

Once back at the inn, he hurries up the stairs to the room where he left Miko and Dave. Opening the door, he finds the room empty. They're both gone. Damn! Nothing to do for the moment but wait, he sits down by the window and pulls out the scroll Ellinwyrd had given him wondering just what was on it.

"I'm tired of staying in this room," Dave complains when Miko tells him that's what Illan wants him to do. "All I've done is sit in here doing nothing and I'm sick of it. James is in trouble and I want to help!"

"But there's nothing you can do so the best thing you can do is sit tight," explains Miko. He ordered a meal brought in for them and Dave's done nothing but complain ever since he awoke. Frankly, Miko is sick of it.

Dave glares at him from across the table as he continues eating his breakfast of eggs and ham steak. "Now, I've got a couple things I need to see to," Miko tells him after he's done eating. "Just stay here and don't get into any trouble."

He can feel the glare of Dave's eyes follow him as he gets up from the table and moves to the door. Without even looking back, he opens the door and quickly shuts it. *I don't know what James sees in this guy.*

At first, Dave seemed to be okay. But ever since coming to Cardri though, he's been a pain. He doesn't do anything, it's just his attitude. Miko can't stand whiny people. Maybe if their lives were reversed, he could understand better where he comes from, but that's neither here nor there. He only puts up with him for James' sake.

Once out on the street, he heads down to where he and the kids were going to meet if they didn't contact him during the night. As he approaches the open market, he sees them near the place where they ate yesterday afternoon.

They see him coming and the little girl gives him a smile as they come to meet him. "Hungry?" he asks. Several nods and an 'of course' meet his question. "Then let's get something to eat." At the nearby open eatery, he gets then all a modest helping of taters and egg. Moving to a table, they bring their food over and begin eating.

The older boy asks, "Did you hear what happened out in the poor section last night?"

"Something about a killing wasn't it?" replies Miko.

"One of the important members of the Empire's trade delegation got himself decapitated," one of the younger boys adds.

"Really?" prompts Miko, very interested in what they may know about it. "Did you see it?"

"I did," the older boy states. "I was in the area with a couple of the older kids and heard a fight was going down out there. So we decided to go and watch the show. It was a regular fight, one guy with two knives against another with two swords."

He pauses a moment as he takes a large bite and then continues through a mouth full of eggs. "It was going pretty good but then it got weird. Both fighters suddenly stopped fighting and began talking to one another. It seems the bigger guy was some sort of fighter for the Empire's men and they got mad when the fight stopped."

"What happened next I'm not really sure about, but suddenly one guy's head went flying and the other men from the Empire pulled out their swords and attacked the two fighters. I tell you, the fighting then got good and the Empire's men were soon taken out. By that time, the whole area was in a panic and the city guards were coming, so me and my friends got the heck out of there."

"Interesting," says Miko. Well that answers one question. The fighter with the two knives had to be Jiron. But just what was he doing and why was he there.

Changing the subject, he asks, "Did you find out anything about the connection between Lord Kindering and the Empire's Ambassador?"

"Not much," he replies. "They have had a few meetings outside the regular trade negotiations, but what they said we were unable to find out. Those always took place at Lord Kindering's estate and couldn't find anyone who knew what went on there."

Nodding his head, Miko says, "Thanks." Digging into his pouch, he pulls out a handful of coppers and proceeds to give each of them two.

After everyone has two of them, he returns the rest to his pouch and then asks, "Did they ever find the men who killed the Empire's men at the fight?"

Shaking his head, the older boy says, "Not that I've heard. They do have someone in the dungeon they believe is part of it, but I don't know who."

That must be James. "Would you all be interested in continuing to find things out for me?"

"Sure," says one of the girls. "As long as you keep feeding us."

"No problem there," he assures them. "See if you can find out what happened to those fighters from the fight. Where they might be."

"Why?" asks a younger boy.

"Why what?" Miko asks him.

"You said your master was a merchant and wanted some inside information," he replies. "I don't see how this has to do with anything."

Remaining silent for a moment as all their eyes are upon him, Miko finally asks, "Can you keep a secret?"

All their heads nod in unison. "Now I'm not talking about an unimportant secret," he tells them. "I'm talking about the sort of secret that if it's told will probably get you dead."

The younger kids' eyes widen at that and the older boy says, "We know when to hold our tongues." To the others he asks, "Right?"

The other kids all nod their heads affirmatively.

"Alright." Miko eyes them all seriously as he says, "The man with the knives is a friend of mine. The man they're holding in the dungeon is another. There are things going on that I'm not at liberty to talk about right now, but believe me, they're serious." He locks eyes with each of them before saying, "Understand?"

They nod their heads.

"I believe this Lord Kindering is up to no good and is probably behind why my friend is sitting in the dungeon. I need to find my other friend and try to work this all out somehow."

"You going to break him out of the castle?" asks one young boy, eyes wide in wonder.

"Let's hope it doesn't come to that," he says. "Are you with me?"

"You can count on us!" the older boy says for the group.

"Good," says Miko with a smile. "Find out what you can but be careful. Again, I'm staying at the Silver Bells, leave word there with a Miss Gilena if you can't find me."

"You got it," the older boy says. To the others he says, "Let's go."

Miko sits there and watches as the group leaves the market area. *James in the dungeon, Jiron mixed up in the slaying of the Ambassador's adjutant. What else could possibly happen?*

Getting up he decides to go down by the docks to see if there might be any scuttlebutt down there. Back in Bearn it always seemed the workers along the river had the most reliable news. And usually before anyone else, too.

He makes his way to the dock area where he finds it a flurry of activity as dock workers transfer cargo to and from the vessels secured there. Strolling along, he keeps his ears open for anything which might relate to what he's hoping to learn.

The conversations he hears is just the usual stuff guys say to one another, mostly about the girl they were with the night before. One ship, a beautiful three masted merchantman has just pulled up to the dock and the dockworkers are still securing the lines.

He misses being out on the water, though on every occasion he's had the fortune to be sailing, something bad has happened. Despite that fact, he longs to return.

"Out of the way!" one porter says as he nudges Miko to the side. At first annoyed at the treatment, he quickly realizes that he had been daydreaming as he stood there blocking the way. Laughing at himself he makes to move further down the dock.

He suddenly stops in his tracks when he sees a girl begin to disembark from the newly arrived merchantman. Dressed in a startling blue outfit with a beautiful dolphin embroidered along one side of her chest, she looks strangely familiar but he can't quite place her. Walking next to her is an older gentleman with a slight limp.

His mind flashes back to a night back in the city of Corillian at the estate of his friend Nate's family. Meliana, that's who it is, the older guy must be her father. *That's the girl James has been mooning about ever since we left!*

Coming out of his startlement, he quickly moves to fall in behind them as they come onto the dock. *Man, is James going to be surprised. That is if we can get him out of the dungeon first.*

"Now Meliana, don't get your hopes up," Miko overhears her father say to her. "There's no way to know if he's even in Cardri."

"I know father," she replies.

She's here looking for him! Miko breaks out into a smile as he says, "Hi!"

They stop in their tracks and turn to see him there with a goofy smile upon his face. "Yes?" her father asks.

"I'm Miko," he says, his goofy smile getting goofier.

Her father looks him up and down, a slight scowl coming to his face. "That's nice," he says and then turns to begin leading Meliana away.

"No, no, you don't understand," he exclaims as he rushes to catch up with them.

Taking a breath to calm his anger, the father turns back to him and says, "I don't wish to be rude but could you please leave us alone? Or I'll have to call for the guards."

"You don't remember me do you?" he asks, looking questioningly to them.

They both shake their heads. "No, I can't say that I do," her father says. "Now, if you'll excuse us."

Miko is at first confused by their reaction until he remembers he really doesn't look the same as he did. The Fire had unnaturally aged him while it was in his possession. So of course they don't remember him.

As they again turn away from him, he exclaims, "Wait! I'm James' friend."

At that her eyes light up and she turns her full attention on him. "James? You know James?"

"I'm Miko," he says, "Nate's friend from the mines."

Her smile begins diminishing as she tries to reconcile what he just told her with how he looks now. "But Miko was much younger than you," she says, confused. "You can't be him." Her hopes dashed, Miko can see sadness begin to well in her eyes.

"Son, I don't know what kind of game you're trying to play here, but we'll have none of it!" he says quite sternly. "Now, if you don't leave us alone, I'll be forced to call for the guards."

Frustrated, he watches them walk away. How can he explain to them what happened? He doesn't really even know what happened. Only James or Jiron could possibly convince them, if he tries anymore they're likely to call the guards and then how will he help James.

If they're here to do trading, then they're going to be here a few days at least. There's no way she'll let him leave until she has a chance to discover if James is here in the city or not.

Decided he's wasted enough time at the docks, he heads back to the inn to see if the kids left any word for him.

The Eye works his way through town. He can feel his agent here in the city. Things were going good until that fool of an adjutant went and got himself killed. Now all the carefully laid plans are beginning to fall apart.

Not only that, but his agent has begun to kill. The need comes at times and it must be satisfied, but now is not the time to draw undue attention. He hates to rely on such an agent but his master said he must.

Dressed as just another commoner of Cardri, he draws little attention to himself as he makes his way to where he knows his agent to be. When he left on this assignment, ostensibly to be part of the trade delegation, his master gave him a ring which enables him to find this particular agent.

What makes him the most angry is that this fool of an agent isn't killing in the poor quarters where such things are almost taken as a matter of course. But he's leaving the bodies in the better sections of the city where such things are given more notice. Fool!

The trail leads him past the outer walls and ultimately through the middle walls into the more affluent areas of the city. He follows the main thoroughfare until the ring indicates to go down an alley.

It's a dead end alley with many shadows and full of garbage. One of the shadows detaches itself from the others and moves forward. What light there is in the alley glints off a long dagger the shadow is holding.

"Just give me your money," a voice comes from the shadow, "and I'll not harm you."

"Of course," the Eye says as he reaches into his tunic. Instead of removing his money pouch, he pulls out a small thin tube and points it at the thief. Depressing the release, a small needle flies out and strikes the man.

"What the hell?" he exclaims as the needle embeds itself in his cheek. His hand brushes his face, dislodging the needle but the damage has already been done. The fast working poison which was delivered by the needle brings dizziness which causes him to begin staggering and then to fall to the ground. In a matter of seconds, he's dead.

Replacing the tube within his tunic, he steps over the dead man barely giving him a second thought. At the end of the alley, a doorway stands open and the ring directs him to enter.

On the other side of the door is a long, dimly lit hallway. He moves into it and follows it down past several closed doors. At the fourth door, the ring tells him he's very close, possibly on the other side of the door.

Opening it, he finds a gruesome sight. A small room, with but a bed and chest. On the floor is a dead girl, bending over her is he who the Eye has been searching for. "You fool!" he exclaims as he closes the door and enters the room.

Chapter Ten

On the way back to the inn, Miko finds Dave sitting at an open air eatery. "What are you doing here?" he asks him. "Didn't I tell you to stay in the room?"

Dave looks up with an annoyed expression and replies, "Relax. All I'm doing is having a meal and getting some fresh air."

The eatery is just down the street from the inn, he can see it from here. Not wanting to cause a scene in a public place, he says, "Very well. But return as soon as you're done."

Sighing, Dave says, "Alright, but you guys are really getting on my nerves."

Wanting nothing more than to take out his anger and frustration on him, Miko instead turns and walks down to the inn. When he passes through the front door, he finds Illan sitting in the common room near a window.

At his approach, he nods for him to take a seat at his table. "You know where that friend of James' is? He's down the street at an eatery!"

"I know," replies Illan as he glances out the window. "I've been keeping an eye on him for some time now. It was a mistake to have taken him with us."

"So why did we?" Miko asks as he sinks into the chair. A serving girl comes over and he orders some ale.

"James wouldn't leave him alone," he explains. "Not after what he's gone through. Plus, Jiron would've killed him if we had left him there with his sister."

Nodding, Miko sees the girl returning with his ale. After he's taken a sip, he asks, "Any word from Jiron and Fifer?"

Shaking his head, Illan says, "No, not yet." In hushed tones, he goes on to relate what Ellinwyrd told him about James. When he's done, he all but has to restrain Miko from rushing to the castle to rescue him.

"We can't just sit here and do nothing!" he exclaims.

"I don't plan to sit here and do nothing," he states. "But we have a day, maybe two and we don't want to act prematurely. I think it's safe to say that they're not planning on killing him here. Most likely they are going to return him to the Empire for interrogation first and find out what he knows."

"About what?" he asks.

"About that certain something you all found and which we just recently put away somewhere," he explains in a roundabout way in case they're overheard.

"Oh right," he says and then mouths 'The Fire'.

"Exactly," he says. "Our first priority has to be finding Jiron and Fifer. Once we have them back with us, we'll be in a much better position to attempt a rescue."

Miko then tells Illan about what he's having those kids of his do, and about the connection between Lord Kindering and the Ambassador.

Nodding, Illan says, "That puts some things in perspective."

"What do you mean?" asks Miko.

"Well, first of all it explains why he was summoned here," Illan explains. "From what we've found out, Lord Kindering and Lord Colerain are bound together in some way. Could be simply trading partners, who knows? Lord Kindering might have gotten the idea that if he managed to get James here and to the Empire's delegates, then they may give Cardri, and thus him, better terms in the negotiations."

"So you're saying they're giving up James just to make more money on trade?" he asks.

"Something like that," agrees Illan. "Though this is all just conjecture on my part, it does fit with what's happening. The fact that it also enables Lord Colerain to extract revenge upon James is probably just an added bonus."

Just then, Dave walks in through the front door. He sees them sitting at the table and simply nods to them as he makes his way to the stairs and up to his room.

"Hope he stays there," grunts Miko.

"We've got more important things to worry about than him," Illan says.

"You're right," agrees Miko.

Jiron comes awake and finds Qyrll sitting against the wall. He turns his head when he sees Jiron sit up. Nodding over to the candle sitting on the crate, he says, "We're almost out of light." Fifer remains asleep over against the far wall.

"Is it light out yet?" Jiron asks.

Shrugging, the Parvati says, "It's hard to tell, but I think the sun's been up for some time now."

Worried, Jiron says, "I was sure James would've found us by now."

"Maybe he's otherwise occupied?" suggests Qyrll.

"Let's hope not." Getting up, he stretches and comes to sit next to the Parvati.

Voices can be heard coming from the other side of the door as footsteps approach and then continue on past. "People have been moving along the corridor outside for some time now," Qyrll states. "Fortunately none have come in here."

Gesturing to the room, Jiron says, "Do you blame them?"

Qyrll just gives him a grin at that as he shakes his head.

More footsteps approach and they become silent. This time instead of passing by, the footsteps stop at the door.

Glancing at one another, they get to their feet just as the door opens. Swinging wide, several girls in their late teens come in and stop with a gasp when they see them standing there.

Jiron is about ready to say they're not going to hurt them when one gives out with a scream at the sight of the Parvati and his extensive tattooed skin.

Fifer starts awake and comes quickly to his feet.

The girls turn and flee out the door and down the hallway all the while screaming for help.

"That tears it!" says Jiron as he moves for the door. "Let's go."

He reaches the corridor on the other side just as a group of six thugs comes at them wielding clubs and swords. "Back in the room!" he hollers. Once they've returned to the room, he shuts the door and puts his shoulder against it.

Qyrll and Fifer lend their strength in holding the door closed as the thugs begin hammering on it from the other side. One of the thugs on the other side shouts for them to open the door but they pay him little attention.

"There's no other way out!" Fifer exclaims.

To Jiron, Qyrll says, "Let them in. We have to face them some time, they block our only way out. We should do it now before more come, or the city guard is summoned."

The incessant hammering on the door by the thugs has begun to produce cracks in the old door. Jiron realizes the truth in what Qyrll's saying. "You guys ready?" he asks.

Standing back, Qyrll draws both swords and nods.

"Alright," he says as he too stands back, knives appearing in both hands, "let's do it."

Fifer draws his sword and they wait.

They don't have to wait long as the next strike upon the door by the thugs outside splits it down the middle. When they again strike the door, it completely comes apart and one of the thugs stumbles through only to be met by Qyrll and his swords. Off balanced, the man has no chance and falls to the floor as Qyrll removes his shortsword from the dead man's chest.

As the thugs pour through the door, Jiron lashes out with his knives and another falls to the floor. The others press on through the shattered door and engage them.

Fifer faces off with one while Jiron and Qyrll each have two. Qyrll's swords dance as they block the attacks from one and strike out at the other.

The thugs are hopelessly outclassed. One strikes out at Jiron with his club while the other strikes out with his sword. Easily parrying the club, Jiron twists to avoid the sword. At the same time, he strikes out with his elbow to the clubber and connects with his chest, sending him stumbling backward. The man with the sword strikes down hard with both hands in an attempt to cleave Jiron in two. Dancing to the side, the sword misses him by scant inches as he strikes out with one of his knives, thrusting it deep into his side.

The man cries out as he stumbles to the side, blood beginning to well from his mouth as his lung fills with blood from where the knife punctured it. Crashing to the floor, he coughs up blood in a vain attempt to clear his lungs and soon passes out.

Qyrll has already killed one of the thugs and is now facing off with another of the clubbers. His shortsword knocks the club to the side and he follows through with his longsword, connecting with the man's neck and sending his head flying.

The torso stumbles around as blood fountains out of the severed neck. Crashing into the crate which had Qyrll's candle resting upon it, it sends the candle flying into a heap of garbage which begins to smolder.

Fifer is having trouble with the man he's facing and Qyrll comes up behind him and strikes him down. Glancing around, they find all the thugs dead. Smoke begins filling the room as the candle ignites the garbage and the flames start to spread rapidly.

"Move!" cries Jiron as he races for the door. A scream greets him as he enters the hallway. People congregating in the hallway to see what's going on begin running away when they see him there with his knife dripping blood. Smoke from the fire behind him begins filling the hallway as well.

Moving in the direction they originally entered from the night before, he breaks into a run, the other two right behind. Those still in the hallway in the direction he's running flee in a panicked run when they see him and his blood red knife coming at them.

Racing out into the alley, Jiron pauses only a moment to grab an old shirt off the ground to clean the blood from his knives before returning them to their scabbards. The smoke is beginning to billow through the doorway as the fire within consumes more of the old building.

Qyrll, hooded cloak once again hiding his features, is already moving down the alley away from the fire. Turning back to where Jiron and Fifer have paused to clean their weapons, he hollers, "Come on!"

Racing for the end of the alley, they collide with a squad of the city guard who were on their way to investigate the commotion. Screaming 'fire', Jiron points back the way they came to the guard captain as he and the others turn and race away down the street. Glancing behind them, he sees the guards moving into the alley to see about the fire. Soon, horns begin blowing as others come to help combat the spreading blaze.

Using the confusion the fire has created, they make their way to the nearest gate leading into the city and slip through at the same time that a fire team was coming out. Once inside, Jiron says to Qyrll, "Keep your hood close to your face. One look and anyone will know a Parvati is in the city."

Nodding, he reaches up and holds the bottom of the hood secure under his chin. Now, only a very close examination will reveal what lies beneath.

Jiron leads them through the city to the gates leading past the inner wall. On the other side is the Silver Bells and hopefully where they'll find James and the others.

As they near the gates, Jiron notices that the number of guards has been doubled. Probably due to the events of last night when the adjutant was killed. They move to a nearby alley and watch the gates for several minutes.

The guards are stopping everyone going in and out, asking them a few questions and then allowing them to continue along their way. Even the carts rolling through are given a cursory examination before they, too are allowed to pass.

"We'll never get through there undetected," he finally concludes.

"What are we to do?" Fifer asks.

"I'm not sure," he says. "There're not many places around here in which to adequately hide like there were outside the walls."

As they stand there in the alley deliberating their next course of action, Jiron takes notice of a young boy staring at them. The boy couldn't be more than fourteen and looks as if he's one of the street kids they've seen roaming the streets. He's sitting on a box further into the alley, eating some bread.

Hopping down off the box, the boy hesitantly makes his way over to them. By this time, both Fifer and Qyrll have noticed his approach and have turned their attention to him. "You guys in trouble?" he asks.

"Our business is none of yours," Jiron tells the boy. "Run along."

The boy just stands there staring at them as he takes another bite of the bread. "You're the fighters they're looking for aren't you?" he asks. "The ones who killed that man last night."

"No," denies Fifer. "I'm sure you've gotten us mixed up with someone else."

"Don't think so," the lad replies, sounding very sure of himself. "Was there. I saw how you took them out. Pretty good fight."

Fifer glances to Jiron and sees him resting a hand on one of his knives. Giving him a shake of his head, Fifer turns back to the boy and asks, "What do you want?"

"Got someone who wants to meet you," he says. "Was asked to keep an eye out in case I ran across you."

"Who?" asks Jiron.

"A friend of mine," he replies as he shoves the rest of the chunk of bread into his mouth.

"And why does he wish to meet us?" Fifer asks.

"Said he was a friend of yours," answers the lad.

"This friend of ours have a name?" Jiron asks.

"Miko," the boy says.

Fifer breathes an audible sigh of relief as Jiron asks, "Where is he?"

"Said at the Silver Bells," replies the boy. "But don't think you should try to get through the gate right now."

"No, I wasn't planning to," states Jiron.

"You wait here and I'll see if I can get him for you," he suggests.

"Very well," replies Fifer.

"Back in a few minutes," the lad says as he strolls out of the alley and walks toward the gate. At the gate, he passes on through, the guards don't even give him a second look.

"Who is this Miko?" Qyrll asks.

"A friend of ours," replies Jiron. "Hopefully we can get ourselves out of this situation."

"Well, well," a voice says.

Cracking an eye open, James sees Lord Colerain and another individual standing next to him outside of his pen.

"Seems the circumstances of our meeting have greatly improved since our last encounter," he continues. To his friend he says, "You have no idea how much satisfaction I have to see him here like this."

"We're getting some very good concessions from the Empire's Ambassador for him," his friend says. "Always pleasant when you can achieve two goals with but one action."

James looks out through the drug induced fog, his mind barely able to even follow what the men are saying. Their voices sound as if they're coming to him through water, probably a side effect of the drug they used on him.

Lord Colerain nods at his friend's comment and then turns his attention back to where James is lying on his side on the bench. "The negotiations will be concluded by this evening and you'll be happy to know that you'll be able to leave these poor accommodations for others."

His friend laughs and then says, "We must return. The negotiations will be starting again soon."

"Very well," Lord Colerain says. Taking one more satisfying look at James, he turns and follows his friend out of the cell area.

Through blurry eyes, he watches them go. When at last they've ascended the stairs out of sight, he slips back into unconsciousness again.

Miko and Illan are still sitting out in the common room when one of his street kids comes walking in the inn. Miss Gilena immediately moves to shoo him out but Miko sees him and says, "He's here to see me."

Eyeing the boy questioningly, she leaves him alone and returns to what she had been doing before he entered.

Coming over to Miko, the boy says, "I found them."

"Where?" asks Illan before Miko has a chance to say anything.

The boy glances to Miko who gives him a nod and then says, "They're out by the gate. I think they were trying to find a way through without being seen. Told them I'd come get you."

"Great!" Miko says as he gets to his feet. Turning to Illan he asks, "What should they do?"

Thinking a moment, he says, "Find an inn close to where they are and have them stay put. Then come get me and we'll figure out what to do."

"Alright," he says. To the boy he adds, "Let's go."

Leaving the inn, the boy takes him along the streets until they come to the gate near the spot Jiron and the others are waiting. Once through the gate, the boy leads him directly to the alley in which they're hiding.

Before he gets to the entrance to the alley, Miko sees Jiron's head poke out and break into a grin as he sees them approaching. He's surprised when he finds not only Fifer there with Jiron but another man in a hood as well.

"Man, are we glad to see you," Fifer tells him once he's in the alleyway with them.

Miko holds up his hand to halt any further questions and then turns to the boy. "Round up everyone and tell them to meet me at our regular spot in an hour," he says. "There's something else I need you to do."

"Alright, Miko," the boy says and starts to walk out of the alley.

"Here," Miko says to the boy. When he stops and turns back to him, he flips a silver over to him.

Snatching it out of the air, the boy smiles and says, "Thanks." Then he turns back and continues out of the alley. He's soon out of sight as he enters back onto the street and disappears around the corner.

"Now, what's going on?" Jiron asks.

"I should ask you that question," Miko replies. "Illan wants me to find an inn to stash you guys away for awhile until he's able to come and talk with you." Nodding to Qyrll, he asks, "Who's your friend?"

"His name is Qyrll," replies Jiron.

At that, Qyrll glances to Jiron who nods. Removing the hood, he reveals the fact that he's a Parvati. Miko's eyes widen and then turns his attention back to Jiron, "A Parvati? This just gets more and more interesting. We'll talk after we get to the inn," he tells them. "I know just the one." As he begins moving toward the end of the alley, he glances back and says, "Follow me."

Falling in behind, Jiron, Fifer and lastly Qyrll with his hood once more in place, follow him into the street. Several blocks down they come to an inn with a sign outside depicting a dancing squirrel. A yellow cat is lying on a nearby window sill and Miko goes over and scratches him on the back of the head. "Good girl, Furball." Furball lets out with an answering purr, obviously enjoying the attention.

Around Furball's neck is a rather plain collar with a small, circular metal disk hanging from it. Upon closer examination, Miko sees an exact duplicate of the dancing squirrel from the inn's sign engraved on it. *So, looks like Inius took James' advice after all.*

The last time they were there, Furball had gotten herself lost. When he and James had come across her and returned her to Inius, James had suggested a collar with something that would tell anyone who found Furball where to take her. Any local who found Furball would definitely know to return her to the Dancing Squirrel.

"Come on," he says to the others as he goes through the open door. He sees Inius there behind the counter and waves to him as he enters.

Inius looks at him with a smile and comes over. "Can I help you gentlemen?" he asks.

Miko expected a more personal greeting and then again realizes he doesn't look anything like he did when last here. Rather than going through what he did with Meliana and her father again, he just says, "I'd like a large room, if you have any. One with three beds maybe?"

"All I have available at the moment are rooms with two beds," he says. "But they are quite large." Looking on hopeful, he awaits their reply.

"Very well," replies Miko. "A quiet one in the back would be nice."

"We have just what you want," he says as he returns to the counter. Reaching for the room key, he says, "It's on the second floor. Only be two silvers and two coppers."

Miko looks to Jiron who digs the money out of his pouch and hands it over. Taking the key, he says, "Thank you."

"If there's anything else you gentlemen require," Inius says, "just let me or one of the servers know."

"We will, thanks," Miko says as they head to the stairs.

Once up to the second floor, they quickly find their room and file in. When the door shuts, Jiron says, "Okay. What's going on?"

"James was arrested last night for the murder of the adjutant to the Empire's Ambassador," he explains. "Which I believe you had a hand in?" He looks from Jiron and Fifer and from their expression, knows he hit the mark.

For the next half hour, Jiron tells him of the fight and what's happened since. Miko for his part, relates how James was arrested in the middle of the night, what Ellinwyrd had said to Illan, and of seeing Meliana and her father down at the docks.

When they're at last done with catching each other up, Miko stands up and says, "Just sit tight until I return with Illan. Maybe by then he'll better know what to do."

"Alright," Jiron says. "You be careful."

Miko looks at him and says, "I'm not the one wanted for murder right now." Turning to the door, he opens it and walks out. Shutting it behind him, he heads to the stairs and descends to the ground level. He's soon out on the street and heading back to the Silver Bells.

Chapter Eleven

"What was he thinking!" exclaims Illan after Miko relates to him what he learned from Jiron. Pacing back and forth, his mind furiously tries to figure out what they need to do next.

Dave sits on one of the beds and asks, "How are we going to get James out of the castle's dungeon?"

"We're not," replies Illan. "To do that would be all but impossible. We'll have to tackle a rescue operation once James is in the hands of the Empire's men and are on their way back to the Empire."

"But isn't that taking a big chance?" he asks, not liking the idea.

"We have little choice right now," he says. "We no longer have a mage on our side so we're going to have to move cautiously. It will do James little good if we act prematurely and wind up getting killed or thrown in jail."

Dave just glares at them. He doesn't like the idea of letting the Empire's men leave with his friend.

"You have a better idea?" Illan asks him. At that, Dave just shakes his head. "Alright then." He paces for another few moments before turning to Miko, "Take us to the Dancing Squirrel first. Then see if your kids can keep an eye on the Empire's camp outside the walls and possibly the gates leading from the castle. Have them find us if they attempt to move him."

Coming to his feet, Illan says, "Let's go." Moving to the door, he glances back and sees Dave still sitting on the bed. "I said let's go," he repeats himself, an edge coming into his voice.

"You're not the boss of me and I wish you would just stop acting like you are," Dave says defiantly.

Illan's eyes narrow as he begins to head back to Dave to teach this upstart a lesson. Miko intercepts him and says, "It won't do any good." Coming to a stop, Illan just stares at Dave and seethes in anger.

Turning to Dave, Miko asks with barely controlled contempt, "Will you please come with us?"

Giving them both a sardonic smile, he says, "I'd be glad to." Hopping off the bed, he moves to follow them.

Illan gives him a look full of anger before he turns to follow Miko from the room. All the way to the Dancing Squirrel, Dave whistles an off tune merry little ditty which does nothing to quell the anger burning within him. Only Miko's sudden intervention and the fact that he's James' friend kept him from beating the living hell out of him.

At the Dancing Squirrel, they find Jiron and the others still in their room on the second floor. When the door opens and Illan sees Jiron standing there, the pent up rage Dave had instilled within him erupts.

"Just what did you think you were doing?" he yells as he and the others move into the room. Miko hastily closes the door so their neighbors along the hall won't be able to hear the interchange. Or at least not as well, Illan can summon quite a loud voice when he wants to.

Jiron has the good sense to blush. "Sorry Illan," he says. "But when I was offered the chance for a fight, I just couldn't pass it up."

"So because of your indiscretion," Illan rages, "James is in jail, you're hiding out and the whole city is looking for you." Then he turns to Fifer, "Why didn't you stop him?"

"I didn't think…" he begins when Illan cuts him off with a wave.

"Of course you didn't," he states. "If either of you had half a brain we wouldn't be in this mess." He glares at both of them and has the satisfaction of seeing them divert their eyes first.

He glances at the Parvati and says, "We have things to discuss which are best said in private."

"He's coming with us," Jiron pipes up.

"What?" Illan asks. "How can you even think that? He's one of them!"

"No longer," asserts Qyrll. "I owe my allegiance to the Shynti. He restored my honor and now I must remain with him until the debt can be repaid."

Illan glances to Jiron who nods. "Great," he says, not very happy about the whole situation. "How are we going to get James with a Parvati? We're not going to be able to remain unnoticed with him along."

"Regardless," Jiron says. "He's coming with us."

"He's good in a fight," adds Fifer.

"I know he's good in a fight," states Illan, "he's a Parvati."

"I'll be back," Miko says as he opens the door.

"Try to return in an hour," Illan tells him. "Sooner if you learn anything."

Miko gives him a nod as he leaves the room, shutting the door behind. While Illan and Jiron begin discussing different strategies for rescuing James, Miko heads for the rendezvous with the kids.

Coming to the open market, he sees most of them congregating around the eatery where they ate before. When he approaches, the boy who was to round them up says, "I couldn't find them all."

"That's alright," he says. Only two of them aren't there, one of the older girls and that cute one that always gives him hugs. "Hungry?" he asks though of course he already knew the answer.

So after buying them each a meal, he lays down what he wants them to do while they're eating. "My other friend is still in the castle dungeon," he begins. "Now it's come to my attention that the Empire's men plan on taking him out of the city and back to their country. I want to stop that."

They perk up at that. To them it sounds like the beginnings to one of the tales of daring do that the bards are always telling. "How?" one boy asks.

"I would like you to keep an eye on their camp outside the city and on the gates to the castle," he tells them. "At some point they're going to be moving him and I want to know when and where."

"Is that when you'll be hitting them?" another boy asks.

"That will be decided when we know exactly what they plan to do," he says. "If you see anything that indicates they are moving my friend, I want one of you to come get me at the Dancing Squirrel. You know where that is?"

"Oh sure," one girl says. "Isn't that the place with the yellow cat?"

Smiling, Miko nods and says, "Yes, that's the one." Getting up from the table, he says, "Just be careful, I wouldn't want anything to happen to you. I'll be back here in a couple of hours if I haven't heard from you first."

"We'll be careful," the older boy assures him.

Nodding, Miko leaves the eatery and makes his way back to the inn. It suddenly occurs to him that he doesn't know any of their names. Inwardly smiling, he recalls how it was to be on the streets. Not too trusting and you never volunteer anything to anyone.

Back at the inn, he finds everyone still in the room. The remnants of the noon meal still sit upon several platters lying on the table. He tells Illan that his kids are going to keep an eye on the doings of the Empire's men and report back to him here.

The fog clouding his mind has slowly been dissipating over the last several hours. Still unable to fully concentrate enough to summon the magic, he's at least regained his equilibrium and the room isn't spinning nearly as bad. Sitting on the floor next to him is a tray of food which was brought in some time ago. Unwilling to trust it, it lies untouched. Still not sure how they managed to drug him, he's not willing to take the chance on a recurrence by eating doctored food.

When all the torches had begun to burn low, a different servant entered and put a single torch in the sconce near his pen. Now, only the light from that one torch is all he has to keep the darkness at bay.

Sitting alone in the cell, he feels the hard round object his magic had formed resting in his pants pocket. It was just a theory, never really had a chance to test it. If his situation worsens, he may try it, but until then he'll let it lie dormant. He's not even sure if it's going to work or not.

Footsteps coming down the stairs herald another visitor on the way. When the man exits the stairwell and begins walking across the floor, he can tell the man comes from the Empire. He's spent enough time down there to readily recognize one of them, even if the man is wearing local clothes.

"Awake I see," the man says as he draws close.

James stays seated on his bench and does nothing more than look at him.

"You should eat," the man tells him. "You have a long trip ahead of you and we must ensure you have the strength to survive it."

"Where?" he asks, breaking his silence.

"To someone who greatly desires to talk with you," the man says.

"Torture and interrogate you mean," replies James. "I hardly think it's going to be a social call."

Breaking into a grin, the man says, "I see you haven't lost your sense of humor."

"Do I know you?" James asks.

"I don't think so," the man says. "Our paths haven't crossed until now."

"Who are you?" he asks.

"Just a loyal servant of the Empire," he replies.

"I see," says James as he leans his head back against the wall behind him.

Gesturing to the food, the man asks, "Are you worried about what may be in your food? Is that why you don't eat?" He waits for a response and when none is forthcoming, he adds, "You needn't be worried, there is nothing contained within other than food. No drugs or anything like that."

James simply stares at him, not believing him in the least.

"We should be leaving in a couple hours," the man says. "The negotiations have been concluded most favorably for all parties. Trade between the Empire and Cardri shall continue."

"Good for you," says James. After a few moments of silence while the man simply stares at him, he asks, "So why are you down here?"

"Just wanted to see you for myself," he explains. "From all that I've heard, I thought you would be more impressive."

James starts laughing.

Turning to leave, the man says, "I shall return when we are ready to leave."

"I can hardly wait," James says, sobering up quickly. He watches as the man walks to the stairs and then ascends to the upper level. Absentmindedly, he rubs the object in his pocket and waits.

Shortly after he arrived at the Dancing Squirrel, Miko set himself in the common room drinking ale. He wanted to be quickly available should the need arise. He worries about James, imagining the worst possible things happening to him and would like nothing better than to storm the castle and rescue him. But like Illan said, that would be foolhardy.

When it draws close to the time when he said he would meet them back at their rendezvous, he gets up from the table and makes his way outside to the street. He doesn't get far before he sees the older boy running up the street toward him.

Upon seeing him, he hollers, "Miko!" and races straight for him. Looking distraught, he comes to a stop in front of him and says, "They've got them!"

"Got who?" he asks.

"Gwynne and little Daria," he replies. When he sees Miko not understanding, he clarifies, "One of the older girls and the little one who took such a liking to you."

Alarmed, he asks, "Who? Who has them?"

"The Empire's men," he explains. "They were down there keeping an eye on their camp while the rest of us met with you earlier. When me and Jerrick went down to join them in watching, they weren't there." Fear evident in his voice, he looks pleadingly to Miko.

"Calm down," he says as he tries to keep his own emotions under control. "How do you know they have them?"

Taking a deep breath, he calms himself and then says, "Just after we got there and began looking for them, the camp started to break up. I think they're getting ready to leave. A coach was sitting in front of one of their tents and I saw children hurriedly being put inside." He pauses for just a second before exclaiming, "I saw Gwynne and Daria being put inside with the others. It looked like they were crying."

Red hot anger begins burning inside him. The thought of those sweet girls going through what he had is more than he can bear. "Try to find out where they're going and then return fast," he says as he turns around to return to the inn and inform Illan what's happening.

"Right!" the boy says. As the boy turns to leave one of the girls comes running down the street. "Miko!" she exclaims.

Turning to see the girl coming, he stops and waits a second for her to reach him. The older boy joins them as well. "They have a boat at the docks!" she tells him. "We saw some of them leave the castle area and followed them to the docks where they began boarding."

The older boy says, "I bet that's where they're taking Gwynne and Daria!"

"Gwynne and Daria?" the girl asks.

To the boy, Miko says, "Send one to keep an eye on the camp to make sure they're not going somewhere else. Round up everyone else and meet us at the docks."

"Right!" the boy says as he takes the girl by the hand and they go racing down the street.

Bolting for the inn, he races through the door and takes the steps two at a time. Upon reaching the room, he opens the door and says, "They're leaving!"

"What?" exclaims Illan as he comes to his feet.

"They have a boat at the docks and they're leaving now!" he replies. "Their camp is being taken down and that's not all. They've taken two of my kids. They're going to make slaves out of them!"

"Damn!" curses Illan. "If they get away from the docks, we'll never catch them." To Fifer he says, "Go down to the docks and try to locate this ship."

"Right," he says as he runs out the door.

To the others he says, "If they try to move James to the ship, that will be our best chance to rescue him." Moving toward the door, he says, "Let's go." Opening the door, he passes through to the hallway, the others following right behind. He glances behind him, glad to see Dave is among them and not being obstinate.

The Parvati is in the middle of their group, the hooded cloak hiding his features. Fortunately it's autumn so relatively cool. If it was the middle of summer, he would attract attention like that.

Each walled section of the city has its own set of docks. It's unlikely the Empire's vessel would be docked outside in the poorer section. That dock is mainly used by simple merchants and fishing boats. The dock for the interior section by the castle is for the royalty and nobility of Cardri and the city. It's possible the ship could be there but most likely it's docked at the dock for the central section of the city where most of the merchants and travelers dock their ships.

It's to this section Illan leads them. Trying not to hurry and draw unwanted attention to themselves, they forge their way through the crowds upon the streets until they're able to see the masts of the docked ships ahead.

"Miko!" a young girl hollers and he turns to see her wave at him.

"One of yours?" Illan asks.

Nodding, Miko disengages from the group and moves to see what she wants.

With a worried expression, she hurries to meet him halfway. "Thank goodness you're here!" she exclaims.

"Why?" he asks. "What happened?" Illan and the others have come up behind him to hear what she has to say.

When she sees them approach, she looks to Miko who nods assuringly, "They're my friends and are going to help me rescue Gwynne and Daria."

"Paul told me to wait here and tell you the ship is called the Black Topaz," she says. "It's tied down at the docks, he didn't say which one it was, just the name."

"That should be enough," he assures her. "You wait here, there might be trouble and I don't want you to get hurt."

With fear in her eyes, she nods her head.

Miko turns back to the others and asks, "You heard?"

Illan nods. "Let's hope Fifer has already located the ship." Continuing down the street to the docks, they leave the frightened girl behind. The street doesn't go much further before they're able to see the harbor open up before them.

The docks are in a mass of confusion as ships are loaded and unloaded either by porters carrying the goods off down the gangplank or by use of one of the several cranes located throughout the dock area. One ship, a smaller two masted deep sailing ship is currently having a coach lifted aboard.

Miko's blood goes cold when he sees the sailors on board that vessel are from the Empire. "I think we've found it," he says and begins moving toward it.

A hand on his shoulder stops him and Illan says, "Patience. They're not leaving yet." He indicates several more coaches and six other wagons which have yet to unloaded. "Let's move closer and see what we can do."

As they make their way closer, Fifer disengages from the crowd and approaches. "That's it," he says as he nods toward the ship. "From what I can gather, most of the Ambassador's group has already boarded. The Ambassador has yet to make his appearance."

"Any sign of James?" Illan asks.

"Not yet," Fifer replies.

"Illan!" Miko exclaims quietly.

Turning to see what he's excited about, he looks to the window of the carriage being lifted on board by a crane and sees a small face peering out. "The kids?" he asks.

Miko nods. "That's the little one, Daria," he tells him. He stands there and watches as the coach is swung over and then lowered onto the deck. Sailors then push it over to the cargo hold where several sailors congregate near the coach's door. Over their heads, he sees the door to the coach swing open but the men there block any view of the children as they're being led into the hold.

"We have to do something!" he says. "We should tell someone."

"And what would anyone do?" Illan asks. "That's a diplomatic vessel and for the authorities to search it would be tantamount to a declaration of war in these shaky times. They'll not risk that on our word alone."

Miko glares at him, his rage wanting to be released. Pushing it back down, he lets it simmer against the time when it can be. And woe to the person who feels its wrath.

A group of kids makes their way toward them out of the crowd. As they draw near Miko can see that Paul, the leader of the group of kids, is very distraught. "They just took them on board!" he states angrily.

"I know," Miko tells him.

"What are we to do?" Paul asks him.

One of the older girls comes toward him tears streaming down her face and says, "Daria's my sister. We can't let them have her."

Laying his hand upon her shoulder, he wipes away an errant tear before it can travel very far and says, "Don't you worry. We'll not let them be taken."

Then from the direction of the castle area, a murmur begins working its way through the crowd and they see a group of important looking people making their way along the docks. The leader of the group is obviously from the Empire, and by his dress he must be the Ambassador.

"There he is!" breathes Fifer as they see James walking within the group of guards behind the Ambassador. His hands and feet are manacled and the short chain between his ankle restraints forces him to move in a shuffle.

"Now?" asks Miko, ready to extract his vengeance.

"No," Illan says. "Let's move a little bit closer." As they move through the throng of people on the dock, he contemplates this foolhardy venture. They haven't made any plans for escape should they even manage to get him free. How are they even going to get out of town? Events are simply moving along too rapidly.

By the time the Ambassador's procession reaches the gangplank to the ship, they've managed to work their way down to the edge of the crowd. James lifts his head and sees them there. He can see in their eyes that they plan to do something foolish. Looking directly at Miko, he shakes his head. He does the same thing with Jiron.

"Is he telling us not to do anything?" Miko whispers to Illan.

"I think so," he replies. "He knows if we do anything here, it'll come to ruin. Too many people and guards."

"Then what are we to do?" Jiron asks.

From behind them, a voice says, "I'd suggest keeping your hand's away from your weapons."

Turning around, they see Lord Colerain standing there, a smirk upon his face. Flanking him are four crossbowmen as well as a dozen armed men. "Now, we don't want to make a scene here," he tells them. "So if you'll follow along quietly, no one will get hurt."

The crowd around them begins backing away when they see what's transpiring between the two groups. The Ambassador's group, having already past their location doesn't take notice of what's going on.

Miko reaches for his sword when Illan grabs him and says, "No! He'll kill us all." Staring into the eyes of Lord Colerain, Miko's anger and rage almost gets the better of him again. "Not now," Illan insists.

Releasing his sword, Miko continues glaring at him.

Lord Colerain gives him a victorious grin and turns as he leads them away from the docks.

Miko glances over his shoulder to where Paul and the other kids are mingled in with the crowd. Paul stares in disbelief as they're being led away. Then Miko sees him say something to another boy who begins running through the crowd toward one of the streets leading away from the docks.

Just before he's led from the dock area completely, he casts one more look toward the ship and sees James as he's led aboard.

Chapter Twelve

_____

"You're not going to get away with this!" Illan tells him as they leave the dock area.

"And who is going to stop me?" he asks. "You? You're wanted for murdering a visiting diplomat. We even have witnesses."

"James' retribution will be hard indeed when he learns of your involvement," threatens Miko.

"I think I have little to fear from him," he says. "It's unlikely we'll ever see him again."

Miko's anger turns to worry for his friend. If he is drugged and incapable of using his magic, just what can he do? In a fight he's pretty useless, he can't use a sword or anything. And then his mind turns to Gwynne and Daria, those sweet girls now in the hands of merciless men who only want to make a profit off them. He feels they'll be safe until they're auctioned off, girls who are untouched tend to go for more. But how long do they have until they stand upon the auction block?

Glancing back, he can see Paul and the rest of his group following along behind, keeping a discreet distance.

They proceed in silence as they're lead through the streets. He's pretty sure they're being taken to the castle area though not entirely. Up ahead the street opens into a wide plaza with a large central fountain where several streets converge. Along the edges are many merchants selling a variety of goods to the people passing through.

"Thief!"

A cry from across the plaza draws their attention. "Guards! Thief!" a fat merchant selling loaves of bread hollers as a boy races away through the crowd with one of the merchant's loaves tucked under his arm.

Members of the city guard in the area give immediate chase. The boy races through the crowd, dodging nimbly as he makes his way to one of the streets which merges onto the plaza.

"Stop!" one of the guards hollers to the boy but the lad ignores the command and reaches the street. Soon, both he and the guards are out of sight.

At first, Miko had thought this some ploy of Paul and the others, but when he didn't recognize the one who stole the bread, he dismisses the idea. As their group crosses the plaza and come near the beautiful fountain of three women who are pouring water out of earthen jugs, he sees the boy who Paul had sent running back at the docks when they were being led away by Lord Colerain. He's standing on the edge of the fountain.

Suddenly, he raises his hand and the crowd around them surges as dozens of boys, ranging from older teens to a couple who couldn't be more than eight or nine, jump the guards surrounding Miko and the others.

As the guards are thrown to the ground, a melee erupts and soon the whole area is one big mass of fighting. Regular citizens scream as they race away from the combatants. Paul appears out of the maelstrom of fighting, struggling people. "Come on!" he cries as he takes Miko's arm.

Leading him away, Illan and the others follow right behind as they make a break for the far side of the plaza.

"Get them!" "Smash their face!" Cries ring out throughout the plaza as the boys pummel Lord Colerain and his guards. Miko glances back and sees a guard run one boy through with his sword just as two more boys tackle him from behind. A knife flashes in one of the boy's hand and the guard soon lies still upon the ground.

"We don't have much time!" urges Paul as they enter the street and leave the plaza behind. Soon, horns can be heard as the city guard makes its presence known. They begin flooding into the plaza from all directions.

"Who were those guys?" Jiron asks him.

"Friends," Paul replies. Taking them through back alleys, he leads them on a circuitous path back to the harbor. When they get there, they see the Empire's ship already away from the docks and heading out to sea.

"Damn!" Illan cries. "We're too late."

Miko turns to him and asks, "What can we do now?"

Illan stands there in indecision.

When no answer is forthcoming, Jiron says, "We have to do something!"

"Jiron?" a voice off in the crowd asks.

He turns to find Meliana standing there in disbelief. "I didn't think I was going to find any of you," she says. Breaking into a smile, she says, "Father said it was unlikely, but I thought..."

"Meliana!" he cries, startling her with the intensity with which he said her name. "You have a ship!"

"Well yes we do," she replies. "It's my father's really. He was nice enough to allow me to..."

Miko comes forward and says, "Take us to your father."

"Quick!" insists Jiron.

Her eyes widen as she recognizes him from when he had originally spoke to her and her father earlier. She glance to him, then to Jiron, "Miko?"

Jiron nods and takes her hand. "Yes. We don't have time to explain. James is in trouble and we need to see your father right away."

Gasping, she says, "Trouble?"

"Yes," replies Jiron. "Now, where's your father."

Turning slightly, she points to a vessel at the dock, "He's just finishing loading our cargo…"

Dragging her quickly, he heads in that direction. The rest of their group follows. "What's going on?" she asks as they run toward where her father is directing the unloading of the last wagon.

"James is being taken back to the Empire," he says. "I think they mean to execute him." He hears her gasp as she begins to understand the gravity of the situation.

As they reach the docks, Jiron sees her father at the top of the gangplank checking off the manifest as the cargo comes aboard.

"Father!" Meliana cries as they reach the ship.

Looking down to her from the deck of the ship, her father says, "Where were you? I was almost ready to send someone to find you."

"James is in trouble!" she cries out as she and Jiron reach the gangplank and run up to the deck of the ship.

"What's this?" he asks. He backs a little away from the gangplank as Illan and the others follow them on board.

Indicating Jiron, she says, "This is Jiron, James' friend."

"Nice to meet you young man," he says as he extends his hand.

Jiron takes it as he glances to the departing ship carrying James. "Sir, we need your help," he says.

"Help?" he asks.

"Father, James is in trouble," his daughter exclaims. "He's being taken back to the Empire. We have to help him." She takes him by the arm and looks pleadingly in his eyes and says, "They're going to kill him!"

"That's right sir," interjects Jiron. Pointing to the ship that's now pulling away from the docks under sail, he adds, "He's aboard that ship."

He glances to the departing ship and recognizes it as the Ambassador's. Looking into the pleading eyes of his only offspring, his will to resist melts away. "But what can I do?" he asks. "I'm not about to have my crew board the Ambassador's ship. We're not pirates."

"But father!" exclaims her daughter.

"No," he says, refusing though his heart would have him do otherwise. "I cannot bring our house to ruin over one man." His voice softens as he adds, "No matter how much you care for him."

Tears begin to well in her eyes as she sees her hopes being dashed upon the sound logic of her father.

"Could you at least follow him?" suggests Illan. "You wouldn't have to do anything, just drop us off wherever they land?"

Meliana looks to her father, hope beginning to spring anew.

He stands there and thinks for a full minute before turning to the captain of the ship and says, "Prepare to get underway."

Having heard the entire conversation, the captain knows just what is in store and begins shouting commands as the sailors bring in the last of the cargo.

"Thank you, father," Meliana says as she gives him a hug and kiss.

Looking slightly embarrassed at this display of affection before everyone on board, he gives her a smile as he quickly disengages from her embrace.

"You should return to shore," Miko says to Paul.

Shaking his head, Paul says, "I don't plan to return to Cardri without Gwynne and Daria." The determination in his eyes forestalls any objection Miko was about to make.

As the last sailor brings aboard the last of the cargo, the captain hollers, "Bring in the gangplank! Cast off the lines!"

One sailor pulls in the gangplank while dock workers untie the guy lines securing them to the docks.

The captain hollers to the men up in the rigging to drop sail. As the sail descends, the wind begins to fill them and they start moving away from the dock. As he gets the ship turned out to sea, Miko, Jiron and the others stand at the bow. The other ship is now far ahead of them and is almost lost upon the horizon.

Once the ship clears the harbor, the captain has the crew in the riggings to drop full sails and the ship begins racing through the water as they work to maintain visual contact with their prey.

When they come to take him from his pen, they remove everything from him but the clothes on his back. His slug belt, plus the entire contents of all his pockets were emptied into a sack before the manacles were put on his feet and hands.

The effects of the drug they used on him have reduced to nothing, though he is still unable to concentrate adequately enough to summon the magic. Helpless to do otherwise, he remains still as they secure the metal around his feet and hands.

Only able to shuffle due to the chain connecting his feet together, he moves as best he can up the stairs and then out of the castle. A crowd has gathered in the castle's courtyard to see the Ambassador off and maybe to take one last look at the mage.

He stands there amidst several guards while they wait for the appearance of the Ambassador and his retinue. When he at last makes his appearance, walking next to him is the man who paid him a visit earlier. That man comes to James and checks the integrity of his manacles before they start to leave the castle courtyard.

As they walk along the docks, he sees Jiron and the others in the crowd. He shakes his head to prevent any ill fated rescue attempt. There are simply too many guards around for it to have any chance of success. Especially with his magic inoperable.

He is then marched up the gangplank and then escorted by several of the Ambassador's guards to the hold where his manacles are secured to the wall by a chain. Over in one corner, ten children sit in a cage looking scared.

Once they are done with him, the guards leave the hold, leaving him there alone with the kids.

He sits there in the gloom of the hold, only a very small amount of light filtering down through the hatch from above. It isn't long before he begins to feel the unmistakable motion of the ship moving out to sea.

One of the girls, a small child, is staring at him with her face pressed against the bars of the cage. He gives her a reassuring smile. She smiles back at him. "Are you Miko's friend?" she asks.

He couldn't have been more stunned than if she started singing the Star Spangled Banner. "What?" he asks.

"Are you Miko's friend?" she repeats. One of the older girls in the cage with her perks up at that and joins her next to the bars.

"Yes," he replies. "I know Miko."

"He's a nice man," she says.

"I've always thought so," he says. *How in the world does she know him? And how could she possibly have connected him to me?*

"We were helping to keep an eye on the Ambassador's camp for him," the older girl explains. "We got a little too close and they grabbed us." After a brief pause, she asks, "What are they going to do with us?"

"Nothing if I can help it," he says. "Miko and the others with him know where we are and where we are going. They'll not sit back and do nothing."

"I hope not," the little one says. "I miss my sister."

"My name is James by the way," he tells her.

The older girl says, "I'm Gwynne and this here is Daria."

"That's me," the younger girl explains to him.

"Nice to meet both of you," he says. "I just wish it wasn't here."

Just then the hatch opens and James looks up to see the man who visited him in the dungeon. The man gazes down at him for a brief moment before stepping aside to allow the Ambassador to step onto the stairs leading down into the hold of the ship.

After the Ambassador has gone down a few steps, the man follows as does three guards, one of which has a crossbow.

The girls move away from the bars of their cage as the men come down the stairs. When they reach the bottom, they come directly to James and stop several feet away. Far enough to keep him from reaching them should he make the attempt.

"So this is the mage which has caused so much turmoil in the Empire?" questions the Ambassador. The guards flank him while the crossbowman keeps his crossbow aimed directly at James' chest.

"Yes milord," the other man says.

The Ambassador gives James a thorough once over before saying, "He doesn't look like much."

"Right now his ability to use his power has been blocked," the man tells him. "If he had his power I assure you your opinion would be different."

"Indeed," the Ambassador says, unconvinced.

After a few moments of silence while the Ambassador contemplates James, the other man says, "We should return to the deck milord. The air down here is most foul for your lordship."

Glancing to the other man, the Ambassador nods his head and says, "Perhaps you're right." Turning back to the stairs leading to the deck above, he moves away from James and the guards follow. As they ascend the stairs, the other man glances back to James just before exiting through the hatch.

When the hatch closes, the hold is once more plunged into darkness.

An hour or so later, he's not sure exactly as time down in the hold is hard to measure, the hatch again opens and the three guards who accompanied the Ambassador earlier enter and come down the stairs.

They approach James and in the hand of one is a small vial. When the man holding the vial stops near, he holds it out to him and commands, "Here, drink this."

Not about ready to willingly consume more of the drug, as that is what this must be, he crosses his arms across his chest and clamps his mouth tight.

"As you will," the guard says. Then he says something to his two companions who grab him. Once they have him tightly secured, the man with the vial comes to him and grabs his hair, pulling his head back.

Keeping his jaws locked securely, James stares at him in defiance.

The guard nods to one of the others who pinches James' nose closed.

Unable to breath but through clenched teeth, the need to draw in a breath becomes greater and greater. Finally, unable to stop himself, he opens his mouth and a piece of wood is inserted between his teeth to keep him from closing it again.

Then he watches as the man opens the vial and brings it to his opened mouth. He upends the vial and James feels the liquid within begin filling his mouth. Keeping the back of his throat closed, he tries to prevent any of the liquid from going down. But the need to breathe becomes too strong and he starts choking as he takes in a breath and the liquid goes down.

They continue holding him for several more minutes to ensure the liquid has in fact been consumed. Then the man nods to the two holding him who promptly releases him.

James immediately bends over and puts his finger in the back of his throat and vomits out the contents of his stomach all over the hold's floor.

"That won't do you any good," the guard tells him. "It's already in your system. The drug is very fast acting."

He looks up at the guards from where he's doubled over and can tell the guard's words are true as his mind begins clouding over. Not as bad as the other time, but bad enough to render him incapable of summoning the magic.

As the guards leave, the drug begins taking its full effect. Though his mind is beginning to be fuzzy, he's at least able to keep conscious. The effect of this drug feels like having a bad fever without the heat.

When the guards have left and the hatch once again closes, the older of the two girls asks, "James, are you okay?"

"Sort of," he replies.

"What did they do to you?" she asks.

Not bothering to reply, he closes his eyes and leans his head against the side of the ship.

Sometime later, the hatch again opens and the man who was with the Ambassador descends down the stairs. From the diminished light coming in through the open hatch, James figures it to be near dusk.

He notices that the man is carrying a sack in his hand as he comes nearer to him. Stopping several feet from him, he pulls a crate closer and sits down. Upending the sack on the crate next to him, James can see it contains the things which were taken from him.

The man holds up the slug belt and says, "Why do you carry this?"

James smiles and says, "I was given a sling by a friend and find that a handy way to keep the bullets for my sling."

He puts the belt down, nodding. The next thing he picks up, James almost can't even see what it is. "And what is the purpose of this?"

Squinting, he tries to make it out in the dim light of the hold. Then recognition hits him when he realizes the man is holding the little round hard object he made with his magic back in Cardri just before losing the ability to do magic.

"Oh that's a toy," he says.

"A toy?" the man replies. "I don't think so. Tell me what it does."

"Would you like me to show you?" James asks, giggling slightly. The giggle surprises him, it must be the effect of the drug.

"Yes," the man replies, "I would."

"Very well," agrees James. He then opens his mouth and says but one word, "Leech."

The round sphere pulses slightly and the man is about to say something when he suddenly gasps. "What?" he cries out as he drops the pulsating sphere as if it was a red hot coal.

The confident expression on his face turns to puzzlement as he begins to sense something is not right. "What are you doing?" he asks.

"Doing as you requested," replies James. "Do you wish to see more?"

Shaking his head, the man pulls out a knife and says, "Stop it now!"

"Very well." Looking to the sphere he says, "Leech by ten."

The man doubles over as if in pain, lines begin forming on his face as he starts to gasp. Raising his knife in one hand, he holds his middle with his other as he lurches toward James in an attempt to kill him.

"Leech by a hundred," James says.

The sphere flashes brightly as the man drops to the floor of the hold and begins writhing. Moaning, he looks to James as his fingers lose their grip on the knife and it flops to the deck when his arm twitches. Shortly after that, he lies still.

"Leech by zero," he says and the sphere, now the size of a golf ball, stops its pulsing and becomes still. An amber glow comes from it, similar to crystals which contain stored magic.

"Is he dead?" asks the older girl.

He glances over to them and sees all the girls staring at him and the dead man with naked fear in their eyes. Nudging the man's body with his foot, he nods, "I think so."

"What did you do?" she asks.

James waves away the question as he takes his foot and snags the dead man's body with his heel. Dragging him a little closer, he reaches out with his hands and pulls the dead body next to him.

Searching the dead man's clothes, he finds a set of keys and as luck would have it, one fits the locks of his manacles. He removes first his wrist restraints, then his feet. Glancing up to the open hatch, he fears that someone up there had heard the man's death. But when no one comes to investigate, he reaches over and picks up the glowing sphere, putting it in his pocket. Taking the rest of his things, he places the slug belt once more around his hip and then gets up, making his way over to the girls in the cage.

"Shhh!" he says, putting a finger to his lips. "We must be quiet."

"How are we going to get out of here?" one of the other girls asks.

Turning the key in the lock, he says, "I don't know. I wasn't planning on being on board a ship." Opening the door, he lets them out and has them move as far from the hatch as possible. They find a spot behind some barrels of tar to hide.

"Stay there and don't come out for anything," he tells them.

The girls just nod, fear on their faces.

Turning back to the hatch, he moves until he's once more by the cage. Unsure what to do, he stands there in indecision as he ponders his next course of action. His mind still fuzzy from the drug, it's hard for him to think properly.

He takes out the sphere and absentmindedly rolls it in his hand. When he had originally made the sphere he had only imbued it with a few simple commands. Leech was the first one, which would draw power from whoever it was near thereby infusing it with power for the other commands.

It was intended to use magic in circumstances when he was unable to, such as now. He only put one offensive spell in it and had he known that he was going to be aboard a ship, he never would have used that one.

Staggering slightly from the effects of the drug coursing through his system, he begins moving toward the stairs leading to the hatch. Suddenly from above, the light coming through the hatch is blocked as a guard begins descending down the stairs.

James halts his forward movement and begins backing up as the man stops abruptly on the stairs when he sees him there. The guard does a quick scan and takes in the scene: James no longer in manacles, the cage empty with the door open and the dead body lying on the floor.

The guard begins hollering up the stairs as he draws his sword. As the guard continues down the stairs, more guards come through the hatch.

Holding the sphere before him, he calls forth the lone offensive spell by saying, "Incinerate!"

The sphere pulses and he can almost feel the magic flow out of it toward the approaching guard. The guard's clothes, hair and it seems his very skin ignites in a fireball. Screams of pain erupt out of the inferno as the man stumbles around until finally coming to rest on the deck. The nauseating odor of burnt hair and flesh permeates the hold. Within the sphere, the glow has been greatly reduced.

James looks to the other guards who have paused on the stairs after seeing the fate of their comrade. They look to him in fear as they back up the stairs and return to the deck above. Voices can be heard arguing up there and though he can't understand the words being said, he has a pretty good idea. The Ambassador wants the guards to come down and subdue him while they feel that's a bad idea.

Finally a decision is reached as the voices become quiet. James glances over to where the girls are hiding and can see their faces peering around and over the barrels they're hiding behind. Turning his attention back to the hatch, he waits.

The light coming through the hatch is suddenly blocked again by several men coming down the stairs quickly. Each is carrying a crossbow and as soon as they clear the hatch, quickly fire.

When he realizes they are sending crossbowmen down, he says, "Shield." The sphere pulses and a translucent, shimmering shield surrounds him. The glow within the sphere diminishes still further until there's only a barely perceptible glow.

The first bolt fired glances harmlessly off the shield surrounding him and he begins making his way toward the stairs. Two more bolts are fired in rapid succession and they too are deflected by the protective shield.

"Leech by a hundred," he says and the closest crossbowman falls to the stairs and suffers the same fate as had the man before. When the other two crossbowmen see their comrade fall, and him advancing they beat a hasty retreat up the stairs, slamming the hatch closed. "Leech by zero," he says when the crossbowman at last lies still.

At the base of the stairs, he glances back to the girls and says, "Stay down here. No matter what happens, stay down here."

An 'okay' comes from the girls and he begins making his way up the stairs. At the top, he finds the hatch has been secured to keep him from escaping the hold and gaining the ship's deck.

Leech, shield and incinerate as well as the degree to which it does those commands, i.e. by ten and by a hundred are the only commands which he had imbued the sphere with when he created it. And until he regains the ability to do magic, those are all that he has at his command. If he ever gets out of here, he'll work on creating something which he can carry that will be more flexible in differing circumstances.

The sphere glows with stored power once again as he tries to figure out what to do. The longer he remains aboard this ship, the closer and possibly further into the Empire he will go. He has to act and act now.

Holding the sphere before him, he gazes at the hatch and says, "Incinerate." Nothing happens. He really didn't think that would work, the spell had been intended for enemies, not inanimate objects.

Coming close to the hatch, he tries to hear what's happening on the other side, but other than muted voices in a language he doesn't understand, he can't tell.

"Shield by zero," he says and the shield surrounding him disappears.

Returning down the stairs, he stares at the grisly sight of the burnt corpse and shudders. He hates what these people make him do. The girls have come out of their hiding place and are coming toward him. "Now what?" one of them asks.

"I'm not sure," he says. "But I'll think of something. Try not to worry." Looking around the hold, he sees many boxes and other paraphernalia which is useful on board a boat. A spare sail, some rope and a box full of tools! *If only the A-Team were here!* Laughing in spite of the gravity of the situation, he begins rummaging around the box of tools.

He finally comes up with a small five pound sledgehammer and takes it with him back to the hatch.

"What are you going to do with that?" one of the girls asks.

"Smash through the hatch and see about getting us off this ship," he explains.

"What if they won't let us?" Gwynne asks him.

His expression turning grim, he says, "Then I'll have to convince them."

"How?" Daria asks.

James glances at her but doesn't reply. Then he resumes moving toward the stairs and up to the hatch. The angle is awkward and his arms aren't all that strong to begin with. Balancing himself as best he can, he swings the sledgehammer with all his might and strikes the hatch with a resounding thud. The other side of the hatch becomes quiet as he brings the sledgehammer back for another strike.

Wham!

He hits the hatch again and begins to hear those on the other side running around.

Wham!

This time he has the satisfaction of seeing a crack begin to form on one of the slats of the hatch.

Wham!

The crack widens and suddenly the hatch is pulled open from the other side. "Shield!" he cries out as three crossbows fire simultaneously. The sphere pulses and the shield forms just as the bolts are released, causing them to bounce off harmlessly.

"Incinerate!" he cries out and one of the crossbowmen bursts into flame, the other two turn and run. The one on fire begins screaming and falls to the deck where he writhes in pain until finally becoming still.

Still protected by the shield, he makes his way out of the hold and onto the deck. The Ambassador is there as is the captain of the ship. "You have nowhere to go," the Ambassador says.

Stepping at last on the deck, James breathes the fresh salt air. It's growing dark, the sun is just now beginning to dip below the horizon. He looks out to sea and can only see water.

"Let me and the girls off in a dinghy and I'll let you live," he warns the Ambassador. Just then, a guard comes up behind him and strikes with his sword. The sword hits the shield and flies out of his hand as it rebounds.

James glances behind him at the guard who's looking at his empty hand in shock. "Don't do that again," he tells him.

Turning his attention back to the Ambassador, he says, "Well?"

"You're not leaving this vessel," the Ambassador tells him. "Whether or not we all survive is immaterial, you are not to be allowed to go free!"

"So be it then," says James as he raises the sphere.

Chapter Thirteen

Miko and Paul stand at the bow of the ship, the wind whipping their hair and the salty spray misting them occasionally. It's cold so they have their jackets pulled tightly. "Think we'll catch them?" Paul asks.

"Hope so," replies Miko. "If we can at least keep them in sight then we'll be able to stay on their tail, possibly attempt to rescue them after they make landfall."

"I'm worried about the girls," he admits.

Miko can hear it in his voice. "It's unlikely they will do anything to them," he assures him for the dozenth time.

"We're falling behind!" Dave's voice reaches them from where he's complaining again to the captain. He's been an irritant the whole way and the general consensus is they'd all be better off if they just tossed him overboard.

The captain's voice can be heard in reply, his tone saying he's had about enough. "We are not falling behind. Now leave me alone!"

Dave glowers at the captain then stalks off to stand by himself near the rail.

Shaking his head, Miko wonders again what James sees in him. Maybe he was different back where they came from?

"Something's been bothering me," he says to Paul.

"What?" he asks.

"Back in Cardri, when we were being led away by Lord Colerain, where did all those guys who jumped him come from?" he asks, glancing at him. "I mean, they appeared in just the right spot and fast."

Paul smiles as he says, "When we knew the girls were being taken to the ship, we spread the word that Gwynne and Daria were being taken. Those of us on the streets have a sort of brotherhood you might say, we look out for each other and take care of our own. The guys you saw had been there for awhile, they just kept their heads low until needed. Didn't want to tip off anyone something might be up, just in case."

Nodding, Miko says, "I see." He certainly understands about the brotherhood those of the streets have.

They stand there continuing to watch the ship ahead of them as the sun drops lower to the horizon. After awhile Illan comes to join them. "The captain says that when it turns dark there's a possibility of losing them," he says quietly.

Miko turns a worried expression to him as he asks, "Lose them?"

Nodding, Illan replies, "A definite possibility. But the captain says they'll most likely stay on this course through the night. That it's dangerous to alter course unless you are familiar with the waters in the area. Something about hitting a reef. So once dawn comes we should be able to pick them up again."

"Let's hope so," Paul says.

"Never did thank you for what you did for us back there," Illan tells him.

"Didn't do it for you guys," he admits. "I figured you were the only hope Gwynne and Daria had."

"Still, I appreciate it," he says as he pats him on the shoulder.

"Where are Jiron and Fifer?" Miko asks.

Nodding his head to the rear of the ship, he says, "In the captain's cabin, asleep. The Parvati is in there with them."

"How can they sleep at a time like this?" questions Miko.

"It's times like these when you get your sleep," he explains. "So you'll be rested when you need to be."

"Maybe," says Miko.

From the mid-section, a bell begins ringing. "Dinner's ready," Illan tells them. Leaving their post at the bow, Miko and Paul follow Illan as he goes to get some food. A wooden bowl full of fish and vegetables along with a single cup of ale is all that's allotted them.

They take their food from the cook and find a place near the stern where they have some shelter from the wind and spray while they eat. Jiron, Fifer, and Qyrll make their appearance as does Meliana and her father. Dave on the other hand takes his food and goes off to eat by himself on the other side of the ship.

When Meliana joins them with her food, she asks, "Have we gained on them any?"

"Not yet," Miko informs her.

"We don't exactly want to be noticed by them," her father says. "It wouldn't be good."

"I know," she says. Ever since they explained to her about the circumstances of James' arrest and being given to the Empire, she's held a deep fear for him. She understands her father's logic, but her heart doesn't care. She glances toward the fleeing ship and is thankful she can still see it in the fading light of dusk.

They sit there, quiet as each dwells silently on what the future may hold while they finish their meal.

"Captain!" a sailor hollers down from his position up in the rigging. "Vessel aflame!"

"Where away?" the captain hollers back.

"Dead ahead," he replies.

"James!" Meliana cries as she drops her bowl and rushes to the bow. The others follow quickly. In the darkening gloom ahead of them, a bright orange light can be seen. "Full sails!" they hear the captain yell. The sailors in the rigging above begin unfurling the last of the sails.

"Mr. Bessin!" the captain hollers.

"Aye sir," his second in command answers.

"Prepare to rescue survivors," he says.

"Aye, aye sir," Mr. Bessin replies and then begins barking orders as sailors prepare their dinghy should the need arise.

Their ship quickly gains upon the other and they can see where the sails have all but been consumed by the flames. It's listing to the side and appears to be taking on water.

"She's not going to last too much longer," Meliana's father says behind them.

"Oh, James," she breathes as she looks for any sign of him.

A massive explosion from within the hold blasts the deck outward, debris sails through the air and splashes into the sea many yards away.

Bodies can be seen floating in the water among the flotsam, none appear to be alive.

"James!" Dave cries out from his position near the bow.

"Daria! Gwynne!" Paul cries as his voice joins Dave's.

"Furl the sails!" the captain cries to those in the rigging and the sails begin to be taken in. Slowing down, the ship draws near the wreckage though the captain still maintains a safe distance so as not to suffer the same fate.

A rattle of chains and the anchor drops into the water with a splash. "Mr. Bessin, lower the boat and search for survivors."

"Aye captain," he replies.

"Incinerate!" James yells as another seaman erupts in flames. The sphere in his hand is now the size of a softball, a deep glow wells from within due to all the power it has stored.

All across the deck are charred remnants of the crew as well as withered husks from whom James drew the power necessary to maintain the spells. The Ambassador and captain lie among them.

At one point during the battle, the ships crew had taken a spare spar that was stored at the base of the ship's rail. Using it as a battering ram, they tried to push him off the boat and into the sea.

Crying "Leech by a hundred," he sucked them dry as they crashed to the deck, the spar hitting the deck and rolling to the side. So much power being absorbed by the sphere had caused it to crackle like static electricity. James begins incinerating crewmen simply to release the pressure. The last thing he wanted was to have it explode in his hand.

Fire rages throughout the ship, most of the crew either lies dead or has jumped over the side. A scream from below rips through the air. *The Girls!*

Racing for the hatch, he sees black smoke billowing up out of it like a chimney. A quick glance around the ship shows it to be almost completely engulfed in flames. Taking a deep breath, he steps through the hatch and begins making his way down to the hold through the black smoke.

Unable to see, he uses the sound of the girls coughing and crying to guide him. "Over here!" he calls to them. "To me!"

A hand reaches out through the thick smoke and takes hold of his shirt. He looks down and sees little Daria there with several other girls in tow. "Where are the others?" he cries out.

"B...b," she says then a coughing fit robs her voice.

Taking her by the hand, he leads her to the stairs and says, "Go up on top. I'll get the others."

A quick nod of her head and she begins leading the others up the stairs.

Coughing badly now, James pulls off his shirt and uses it to try to filter out the smoke. Helping only slightly, he begins working his way further to the back. "Where are you?" he hollers but there's no answer.

In the thick smoke, he can barely see anything. A crack from above and a portion of the flaming deck falls in, crashing to the bottom of the holds several yards away. "Girls!" he cries again.

Moving as quickly as he dares, he tries to see through the smoke but his eyes are so red and burning now it's all a blur. Useless, he keeps them closed, only peering out of them every now and then.

Suddenly, he hears coughing from up ahead. The coughing and crying of a small child. Using the sound as a guide, he comes to the barrels he told the girls to hide behind earlier and finds a small girl lying with her head on the chest of a larger. The older girl looks to be unconscious, the smaller one not much better.

"You okay?" he asks her when reaches their side.

The small girl looks up at him with red rimmed eyes and tries to say something but only breaks into a massive coughing fit.

All around them, the heat from the fire is increasing as more of the ship becomes engulfed.

"Can you crawl?" he asks her.

When the coughing spell lets up a little, she manages to nod.

"Follow me then," he says. Grabbing the older girl, he gets on his hands and lays her across his back. Moving on all fours with an unconscious girl upon his back, he begins leading the other little girl to the stairs.

At this level, the smoke isn't nearly as bad, though it is still thick. Glancing back every other step, he makes sure the little one is keeping up.

They make it about halfway to the stairs when he suddenly feels the ship lurch slightly and cold seawater flows across the floor. The hold begins to fill with water. He doesn't have that much time.

"Come on!" he manages to yell to the girl behind him. He removes the girl from his back and then stands up. The water is now about ankle deep and rising. Picking up the unconscious girl, he carries her toward the stairs, the little one following, holding onto his shirt.

As they reach the stairs and start to climb up, the ship lurches again and begins to tilt. Scenes from Titanic run through his head as he climbs the stairs. Before he makes it to the top, another section of the burning deck caves in and lands upon a small stack of barrels lining one wall. He hopes they aren't flammable.

Clearing the hatch, he sees an inferno all around him. The girls who had come out before are huddled against one side of the ship. It's the only area yet to be consumed by the fire and it's not going to last very much longer.

When he reaches them, he asks, "Is this everyone?" Several heads bob affirmative.

He glances over the side to the water below. Debris has already begun to dot the surface. "Over the side!" he yells.

"I can't swim!" one girl screams, terrified.

"You got no choice!" he tells her. One of the older girls goes to the rail and jumps over, a couple others follow. Finally he's left there with the unconscious girl in his arms and the frightened girl who won't go over. The heat from the fire consuming the ship is beginning to burn his skin. The central mast suddenly cracks and topples over sending sparks and embers flying.

One ember lands in the frightened girl's hair and James quickly puts down the girl in his arms and brushes it out before it has a chance to catch. He then looks over the side and sees that Gwynne and the others have all managed to find something to grab a hold of to keep from going under.

"Gwynne!" he yells.

She looks up at him.

"One girl can't swim," he hollers. "You'll have to help her!"

She gives him a nod.

Turning to the frightened girl, he says, "You can't stay here!"

Looking at him with fear in her eyes, she says nothing, just stands there with her bottom lip trembling.

He picks her up and she begins fighting him. Struggling, he manages to get her to the rail and then tosses her over. She lands with a scream and a splash near Gwynne.

Gwynne immediately dives under the water and pulls her up. Helping her, they both grab hold onto the flotsam floating nearby.

Suddenly, the deck under which James is standing gives out with a crack, but doesn't collapse. Picking up the unconscious girl he jumps over the side and together they hit the water.

The impact knocks the breath out of him and he loses hold of the unconscious girl. Little hands begin reaching for him and help him to the surface. When he breaks through the surface, he looks around in a panic and sees another girl having already rescued the unconscious girl.

"Away from the ship!" he hollers. "We've got to get away before it goes down!"

Bam!!!

An immense explosion sends wood and other debris through the air. The ship begins to tilt even more precariously in the water.

"Now!" he yells as they begin kicking and swimming away from the burning wreckage. From behind them, a groan and a crack can be heard as the second mast topples over.

They continue swimming away and soon, the ship upends before sinking completely under the water. Steam and hissing sounds erupt as the flames meet the water. Then, all is quiet.

As the second mast falls, the dinghy with six sailors in it begins moving carefully toward the wreckage. All the while keeping its distance from the raging inferno.

"There she goes!" one sailor hollers as the ship upends and sinks below the surface.

The flaming ship produces a massive amount of steam as its burning carcass enters the sea. When the steam begins to dissipate, Meliana screams, "There!" The others look to where she's pointing and she sees several forms floating in the water. One of them is waving, trying to gain their attention.

"Is it James?" Miko asks.

"Hard to tell from here," Illan says. "But I think so."

"James!" Dave yells from his position by the rail. Waving madly, he looks as if he's about to have a fit from jubilation.

The dinghy makes its way through the flotsam scattered about the surface of the water as it continuous to head for the survivors. When they draw close, those still on the ship watch as they haul them out of the water. After they're all in the dinghy, they turn and start returning to the ship.

"It is James!" Meliana exclaims happily. She turns and gives her father a hug and kiss.

"But what happened?" he says to no one in particular.

"James happened," Jiron tells him. When her father glances at him, he adds, "This is why the Empire wants him so badly."

"But you said he had been drugged?" he asks.

"True," replies Jiron. "That's what we were told."

"Then, how?" he wonders.

Jiron just shrugs and turns back to watch the dinghy as it returns to the ship. It suddenly alters course and begins returning to the wreckage. Two crewmen of the sunken ship are found hanging onto one of the spars. After they haul them aboard, they return to the ship.

Meliana rushes to the side where they'll be coming abreast and watches as they draw near. Her eyes and James' lock for a minute and she's pleased to see a smile break across his face when he recognizes her. He gives her a wave.

Next to her, Paul waves to the approaching dinghy and shouts, "Gwynne! Daria!"

The girls see him and begin shouting, "Paul! Paul!"

When the dinghy comes to rest against the side of the ship, a rope ladder is let down to them and they begin climbing up. The girls are the first to come up, Paul gives Gwynne and Daria each a hug. The other girls know him as well and in turn give him a hug, several break down and cry.

As James takes his turn in climbing the ladder, Meliana positions her self to greet him. The others know what's between them and allow her to be the first to greet him. When he finally reaches the top, Dave comes over and nudges her out of the way as he extends a hand down to him.

"Man, I didn't think to see you again," he says.

Meliana gets a hurt look on her face and her father's demeanor turns dark.

"Thanks," James says to him as he takes his hand and makes it over the rail.

Dave tries to say something else but Meliana rushes past him and gives James a hug. Burying her face in his shoulder, she lets out the pent up fear and frustration she's felt ever since learning of his fate.

He pats her on the back and says, "Here now, I'm okay, there's no reason to fret."

"I was just so scared for you," she cries.

James looks at the others slightly embarrassed at this display of emotion in front of everyone, though he does rather enjoy it. Dave is giving him an odd look and it doesn't look like a pleased one.

"What happened?" asks Jiron.

"That's a long story," he replies. "Best if we talk about it later."

The two rescued crewmen climb aboard and begin talking to the captain. Meliana's father goes and joins in the conversation. After a few words are exchanged, her father says, "Captain?"

"Yes sir," the captain of the ship replies.

He glances at his daughter and as if the words are painful to say, points to James and says, "Place this man under arrest."

"Father!" she cries.

"What?" Illan asks as he rounds on her father in disbelief.

Nodding to the rescued crewmen, he says, "He killed the Ambassador and everyone on board except these two sailors. We must take him to the nearest port in the Empire and hand him over to the authorities."

"But they'll kill him!" Meliana exclaims. "We can't!"

"We must!" he shouts at her. He sees the pain in her eyes, the look of betrayal but he has no choice. "We are loyal citizens of the Empire."

James looks at him and then at his friends. He sighs and says, "I understand." To his friends he says, "I don't want any trouble from you while we're on this ship." Locking eyes briefly with each of them, he says, "Alright?"

Each in turn gives him a nod. Miko looks outraged and about ready to protest when Illan lays a hand on his shoulder. Giving in to his wishes, he gives James a nod.

"This way," Mr. Bessin says.

Disengaging from the crying and on the point of hysteria Meliana, he follows Mr. Bessin to one of the cabins and goes inside. The door shuts and he hears a key turn in the lock. At least this is better than where he had just been.

When James is locked away, they gather around her father. "You can't just hand him over to the Empire's men," Dave says. "They'll kill him."

"Young man," her father says, "shut up and get out of my face before I have you thrown overboard."

"But…" he begins when Fifer comes and escorts him away.

Illan starts to say something, when her father cuts him off and says, "I can't ruin my house over this. When we arrive at a port in the Empire, I must hand him over. I'm sorry." He then turns and walks away.

"What are we going to do?" Miko asks him.

"I don't know," Illan replies. "We'll have to wait until he's off the ship, then we'll see."

Meliana's father keeps James locked up in the cabin with only brief respites out to answer the call of nature and to get some fresh air. It was during one such time when Meliana comes to him with something in her hands. As she draws close, he realizes it's the ceramic dolphin figurine he had shipped to her during their brief stopover at Maradan when they left Corillian.

He smiles at her and says, "I see you got it."

"Yes," she replies with a smile. "You can't imagine how surprised I was when Miriam came over and gave it to me. How did you know I liked these?"

"I didn't," he admits. "I just liked them too, and I wanted you to have something to remember me by."

She comes close to him and he slips his arm around her. They stand by the rail watching the waves roll by. "What's going to happen?" she asks him.

"What do you mean?" he replies.

"My father meant what he said," she tells him. "At the next port we visit in the Empire, he will hand you over to the authorities."

"I know," he says. "I harbor him no ill will, he's just trying to protect his house…and you."

She lays her head on his shoulder as they stand there in silence, simply enjoying each other's company.

"James," an annoying voice interrupts this peaceful scene.

Turning, he sees Dave standing there. "What?" he asks.

"Can I talk to you?"

Sighing, he says, "Sure." Then to Meliana, he asks, "Will you excuse me for a moment?"

"Of course," she says though in her heart she wanted to say no.

He and Dave move a little ways from her, the two sailors who are set to watch him follow. Like her father said, the guards are more for show. If James wanted to kill them all there's little any of them could do about it.

"What?" he asks when they reach a spot of relative privacy.

"Let's get out of here," he says. "I know you can do it, they've told me enough tales about you."

"I can't," James tells him.

"Why?" he asks. Pointing to Meliana he says, "Is it because of her?"

"Partly," he admits.

"You and me go way back," Dave says. "We've been friends a long time."

Holding up his hand to forestall any further comments, he says, "I know, Dave. Your friendship has always meant the most to me. But no matter what, I have to do what I feel is right. You know that."

True, throughout his friendship with James, he's always known him for doing what he felt was right. No matter what the consequences were. "Yeah, I know," he says. "But this could be your life we're talking about. Not to mention mine. You're all I have in this crazy world." He looks into James' eyes a moment and then says quietly, "I just want to go home."

"I know you do," he says. "So do I. But right now we can't and are simply going to have to do the best we can."

One of the sailors comes up and says, "It's time to return to the cabin."

"Everything will be alright," he assures his friend.

"I hope so," he replies.

Meliana comes and walks with him back to the cabin and gives him a quick kiss on the cheek before they put him in and lock the door. Once the door is closed, she turns around and sees her father there looking at her. She gives him a look of betrayal and then turns around and goes the opposite direction.

Later that afternoon, they make a course change and land begins to appear on the horizon. Shortly after that, a major port city comes into view ahead of them.

Illan is standing next to Kendrick, Meliana's father. "So," he says, "you still plan to hand him over when we dock?"

"Here?" he asks. Shaking his head, he says, "Not here. That's Westerlyn, a port city still within the borders of Cardri. If I were to take him ashore here and he got away, I wouldn't very well be able to take him on into the Empire, now would I?"

Illan's eyes move to his and they lock for a moment before he says, "No, you wouldn't."

"There's some trading we will be doing here before returning to the Empire," he tells him. "Probably won't be staying more than the night. Should have our business concluded by then." He then turns and heads to the other side of the ship to confer with Mr. Bessin.

Illan watches him go and then he turns back to watch Westerlyn approach.

Chapter Fourteen

In the late afternoon, the ship comes to rest at the dock and Kendrick's sailors begin transferring cargo. By the time night falls, the cargo for Westerlyn has been transferred off and the cargo they are acquiring brought aboard. Their next stop being far into the Empire, Kendrick allows most of the crew to go ashore, keeping only two on board to watch James. He and his daughter leave for the evening to find an inn and have a good dinner, perhaps listen to a bard.

While the ship was unloading, Illan and the others took Paul and the girls to find a way back to Cardri. They eventually came across a caravan going in that direction and arranged passage for them. Fortunately one of the wagons was only half full and the merchant was more than willing to have them use that space, for a price.

Miko and Paul exchange goodbyes, Daria giving him a hug and a kiss. "Some adventure," Paul says as they get loaded onto the caravan.

"Yeah," Miko replies. "At least it all worked out well."

"You coming back to Cardri?" he asks him.

"Maybe," Miko tells him. "If I do, I'll be sure to look you up."

"You do that," he says as he takes his place in the back of the wagon.

The caravan master calls for the wagons to begin moving and their wagon starts rolling down the road. Miko watches for a while as they move away, Paul and the girls waving goodbye to him. He waves back until they've rolled out of sight.

All afternoon, Illan has been contemplating the words Kendrick said to him. Not just the words but the tone of voice. That, along with the fact he sent most of his crew away on shore leave, seems to indicate he wants them to get James off his ship.

He mentions his observations to Jiron and he readily agrees. "He doesn't want the Empire against him, he lives there. But at the same time he wishes to please his daughter so is creating a situation for us to get him off without seeming to. He won't be considered at fault and James will be free."

"That's how I see it too," he adds.

They have Fifer take Dave into town to keep him out of the way while they wait nearby on the docks for everything to become quiet. The two sailors who survived the destruction of the Ambassador's ship have gone into town with Kendrick's crew and aren't expected back until late or maybe not until the following morning.

Illan, Miko, Jiron and Qyrll wait in the deepening shadows of the dock as the crew from a neighboring ship disembarks. Once they've passed from the dock area, it grows quiet.

"Now?" Miko asks.

Illan nods his head and they make their way through the dark and to the gangplank leading up to the ship's deck. The two guards posted outside James' door sees them come aboard, one of them breaks into a grin. "Can we help you?" he asks.

"You know why we're here," Jiron states as he draws one of his knives.

The two guards step aside. As Illan moves to open the door, the other guard says, "You better rough us up. Gotta make this look convincing."

Jiron nods understanding before lashing out, catching one in the stomach. As the man doubles over, he cracks him in the head with the butt of his knife, dropping him to the floor.

Miko turns to the other guard who says, "You better cut me." Pulling out his knife, the other guard exposes his side for Miko as he strikes out. A red line forms in the sailor's side from where Miko's knife opens a four inch long wound. Then Jiron strikes him in the back of the head and he falls to the deck.

By this time Illan has the door open and James walks out. Upon seeing the guards lying on the deck, his expression darkens.

"We had to," Jiron assures him. "We didn't want anyone to believe Meliana's father allowed you to be taken off his ship. This way, it looks like we came and rescued you."

"He still may get into trouble," Illan tells him, "but hopefully not nearly as bad."

James looks down at the guard who isn't unconscious and sees him nod agreement to what Jiron had just said.

"Alright," he says. "Let's get out of here."

They move off the ship and cross through the docks. "Just where are we?" he asks.

"A port city called Westerlyn," Illan explains. "It's somewhere south of the city of Cardri, but still north of the Empire."

As they make their way along the avenue through the warehouses bordering the docks, a shadow disengages itself from the darkness. James comes to a stop before he realizes it's Mr. Bessin.

"Hope you didn't kill the men standing guard," he says.

Shaking his head, James replies, "Only roughed them up a little. Had to make it look convincing."

"Indeed," he says. He pulls a small sack out of his shirt and hands it to James.

"What's this?" he asks as he takes the money.

"Something from a friend to help on your journey," he explains. "Also, this friend said for you to find the horse trader, Ellias. That you should tell him 'your ship left without you'."

"Tell this friend we appreciate all he's done for us," says James.

Nodding, Mr. Bessin abruptly moves into the avenue and walks back to the ship.

James lightly shakes the sack and hears the coins within clinking together. "That was nice," he says to Illan.

"Probably doesn't want us captured anywhere near where he is," Jiron says.

"Probably," he agrees.

To Jiron, Illan says, "Go find Fifer and Dave and meet us at this horse trader Ellias' place."

"Will do," he says. Moving away down the street, he is soon out of sight in the darkness.

They move further into town and after asking directions, find themselves at the eastern edge of town. Ellias' place is one of the largest horse trading establishments James has yet encountered. Dozens of horses stand in the open corral outside the office building. A light shines from within and they enter through the front door.

A short man is there and looks up from where he's jotting down notations on a piece of parchment. "Yes?" he asks.

James steps forward and says, "Our ship left without us."

"Did it indeed?" he says. Resting his quill in the inkwell, he gets up and gestures for them to follow him through the back door.

Seven horses are saddled and ready for them. "Which one of you is James?" Ellias asks.

"I am," James replies.

He pulls out a rolled letter and hands it to him.

Taking the letter, he says, "Thanks."

"You're welcome," Ellias tells him. "These are yours and already paid for." Turning around, he leaves them there and returns to within the office.

Having a wait before Jiron returns with the others, he unrolls the letter and moves over to take advantage of light coming through one of the office's windows to read it.

James,

At first I was so mad at my father that he would hand you over. It wasn't until we left the ship that he explained to me what was going to happen. I so much wanted to be with you, but understand why that cannot be right now.

I will return home with my father and hope one day to see you again. We will have other voyages to Cardri in the spring, this is to be the last one before the winter storms set in.

I wish you safe journeys and will always hold the memory of you precious. Thank you again for the figurine, it is special to me.

I love you,

Meliana

"I love you too," he whispers to himself after reading the last word. He didn't actually think he felt that way until he read this letter.

"Good news?" Miko asks him when he sees he's finished.

Nodding, James rolls the letter back up and puts it inside his shirt for safe keeping.

Just then, they hear voices coming from the office and soon the back door opens as Jiron and the others join them.

"We got horses," Miko tells Jiron.

"I see that," he says.

Mounting, Illan says, "We better get out of here. When it's discovered we're gone, a search may develop."

"I doubt it," argues James as he gets in the saddle. "By the time the authorities here could be contacted and convinced a search should be implemented, we'll be gone. They'll know that. Plus I doubt if any of Kendrick's crew is likely to go against him. He may not have publicly stated that he supported my release, but I'm sure they know. Woe to any of them who speaks out against me to his daughter."

At that several of them laugh. Dave gives him a grin.

"What about you my Parvati friend?" Jiron asks Qyrll. "Are you going to return home?"

Shaking his head, he says, "I must stay with you until my debt is repaid."

Moving away from the horse trader's establishment, they head through town and take the road to the northwest along the coast.

"Where are we going?" Fifer asks from the rear.

"Home," James said. "I presented myself as requested and the court did what it had to do. Now I just want to go home."

Illan reaches into his tunic and pulls out the sealed letter Ellinwyrd had given him when he went to see him about helping James. Handing it over to James, he says, "In all the excitement, I forgot about this."

Taking it, James sees the wax seal bearing Ellinwyrd's symbol. "Where did you get this?"

Illan proceeds to relate to him the events leading up to his meeting with the Archive Custodian. "He said it had something to do with your last meeting," he explains.

His orb suddenly blossoms to life as he breaks the seal and unrolls the letter.

"What does it say?" Dave asks as he pulls up next to him.

"It only has one word," he says.

"What?" Illan asks.

"Ironhold."

"Ironhold?" Illan asks.

James glances to him and asks, "Ever heard of it?"

Shaking his head Illan turns back to the others and raises his voice, "Any of you heard of a place called Ironhold?" When he gets nothing but negative responses, he turns his attention again to James.

"I told Ellinwyrd of what happened in Saragon and of the cryptic message that I discovered there," he explains. Holding the letter up, he adds, "This must in some way have to do with that. Just have to figure out what."

Shortly after leaving town, they come to a crossroads. They can either continue along the coast or head due north, James chooses to go north. "The coast road would lead us back to Cardri, and after all that's been done there, I think it wise to avoid the place for awhile."

"Plus this road should lead more directly home too," adds Miko.

An hour later, they come to a cluster of buildings, one being an inn and they decide to stop for the night. It being so late, the inn is all but deserted. Only two workers are cleaning up and getting the place ready for the morning customers.

James and Illan enter and get rooms for everyone. After stabling their horses around back, they head up to their rooms and go straight to sleep. Dave shares James' room again.

"Why do we need to find this Ironhold anyway?" he asks as they get ready for bed.

"There are many questions that have arisen since I've come here," he explains. "and I need to find the answers."

"Why?" he asks.

James opens his mouth to reply when he suddenly realizes he doesn't have a good answer for that. He doesn't know why, he just feels he needs to. Turning to Dave, he says, "If I do what I'm here to do, maybe we can go home."

"You haven't really explained it all to me yet," he says. "I'm your best friend and I think you should clue me in as to what is really going on."

"You're right Dave, you are my best friend," he says. He then gives him a general rundown as to what's going on and the visits by Igor. He makes no mention of the Fire or anything about his experiments. When he's done, Dave is satisfied and they drift off to sleep.

Early the following morning, a commotion outside wakes them and Dave goes to the window overlooking the rear courtyard. A group of people are congregating near the rear of one of the other buildings. "Something's going on," he says.

"We better go check it out," James says as they begin getting their clothes on.

Before they're finished getting dressed, there's a knock at their door.

James hollers, "Come in," and the door opens. Illan walks in and says, "Some girl was murdered last night."

"What?" asks Dave and James at the same time.

"It was the younger daughter of the innkeeper," he says. "She was torn up pretty bad. At first they thought it was an animal attack, she looked like she had been chewed on. But then they found bloody tracks from some man's boot walking away from the scene."

"That's terrible," James says.

"We better get out of here before anyone starts asking questions," he says.

Nodding, James gets his pack and stands up. "Yeah. Good idea."

As they leave the room they begin to hear yelling coming from downstairs and they rush down to find Qyrll encircled by an angry crowd. His hood has fallen back allowing all to see his extensive tattoos.

"Monster!" one woman cries as she breaks down into tears.

"He is not to blame for the death of the young girl!" Jiron shouts to be heard above the noise of the crowd.

He and Qyrll have their backs to the wall as they face the angry people. They haven't yet pulled their weapons out, but James can see he's about ready to if they get much closer.

One man draws his sword and says, "He killed my little Elenda!"

"He was with me all night," responds Jiron.

James can see the situation beginning to blossom out of control. If he doesn't do something, it's going to escalate into a flat out riot and all these people are going to get hurt. Jiron and Qyrll could wade through them like a hot knife through butter.

Summoning a little bit of magic to magnify his voice, he yells, "Enough!"

His voice rolls over the crowd and Jiron looks to him in relief. As one, the onlookers turn to face him. Their anger is plain on their faces and he hasn't long to diffuse this situation.

"This man is not to blame for the death of your daughter," he says to the innkeeper as he makes his way through the crowd to stand before them. "I have known him to be only a gentle man. Let not his visage frighten you. From where he comes from, these markings are a sign of manhood. His people are not bloodthirsty killers." *Well, they are but not in this way.*

"Before you kill an innocent man, make sure of the facts!" he hollers to them. "You say that whoever killed your daughter walked away through blood?"

Several heads in the audience nod in agreement.

Turning to Qyrll, he says, "Remove your boots."

While he's removing his boots James turns his attention to the crowd and says, "If he did in fact walk through blood, then there should be some indication on his boots that he did." He's thankful to see a couple people nod their heads at his logic.

"Here," Qyrll says as he hands him his boots.

James examines them and with profound relief finds them completely devoid of any blood. He didn't know what he would do if there had been any on them. Holding the boots toward the crowd, he says, "See. There is no blood!" He moves them first one way and then another as everyone in the crowd presses forward to see.

Unconvinced, the innkeeper says, "He could've cleaned them off!" Several, people grunt their agreement.

Despite the fact that some of the crowd are unconvinced, he begins to notice the overall mood has changed from one of mob violence to restless curiosity. He has to keep this going or that innkeeper will stir them up again.

Pulling an idea from a crime drama on television, he says, "Let's go and compare this boot with the one which walked away from the scene, to see if he could even have made the tracks."

"Alright," the innkeeper says. "But if they're the same, he dies."

James isn't too worried about that, this Parvati is larger than most and it's unlikely his boot is going to match that of the killer's. Unless of course he really is the killer. There is a kernel of doubt in his mind, he remembers the deaths back in Cardri that seemed to have occurred around the time they were all there. He knew Parvati's were not murderers. Killers, yes, but not murderers.

Leading the crowd out to the scene of the crime, he carries the boots. Qyrll and Jiron follow along behind him.

"The tracks are over here," one person says.

James follows him and they come to three very clear imprints in the dirt. Bending down near the clearest of the three, he says, "Now, let's see." Putting the boot on the ground next to the print, he lines up the heel of Qyrll's boot with that of the bloody imprint. Once aligned, he looks up to the crowd.

A murmur begins running through the onlookers as they see the toe of Qyrll's boot extends two inches past that of the imprint. One says, "He couldn't have been the one."

The innkeeper's anger toward Qyrll dissipates quickly. Looking to the Parvati, he grudgingly says, "Sorry."

Qyrll makes no reply as he puts his boots back on.

"But who killed my daughter?" he wails as his wife comes over and embraces him, her sobs adding to his own.

"I don't know," James replies, "and we're all sorry for your loss." To Fifer, he whispers, "Get the horses ready to leave."

"Right," he whispers back and takes Miko with him to get it done.

Many of the onlookers come to the grieving family and offer words of sorrow and encouragement. James glances to Jiron and Qyrll and nods to the stables. As they leave the crowd behind, he says, "Let's get out of here quickly before something else happens."

With Dave walking beside him, he and the others make their way to the stables. Those who had left their things in their rooms hurry back to the inn to retrieve them. Before too much longer, they are all in the saddle and making their way down the road.

"That was quick thinking," Illan tells him after riding several minutes in silence. "I never would've thought of that."

"Where I come from, solving crimes and stories of the same nature are very popular," he tells him. "Frankly, if his boot had matched the bloody footprint, I don't think bloodshed could've been avoided."

"I'm glad you were able to avert a conflict," Qyrll says. "Killing people such as those would bring little honor."

They ride on for several hours, a few travelers share the road with them, but otherwise it's empty. A caravan passes them coming from the north and James asks them how far the next town is.

One guard pauses long enough to say, "The next town lies a full day's ride to the north."

"What's it called?" he asks.

The guard replies, "Willimet."

"Willimet?" James asks. When the guard nods yes, he begins seething inside. He hasn't forgotten what happened to him the last time he passed through there.

Miko remembers as well and comes to ride next to him. "What are you going to do?" he asks.

Turning to him, he says, "Going to go and talk with her."

Serenna, that was her name. The fortune teller who had run him out of town. The one who is telling everyone he is possessed by a demon. He intends to get her to stop!

Chapter Fifteen

The rest of the afternoon, James rides in silence, his mind only on what he will do at Willimet. Miko on the other hand is more than happy to tell the story in its entirety to the rest of the group. When he gets to the part about how they learned the following day the way she had distorted the truth, several of them chuckle which only darkens James' mood further.

To make matters worse, during the late afternoon while they are still several hours away from Willimet, they encounter a man.

They first see him approaching down the road and don't pay him very much attention. He's a bit scraggly and when he draws close, can see a wild look in his eye.

Stopping right in front of them, he raises his hands and asks, "Where are you bound to on this fine day?"

Bringing his horse to a stop so as not to run over the man, James replies, "To Willimet."

The man's face lights up, "To see the great Serenna? Truly she is sent by the gods to guide us in these dark days."

At that, the entire company comes to a stop and gathers around to hear this man. "Sent by the gods?" scoffs James. "I don't think so."

The man immediately grows indignant and cries out, "Scoff not the wise Serenna. Only her wisdom can deliver us from the demon which walks the lands."

"Demon?" Illan asks him. He casts a quick glance to James and can see the anger seething behind his eyes.

"Yes my friends," he says. "A demon disguised as a man. Evil are his works and through Serenna, the gods work to counter his most malign plans." He gazes into their faces, eyes wild with a crazed look to them. "You will see for yourself," he says. Beginning to mumble to himself, he suddenly walks forward and James has to back his horse quickly out of the way to keep the man from walking into it.

He sits there a moment and watches as the man continues down the road. "Great!" he exclaims. "What in the world is she saying about me now?"

"Looks like it's getting pretty serious," Illan says. "I've seen religious zealots before, and that man certainly acted like one. We better be careful while we're there."

"What is she doing?" asks Fifer. "Creating a new religion?"

"We'll find out shortly," he says.

"Wonder how come word of this hadn't reached us before?" Jiron asks.

Shrugging, James says, "Who knows? Maybe she's just recently stepped up what she's telling people. Or maybe she's come to believe it as well."

"What are you going to do?" Miko asks as they resume their way north.

"I don't know," he replies. "But I can't just let this whole thing fester and rot. Who knows where it might lead?" *Or where it already has?*

They continue on down the road and it's well after dark when the lights from Willimet appear ahead of them. Off to the east of town, a large pavilion has been erected in which numerous people are congregating. Many fires dot the area around the pavilion where those not within can keep warm.

"What's that?" Dave asks as they ride closer to town. "Looks like a revival meeting from back home."

"It does, doesn't it," agrees James. "It's probably where she's preaching."

Suddenly a great cheer and cry can be heard coming from the pavilion. "Wonder what she's telling them now?" he hears Miko say behind him.

"Probably that I'm going to eat their souls or something," he says.

Jiron chuckles, "Maybe."

James turns his horse toward the pavilion, intending to go see what's going on but Illan stops him. "I don't think it would be such a good idea for you to go over there right now."

"Why?" he asks.

"If you're recognized as the person of whom she's talking about, they'll try to tear you apart," he says. "Or you'll be forced to kill them." He pauses a moment as James digests that. Then he asks, "Do you want a bloodbath?"

"No," he replies.

"Alright then," Illan says. "Let's find an inn and the rest of us will find out what's going on and let you know while you stay out of sight in your room."

James definitely doesn't like the sound of the plan, but can see the wisdom in it. "Very well," he says. Turning his horse back to the road, he leads them toward Willimet.

The first thing he notices upon reaching the outskirts of town are the many lean-tos and makeshift dwellings which have sprung up since he was here last. When they reach the outer edge of the main buildings of town, the number of makeshift dwellings decline rapidly until they disappear altogether.

The few citizens still on the street hurry along as if they're afraid to be out after dark. "There's a definite uneasy feeling here," observes Jiron.

"I know," agrees Fifer. Watching one fellow hurrying along, he sees him continuously darting nervous glances this way and that. When he notices Fifer looking at him, he stops in his tracks, then darts quickly down a side alley.

"Wonder what has them all spooked?" Dave asks.

"The answer is probably in that pavilion sitting outside of town," replies James. "From the look of that one guy we ran into earlier, it isn't surprising the townsfolk have grown wary."

They come to an inn and James has everyone wait by the horses while he and Illan go inside to see about getting some rooms. He dismounts and with Illan right behind him, goes through the front door.

As he enters, a man behind the counter turns with a start, his eyes wide. When he sees them entering, his demeanor subtly relaxes and he asks, "Travelers?"

James nods and says, "Yes we are. Just passing through on our way north."

At that, the man completely relaxes. Illan asks, "What has everyone around here so afraid?"

The man's eyes dart around for a moment, as if he's looking to see if anyone is listening. Waving for them to come closer, he says in a soft voice, "It's the woman out in the big tent in the center of the pavilion outside of town. She and her followers have everyone on edge."

"Why?" James asks. "What's going on?"

"Before summer, she had been a simple fortune teller who gave bad advice," he says. "Everyone knew she was a fake but as she was very nice, we didn't say anything. One day that all changed."

James glances to Illan as the man continues.

"As the story goes, and let me tell you it's different depending on who tells it to you, a man came to her and asked for a reading. He was a stranger in town so didn't realize she was a fake. What happens next no one is sure about, but the next morning her crystal ball is shattered and she has this streak of white hair where the day before it had been black."

"She begins telling this story about how some demon showed up and tried to take his soul but that she fought him away. Now those of us who knew her didn't believe it for an instance. I mean really? What a wild tale. But as time went on, she continued telling it and some came to believe in it. I think even after a while she did too."

"Up until about a month ago things were fine. She had her little following and most of us were rather amused by the whole thing. Oh sure, for a lark we would at times go and listen to her but none took her serious. Most of us still don't."

"What changed?" James asks.

"Things started happening," the man says. "People who went to hear her talk all of a sudden became ardent believers. Those who became believers would entice travelers passing through to go and listen to her. Then they too, became believers. Before we knew it, she had amassed hundreds of people and one day that large pavilion and the big tent sprung up."

"Interesting," Illan comments.

"This city is falling apart rapidly," he tells them. "People are afraid to be on the streets for fear of being 'asked' to attend one of her talks."

"Why should that be a problem?" James asks.

"If you refuse, sometimes they go away, sometimes not," he replies. "One man refused and a pack of her believers fell on him and beat him to a pulp right here in the center of town."

"Didn't the guard try to stop them?" Illan asks.

"Some were in the vicinity, but word has it they've been bought off by someone, maybe her. Now they patrol the streets but do nothing to stop her people if they get violent." Leaning closer and lowering his voice even more, he says, "I've even heard that some who spend too much time within the tent go mad."

"Really?" prompts Illan.

"Really!" he says. "A friend of mine became a believer and spent a week straight within her tent, listening to her talk. When he came out, he wasn't himself and all he could talk about was her and her mission to thwart the demon that walks the land."

James glances to Illan who nods. They both remember how that man who they encountered on the road here had acted.

"Anyway," he says. "Stay here in the inn, maybe in your rooms and don't go out until dawn. Her people are most active at night though can be encountered anytime."

"Thanks for the information," James says.

"Do you still plan on staying?" the man asks.

Nodding, James says, "We have to."

"It'll be three coppers per room," the man says. "How many will you require?"

"Four," he tells him as he counts out the coins. The man hands over the room keys and says, "If you're hungry, I can send something up."

"That would be good," Illan says. "Maybe in about a half hour, there are seven of us."

"Very good," he says. "The stable is around back."

"Thank you," James says as he and Illan turn to leave the inn.

Stepping outside, he comes to a stop when he sees the others engaged in conversation with three other individuals.

"...come, the wisdom of the lady is great."

Jiron hears him leaving the inn and turns toward him. Indicating the two men and woman standing next to him, he says, "They've just invited us to hear her speak at the pavilion."

The lady turns to him and says, "Yes, she welcomes all to hear her words of wisdom."

"All who come are filled with the knowledge to combat the evil walking the world," one of the men says.

After hearing what the innkeeper inside just said, the last thing he wants to do is expose any of his group to whatever is going on in the tent. "We need to get settled in right now," he tells them. At that, the three become visibly agitated and the words of the innkeeper comes back to him. *"If you refuse, sometimes they go away, sometimes not."*

While not worried about what these three would do to his group, he's more worried about what his group would do to them. Hoping to diffuse the situation, he says, "We may stop by later this evening after we have something to eat."

His words have a somewhat calming effect on them. "The lady's words are greater than any food. Take not long in coming," the lady says as they abruptly turn away and move down the road.

Fifer glances to James and asks, "What was all that about?"

"Are we going to hear her speak?" Miko asks.

James glances at the departing trio and says quietly, "Not here. Let's get our horses settled in first and we'll talk where we won't be overheard."

They all turn somber at that. Not exactly what they were expecting to hear. Fifer glances to Illan who nods his head gravely.

Taking the horses around back, they find only one other horse in the stable. Visitors here must be few, with all that's going on it isn't too surprising. No stableman is around so they choose a set of stalls together and get their horses settled in. Then they take their packs with them and return to the inn where they head upstairs to their rooms.

James has them all come into his room and they close the door. He gives the others a rundown of what he and Illan were told by the innkeeper. When he's done, Qyrll asks, "Do you plan to go and listen to the lady's words?"

He sits back a moment and considers the question. "Maybe," he finally says.

"What?" asks Jiron. "You can't be serious."

James looks to him and says, "I am. Something is going on here and it's possible I could be the cause. Also, consider this. If she finds out where The Ranch is, she could send all her crazies there to 'destroy the demon' which would mean a bloodbath. No, I need to stop this now. She and her followers could become a veritable plague upon the land."

"So what do you propose to do?" Illan asks.

"Later on, I'm going to go and see what's going on," he says. "After I get a little rest and some food."

"We're going with you," Jiron says, several of the others nod their heads in agreement.

"It wouldn't be wise for you to go in there alone," Illan agrees.

James considers it for a moment and then says, "Very well." To Miko he says, "Go downstairs and see if we can get our meal up here." He hands him some coins to cover it.

"Alright," replies Miko, taking the coins. "I'll be right back." Leaving the room, they hear his footsteps going down the hallway to the stairs.

"What are you planning to do there?" Fifer asks.

"I don't know, really," he admits. "People don't go mad such as we've seen in so short a time unless something is causing it."

"Magic?" suggests Fifer.

Shrugging, James replies, "Maybe. Who knows?"

"Have you felt anything since coming here?" Jiron asks.

"No, but the pavilion isn't exactly close either," he replies, shaking his head. He sits in contemplation for several minutes until Miko returns saying their food will be up shortly.

"What did I miss?" he asks.

"Not much," replies Jiron. He goes to the window and looks out onto the courtyard below. Nothing is stirring out there. The only thing which disturbs the night is the light coming from the pavilion area.

It isn't long before there's a knock on the door and the innkeeper's son arrives with their food and plates enough for all of them. James gives him a few coppers for a tip before he returns downstairs. Roasted chicken, bread and ale, not much variety but there's a lot of it.

Each of them fills a plate with a portion of the chicken and then finds a place to settle down to eat. James and Illan take the small table and the only two chairs in the room while everyone else makes do with either the bed or floor. Jiron just stands.

Illan glances across the table to James and after swallowing, says, "You know, if you go over there, there'll probably be trouble."

James sighs before replying. "I realize that. But how much more trouble will there be if I do nothing? She and her followers are a cancer which must be stopped before it has a chance to spread further."

He takes a few more bites before replying, "Already we've seen one of her people heading south. Who knows why he left and what he plans to do?"

"Finding more people to come hear her?" offers Fifer.

"Probably," agrees James. "If nothing else will just stir up mischief."

Crash!

The sound of pots clattering on the floor can be heard coming from below.

"You can't take him!"

Everyone comes alert when they hear the innkeeper cry out. Illan motions for Fifer to see what's going on. Qyrll goes with him.

"What happened?" Miko asks.

"Think they came back?" Jiron asks as he moves toward the door Fifer and Qyrll left open when they left.

"It would seem so," Illan says.

They begin moving out into the hallway, Illan turns to Dave and says, "Stay here and lock the door."

Dave gives him a dark look but remains within the room.

From the stairs they hear footsteps running up them. In a moment they see Fifer and the innkeeper's son reach the top.

"They've taken my father!" cries the boy, tears running down his face. A long cut is welling blood on his forearm. Jiron returns to the room and rips a section of sheet off and ties it around the wound to stop the flow of blood.

As Jiron ministers to him, the boy continues, "They came to take me but my father fought them and they took him instead."

"Qyrll's following them," Fifer says.

"Damn!" curses James. "He might become like them." Turning to Illan he says, "We have to move fast."

"Agreed," he says. To the innkeeper's son, Illan indicates their room and says, "Stay in here. We'll find your father."

"Please hurry!" the boy says.

As the boy enters their room with Dave, James tells his friend, "You stay here and look after the boy."

"Why do I always have to stay behind?" he asks, voice full of hurt.

"There could be fighting," he tells his friend. "Just promise me to stay here?"

Nodding, Dave says, "Alright. But you come back!"

"I will," he assures his friend. Closing the door he begins heading for the stairs. Jiron moves ahead of him and takes them two at a time. He then makes it to the door leading out to the main street first.

The door is standing open, the street on the other side deserted. After a nod from James, he leaves the inn and begins making his way toward the lights of the pavilion.

Hurrying along quickly, they move through streets strangely quiet. Usually there are people out and about even at this hour, the sun hasn't been down all that long.

They come to a junction of streets and from out of the cross street to the right, a band of a dozen of her followers suddenly appear.

Jiron draws his dagger but James lays a hand on his arm and says quietly, "Not yet."

They're immediately noticed by the followers who move to intercept.

James steps to the fore and asks, "We heard about the lady and her message, would you know where we could find her?"

The band stops and one points to the lights of the pavilion before saying, "There you will find the lady." His eyes are slightly wild and foam flecks the side of his mouth.

"Thank you," replies James as he gives the band a nod and gestures to the others to continue toward the pavilion.

Miko glances backward repeatedly until her followers are out of sight behind. He keeps one hand on the pommel of his sword, just in case.

Jiron again takes the lead as they continue to make their way toward the lights. Twice more they're intercepted by roving bands of her followers and each time he handles the situation just as James had. Once her followers are told they mean to go to the lady, they leave them alone.

"How far ahead do you think the innkeeper is?" asks Fifer.

"Can't be too far," Jiron states, "we've kept a good pace."

They finally reach the ramshackle area of lean-tos and hovels where her followers seem to live. The stench from this area is wretched, refuse having been deposited wherever convenient. This is the most deplorable state of sanitation James has yet to experience.

When they pass the last building, they see the pavilion before them. A tingling sensation begins as they draw closer to it and James says to the others, "Magic."

Jiron nods as he resumes making his way to the pavilion. Her followers are more numerous here. Many eye them, but none try to hinder them in any way. After all, they're going to go see the lady. If they were to turn around, that might be an altogether different situation.

As they draw closer, the people begin to change subtly with more vacant eyes and emaciated appearances. It almost looks like they've done without food for quite some time. One group of individuals look as if they're sleeping near one of the campfires but when they come near find they're actually dead.

"What's going on here?" asks Illan.

James glances to him and replies, "I don't know. Whatever it is has to be stopped."

Nodding, Illan says, "I agree."

When they're only a dozen yards from the entrance to the great tent in the center of the pavilion area, a large figure detaches itself from a group of onlookers at the opening and comes toward them.

"Qyrll," Fifer says with relief. "I was worried about you."

Giving him a smile, Qyrll replies, "No need to worry." To Illan he gestures to the tent opening and says, "They took him in there."

"What's going on in there?" James asks. The prickling sensation has continuously increased as his proximity with the tent decreases.

"Bad things," he says.

Murmuring can be heard coming from within. James darts a quick glance inside and sees the entire floor space of the tent covered with people. An aisle of sorts extends from the tent opening all the way to a central platform erected in the center. Standing at the base of the platform is the innkeeper and several followers. Two of them hold his arms and James can see him struggling to get away. Standing on the platform is Serenna, the fortune teller whom he had been so nice to on his last visit.

"The lady awaits."

Startled, James turns to see several dozen of the faithful gathered around him and his party.

"She grows impatient," another says, though James isn't sure just which one of them said it.

Turning to the others, he says, "Watch each other and if any start acting weird, or if you feel yourself slipping away, tell me at once." After he receives a nod from each, he turns to the opening. Taking a deep breath to calm his shaky nerves, he enters.

Chapter Sixteen

As he enters, the prickling sensation intensifies. The smell of unwashed bodies mingles with that of feces making the resulting odor nigh on unbearable.

James looks at the surrounding mass of people and takes notice of motionless forms lying here and there about the floor. More of her followers who have died.

Bringing his attention to bear upon the platform, he sees a dark globe sitting next to her on a pedestal looking to have been made of marble. A dark stone three feet high, it allows the globe to sit perfectly for her to rest her hand upon it.

"Listen to my words," she says and the crowd grows hushed. Laying her hand upon the globe, James feels a sudden spike in the tingling sensation. The globe must be the source of her power and control over these people.

"It's the globe," he says to the others with him.

Nodding, Jiron replies, "Can you destroy it?"

"Need to be closer," James tells him as they continue toward the platform.

"Protect James," he hears Illan say to the others. They then form a circle around him as he continues forward.

"The demon walks among you," her words float upon the air from the platform. His mind suddenly begins to cloud as the magic from the globe makes its way into his thoughts.

At the foot of the dais, the innkeeper becomes docile as his struggles against his captors cease. Her eyes are directly upon him.

James calls forth the magic and pushes it from his mind, erecting a barrier which causes the magic from the globe to flow around him. It's the same principle as the concealing spell he developed for hiding the Fire. Suddenly, he realizes the others with him have stopped. He almost runs into Jiron who was ahead of him.

"Jiron!" James says, as he shakes him by the shoulders.

Jiron turns his head and looks at him but his eyes don't appear to really focus on him.

James summons a burst of power and erects shields around the others' minds as well. Snapping out of their lethargy, they look around confused for just a moment before realizing what had almost happened.

"Thanks," Jiron says.

James nods and takes the fore as he moves further toward the platform. Looking to Serenna, he sees her eyes locked on him. She's aware of his presence.

Pointing to him, she cries out, "The demon has come!"

As one, the followers turn their attention to him. A growl can be heard coming from them as the throng closest to the stage closes off the aisle, preventing him from continuing further.

"Thou hast come to thy doom!" Serenna cries out. Magic crackles in the air and the prickling sensation suddenly spikes. "Kill him!" she screams to her followers.

"Ready!" cries out Illan as he draws his sword. The others follow a split second behind.

James looks at the people coming toward him, townsfolk and farmers, simple folk. When they reach the men protecting him, they begin to fall as swords strike out. Limbs fall to the ground, heads are separated from shoulders and still they come. Trusting to Illan and the rest, he turns his attention to the platform.

Serenna stands there, eyes blazing hate as she watches her followers being cut down like stalks of grain to the scythe.

From the corner of his eye, James sees the innkeeper fall to Jiron's knife as he reached out for him. Anger suddenly flares up within his breast, taking a slug from his belt he launches it toward her. Before it comes close, he feels a surge of power erupt from the globe and his slug explodes before it even reaches her.

The pile of bodies surrounding the men protecting him is beginning to rise. The remaining followers who are trying to get to him have to step over the dead which allows the defenders to take them out more easily. From the tent opening, more of her followers enter as they join with those already attacking.

"James," Jiron hollers as his knife takes a woman through the chest. Kicking her back into the ones behind her he continues, "Do something!"

The globe is the source of the power here. It's going to defend itself and Serenna against whatever I try to do. Just then, the darkness within the globe begins to pulsate. A dark light seems to emerge from it and then suddenly, a shadow is standing next to Serenna on the platform. She appears to take no notice of it.

A shiver courses through him as the shadow turns its head in his direction. Dread fills him when he recognizes the shadow as being similar to the ones in that other world where Igor found him. He can't even begin to imagine the ramifications of that.

Steeling himself, he summons the magic and unleashes a wave of energy. When the wave hits the shadow it appears to have little effect. Taking a step forward, it begins making its way directly toward him.

Crumph!

The ground under the front edge of the platform where the shadow stands explodes outward, causing the platform to buckle and break. Serenna cries out as she stumbles away from the pedestal and breaks contact with the sphere. As soon as her hand is no longer in contact with the sphere, the pressure on the shields around their minds disappears.

James stops maintaining the shields around their minds which frees up a lot of power and concentration.

The shadow remains unaffected by the explosion and continues toward him.

Crumph!

As the shadow steps off the bottom step, the ground once again erupts. Still not being affected by the blast, it continues on. Serenna is nowhere to be seen and the globe begins to pulsate again as another shadow disengages itself from the globe.

"Dear god!" Jiron exclaims when he finally takes notice of what's transpiring upon the platform. Serenna's followers begin losing the will to fight. Some continue unabated, while others begin wandering away as if lost in a daze. Still others seem to come to their senses and race from the tent.

The first shadow has now reached the followers who are standing dazed and confused. When it brushes up against someone, they cry out and fall to the floor as if they had the life sucked out of them.

Jiron stands his ground, attempting to keep his fear of the approach of the shadow from taking over and causing him to flee. Both knives, red with the blood of Serenna's followers, are in hand as he readies himself to meet this new foe.

"James!" Jiron yells as he kicks a follower away from him. "The Star! Use the Star!"

The Star! Of course! Reaching into his shirt, he brings forth the Star which bursts into a blinding white light. The followers who are attacking suddenly break off as they shield their eyes from its brilliance.

"Stand your ground!" Illan cries as Qyrll was about to step away from the group and continue the attack on the dazed people. Qyrll glances to Illan and then resumes his place in the circle around James.

The two shadows emit a scream as the light from the medallion touches them. A slug flies from James' hand and passes harmlessly through the first one.

They have no substance! They really are just shadows, but deadly nonetheless. Holding the medallion above his head, he begins moving toward the platform. The globe begins pulsating again.

Crumph!

The section of the platform upon which the globe's pedestal sits suddenly explodes upward. Launched into the air, the globe leaves the pedestal and flies for several yards before hitting the ground. It rolls for a few more feet before settling to a stop.

"Jiron!" James hollers. "Smash the globe!"

"With what?" he asks.

"I don't know," he replies. "It's the source of the power." Keeping the medallion held aloft, he continues toward the first shadow. "But don't touch it!" he warns.

Out of the corner of his eye, he sees Qyrll making his way through the crowd toward it. His swords out and ready but none of the followers seem to even take notice of him in their midst. Without Serenna's will to control them, they're nothing more than mindless zombies.

The shadows screech painfully as the light from the medallion burns into them. James almost imagines he can see smoke rising. Illan appears at his side and asks, "What is it?"

"Not entirely sure," replies James. "Demon maybe. Encountered them once before."

Fifer has joined Qyrll who has climbed up onto what's left of the platform. Together they're lifting the pedestal upon which the globe at one time sat. The second shadow appears to be moving in their direction but the light from the medallion seems to be affecting it so badly it can barely move.

They take the pedestal over to the globe and raise it high. Then they bring it down as hard as they can, smashing it onto the globe. With a crack, the globe shatters.

Kaboom!

The shattering of the globe releases a massive explosion which lifts them off the ground and throws them across the room. Followers fall to the ground, James and the others are knocked from their feet by the force of the explosion.

Landing on his back, he still retains hold of the medallion and the light still shines forth. One final shriek and the two shadows dissolve into nothingness. The light from the medallion goes out and the tent is suddenly quiet.

As Illan gets to his feet, he hollers to Miko, "Go see about Fifer and Qyrll." Turning to James he asks, "Are you okay?"

"Think so," he replies. "Anyone hurt?"

Illan glances around and sees Fifer and Qyrll beginning to get to their feet. Jiron is already standing near James as he keeps his eye on the remaining followers in the tent. "Looks like other than some minor cuts and bruises, we're alright."

"Good," he sighs in exhaustion. Replacing the medallion beneath his shirt, he gets to his feet and surveys the damage. Dozens of dead men and women lie in heaps from their ill fated attack on James and the others. Others wander aimlessly through the tent while a few continue regaining their senses and make their way outside.

"Where is she?" James suddenly asks. Looking around, Serenna is no where in sight. "Damn! We've got to find her!"

Raising his voice, Illan hollers, "Fan out! Locate the woman."

As James and Illan head toward the shattered remains of the globe, the rest move out and hunt for Serenna. Coming to the shards, James bends down to examine them. No presence of magic or a malignant presence remains. He reaches out and picks up a two inch long piece. Holding it close it appears just a simple glass shard. Tossing it back with the others, he gets back to his feet.

"What happened here do you suppose?" Illan asks him.

"I don't know?" he replies. "Maybe she tapped into a force which got the better of her? Who knows?"

Jiron comes running back in and says, "There's no sign of her."

"Continue the search," Illan tells him. "Fan out through the city if you have to but we must find her."

Jiron nods his head then returns to the hunt. Illan turns to James and asks, "Can you find her with magic?"

"Too tired to attempt it now," he says. "Let's go back to the inn."

As they make their way back toward the entrance, they pass by the pile of bodies lying on the floor and he catches a glimpse of the innkeeper's dead face where he's wedged in among the others. Sadness overcomes him as he realizes he's going to have to tell the innkeeper's son that his father is dead.

Outside the tent, they see a group of townsfolk at the edge of town looking toward the pavilion. "What should we tell them?" Illan asks.

"As little as we can," he replies. "In the morning let's get out of here as fast as possible. I would leave now but I'm just too tired."

"Understandable," he says. "Fifer!" Illan hollers when he sees him poking through the ramshackle houses which have sprung up around the pavilion.

He looks up to see Illan waving him over. Making his way to him, he asks, "Yes?"

"Tell the others to keep searching," he says. "We're going back to the inn. If you can't find her soon, head on back as well."

"I'll tell them," Fifer assures him as he heads off to find the others.

James looks to the townsfolk as he and Illan draw closer, each have the look of fear and uncertainty on their faces. When he reaches them, he says, "Serenna and her followers will no longer be bothering you."

Seeing the blood on his clothes which Illan acquired during the battle, one lady asks, "Did you kill them all?"

Shaking his head, Illan replies, "No. No more than we had to." Gesturing back to the pavilion, he adds, "Many are coming out of the hold she had on them and are going to need your assistance."

Suddenly one of the men cries out, "Hera!" and rushes toward the pavilion. A woman is emerging from the tent and he runs to her, wrapping his arms around her. The others begin seeing others whom they know emerge or are already wandering around on the outside and go to them.

"Let's go," James says.

He and Illan work their way through the town until they see the inn appear down the road ahead of them. Entering through the front door, they make their way up the stairs to their rooms.

The door to where Dave and the innkeeper's son had remained is ajar. Illan places his hand on James' shoulder and draws his sword. Motioning for James to remain where he is, he moves closer to the door. Placing his hand upon it, he slowly pushes it open and gasps when he sees what's inside.

The innkeeper's son, or rather what's left of him, lies on the floor. At his gasp, James comes forward and takes in the scene. Glancing around, he says, "Dave's gone."

The room is a shambles, the table is overturned and only one chair remains. The shutters for the window are broken and James moves to the window to find the other chair lying broken on the ground below. "Dave!" he cries.

"Damn!" curses Illan. "Where could he have gone?"

"I don't know," replies James as he turns from the window. "If they broke in here to get them, he might've made it past and escaped. Hopefully he's holed up somewhere. When the sun comes up and he sees the townsfolk on the streets, he should return."

"Let's check the other rooms just in case," suggests Illan.

James nods and they begin searching the inn room by room. Neither on the top floor nor the bottom do they find Dave. The downstairs looks the same as when they left earlier so whatever occurred happened upstairs.

They finally return upstairs and enter the room across from the one with the dead innkeeper's son. Illan suggests leaving the door open so they can keep an eye out for the others. James concurs.

"Get some sleep if you can," Illan tells him. "I'll stay up and watch for the others."

"Alright," he says as he goes over to the bed and lies down. As active as his mind is right now, he has little hopes of falling asleep any time soon. *What happened to Dave?* He worries about him all alone out there and hopes someone will run across him and bring him back. The fact that he's here in this world at all is his fault so it makes him his responsibility.

If he should run across her, he's going to kill her. Jiron made that decision the instant he saw the inside of the tent. Miko walks beside him. It was decided that it would be prudent if they broke up into pairs. He and Miko would search inside the town while Fifer and Qyrll hunt her in the outer section.

"Do you think we'll find her?" Miko asks while they're checking an abandoned storehouse.

"I don't know," he replies. "I doubt it, the town is simply too big."

The townsfolk have all come out into the streets to see what's going on, many have made their way down to the pavilion after hearing Serenna's been dealt with. Crying and wailing can be heard throughout the town as loved ones are found either dead or with vacant eyes. Some come out of it, but for those who were under her spell the longest, it might take longer, if ever.

"We'll try a few more places then head back to the inn," Jiron tells him.

Miko nods as he follows him to a rundown tavern on the outskirts. The windows have been boarded up and the shantytown of the followers has grown up around it. "This would be a good place to hide," he remarks.

"Does look like it doesn't it," agrees Jiron as he approaches the front door. A couple boards have been nailed across the entrance and it's easy enough for them to rip them off. He then tries to open the door and finds it locked. Kicking out with his foot, he breaks the door in. It flies inside as one hinge breaks off and lands crooked as it's only being held by one hinge now. Partially blocking the doorway, they have to step over the door as they enter.

The interior is dark, the light coming in through the broken doorway is little help in dispelling it. Moving inside, Jiron keeps a knife in one hand while he feels his way with the other.

Miko stays right behind him as they make their way around the inside of the walls. Jiron keeps his hand against it to feel for doorways. When he comes to one, he tries to open it but finds it locked. Using the same key as he had on the front door, he kicks it. Swinging open, it smashes into the wall with a resounding thud.

Jiron stays motionless for a few seconds, cocking his head to the side he tries to hear if the sound of the door slamming against the wall disturbed anyone. A slight rustling noise can be heard coming from down the darkened hallway.

"Jiron…" Miko begins and is cut off by Jiron.

"Shhh…" he says. Moving cautiously forward with knife at the ready, he softly walks toward the sound. Unable to see anything, he has to use his other senses to find the source of the noise. Step by slow step he moves down the hallway, ears alert for even the slightest sound.

Suddenly, a body lurches from a side room and knocks him backward a few steps and then he hears footsteps running away. Regaining his balance quickly, he breaks into pursuit, the person ahead of him but a dim shadow in the dark as Jiron races to catch him.

The person fleeing smashes through the door at the end leading outside and they see that it's a lad of about twelve as he races off down the street in the moonlight. Coming to a halt, he lets the boy go.

"That wasn't her," he hears Miko say from the back.

Turning back to him, he says, "I realize that."

Moving down the street they come across another dilapidated building that has seen better days. Jiron comes to a halt as he stares at the building. "What?" asks Miko quietly.

Pointing to the rear of the building, he says, "There's light coming from the rear window."

"So?" Miko asks not sure why that would require special attention.

Jiron glances back to him as he says, "The building looks like it's about ready to fall apart. I wouldn't be in there unless I had no choice."

"Could be just another street kid like we found back there," suggests Miko.

"Perhaps but we better check it out anyway." Moving toward the window, Jiron steps quietly. The light is none too bright, most likely coming from but a single candle.

They reach the edge of the building several feet away from the window and he motions for Miko to remain there while he goes to investigate. When he sees Miko's nod, he moves to the window. Peering inside, he sees four men standing around another seated in a chair. His breath catches when he sees who it is seated in the chair, James' friend Dave. He has half a mind to leave him there.

The men are saying something to Dave but Jiron can't quite make it out. Suddenly, Dave looks toward the window and sees him there. "Jiron?" he asks.

The four men as one turn to see him there at the window and they draw their swords.

"Damn fool!" he exclaims as he backs away from the window and draws his knives.

"What?" asks Miko when he hears him curse and sees him draw his knives.

Jiron glances back to him for just a second and says, "Trouble."

The door to the building crashes open as three of the four men rush out onto the street. Jiron moves to engage them and hears Miko's sword leave its sheath as he too joins the fray. "They have Dave!" he tells him.

The first man to reach him tries to bull his way through his defenses as he hacks down with both hands on the hilt of his sword. Jiron easily sidesteps and lashes out with a return strike as the man passes and scores a deep cut on his left shoulder.

The second man comes at him with a thrust which he dodges backward to avoid. He hears the first man cry out as Miko takes him through the chest with his sword and moves to engage the third.

Now one on one, Jiron is able to block the man's attacks. After three exchanges of attacks, he has the man's measure. When the man thrusts as he knew he was going to, he sidesteps the sword and strikes out with an attack so fast it's but a blur. His knife sinks into the man's throat and severs the larynx. Choking on his own blood, the man is unable to properly defend himself and Jiron kicks out, connecting with his knee and shatters it. Falling to the ground, the man gurgles as blood fills his lungs.

Miko parries the third man's attack and follows through with one of his own. His reflexes having been honed by his time with the Fire, his sword flies at the man horizontally and severs his leg at the hip. As the man topples forward, he strikes out one more time and runs his sword through his chest. His sword gets wedged in between the man's ribs and is ripped from his hand.

After the man hits the ground, he puts his foot on his ribcage and draws out his sword. Looking around quickly, he sees Jiron wiping his blades on one of the dead men's shirts.

"Dave!" Jiron says and moves toward the doorway. He stops suddenly when he sees Dave peering around the corner.

"Are they dead?" he asks, a tremor of fear in his voice.

"You can come out now," Jiron tells him. "Where's the other guy?"

"He ran out the back," he says. Looking at the dead bodies, he can't help but hide his revulsion at the sight.

"Let's get back to the inn," Jiron says.

"Yes," he says, "I'd like that."

"Who were they?" Miko asks as they begin moving back toward the inn.

"From the Empire, I think," he says. "They said they were going to kill me if I didn't tell them where the Fire is."

Jiron glances to Miko who gives him a knowing look.

"Just what is the Fire?" he asks. "They knew I was his friend. How could they know that?"

"I don't know, but we better hurry and tell James about it," Jiron says. Picking up the pace, they make their way straight toward where the inn lies.

When they go upstairs they find Fifer and Qyrll have already returned, having no better luck in finding Serenna than they had.

James gets to his feet as Dave walks into the room ahead of Jiron and Miko. "Are you alright?" he asks.

"I'm fine," Dave replies, sinking into one of the chairs by the table. Illan gets up so James can sit next to him.

James turns his attention to Jiron and asks, "What happened?"

"Found him in some old building on the outskirts of town," he replies. "Looked like he was being questioned."

Turning back to Dave, James says, "Tell me everything."

"Several minutes after you left, more of those people showed up," he tells them, a haunted look coming over him. "They demanded us to go with them and when we refused, they fell upon the boy and started killing him. I grabbed a chair and smashed open the window and climbed down to the street below. I didn't know what to do or where to go. There were more of them on the streets so I just starting running, I was hoping to find you."

"But instead, I ran into those other guys. They recognized me as being your friend," he says, bringing his eyes to meet James'. "How could they know that?"

Startled at that, James glances around to the others in the room and then says, "I don't know. It wouldn't seem likely."

"They've probably had spies on us for awhile now," offers Illan. "It wouldn't have been too difficult for them to find out who we all are and our relationship to you."

Nodding, James says, "Possibly."

Laying his hand on James' arm, Dave says, "They wanted to know about something called 'The Fire'. Do you know what they're talking about?"

James sits back in his chair and contemplates what he just heard.

"They haven't given up," states Jiron.

"No they haven't," he replies. Looking to Dave, he can see the questions behind his eyes but can he afford to give him the answers? "The Fire is an artifact of power here in this world. I have it on good authority that should the wrong people acquire it, this world could end. Or at least those who live here would wish it had."

"So you have it?" he asks.

"Not any more," he answers. "It's hidden away for all time."

"Where?" he asks.

James looks to his friend for a minute as he considers his reply. Finally, he says, "I can't tell you."

"But I'm your friend!" he exclaims. "My life is in jeopardy because of it, I have a right to know!"

Shaking his head, James says, "Dave, you are my best friend. We've been through a lot together but I can't tell you. I can't tell anyone."

Indicating the others, he asks, "Do they know?"

Shaking his head, James says, "No, they don't. No one does but me and it's going to stay that way."

Somewhat mollified at knowing he isn't the only one who doesn't know, he calms down.

James hated to lie to his friend, but he's too vulnerable. This latest escapade shows him that not only himself, but those around him are likely to be sought. And how did they know he was here. Something's afoot and he needs to figure out what.

He gets to his feet, tired and exhausted. Looking at everyone in the room he says, "As much as we all need to rest, we better get out of here. If there are agents from the Empire here, there's no telling what they may be planning next."

"I agree," Illan says. To Fifer and Qyrll he says, "Go down to the stables and get the horses ready for travel." As they move to leave the room, he adds, "Be alert."

"Count on it," Fifer says. Then he and Qyrll pass into the hallway and move to the stairs.

Turning back to James, he says, "Now that they've tipped their hand, we'll be on guard."

"That's something at least," James replies. Getting up from the chair, he says to Miko, "Go down to the kitchen and fill several packs with food."

Miko looks at him askance as he says, "Isn't that stealing?"

"Stealing from whom?" Jiron asks. "The innkeeper and son are dead and we haven't seen anyone else around the whole time we've been here. Likely as not, if we leave the food it'll just spoil."

"Right, I hadn't thought of that." Miko grabs his bag and heads down to the kitchen.

James glances to Jiron and says, "I hope there're no tarts down there or that's all he'll get."

Breaking out into a grin, he says, "I better go help him." Taking his pack, Jiron leaves the room and follows Miko down to the kitchen.

James, Illan and Dave make their way down to the stables where they find all but two of the horses already saddled. Fifer and Qyrll are getting the saddles ready for the remaining two.

Taking the reins of his horse, he leads him out into the inn's courtyard as does Dave and Illan. They wait there a moment before Miko and Jiron exit the back door of the inn, each with two bulging sacks of food for their journey back. One small pouch hangs around Miko's neck and Jiron nods toward it and mouths, 'Tarts'.

James gives him a grin and by the time they have the food secured to the horses, Fifer and Qyrll come out with the others. Once mounted, they follow the north road through town.

Several townsfolk watch them as they ride by. Whether or not they realize they were the ones who took care of Serenna or not, they make no move toward them nor do they offer a greeting. It's going to take some time before this town is back the way it was before all the unpleasantness.

They finally reach the outskirts and break into a fast trot as they leave Willimet behind.

Chapter Seventeen

While he rides through the night, his mind continues going over the events during the battle with Serenna and her followers, mainly, the shadows which came from the globe. They were identical in look and feel as the ones he encountered that time Igor came to save his butt. He's still not sure where he was. Whether it was another plane of existence, another world or maybe just a terrifying dream, he's not sure. But after seeing the shadows appear from the globe, he's convinced it wasn't just a dream.

Since coming to this world, he's encountered several forces, malignant in nature. By far the worst experience was the one on that other world. From the various books he's read back home, he has a couple theories as to why these things may be happening, none of which will be pleasant if they're true.

Two hours from Willimet, they come across another of the areas catering to travelers. This one has but an inn and one other building behind it which looks to be the innkeeper's home. Both buildings are dark.

Illan brings them to a halt before coming very close. He sits there for a moment.

"What's wrong?" James asks him.

"Doesn't feel right," he says. "There's usually always a light of some kind at an inn." To Jiron he says, "Go check it out."

"Right," he replies and then dismounts from his horse. While the others wait there in the road, he makes his way toward the inn.

The front door is ajar. Removing a knife from his belt, he steps toward the door. Pausing a few feet from the door, he looks inside but all he can see are shadows cast by the faint light of the moon shining in through the windows. Placing his hand against the door, he slowly pushes it open. The hinges of the door squeal slightly, giving an eerie feel to the place.

When the door is open far enough to allow him to enter, he releases the door and steps through. The stench from within hits him like a wall, death has been here. Moving inside, he tries to breathe through his mouth to minimize his reaction to the odor. On a nearby table he sees a candle silhouetted by the moonlight coming in through a window. Making his way over to it, he sets his knife on the table and removes his flint from his pouch. After two tries he manages to get the candle lit.

The candle's light reveals a macabre scene. Several people lie dead on the floor, another is slumped across a table. A quick survey shows none of the people are still alive. "Hello?" he hollers. "Is anyone here?" Listening for a moment, he fails to hear anything and then makes his way back to the door.

Sticking his head out, he hollers to the others, "I think everyone here is dead!"

The others come to the inn where they dismount and secure their horses to the front hitching post. "James," Jiron says from the front door, "you better come in here."

Coming to the door with the others following, James sees the ghastly scene in the common room. "Looks like the work of Serenna's followers," he says. When the smell hits him, he takes out a cloth and puts it over his nose.

Suddenly from upstairs, they hear a floor board creak as if someone is walking around. Without hesitation, Jiron moves to the stairs and cautiously ascends to the second floor with Fifer and Qyrll right behind.

"Be careful," offers James.

Jiron ignores him and continues up. At the top of the stairs is a hallway running the length of the second floor with doors lining both sides. The noise had to of come from either the first or second room on the left. The first door is open, the second one is closed.

Motioning for Fifer and Qyrll to follow, he edges toward the first door and glances through the doorway into the room. Standing in the middle of the room is a person, silhouetted by the light coming in through the window. The smell of death is in this room as well.

"Are you okay?" Jiron asks the person in the room.

Other than shifting its feet, the person makes no reply.

"Are you hurt?" When no reply is forthcoming, he hollers to those downstairs, "Bring up the candle, we need some light."

Jiron stands there in the doorway and keeps an eye on the individual in the room as James brings the candle up from below. The others follow as well. When the light at last illuminates the room, they see the person is another of Serenna's followers. The man looks emaciated and has the same lost, dazed look the others had when her hold over them was broken.

Illan comes behind James and when he sees the man, turns to the others and says, "Search all the rooms, there may be more."

One by one they search the rooms and find five others in the same state as the first man. "What should we do with them?" Fifer asks.

They look to James who shrugs, "I don't know what we can do. They may snap out of it, or they may not."

"Are we just going to leave them here?" Jiron asks.

Nodding, James says, "I think that would be the prudent thing to do. At the next town up the road we'll tell someone who can come back and take care of them."

"You're not still planning on staying here are you?" Dave asks from where he stands at the top of the stairs.

"Hardly," he replies. "Let's bury the dead and then get out of here."

Dave stops him at the top of the stairs and asks, "Why?"

James looks him seriously in the eye and says, "I can't believe you just asked me that." Brushing past him, he goes downstairs to find a shovel.

They find several out back by the house and commence digging one large communal grave. Once it's large enough, begin to fill it with the dead from the inn. During the process, the mind dead wander around aimlessly, one actually falling down the stairs and ends up breaking her neck. So they pick her up and add her to the grave.

When at last all the dead are buried, they have a moment of silence and then get mounted. They ride for an hour before pulling off the road and making camp near a small stream. Exhausted beyond measure, James finds a good spot to rest while the others volunteer to see to his horse. He no sooner gets his head on his pack than he falls asleep.

Early the next morning when the sun begins to rise, he wakes to find Fifer on watch. The others are sound asleep and snoring up a storm. He gets up and comes to the fire and sits down next to him.

They break out some of the food which was appropriated from the inn back in Willimet and have breakfast. It isn't long before everyone is up and eating. Dave is the last one to rise.

"Are we heading home now?" Miko asks him.

Nodding, he says, "That's the plan. Need to talk to Ceryn about something then may be going on another trip."

"So soon?" he asks.

"Yes," he replies. "Have to find out what Ironhold is and where. Ceryn's been around so I'm hoping he may know something about it."

"We're probably two or three days from The Ranch," interjects Illan.

"Can't wait to get back," Jiron says. "Tersa must be worried sick about me."

Just then from the north, they see a dozen or so riders coming their way. When they get close enough, they see that they're part of the Cardri cavalry. James comes to his feet as they approach and the officer comes forward and says, "Heard there's some strange happenings going on around here. Have you seen anything out of the ordinary?"

Nodding, James says, "An hour or so to the south is an inn. We found the occupants slaughtered and several mindless people wandering around. Buried the dead and left the mindless to continue wandering."

"Slaughtered you say?" he asks.

"That's right," he replies. "Same thing was happening down in Willimet. Those people down there need some help that's for sure."

The officer waves over a subordinate and has a few quiet words with him which James cannot make out. When he's done, he turns back to James and says, "Thanks for the information."

"You're welcome," he says.

The officer then calls for his men to begin moving and they double time it down the road.

"Looks like those people are going to get help after all," remarks Fifer.

"Maybe," says James, "if they don't just kill them."

"True," adds Illan. "At least it's not our problem anymore."

James nods his head as he returns to the campfire and finishes eating.

On the road again, they continue their northerly course, anxious to get home. Setting a quick pace they manage to reach the city of Guellin by the night of the second day. The sheep ranches come into view long before they see the skyline of the town. Shepherds are out among them, minding their flocks. Some wave a hello while others pointedly ignore them.

As the road enters town, a large three story building sits on their right with a sign of a sleeping sheep hanging by the front door.

"Looks like a good spot," says James. The grounds are relatively free of debris and the inn has an overall look of having been well maintained.

"Shall I see if they have any rooms?" Jiron asks.

Getting down from his horse, James stretches his sore muscles and says, "Sure. See if they have four. I'd like one on at least the second floor."

"You got it," he says as he goes up and enters the door.

"Just another day to Trendle," Illan tells him as he comes to stand next to him.

"Good. I'm tired of riding," he admits.

Miko gets down and has the last of his tarts in his hand. James can't believe he's still eating them. Last night they seemed a bit off but Miko wasn't swayed by the chance of food poisoning. James tried to explain it to him but the concept was simply too far beyond his understanding. He couldn't see how something which doesn't smell or taste bad could be. So James just shrugged and hoped for the best.

"James, look," Says Miko as he points across the street.

A woman walks along the far side of the street with a small girl behind her. His eyes widen and a smile comes to his face when he sees the little girl carrying what has to be one of Tersa's teddy bears. He nudges Illan and nods in their direction.

"Guess you really had something there," he says.

"I'm going to go find out where she got it," James tells him as he steps into the street. Making a beeline for her, the mother soon becomes aware of his approach and stops. She puts herself in front of her daughter as he comes close.

"Excuse me," he says and then points to the teddy bear, "but could you tell me where you got that?"

Visibly relaxing, she replies, "Argoth's down the street has them." She then points to the right.

"Thank you," he says and gives her a nod as he leaves.

"Be right back," he hollers over to the others as he makes his way to Argoth's. He barely takes four steps before Fifer, Qyrll and Miko join him. When he looks questioning at them, Fifer says, "Illan doesn't want you out alone."

He glances back to see Dave standing with Illan, a sullen expression on his face. "Very well then." They continue down the street until they see a store with a large window. Four of Tersa's teddy bears are displayed there. He grins to Fifer when he sees them.

Walking in, he finds a portly man organizing small pouches into a neat pile. As they enter, he turns to greet them. "Good day to you gentlemen," he says with a warm smile. "How may I help you today?"

James gestures to the teddy bears in the window and says, "I saw a woman with a little girl who had one of those and wanted to find out about them."

"We just got them in a few days ago," he says. "At first I didn't really think they would do much, but so far I've sold half."

"People really like them?" he asks.

Nodding, he replies, "The kids do. The trader lady who sold them to me suggested that I give one away and just see what happens. I thought that a rather foolish thing to do so before she left, she gave one to a little girl. After the girl left, she said, 'If you sell all those in a week, you pay me for the one I just gave away.' Of course I told her I would, but I didn't think it would work. But sure enough, I sold three more that day just from people whose kids saw the little girl with hers."

He looks to James and asks, "Are you interested in buying one?"

Shaking his head, he says, "No. I was just curious. Thank you."

"You're welcome," the shopkeeper says as they turn to leave.

When they're back outside the shop, Miko asks, "Why did you want to know about them?"

"Just doing a little market research," he says. He smiles at Miko's blank look of not understanding. Who would have thought Mr. Edward's class on economics would have come in handy here. Unable to stop himself, he breaks into a short laugh.

The others look at him a bit oddly.

Back at the inn, they find Jiron has already arranged for their rooms. Taking their horses around back to the stables, they get them settled in for the night before returning to their rooms.

Later on when they convene in the common room for their evening meal, they take a large table off to one side. The room begins to fill as other travelers as well as locals come to have their meals. A bard sets up and begins playing by the time the server has brought them their food.

"I doubt if they've given up yet," Jiron suddenly says.

"Who?" Fifer asks.

"The people who were interrogating Dave," he explains. "It still bothers me that one of them got away."

"True," agrees Illan. "But if we stay together and keep alert, we should have no problem."

"Wish they would just stop," says Miko.

Dave gives a short laugh at that.

Turning to him, Jiron asks, "You got something to say?"

Giving Jiron a sardonic look, he replies, "They're never going to stop! They will keep at him until they have what they want." To James he says, "Would it be so bad to give it to them if it would mean living without the fear of being attacked at any moment."

Jiron gives him a look of barely disguised disgust.

Shaking his head, James says, "Never. They could give me no guarantee that I would believe. Besides, giving it to them may prove more disastrous than the possibility of continued attacks."

Face turning into a frown, Dave glances at the others and can see them united against the idea of returning the Fire to the Empire. Getting up, he says, "I'm going to my room and go to sleep."

"Be careful and lock the door," James tells him.

"You needn't point out the obvious," he replies then begins making his way to the stairs and up to the room he and James share.

"Coward," can be heard though James not sure which one of them said it.

Turning his attention to the others, he says, "You guys should cut him a break."

Jiron looks at him with a serious look on his face. "Are you sure he's the type of person you want around? Things are afoot and he's just a liability." Around the table others nod their heads in agreement.

Sighing, James says, "I know. But where would he go? What would he do? I'm almost as lost here as he is."

"But you're handling it well," Fifer interjects. "And you sure don't back down from a fight."

Shaking his head, James says, "Given the choice, I wouldn't fight at all and would avoid any conflict to the best of my ability." He sighs then continues, "But I am not given that choice. I know what's right and I do it even though sometimes it pains me. He's just gone through a bad time, worse than any I can imagine. Maybe he'll find his niche here, but until then, he stays with me."

"As you will," Jiron says. "I just wanted you to know how we feel."

"I understand full well how much you all dislike him," he replies.

The rest of the evening they sit and enjoy the music and tales the bard relates. When James finally can't fight off sleep anymore, he heads up to his room. As he clears the stairs and begins walking down to the door, it opens and a girl comes out.

He freezes for a moment as she makes her way toward him and then moves quickly down the stairs. Muffled sobs can be heard coming from her and tears dot her cheek. Confused and speechless, he stands there as she disappears down the stairs.

Moving quickly, he comes to the door to his room and opens it. Dave is lying in bed and turns to look at him as he enters the room. "What happened?" he asks his friend.

"What do you mean?" replies Dave.

"You had a girl in here," he says.

"So?" replies Dave. "Just because you're happy being a virgin doesn't mean I am. Relax, she got paid."

"She was crying when she passed me by out in the hall," he says accusingly.

Shrugging, Dave says, "Don't know why, she enjoyed herself well enough earlier." Lying back on his pillow, he says, "Now if you'll excuse me I'm quite tired." Closing his eyes, he lies there quietly.

James stays standing by the door staring at his friend for a minute then moves over to his bed and undresses before getting under the covers. With a final glance over to his friend, he blows out the candle and tries to go to sleep. Sleep is long in coming, the memory of the sobbing girl keeps him awake.

The following morning, they head out early. "Should reach Trendle by the time it gets dark if we keep a quick pace," announces Illan as they leave the outskirts of town.

"That would be nice," James says with a grin.

Breaking into a fast trot they take the road to the northwest. Three hours out of town they come to a crossroads and take the northerly direction which will take them through Osgrin on the way to Trendle.

Ironhold. James ponders the significance of that lone word Ellinwyrd had inscribed on the scroll. What significance does it play? Where is it? He hopes Ceryn will be able to help him in discovering the answers.

Shortly after noon the party makes it to Osgrin where they find an inn to have their lunch. During the meal, Jiron suddenly says, "Wonder if there're any assassins here?"

The others with him chuckle at that, all but Qyrll, Miko and James. Qyrll doesn't understand, but Miko and James do all too well. "Enough of that," James scolds him.

"Sorry," he replies. The last time Miko had been here he overheard what he thought was an assassination plot aimed at James but which in fact was a betrothal party on their way to a wedding. The others still give him a hard time about it now and then despite James' efforts to get them to stop. At least it's fairly harmless jesting and Miko doesn't seem to mind as much as he had.

After leaving Osgrin, they continue north, next stop hopefully will be Trendle. Illan informs them it's still many hours away but that they should be able to make it by dark if not before.

As it turns out, they reach the outskirts of Trendle just as the sun hits the horizon. The people on the streets pause as they see him ride through, some offering greetings or well wishes. He returns them and continues on.

Passing the Squawking Goose, the favored inn of most of the townsfolk, they see young Devin coming out in the company of his family. His face turns pale as he sees them riding toward him.

"Why James," Mary says once she sees him approaching, "thought you were out of town for awhile?"

"I was," he replies. "I'll be in town for a short while before I have to be off again."

Illan is eyeing Devin who's withering under his gaze. Obviously he isn't supposed to be in town.

Corbin notices Illan's gaze and says, "Today's Devin's birthday. We went out to your place and asked Yern if we could take him into town to celebrate. He said it wouldn't be a problem."

Illan's face softens slightly as he says, "Just return before too long."

Relaxing with relief, Devin replies, "I will sir."

"I wish we could stay to share your celebration," James says. "But we've been on the road for several days and are extremely tired."

"I understand," Corbin says. "Nice to have seen you again."

"You too," he says. Then to the two girls he adds, "You two, too."

They just giggle and cast him shy glances.

Kicking his horse into a trot, he heads down the road out of town and to The Ranch. The shack for the guard stationed at the end of the lane leading to The Ranch has been completed. A lit lantern hangs from a post nearby to shed light on any who approach.

"Ain't you a sight for sore eyes," Jorry says as he steps from the guard shack.

"How've things been?" James asks him.

"Quiet," he replies. "Still get the curious every now and then but it seems to be tapering off." He notices Qyrll there but the darkness prevents him from being able to see his features well.

"Good," he says.

"How did things go in Cardri?"

"Tell you later," replies James. "I'm for bed."

"Good to have you back," he says as he returns to the guard shack.

Heading down the road, he sees Errin and Aleya sitting on the front steps fledging arrows. When they see him coming down the lane, Errin bolts to her feet and rushes into the house. Shortly, Roland and everyone else come out to greet him.

"Welcome back," Roland says as James and the others come to a stop. He casts a glance toward Qyrll but doesn't comment. James can see the others taking in his tattooed visage in uncertainty.

Errin and Caleb come to take the horses. James hands Errin his reins and says, "Can't tell you how glad I am to be back."

To Errin and Caleb, Illan says, "Take the horses to the barn and get them settled in."

Taking the reins from him, Caleb says, "Yes sir." They then lead the horses to the barn.

"Let's go inside and I'll give you a brief rundown of what happened," James says as he makes for the door.

"Something wrong?" Yern asks.

"You could say that," replies Jiron.

Everyone moves inside the house and takes their usual positions in the front room for when they have the evening gathering time. After settling into his chair, James gestures to Qyrll and says to everyone, "This is Qyrll. He's a Parvati from a land deep within the Empire. Fierce fighters but loyal to their friends."

Launching into what happened at Cardri, he as well as the others relate the events which ultimately culminated with the rescue at sea. When he's done, Yern just shakes his head and says, "You can't go anywhere without something major happening to you."

Turning toward him, James sighs and replies, "It looks that way."

"What are they going to do now?" Tersa asks from where she sits with her brother. She sits next to him on one side while Aleya sits on the other.

"Who?" he asks.

"Cardri," she clarifies.

"I doubt if they'll do anything," he explains. "After all, they did as requested and handed me over. As much as that upset me, I don't hold any ill will toward them. They only did what they did to insure peace. I can understand that mentality. From their point of view, what happened on the open seas is none of their concern. I don't think we need fear any reprisals from them."

"What about the Empire?" interjects Jorry.

"That's an entirely different matter," he says. "I expect them to continue in their efforts to do me harm. Since the political maneuver didn't work I think it's likely they will try something more direct again."

Nodding, Illan adds, "I agree." He then looks around to the others, "We need to be more vigilant from here on out. Assassins or another kidnapping plot may be in the offing."

"What should we do?" Tersa asks nervously.

"Don't go anywhere alone," replies James, "unless it's close to The Ranch. And by close I mean within sight. If someone goes into town, they take another with them. Tomorrow I plan to go see Ceryn early in the morning."

"I'll come with you," Jiron says.

"Fine," he says. Suddenly a big yawn escapes him. "Any questions?" He can see they have questions in their eyes but none speak them. "In that case, I'm heading to bed."

"Good night James," Tersa says.

"Good night to you all," he replies and then heads to his room. After he leaves the front room he can hear them beginning to talk in greater detail about what went on as well as the events in Willimet. He finally makes it to his room and closes the door. Getting undressed quickly, he wriggles under the covers and is soon asleep.

Chapter Eighteen

The following morning finds Illan out with the recruits putting them through drills. Ever since he moved the practices from outside of James' window, he has been able to get a good night's sleep.

Getting out of bed, he puts on his clothes from yesterday and goes to the kitchen to have breakfast. Ezra has a plate ready for him and he takes a seat next to Arkie who is in his high chair. "Has Dave come out of his room?" he asks her.

"Haven't seen him sir," she replies. While they were gone she had Roland fix an oversized pantry with a pallet for Dave. She felt the master of the house shouldn't have to share his bed.

He's worried for his friend. The last few days on the way back, he had been quiet and moody. He continues to think on his friend until something wet and soft hits him in the side of the face, the side facing Arkie.

He turns to see Arkie there with a big smile on his face and another handful of his breakfast arched back and aimed at James. "Don't you dare," James says to him, amused.

"Arkie!" his mother cries just as he throws it at James.

He ducks but not fast enough and a handful of squishiness hits him in the head just above the ear. Arkie lets out with a jubilant squeal as he reaches for yet another handful.

Ezra rushes over to him, intending to punish the boy for treating the master of the house in such a manner. She begins talking to him rapidly in the Empire's tongue and the smile on his face quickly disappears. Grabbing the arm which has the handful of food poised to hurl at James she slaps his hand.

Dropping the food, he looks to his mother, eyes beginning to well tears and lets out with a cry.

"I'm sorry sir," she says to James.

"It's okay," he replies, more amused than upset. "I was going to head out for a bath anyway. Don't be too hard on him."

"He has to learn right from wrong now," she says. Giving her son a stern glare, she sees him reaching for another handful of food. She brings her hand close to the one reaching and holds it over his hand as she gives him that look. The look all mothers give their kids when threatening a punishment if they don't stop what they're doing. Obviously Arkie hasn't learned the subtle nuances of facial expressions yet and takes the handful.

Slap!

Her hand comes down and strikes his hard. Not hard enough to hurt, just hard enough for him to know he did wrong. "No!" she says sternly.

After getting the food mostly out of his hair, he hurriedly eats the remainder of his breakfast as he watches mother and son out of the corner of his eye.

Crying, Arkie looks to his mother, hurt and upset. His bottom lip is out and tears stream from both eyes. He begins reaching for another handful and her hand again moves to hover over his.

You better learn kid, James thinks as he puts the last forkful of eggs in his mouth.

Never taking his eyes from his mother, Arkie moves his hand closer to the food and she raises her hand slightly while at the same time cocking her head to the side. "No," she says.

Pulling his hand back, he gives James a hopeful look.

"Don't look at me," he says. "I may be master of the house but she's your mother." To Ezra he gives her a quick smile and then gets up from the table. Patting Arkie on the head he returns to his room and collects a set of clean clothes as well as a cupful of soap.

After he passes back through the kitchen and goes outside, Miko sees him and hollers that he'll join him. Racing back to get his things, he soon catches up with him at the bathing pool.

The morning air is crisp, he's not sure how many more mornings he'll be able to endure the cold water. Each day seems to be getting colder and colder. The days where he would linger in the water are past. Scooping out some of the soap, he quickly cleans himself as well as his hair.

"Arkie get you this morning?" Miko asks amused.

"Twice," he replies.

"He nailed me earlier," he tells him with a grin. "Ezra sure has her hands full with him."

"It's just a stage, I hope," he says.

"Coming with me to town today?" James asks.

Shaking his head, he says, "No. Roland says I've missed too much time at the class and am starting to fall behind the others. He wants us all to be doing the same, says it's easier that way."

"I can see where he would want that," he replies.

"Seen Dave yet today?" he asks Miko.

Shaking his head, he replies, "No. He was gone when I got up."

"Gone?" he asks, worried.

"He does that some times," Miko explains. "I think he likes to get away by himself or something."

"Maybe," replies James, worry for his friend increasing. Dave has never been one to wander off by himself. He would always try to be the life of the party and garner attention. He continues to think on Dave while he finishes his bath.

"This water is simply getting too cold," he says when he's finally done washing. Getting out, he dries himself off quickly. The slight breeze has caused goose bumps to arise over a good portion of his skin. Once he's dressed, he leaves Miko in the water and returns to his room where he takes out his shaving knife and scrapes off the stubble which has grown scraggly ever since he left. *Got to remember to take this with me.*

Once he's done, he rubs his face and feels much better now that it's once again smooth. He leaves his room and goes outside where he finds Jiron has already readied two horses. Fifer is talking with him and breaks off when James approaches.

"How do you feel this morning?" he asks.

"Fine," replies James. "Always feel fine after a good night's rest."

"I think Illan's going to have us out and bring in some meat to smoke after the morning drills so may not be around when you return," Fifer explains. Qyrll comes around the corner, swords swinging at his hips and stands beside Fifer. A definite friendship has developed between the two.

"Running low are we?" James asks as he mounts.

Looking up at him, Fifer nods. "That's what Ezra is telling us," he says.

"Good luck."

"Thanks," replies Fifer.

Jiron mounts and then they head down the road. As they make their way up the lane to the main road, James glances over to the construction site of his new house and stables. The stables are complete, except for a few of the interior walls separating the stalls. It should be done by the end of the week. The house still has another two or three weeks to go.

Sean the master builder in charge of the construction sees him looking his way and gives him a wave. James returns it.

They find Uther at the guard shack looking bored and tired. As they approach, he asks, "How much longer do we need to have someone out here?"

"Until we no longer get unwelcome visitors," James replies. "Have there been any today?"

Nodding his head, Uther says, "One. He said he would pay you to remove a wart from his face."

"Bad?" Jiron asks.

Chuckling, he nods and says, "Very."

"Where are all these people coming from?" groans James.

"Who knows?" replies Jiron. "They sure are an irritant though."

"Tell me about it," he says. Then to Uther he adds, "Be back in awhile."

Uther gives them a nod as they leave the lane and turn onto the road heading to town.

On the outskirts of Trendle, they find a group of men standing and talking to one another against the outer wall of the last building. As he draws closer he sees it's the mayor and a few members of the town council along with several other men from town. Corbin is among them.

"James!" Corbin says as he approaches.

"What are you all doing here?" he asks as he pulls to a stop. Then he asks jokingly, "Are you hiding?"

The mayor's face flushes a little bit red and Corbin says, "In a way."

Then it hits him. The mayor is meeting with his old drinking buddies his wife doesn't want him to associate with. Feels he's above that now. "I understand," he says not pursuing the matter. "Do you know if Ceryn's around anywhere?"

"I think he left for a couple days," the mayor replies. "Seems there have been some problems on the road to the east."

"Nothing serious I hope," James says, concerned.

"We may have another band of robbers out that way," Corbin explains. "One man said a band of six men waylaid him and took all his coins. Ceryn's gone to investigate and isn't expected to return for a couple days. Did you need him for something?"

"Just wanted to ask him if he knew of a place called Ironhold," he says. "Have any of you heard of it?"

The blank expressions they give him tell him they haven't. "You might try Kraegan," suggests the mayor. "If it has something to do with iron, being the blacksmith he may know."

"Thanks," he says. "I hadn't thought of that." To all of them he adds, "Good day to you."

"Take care James," Corbin says.

He and Jiron then turn their horses and head into town to see Kraegan. "What will you do if he hasn't heard of it?" Jiron asks as they make their way through town.

"Wait for Ceryn's return I guess," he says.

The sound of hammer on metal reaches them long before the sight of Kraegan's shop appears down the street ahead of them. James has them stop in front and goes to the back while Jiron waits with the horses. He finds the blacksmith instructing an apprentice on the proper way to repair a plowshare.

Not wishing to intrude, he stands to the side and waits. Kraegan takes notice of him and gives him a nod but continues working with the apprentice. After two minutes and several rounds of hammering, he gives his apprentice a few more instructions before leaving him to finish.

Walking across the forge area to where James waits, he says, "Need another box made?" Grinning, he comes to a stop.

"Not this time," replies James. "Rather I am looking for information."

"What place?" asks Kraegan.

"Ironhold," he says. "Ever heard of it?"

"Ironhold huh?" he asks, eyeing James oddly. "Why would you be interested in that place?"

"You've heard of it then?" he asks excitedly.

"Sure," he says. "Never been to it, but my master when I was an apprentice talked of it once in awhile. It's to the north, I think on the other side of the Silver Mountains though I'm not exactly sure."

"What is it?" he asks.

"Ironhold is an old town that once had several iron mines," he explains. "It used to be a large supplier of iron but that was centuries ago. I think the mines finally played out and the place was abandoned."

"Abandoned?" questions Jiron.

"That's right," replies Kraegan. "My master said that over the years people tried to get the mines restarted but nothing ever came of it."

"Thanks," James tells him.

"Any time," he assures him. "Is there anything else?"

Shaking his head, James says, "No. I appreciate the help."

Giving him a nod, Kraegan returns to his apprentice and the plowshare.

James returns to Jiron and the horses and fills him in on what he learned.

"What do you think?" Jiron asks as they mount their horses.

"Seems reasonable," he says. "If the mines were played out as he says, then it might be likely that the priests of Morcyth went there."

"Do you mean to go there?" Jiron asks.

Nodding his head, he says, "Absolutely." He turns to look at his friend and says, "It's all I have to go on."

"Going to leave tomorrow?" he asks.

"May as well. No reason in putting it off," he says. "If winter's on the way, we want to get this done and return before it hits."

"You have a point," states Jiron.

As they leave the blacksmith's shop, James notices a woman walking with a grim expression down the opposite side of the street. She stops at the various windows and doors, peers inside for a moment and then continues down to the next.

"That's the mayor's wife," Jiron says amused.

"Glad I'm not married to something like that," James says.

"She's nice enough though," Jiron states.

Nodding, James watches her as she steps in through a door and then returns to the street a moment later. They continue through town, eventually leaving her behind. When they get to the edge of town where they last saw the mayor and his buddies, James glances over and finds them still there.

"Ahem," clearing his throat loudly, he gets their attention. He then jerks his thumb back behind them as he continues riding.

One of the men looks around the building and sees the mayor's wife coming down the street. "It's your wife John!" he exclaims.

"Thanks James!" the mayor hollers as he and the others move quickly around the other side of the building to avoid being found.

"I suppose it keeps his life from getting dull," Jiron says with a grin.

Laughing, James replies, "I guess so." Glancing back, he sees her get to the edge of town and stop after passing by the last building. With hands on her hips, she looks both ways and then turns around as she begins combing the other side on her way back.

Ahead of them playing among some trees near the side of the road are five young children, three boys and two girls. When they see him coming, they group together and stare at him approaching. Several of them whisper among themselves and finally one of the younger boys is pushed forward. Glancing back to his friends nervously, James sees the others prompting him to come forward.

Turning back to the road and James, the boy steps forward nervously. As James comes to him, he asks, "Are you the mage what lives outside of town?"

Nodding, James slows down and comes to a halt. "Yes I am," he tells the boy. He can see he's nervous so gives him a reassuring grin.

Glancing back to the others, the boy sees them nodding at him encouragingly and then turns back to James. Shuffling his feet back and forth, he asks, "Could you do some magic for us?"

James glances to Jiron and then looks around to see who else may be watching. Not seeing anyone, he turns back to the boy and nods. He holds out his hand palm up. The other kids edge closer when it looks like he may be doing something. Suddenly, his orb appears and the little boy says, "Oooohhhhhh!"

He throws it up into the air and it splits into three. The three orbs hang there suspended for a moment as the other kids approach. Slowly at first, the three orbs begin circling above the heads of the children. Gradually picking up speed, the swirling orbs begin looking like a circle of light above them.

Then the orbs suddenly explode in a burst of sparkles and disappear. "Wow!" one boy says. "Do it again!" a girl exclaims.

Grinning he says, "Sorry. I must be on my way. Maybe next time."

"Bye!" the kids say as he begins riding away.

Jiron glances at him and sees the grin on his face. "Why did you do that?" he asks.

"Just having some fun is all," he replies. "Why?"

"Now they're going to spread even more stories about you," he warns.

Sighing, James says, "I know. But sometimes you just have to do what you want and damn the consequences." Turning to him, he says, "It's for the kids."

"You have a soft spot for kids don't you?" he asks.

"I do like to make them happy," he admits. "I love to see their faces light up."

"You're a good man," states Jiron.

"I try to be." Glancing back, he sees the kids still standing there watching him. One waves when he notices James looking back. Giving them a wave in return, he then turns back and hurries down the road.

Back at The Ranch, he finds Uther still at the shack. "Tired of guard duty yet?" he asks.

"That's a dumb question," retorts Uther. "Of course I'm tired of it. All you do is stand and do nothing. Cant' go anywhere…"

Holding up his hand, James stops his tirade. "Alright, sorry I asked," he says. Moving down the lane, they leave Uther behind and come to the house. The morning practice is already over but he doesn't see any of the new recruits around. Seeing Illan over to the side where he's sparring with Jorry, he walks over and asks him where they are.

Stopping the sparring, he turns to James and wipes the sweat from his brow. Nodding to the old barn, he says, "They're in there with Roland working on their letters."

"Oh, right," replies James understanding.

"Did you find out what you wanted to know?" Illan asks.

"Yes I did," he replies. "It's in northern Madoc, used to be a mining town before the iron ore played out."

"Planning on going?" he asks.

"Tomorrow," says James. "I would like to find it before winter hits."

"Should be a month or more before you have to worry about any real bad weather around here," Jorry says.

"It's not around here I'm concerned with but where I'm going," he explains. "Not sure how far north it is or how long it will take."

"Who are you planning on taking with you?" he asks.

"Dave for sure," he replies. "Don't think I could leave either Miko or Jiron behind."

"You got that right," says Jiron from where he stands behind him.

"Also I was thinking of taking Jorry and Uther as well," he says.

Jorry brightens up when he hears that, "About time we get to get in on some of the fun!"

"Are the recruits improving?"

"Little by little," replies Illan. "Some will never amount to much more than sword fodder in a real conflict. But I think they'll suffice for here."

"Good. Keep up the good work," he says as he leaves them to return to their sparring. Moving toward the barn, he says to Jiron, "I'm going to check in on Roland."

"Alright," he says and then moves toward the house.

The barn is surprisingly quiet as he nears the door. Stepping through he finds Roland's 'students' sitting on benches bent over a shingle on their lap. The thin slice of wood seems to be what they're practicing writing on. Each of them has a thin, blackened stick with which to write and are currently shaping letters.

Roland looks up from where he was examining Errin's work when he enters and hands her back her shingle. Heading over to James, he rolls his eyes.

"Everything alright?" he asks. Every head immediately turns at the sound of his voice.

"Get back to it please," Roland tells them. "I have you little enough as it is." They all return to their writing with only the occasional, brief glance his way.

Sighing, he indicates for James to follow him outside. Once outside, he keeps his voice low so as not to be overheard by those within the barn. "Some are doing fine. Others not so."

"That's to be expected," replies James, nodding.

"It's slow going," he says. "They're fairly tired out from the hours of practice they've put in with Illan before they get to me."

"Just do what you can," offers James.

"I do, and they are improving," he states. "Some have their letters down and are moving onto whole words. Errin is the brightest, I think Miko may be the next brightest in this but he's not here enough to keep up with the others."

"I know and we'll be leaving again tomorrow too."

"Off again?" he says. "You don't like to stay in one place very long."

"It's not that I don't want too," asserts James. "Just that circumstances warrant it."

"I know," he says.

"Everything going well with The Ranch and the finances?" James asks.

"Actually," he says, "while you were gone, Delia returned and dropped off the coins she received from the sale of the gems. It was quite a sum. That alone should last us almost a year. With Tersa's bears we should be fine through next summer."

"I'll have Jiron or Fifer go back for more gems," he says. "But not until after winter."

"I understand." Making to return to the barn, Roland says, "I better get back in there. I only have them another half hour before they have to start their duties."

"Very well," says James.

He leaves as Roland enters the barn and goes into the house to check when lunch will be ready. Ezra tells him still another hour or so. Telling her he'll be in his workshop, he leaves through the backdoor. Crossing the yard he's soon inside with the door shut.

First thing he checks is the receiving crystal. That's the crystal which should emit a light if the hiding place of the Fire is disturbed in any way. At some point he'll have to get this crystal set up in a secure spot where it'll be visible yet at the same time safe from accidental loss or destruction. When he gets back from his trip to Ironhold, he may try to create a relay which will inform him no matter where he is should the receiver crystal receive the signal. But he doesn't have time before tomorrow.

Sitting down at his workbench, he pulls out a crystal from the sack sitting on the floor next to his workbench. Holding it absentmindedly, he rolls it through his fingers as he contemplates what happened in Cardri.

From what Illan told him, he was drugged by fumes coming from one of the torches which were burning in the dungeon. If they can render him powerless without so much as touching him, he's got problems. Fortunately he has been considering just such an occurrence and was able to realize what was happening before he completely lost his abilities.

He made that little sphere which held three simple spells, all of which were voice activated by him. No power or even conscious thought was needed to activate the spells. Since long before he ever went to Cardri, he had been thinking of just such a thing. The question he had was, 'If he was drugged how could he defend himself?' The answer was the sphere, of course the spells which he had embedded within it had disastrous repercussions when used on board a boat.

As he sits there and goes over the events on the boat, he comes to the conclusion that maybe it would be beneficial to have an ongoing spell which monitors and if certain things happen, automatically counters hostile spells or actions. It can't be too complicated or it might not work. Just some simple spells. First he'll try an automated shield, that should be easy.

First he casts his leech spell upon the crystal in his hands and allows it to absorb power from him for a few minutes until it has a small glow. Then he cancels the leech spell and after working out the details embeds an automated spell which will detect anything flying toward it at a rapid rate and throw up a shield before the object comes close.

Once it's done to his satisfaction, he takes the crystal across the room and sets it on a box sitting against the wall. Returning to his workbench, he activates the spell and removes one of his slugs from his belt. Just throwing it naturally without the added magic behind it, he watches as it arcs through the air toward where the crystal lies.

As it nears, he feels a spike in the tingling sensation and watches as the slug bounces off an invisible shield which springs up around the crystal. Once the slug was deflected, the tingling sensation subsides and the shield disappears.

He walks over to the crystal and slowly reaches his hand out toward it. Moving slowly, his hand is able to reach the crystal and take hold of it. The glow within is greatly diminished, but still perceptible.

It worked. However the tingling sensation still resonates through him and that isn't good. Any mage in close proximity will recognize that another mage is in the area. This may not work as well as he hopes. He can't afford to declare to any mage that he's one, could have unfortunate results should the other mage be unfriendly. He may have to stay with the voice activated one.

In situations where his presence is already known, then this would be a viable protective device. He'll have to think on it.

From outside, he hears Ezra calling in everyone for lunch. He didn't realize he had spent that much time on this. Deactivating the shield spell, he sets the crystal down on his workbench. Leaving the workshop, he heads over to the house and is soon sitting down at the table.

Dave is not present. Miko sees him wondering about it and says, "He returned awhile ago and went back to bed. Said he wasn't feeling good."

James commences eating, his mind on his friend. What can be wrong with him? It's not like him, maybe the time as a slave really messed him up. They're not five minutes into eating before Arkie nails him in the side of the head with a piece of slightly mashed tuber.

"Arkie!" Roland scolds his son.

Not looking the least bit sorry, Arkie grins at him as James wipes off the residue of the impact from his head.

"I'm sorry James," Roland says as he slaps his son's hand. The grin from Arkie quickly vanishes as his father reprimands him.

"Seems he has it in for you," Miko says from his place down the table. Giving James an amused grin, he holds up one of the boiled tubers in salute then commences eating it.

At first it was amusing now it's getting downright annoying. An idea comes to mind and James excuses himself for a moment and leaves through the back door.

"Think he's getting a helmet?" Uther jokes.

"Maybe full body armor," retorts Jorry which causes everyone in the room to chuckle. As soon as the door opens again and James returns to the table, everyone quiets down.

"What did you do?" Miko asks with a smile.

"Just got something from the workshop," he says. Taking his fork, he commences eating. All the while he keeps an eye on Arkie from the corner of his eye. Sure enough after he's begun to eat, Arkie starts glancing in his direction. He sees Roland begin to say something to his son but James shakes his head, indicating for him to leave the boy alone.

Everyone in the room is watching the unfolding event to see what's going to happen. They know Arkie is about to throw, but James appears unconcerned. Ezra is simply beside herself. She wants to stop him but had seen James' indication to Roland to leave him alone. Hitting the master of the house with a mushy tuber simply is not to be encouraged.

Then all of a sudden, Arkie grabs a tuber from off his plate and with a squeal, launches it at James. Just before the tuber reaches him, he feels a tingling spike as the crystal in his pocket creates a shield around him.

Splat!

The tuber strikes the shield three inches from his head. Everyone looks to James in surprise and he returns their gaze with a satisfied smile. Then all of a sudden, the shield disappears and the tuber, now no longer upheld by the presence of the shield, falls. Striking his shirt, it leaves a trail all the way down to his lap.

He sees Arkie again pick up a tuber and this time he doesn't interfere in Roland's attempt to discipline his child.

"What happened?" Miko asks incredulously.

"Just something I was working on," he replies. "I'll not go into detail about it."

"It stopped the tuber," Illan says.

"And anything else speeding toward me," replies James.

"Anything?" asks Miko.

"Anything," confirms James.

Miko suddenly grabs a large tuber and launches it at James.

Surprised by the attack, he leans back in his chair as the shield suddenly springs to life and stops the flying tuber. The tuber disintegrates and plasters the shield with a large area of tuber pieces. Then, just as it had before, when there was no longer something coming at him, the shield disappears. James scoots back quickly but not fast enough to avoid being hit when the mashed tuber is no longer supported by the shield and falls.

"Miko!" cries out Ezra. Enough is enough.

He looks and sees the anger in her eyes. No one acts that way at her table. "Sorry," he says in his most apologetic tone.

"It's nice to see I'll have some help cleaning the dishes after the meal today," she says, never once taking her eyes off him.

James stands up, tuber coating him from chest to groin. The others on the table break into a laugh. Arkie looks around at everyone, thankful that the attention has been diverted from him, and joins in with a high pitched squeal of delight.

"Guess I'll have to work on that," he says. Taking one more piece of meat off his plate, he leaves the kitchen and heads to his room to get a change of clothes. He's not about to bathe twice the same day, at least not unless it's warmer outside.

While he changes his clothes, he thinks he may need to make it that once the shield is activated, it will need his vocal authorization to cancel itself. He remembers back to when he and Jiron were coming back from Saragon and that magical attack he fought off by the other warrior priest. There are definitely times when it would be bad for the shield to disappear, such as when a flesh eating goo is covering it. He can still recall what happened to that captain at Mountainside when the shield disappeared and the goo hit him. Wasn't a pretty sight.

Before he's done, Miko appears at his door and says, "Sorry."

James gives him a smile and says, "I'm not mad."

"I didn't think you would be, but Ezra told me to come and apologize," he says with a grin.

"You don't want to be on her bad side," James tells him.

"Don't I know it," he says, rolling his eyes. "I have a whole afternoon of cleaning and other chores I'm sure." Then his mischievous grin appears and says, "But it was worth it!"

James laughs, claps him on the shoulder and they both return to the kitchen. On the way, he stops by the door to the room Dave now calls his own. Not much more than a walk-in closet really but at least it's private.

"Good luck," Miko says as he continues on to the kitchen.

Opening the door, he finds Dave lying curled up on his bed. His eyes open at the sound of the door opening. When he sees James standing there, he says, "Come on in."

James enters and closes the door. A very little amount of light enters through the cracks in the wall, giving them enough to see each other. He comes to sit on the edge of the bed as Dave sits up. "You okay?" he asks, concern in his voice.

Dave is silent for a moment and then replies, "I just want to go home."

"I know," replies James. "So do I."

"Do you?" he asks. "Do you really?"

Taken aback by the question, James asks, "How can you even ask that? Of course I do."

"Why?" he asks. "You were nothing there. Here you are a powerful mage, have a house and many friends. I remember you always used to say how great it would be if you had magical abilities. The things you would do. Can't imagine that you would want to give all that up."

James sits back a moment and thinks about what Dave said. Does he really want to go back home? Up till now, he thought the answer would be a resounding yes. But after what Dave just said, he now understands what he would be giving up if he went back.

"Thought not," Dave says. "If you'll excuse me now, I'm feeling kind of tired." Lying down in bed, he turns his face to the wall.

James sits there a moment before getting up. "You get some rest, tomorrow we're heading north."

Dave doesn't comment just lies there quietly.

Opening the door, James takes another glance at his lifelong friend and feels like a wall of some kind has grown between them. Saddened, he closes the door and leaves his friend to rest.

As he passes through the kitchen he finds Miko already clearing the dishes from the table. He pauses a moment intending to tell Ezra to go easy on him, but then decides against it. She can always use the help. Arkie has been removed from his chair and is now over in the corner on a pallet nestled with his teddy bear. He often takes a nap there right after lunch.

Leaving the kitchen he heads over to his workshop where he continues working to perfect his automated defensive device. Trying to put Dave out of his mind, he works on making it so the shield will remain active once it's been activated even if nothing further is flying toward him.

When at last he has it just the way he wants it and has tested it several times, there still remains one small problem. He can sense it while it is active. Of course when it is deactivated, it doesn't work. So the problem is, if he has it active to protect him, then any mage in the vicinity will pick up on it. The tingling is slight, but there none the less.

He then works on applying several other spells into it that may be useful in different circumstances. Not too many, the more complicated it becomes, the more chance of something going wrong. It takes awhile but he at last gets it pretty much the way he wants.

When he finally leaves the workshop for the night, he takes it with him and puts it into his pack. He intends to take it with him on the way to Ironhold in the morning. It may come in useful. Returning to the house, he finds Dave still in his room. He joins the others in the front room as they spend their evening time together.

The rigors of the day at last begin to catch up with him and he heads off to bed, again the first one. Once in his room, he's quick to undress and slip under the covers. Worries of Dave and what may be found at Ironhold spin through his mind as he fades away to sleep.

Chapter Nineteen

The following morning dawns bright and sunny. When James leaves his room there's a slight chill in the air despite the sun having been up for an hour. On the way to the kitchen for his breakfast, he stops by Dave's room and finds it empty. He worries about his friend until he arrives at the kitchen and finds him there eating breakfast with the others.

"I would like you to take Fifer and Qyrll with you as well," Illan tells him after he's taken his seat. "The Empire still wants you. Also, if you're going to Madoc, there's no telling what may happen."

"Sure," replies James. He glances over to Dave and when their eyes meet, gives him an encouraging smile. Dave's face breaks into his familiar jovialness which greatly relieves him. Hopefully last night was simply a low ebb in his mood and he's now out of it.

"Where's Jiron?" he asks.

Roland nods his head toward the door and says, "Outside with Aleya. Seems they've been getting into it since your return."

"Nothing serious I hope?" he says.

Shrugging, he replies, "Who knows? They're both in love but too stubborn to admit it. At least Aleya won't, Jiron wears his heart out on his sleeve for all to see."

He shakes his head. Then it dawns on him that it's still early yet and Illan isn't doing the morning drills with the recruits. "No drills today?" he asks.

Illan shakes his head and says, "They need at least one day every other week away from drills. Keeps them fresh and better able to learn. Half have returned to their homes for a brief visit, the others will have their turn later this afternoon."

"You're not keeping yourself too low in the event of an attack are you?" he asks worried. Already they've had to fend off two attacks since the founding of The Ranch.

"Shouldn't be a problem," he assures him.

For the remainder of the meal, they talk about small things having to do with The Ranch. Tersa tells him that Delia is finding wide demand for her bears and that she can't make enough.

"Just make what you can," he says. "Don't short the customer on quality and they'll always be back."

"I don't," she says. "It's just that Delia always wants more than what I've done."

"Don't worry about it," he tells her. "Just means the ones you do make will sell all the better." Finishing up the last bite of eggs on his plate, he stands up and announces, "We're leaving in ten minutes."

The others quickly finish what's left on their plates and proceed to the barn to get the horses ready for travel. James gestures for Dave to accompany him and they head out to the workshop.

"You doing better this morning?" he asks.

"Much," he replies. "Don't know what got into me last night." They walk the rest of the way to the workshop in silence. When James opens the door and enters, Dave adds, "I've had bouts of depression ever since I got here."

"Could be just a reaction from your time in the Empire," James suggests.

"Probably," he replies. "I have nightmares almost every night about what happened." He takes James by the arm and says, "I'm sorry if I haven't been much of a friend lately."

Pausing, he turns back to his friend, "Don't worry about it. If a friend can't help another out when they're going through a hard time, what good is he?"

He checks the receiver crystal and finds it still quiescent. It's unlikely he'll ever see it active, but you never know. Moving to his desk, he reaches down to the sack of crystals and takes out six and puts them into his belt pouch.

"What do you need those for?" Dave asks.

"Emergencies," he explains. He also has the automatic shield one as well. He takes a small swath of cloth and wraps it to keep it separate from the others.

By the time they leave the workshop and head over to the barn, the others have the horses saddled and are waiting. James and Dave come over and mount the two ready for them.

"Be back when I do," he tells Roland. "Not sure when that will be, though I'm hoping before winter sets in."

"We'll keep things going here," he says. "At least the house will be done when you return."

"That will be nice." Turning to the others who are coming with him, he says, "Let's go. Jiron, take the lead."

As they move out, Jiron moves to the fore with James right behind, Dave on one side and Miko on the other. Behind them ride Jorry and Uther, Fifer and Qyrll bringing up the rear.

Since Kraegan said Ironhold lies in the north of Madoc, they're going to the more northern pass through the Silver Mountains. With any luck, the war over there hasn't reached that far and they'll avoid any and all Empire forces.

Once on the other side, he's hoping to be able to ask the locals for directions to Ironhold.

Keeping a brisk pace, they're able to make it to the town of Wurt on the shores of Crystal Lake that first night. So far the trip has been uneventful and they stay at the same inn they stayed in that first night back when they were on their way to hide the Fire.

Dave remains cheerful all day, even managing to crack a joke now and then. To James, this is the old Dave, the Dave he remembers from back home. Seeing him act this way eases the worry he's been feeling for his friend.

The following morning when he rises, he finds clouds moving in from the west. How he misses riding in cars. The radio, the speed and not to mention the fact that when it rains you don't get wet. Sighing, he wakes up Dave and they head down to the common room for breakfast.

A quick meal and they're once more on their way. They continue along the road as it follows the shore of Crystal Lake. By noon the clouds have completely blotted out the sun and not long after that it begins to rain. Not a hard rain, but enough for them to break out their rain gear.

James acquired a wide brimmed hat and poncho for just such an emergency. When he has it on, Dave says, "You look like some Mexican out of the old west."

Grinning at his friend, he says, "Better than being wet."

When the light begins fading with the coming of dusk, they come to a town situated on the northern shore of Crystal Lake. "Should we stay here or continue on?" Jiron asks.

"We're not in any hurry," James says, "Let's find a spot here. Beats the heck out of sleeping on the ground in the rain."

"Thought you might say that," he says.

The town as it turns out is called Crystal City. Despite such a name, it is just another fishing village, though larger than most they've come through since leaving Wurt. They find an inn with a sign outside depicting a fat fish lounging in a bed.

Inside, they find the proprietress of the Fat Flounder, a rather jovial fat woman who greets them warmly. Arranging for rooms and stall space for their horses, they're soon settled in and having dinner down in the common room.

Outside, the sound of the rain beating against the windows tells them it's increased in severity. James is quite glad they didn't decide to continue on in this weather. Tomorrow will be soon enough.

No bard makes an appearance while they eat so they make do with conversation. During the course of their meal, a serving girl is bringing over another round of ale to their table when she's accidentally tripped by another customer who stood up from his chair abruptly.

Two of the mugs she was carrying on her platter fall off and hit Dave in the head, dousing him with ale.

James begins to chuckle at the sight but then it dies on his face when he sees the expression coming to Dave's face.

"You stupid girl!" Dave says as he comes to his feet. Red faced and dripping with ale, he turns on her and strikes her across the face. "Don't you know how to carry a few measly mugs?"

"Dave..." James begins to say when Jiron comes to his feet.

"Relax," Jiron says to Dave. "It was just an accident."

The room has grown silent as everyone there watches the events unfolding at their table. Face turning red from where Dave had slapped her, the girl begins to tear up as she says, "I'm sorry."

"Sorry!" yells Dave. "I'll show you sorry!" He makes to step toward her when Jiron grabs his shoulder. Turning around, he looks with eyes burning in anger at him and throws a punch.

Almost without effort, Jiron blocks the attack and in two lightning fast punches has Dave on the ground. "Apologize to her," he says as he stands over him.

"Jiron," James says trying to calm the situation down.

From the kitchen the large proprietress enters the common room. Upon seeing the whole room staring at Dave and Jiron, she makes her way over to their table. That's when she sees the serving girl with tears in her eyes and face turning red from where Dave had slapped her. All jovialness leaves her as she demands, "What's going on here?"

"Mother, it was my fault," the serving girl explains. "I spilled drinks on this gentlemen and he became angry."

"Did he hit you?" she asks her daughter. When her daughter nods yes, she turns an angry expression upon the supine Dave.

"He was about ready to apologize to your daughter," Jiron says. Then to Dave he asks with an edge to his voice, "Weren't you?"

Eyes dark from the smoldering rage bottled up behind them, he looks to James who nods his head. With absolutely no sound of feeling sorry for what he did, he says to the girl, "I'm sorry."

Jiron reaches down and takes Dave's money pouch. When Dave tries to stop him, he slaps his hand out of the way. Opening it up, he pulls out two silvers and hands them to the girl. "Here," he says to her in a kind voice, "take these as recompense for what transpired here."

She looks to her mother who nods. "Thank you," she says as she takes the offered coins.

"Go back to the kitchen," her mother tells her and she turns and quickly disappears through the kitchen door. To their group, she says, "Any of you strikes my daughter again and you'll be out the door. Understand?" She looks from one to the other.

"It shall not happen again," Jiron assures her. "I'll see to that."

"Very well." She then turns and walks back to the kitchen to console her daughter.

Reaching down he grabs Dave by the shirt and hauls him to his feet. "You and me got to step outside," he says and shoves him toward the door.

James starts to get up when Fifer puts a hand on his shoulder and says, "This needs doing."

"But Jiron will kill him!" he exclaims.

Shaking his head, Fifer says, "No, he won't."

Looking around at the others, he can see they're all in agreement with Fifer. Sitting back down, he watches as Jiron pushes Dave outside. After they leave, the room maintains a hushed silence for only a moment before the normal murmur of conversation resumes.

Shoving hard, he propels Dave out the door and outside into the pouring rain. People standing near the entrance give them room as it appears they're about to get into it.

"What the hell's the matter with your?" Jiron shouts at him as he comes to a stop two feet from where Dave lies sprawled in the mud of the street. The rain plasters his hair against his face as he confronts him.

Turning a gaze burning with hate and anger, Dave gets to his feet. "This ain't none of your business!" he spats back at him.

"Whatever effects James is my business," replies Jiron. "He's my friend."

"He was my friend first," he says.

"That is true, he was," agrees Jiron. "But how someone like you could ever be a friend of his I'll never understand." Looking at Dave, he adds, "The only reason you're even alive is due to him."

"You're all trying to turn him against me!" Dave accuses.

The crowd around them begins growing despite the downpour as they yell at one another, attracting everyone in the immediate vicinity.

"I haven't even tried yet," he retorts back. "None of us have."

Dave glares back at him, not responding.

"You want to take a swing at me?" Jiron asks.

"No," replies Dave. "Just to rip your head from your shoulders."

"Then let's have at it," he says.

A murmur runs through the crowd as they await Dave's response. Even though his anger is red hot, his wits are sharp and he knows that to go against Jiron is a death sentence.

"You all don't even seem to care what I went through before I met up with James!" he shouts out accusingly.

"What? That you were a slave in the Empire?" he asks back. He spits on the ground and hollers back, "My sister was a slave in the Empire as was Miko! Don't you even think to play that card with me! If you were any kind of man you would get over it and start living your life."

Dave glares back at him, rage burning within him.

"But no," he continues, "you keep whining about it like yours is the only life ever to experience hardship. The difference between you and the others is that they had the strength to carry on."

"You don't know what you're talking about!" he cries out. "Your sister and Miko went through nothing like what I did. Don't even think for a moment to compare their pain with mine!"

Jiron can see a subtle change come over Dave, his rage beginning to subside and something else taking its place.

Dave's voice gets a faraway quality, "The darkness." His eyes get wide and tremors seem to shake his entire body. The crowd around them begins to sense things are not going toward the fight they had been expecting.

Looking at Jiron, his eyes almost get a pleading look, "Pain in the dark. The biting and tearing. Voices, voices saying words you don't know, but yet do. I…" His eyes dart around, almost as if he's looking at something that's not there. "They come for you. They are coming for you but you can't escape. Wh…" He backs up several steps and then…

Noooooooooo!

…a blood curdling scream is ripped from his throat and the crowd nervously edges back from him.

James is suddenly there running past a shocked Jiron as he comes to his friend's aid. "Dave!" he cries as he grabs his shoulders. "Dave, it's James," he says as he looks into Dave's panic stricken eyes.

Noooooooooo!

Dave's scream again echoes through the night. James strikes him across the face with the palm of his hand and it seems to bring him back to the here and now.

His eyes focus on James' face and he asks in a raspy voice, "James?" then passes out.

James is quick to catch him before he falls. Looking to Jiron he says, "Help me get him up to our room."

Nodding, Jiron comes over and between them, they carry him up to the room James and he are sharing. Removing the wet clothes from him, they lie him down on one of the beds. Again they see the patchwork of scars and burn marks from his time as a slave. James looks to Jiron and asks, "What happened?"

"I'm not entirely sure," he says. "We were arguing and then he started talking about his time as a slave and then things went from bad to worse."

"He must have had a flashback," explains James. Using a finger, he pushes a lock of Dave's hair that had strayed across his face to the side.

"A flashback?" Jiron asks.

Nodding, he says, "In his mind he was reliving his time as a slave." Looking up, he sees the others there gathered in the doorway. "I think he'll be alright," he tells them.

"You need anything?" Miko asks.

"I don't think so," he replies. "Maybe some ale for when he wakes up."

"I'll get some," he says and leaves to head downstairs.

To Jiron, he says, "It might be best if you all weren't here when he comes out of it."

"You going to be okay?" Jiron asks.

"I think so," James assures him. Then looking to Dave, he says, "Him I'm not so sure about."

Jiron moves to the door and before he leaves says, "If you need something I'll be in the room next door."

"Thanks," he says.

Jiron closes the door and James can hear them outside as he relates to the others the gist of the conversation he and Dave had out front of the inn and what happened after.

A minute later a quick knock on the door and Miko walks in with a pitcher of ale and two glasses. "Thanks Miko," James says.

"Anything else you need?" he asks, casting a quick glance at the comatose Dave.

"Nothing right now," he replies.

"Alright." He moves to the door and pauses before opening it. "Are we still leaving in the morning?" he asks.

"Maybe," replies James. Nodding to Dave he says, "We'll have to see."

"I'll let the others know," he says as he opens the door and walks out.

When the door closes, James creates his orb for light and then sits there with his friend.

He must have fallen asleep for the sound of sobs wakes him up. Dave is there, lying in a fetal position sobbing into his pillow. "You okay?" James asks him.

Dave's eyes glance to his friend and another sob wracks his body. James gets up from the chair he's sitting in and takes his place on the bed next to his friend. "It's okay Dave," he says.

"I'm sorry James," he says between sobs. "I don't know what came over me!"

"I understand," he replies soothingly. He puts his arm around him and pats him on the back.

"You're all I have here," he says despondently. "I want to go home." His sobs are beginning to quiet down.

"Don't worry Dave," James assures his friend. "I'll always be there for you."

"No matter what?" he asks.

"No matter what," he says with conviction.

The rest of the night they stay there in the room together, talking of old times. They tell each other favorite scenes of old movies, remembrances of food long gone, and things they once did together before that fateful trip downtown. Sometime around midnight they finally fall asleep and when they wake up in the morning, Dave seems to be more of his old self. Still wearing a solemn expression, he at least can crack a smile when James tries to joke with him.

It's a little after sunup when they leave their room, the others have already congregated downstairs. When they join them Dave is quiet, casting occasional glances to Jiron and the others while he eats.

"Everything okay?" Fifer asks.

"As well as can be I suppose," James replies.

"We leaving?" Uther asks.

Nodding, he says, "As soon as we finish eating."

Standing up, he says, "Me and Jorry will get the horses ready." Jorry comes to his feet and together they cross the common room and exit through the door leading to the stables out back.

Much to James' relief, no one makes any mention of the events of the night before. They finish their breakfast quickly and are soon on the road. The rain from the night before has stopped, leaving the world wet and soggy, their horses splatter mud as they move along the road. The sky above still threatens possible rain with dark, ominous clouds.

Taking the road leading north, they soon leave Crystal City behind them and after but a half hour, the lake as well. Coming to a crossroads just north of the lake, Fifer tells him they need to continue along the north road, that it will lead them to the northern pass.

"A fellow back at the inn said the road would follow along the Three Sisters," he explains. "It's a series of three lakes set against the foot of the Silver Mountains connected by a single river."

"Wonder why it's called Three Sisters?" Miko asks.

"Who knows how anything gets its name?" Jorry says.

An hour after the road begins curving to the east, they see the first of the Three Sisters to their east, the spires of the Silver Mountains rising majestically behind it. The lake looks to be of fair size, nothing as grand as Crystal Lake.

"Might be a good spot for fishing," announces Uther.

"Perhaps when we have time we can do some fishing there next summer," James says. "A campout would be fun." Looking to Dave he asks, "Wouldn't it?"

"Sure," his friend replies.

Throughout the rest of the day they continue along the road, passing the second sister and reaching the third by nightfall. Raindrops have peppered them occasional while they rode, but not with the intensity of the night before.

With the light failing, James decides to pull off the road and camp at the last of the sisters. It's neither the largest nor the smallest of the three, perhaps a mile or more across at it's widest. Trees dot the area and they find a suitable spot to make camp along its shores.

While Miko takes his crossbow along with Uther and Jorry to scare up some dinner, he and the others begin gathering what dry firewood as can be found. "Not much to start a fire with around here," comments Fifer as he brings in his first load.

"We'll get a fire going then set wood around it to dry," Jiron says. He was fortunate to have found a section of moss hanging from the underside of one of the trees that is relatively dry and is using that as the base for the kindling.

Taking out his flint, he strikes a couple sparks and then gently blows as he tries to coax a fire to life. At first a small amount of smoke appears, then a fire catches and begins to consume the moss. Putting several smaller relatively dry pieces on, he gradually gets a fair sized fire going.

When Miko and the others return with a small game animal, the fire is going well and enough firewood has been gathered to last through the evening. By the time the animal is roasting over the fire, the sky has grown dark and the occasional baying of wolves can be heard from the nearby mountains.

Dave appears to be doing better, his jovial mood having returned which soothes the worries James has had over his friend. If there was a way to get him home, he would send him there in a heartbeat. As for himself, ever since Dave raised the question as to whether he wanted to return home or not, he's begun to wonder.

Despite the ruggedness of this world and the small fact that several groups out there are bent upon his destruction, he rather likes the life he's living. And Dave's right, here he is someone. Back home he's just another teen looking for a job with little prospects for a future, job market being what it is and all.

Do I really want to go home? No, I don't think I really do. It surprises him that he thinks that way, there are many things from back home he misses. His family for one, sure they were a bother, but whose family isn't? They loved and cared for him and he hates what they may be going through on account of his disappearance. He wouldn't mind returning briefly if for no other reason than to put their minds at ease.

Computers. Man does he miss his computer and all the games. Aside from reading, that was the one thing he really liked to do. Empire building was his favorite type of game and it occurs to him he may have inadvertently been doing the same thing here.

Starting out with nothing, he now has a place to live, a small army and enough money to do what he wants. However, the stakes of the game have changed. Where before on his computer he was out for either world domination by conquest or for accumulation of wealth, here he wishes to simply be left alone. Of course that doesn't look as if it's going to happen for quite some time.

When it's time to bed down for the night, he finds a spot under a tree which will afford some protection from the rain should it begin again in the night. Dave takes a spot close to him and is soon out. The others take turns at watch throughout the night, they don't bother James with it and they don't trust Dave to do it.

Uther has the first watch and his moving around the camp is the last thing James sees before succumbing to sleep.

Chapter Twenty

The next morning they rise to another dismal day of rain. The tree under which James had spent the night kept most of the rain from him though he is still slightly damp from what did reach him. A quick breakfast and they're on their way.

Several hours after they leave the last of the sisters behind, they come to a small community situated at a crossroads. Not much more than an inn and a chandler's shop, they continue on through, taking the road heading to the northeast. Just before they pass the last of the buildings, Uther pauses and asks one of the locals how far it is to the pass.

"You should reach the town of Feld in a couple hours," the man tells him. "It lies just before where the road begins its climb up into the mountains."

"Thank you," Uther says and then they continue along the road out of town.

"We should make Feld in time for the noon meal," Jorry announces.

"Might be a good time to find out what to expect before we start through the pass," James says. "Whether we should expect trouble or not."

"We should always expect trouble," states Jiron. "As soon as we become complacent and think we're safe, that's likely when the Empire or others will strike."

Sighing, James nods his head and says, "You're right."

They make good time, but the road is fast becoming a muddy mess and they all have a coating of mud from where the horses have kicked it up on them. Jiron isn't as bad as the others since he rides point for the most part.

The road continues to follow the base of the mountains and as the miles pass, the trees become increasingly denser. When noon has come and gone, and Uther has begun to complain about the lack of sustenance in his stomach, the town of Feld finally appears through the trees ahead of them.

They find an inn and after securing their horses, make their way inside. The inn is fairly clean and orderly, they find an empty table to the side of the room large enough to accommodate them all. A serving girl comes over once they've taken their seats and soon has them all set with a platter of their special, roast squirrel. Bread and a few vegetables, as well as ale, rounds out the rest of the meal.

Two men who have the look of locals are seated at the table next to them. James turns in their direction and says, "Good day gentlemen."

They glance at him but make no other comment.

"We are planning on heading through the pass," he tells them. "Would either of you know how the conditions up there are?"

One of the men, the older of the two nods his head and says, "This time of year it shouldn't be too bad, the snows have yet to fall. That usually doesn't happen for another month or so." His friend grunts in agreement.

"How long will it take to make it through?" Miko asks.

"Two days, roughly," the younger of the two states. "But we've heard tales of travelers being accosted going through lately."

"Accosted?" James asks. "As in robbers?"

"That's right," the older gentleman replies. "Not everyone who goes through is troubled however." He eyes their group a moment and then adds, "I doubt if anyone would bother a group such as yours."

"True," agrees the younger. "It looks like you know how to take care of yourselves."

"We appreciate the information," James tells him.

"No problem," the older man says. "Good luck." He then turns back to his meal.

"He's right you know," Jorry says. "No one in their right mind would tackle a group such as ours."

"Especially not one with as scary mug as you've got," Uther says with a grin.

Jorry gives him an annoyed look before breaking into a grin himself.

All through the meal, James takes notice of a couple sitting near them, a young man and woman. Neither of them could be more than sixteen or seventeen. From the way they sit close to one another, it makes him think they may be newlyweds. She keeps laying her head on his shoulder and snuggling close.

Once lunch is over and they begin heading to their horses, the couple gets to their feet as well and follows them out. When they're outside the inn, the young man approaches and says, "Excuse me."

They all stop and turn toward him. "Yes?" asks James.

The girl is attached to his arm as he says nervously, "I couldn't help but overhear your conversation with those other gentlemen." His eyes flick first to James then to the others, finally coming to rest back on James. "Am I to understand you are planning on taking the road through the pass?"

"That's right," he replies. "Why?"

Jiron draws close as do the others which only makes the man more nervous. The girl says, "Maybe we shouldn't bother them, dear." She pulls on his arm as if she wants to move away.

Turning to her he pats her arm and says, "It's alright." Then to James he asks, "We were wondering if you would allow us to accompany you over the pass. It's just the two of us and I'm afraid of what might happen if we go it alone, what with all the talk of troubles."

James glances to Jiron and Miko who both shrug, Dave gives an emphatic negative shake of his head. "Are you ready to leave right now?" he asks once he's returned his attention back to the couple.

Bobbing his head, the young man asks, "Yes sir. Our wagon is around back." The girl doesn't look very happy about this but will not gainsay her man.

"Sure," he replies. Holding his hand out, he adds, "Name's James."

With relief evident upon his face, the young man takes his hand and replies, "I'm Kerrin and this is my wife, Gayle."

"Nice to meat you," says James. "If you wouldn't mind going to get your wagon, we would like to leave as soon as possible."

"Yes, sir," the man says. "Right away and thank you." The woman gives him a slight courtesy but still doesn't look happy about the situation.

As the couple goes to get their wagon, James and the others begin mounting. "Are you sure this is such a good idea?" Dave asks.

"What are you worried about?" exclaims Jiron with a grimace. He hates the negativity which always seems to come from him lately.

"Relax Dave," James says. "It'll be nice having them along. The more we have, the less likely anyone will trouble us."

"True," Uther interjects. "Not to mention giving us something better to look at than Jorry's sorry mug."

Turning to his friend, Jorry says, "I wish you would retire that sorry old joke. No one laughs anymore."

Uther glances around the group and sees them all staring at him, some with disapproving expressions. He says, "Very well."

Just then from around the corner a wagon turns onto the street, the couple is seated upon the seat. "You know that wagon is going to slow us down a little," Miko says.

"Some," replies James with a nod. "But I just couldn't say no."

As the wagon draws near, the riders take up position around it and they make their way through town, toward the entrance of the pass.

This pass isn't nearly as steep as the Merchant's Pass had been. The road rises much more gradually as the mountains are not as tall. For the first couple of hours they steadily rise toward the summit which looks to be a day or two away.

Riding along, James casts glances back to the couple on the wagon behind them. The man always gives him a cheery smile while the woman simply looks scared. She looks as if she thinks they are going to fall upon them and attack them at any moment.

Miko is riding beside them and is regaling them with stories of their exploits. James smiles at the embellishments which have already crept into the often repeated tales. At least he's not making any mention of anything important, like the fact he can do magic. He knows James doesn't like that little tidbit to be talked about, so glosses over those parts. Try as he might, nothing Miko does seems to put the girl at ease. If anything his stories are only making her more nervous.

Maybe it's the heavily tattooed Qyrll that has her spooked. He does make a rather menacing sight. Qyrll generally keeps his hood over his features since he realizes the reactions people in this part of the world have to him. So it wasn't until they were an hour into the pass when the hood came off for one reason or another. She gasped in fright when she saw his visage and the others tried to put her at ease but to no avail. Her husband grew nervous for a time but his good natured personality resurfaced and came to accept Qyrll as non threatening.

Near the end of the day, a river appears. It flows through the pass ahead of them alongside the road and then turns more northerly before disappearing into the mountains again. From where the river disappears to the north, the sound of a mighty waterfall can be heard.

They continue along the road as it makes its way along the banks of the river for another hour until the light begins to fade with the coming of night. Finding a suitable spot, they make camp at the edge of the river under the cover of a cluster of trees. Their overhanging branches afford them some protection from the rain that's still coming down. It's been falling continuously all day and even though they've worn rain gear, it has managed to infiltrate and soak a good portion of their clothes underneath.

Other than the occasional drops of water which make it through, the area under the trees is relatively dry and large enough to accommodate them all. Off to one side they stake the horses near the wagon and then begin setting up camp.

When Kerrin notices them taking their food out in preparation to fix their meal he says, "You let us handle dinner tonight. It's the least we can do for you allowing us to travel with you."

His wife gives him a glare behind his back which says feeding them is the last thing she wants to do.

James notices the look on her face and says, "We don't want to be a bother."

"It's no bother," Kerrin assures him as he turns to his wife. "Is it dear?"

As he turns to look at her, her expression changes from one of annoyance to that of willingness. "No," she says. "No bother at all."

Before James can come up with a way to turn him down, Uther says, "That would be wonderful."

"Good, good," the man says and then turns back to his wife, giving her a smile. She smiles back until he begins walking from the trees to hunt for firewood, then her smile disappears. With a brooding expression, she goes to the wagon and begins removing several pots in which to cook their dinner.

Jiron comes up behind James and says with a grin, "I don't think she wants to cook for us."

Glancing back to him, he replies, "I got that feeling as well. But it's too late now, Uther's gone and accepted for us. Set up the watch for tonight, we can't afford to be caught unawares if bandits make an appearance."

"Already taken care of," he says. "Uther gets the first watch and you'll take the last. Everyone is taking a turn but Dave."

James arcs an eyebrow at that. "Why?" he asks.

"We don't trust him to stay awake," Jiron replies. Lowering his voice, he adds, "Actually some of us just don't trust him at all."

"I know," James says sadly. He glances over to his friend who has staked out a spot with his bedroll near the center of the trees. Lying down on his back, he has his arms crossed behind him under his head as he stares up into the trees. James goes over and sits down next to his friend.

"You okay?" he asks.

"A little depressed is all," Dave admits. "Homesick."

"I know how you feel," he says.

Turning on his side, he props his head on one hand and looks at James. "I miss the arcade," he says. "Not to mention tv, pizza and milkshakes."

"Pizza we might be able to manage here," James says. "Maybe a pepperoni one when we get back to The Ranch."

Perking up a little, Dave says, "You think so?"

Grinning at his friend, he says, "I don't see why not, it's just dough, sauce, cheese and toppings. In the winter we may even be able to do milkshakes."

"Or snow cones," adds Dave with a grin.

"Now sure what to flavor them with but we'll figure something out," he says.

"Would be nice to have some things from home like that," Dave says. "Maybe it wouldn't be so bad."

"That's the spirit," James says encouragingly. "Since we're stuck here, we may as well make the best of it."

"When life gives you lemons make lemonade?" asks Dave with a grin.

"You know it," agrees James with a nod. "Remember that time..." It's an hour before Gayle has dinner ready and all the while he and Dave reminisce about the old days back home. Seems they've been doing that a lot lately. Those are the times when Dave seems to perk up the most and be his old self.

Gayle finally calls everyone to eat. She's made a stew with plenty of meat and vegetables. They bring their bowls over and are given a hearty portion, then take position around the campfire.

"We are very grateful that you have allowed us to accompany you," Kerrin says as he takes his place near his wife.

"Glad to have you with us," James assures him.

Through a mouthful of stew, Jorry says, "You make a good stew ma'am." The others offer their praise as well.

"Thank you," replies Gayle, a shy smile coming to her face.

"My Gayle is one of the best cooks anywhere," Kerrin says as he gives her a one armed hug about the shoulders. "Don't know what I would do without her." She blushes from his words and lowers her eyes as she continues eating.

"May I have more?" Uther asks, holding his bowl out.

"Of course," she says as she gets up to ladle more into his bowl. "Anyone else?" she asks when his bowl is full. Miko of course comes to his feet quickly and gets more. Qyrll stands and comes forward with his bowl as well.

She glances to his tattooed face coming toward her and gets a nervous look on her face.

"I would like some more too if you don't mind," he says to her.

Her hand has a slight tremor in it as she ladles more stew into his bowl. "Thank you," he says when his bowl is again filled and retakes his seat. All they have to go with the stew is some slightly stale bread. But you dip it into the stew and it's edible.

By the time the meal is over, night has settled in and the temperature continues to drop. They throw more wood on the fire to keep the chill at bay as they begin to settle down for sleep. All that is but Uther who has pulled the first watch.

James lies his blanket down next to Dave, Miko settles in on his other side. Soon they're all fast asleep.

Suddenly awakened by a tugging sensation, James comes awake. He opens his eyes and the world swims in front of him. He looks up to see Kerrin standing above him, his hand around the chain securing the medallion around his neck. He tries to stop him but his movements are lethargic, his muscles not responding well to his commands.

"Get the rest of their money," Kerrin says.

"Yes dear," he hears Gayle reply.

"You did good work," another voice says. James scans the area and finds the voice belongs to another man. He starts in shocked recognition when he realizes it's the older gentleman from the inn back in Feld. The one who had warned them about the bandit attacks in the pass.

"Was easy enough," replies Kerrin as he finally manages to remove the medallion from around James' neck. Holding it up, he mumbles to himself, "Might bring a couple silvers."

He then reaches down and removes the pouch from James' waist which contains the crystals. At first excited when he opens it thinking he's found a stash of gems, he's quickly disappointed when he finds all there is are some common crystals of little value. "Don't you know what real gems are?" he asks James. Grunting in disgust, he dumps out the crystals on the ground next to him and continues rummaging through his pouches, removing all things of value. The necklace James had found in the underground temple near the fortress of Kern goes into Kerrin's pouch as well.

When at last he finishes with James, he moves to Dave and begins going through his things.

"Gather the horses," the older man says. James notices the younger one from the inn is there as well and begins putting the reins on their horses and securing them in a line to the back of the wagon.

Unable to move other than small movements, he tries to look around the campsite. He finds most of the others are passed out, Jiron seems to be the only other one besides him even conscious. He fears the others may be dead, no way to be sure.

They must have drugged us! His eyes come to rest on the stewpot and the realization hits him that that must be how they did it. But Kerrin and Gayle had eaten too, maybe they had taken the antidote before they consumed it.

Gayle is remaining by the wagons while the three men continue removing everything of value from their victims. Once Kerrin is finished with Dave, he stands back up and moves to the wagon to deposit the items he's removed. The older gentleman joins him and together they help to get the horses secured in a line behind the wagon.

When they at last have all of them tied behind the wagon, Gayle points to James and the others as she asks, "What are we to do with them?"

"Can't leave them to come after us," Kerrin says to her.

"You're going to kill them?" she asks aghast.

"You don't worry about that," he replies.

James tries to move after hearing that but whatever drug they used on him has almost completely immobilized him. All he can manage are weak movements which don't get him very far and exhausts him in the process.

Out of the corner of his eye his gaze settles on the crystals spilled on the ground next to him. Hope springs to him as he sees the one wrapped in cloth lying not six inches from his hand.

The last horse is secured in line and he hears the older gentlemen say, "You and your wife take the wagon and horses. We'll meet up with you in a few minutes." As the wagon begins to roll away, the unmistakable sound of a sword leaving its scabbard can be heard followed shortly by another.

James sees them moving toward them, intent on ending their lives. He again focuses on the crystals lying next to him and with a sheer force of will begins inching his hand toward the crystal with the embedded spells. His finger finally comes into contact with it just as they reach the unconscious men lying on the ground. He watches in horror as the older gentleman raises his sword to end the life of one of his comrades.

In a bare whisper, he says "Leech" and can feel power being absorbed from him by the crystal. Then before the sword can fall, he cries out in a gasp, "Incinerate!" More power is sucked from him as a red flare flies from the crystal toward the man.

The light from the flare causes him to pause a moment in his swing and that's all the time it needs. Striking him, the flare erupts in a flaming ball. Screaming, the man begins running around, a veritable human torch.

Startled, the younger man cries out, "Father!" Running to his aid, he attempts to put out the fires to no avail. Finally his father slumps to the ground, and lies still as his screams of pain come to a stop.

With a cry of rage, the son stands up and with a primal scream runs toward the nearest of the drugged men, intent upon venting his anger.

"Shield radius twenty!" can barely be heard as James gasps another command to the crystal. Springing up around the men lying on the ground is an invisible barrier.

Aaaaaahhhh!

A cry of pain and agony rips through the night, drawing James' attention. The son had been caught by the creation of the barrier and a portion of his face, chest and one leg had been severed off by it. Falling backward away from the barrier, he collapses to the ground where he writhes in agony until finally dying.

James says one last command before succumbing to unconsciousness, "Maintain."

Chapter Twenty One

_____

When he at last awakens again, morning has come. The rain has stopped and the sun is just beginning to break through the cloud cover. Sitting up, his head begins to spin and realizes how weak he is. That's when he feels the drawing of power from him by the crystal while it maintains the barrier around them.

"You okay?" he hears behind him.

Glancing back he finds Jiron walking toward him. Nodding his head, he asks, "You?"

"Still a bit dizzy but otherwise fine," he replies. He sees James glancing at the others and says, "They're all still alive but unresponsive. I think they may have been affected more than you and I."

"Gayle must have put something in the stew," he says as he comes to his feet. "Any sign of her or Kerrin?"

Shaking his head, Jiron says, "I don't think so." Then he motions over to one side of the camp and adds, "We have one stiff over there that's charred beyond recognition. At the edge of the barrier next to it is what's left of some guy your barrier cut in two. May be them."

"Cut in two?" James asks.

"Yeah," he says. "Come here and I'll show you." Reaching down a hand, he helps him to his feet. They make their way over to where the man had been sliced by the materialization of the barrier.

Turning away from the grisly sight, he says, "It's one of the men from the inn."

Instant recognition comes to Jiron who points over to the burnt corpse and before he can say anything, James adds, "That's the other one."

"Then they were in it together from the start?" he asks.

"It looks that way," he says and then begins making his way to the others where they lay on the ground, making sure they're alright. He finds them all asleep but unresponsive just as Jiron had said.

"We got a bigger problem," he tells him.

"What?" Jiron asks.

Turning to face him, he pulls down the collar of his shirt and says, "They took the medallion."

Jiron gasps in shock. This is the first time he's ever seen him without it. "What are you going to do?"

"Get it back," he says.

"They're going to be long gone by the time the others are ready for travel," he states.

"Be that as it may, I have to retrieve it," he asserts. No longer seeing the need to maintain the barrier, he returns to where the crystal lies on the ground and picks it up. Holding it in his hand he says "Cancel" and it disappears. He rewraps it in the cloth and then gathers the other crystals, putting them all in one of his pockets.

When the barrier goes down, Jiron moves and collects the two horses which are still tied to a nearby tree. They must have belonged to the two dead men. Bringing them closer he secures them nearby and then starts a fire in the now cold fire pit.

Over the course of the next several hours the others begin to regain consciousness. When they find out what happened they're all set to go and extract their vengeance upon them. The last one to come out of it is Miko, probably because he had eaten the most of the drugged or poisoned stew than the others.

During this time, it has been determined that Kerrin and Gayle proceeded further into the pass rather than return to Feld. The ruts created by the wagon are still visible in the mud and they head further up the pass.

Once they have a light meal, James announces that he and Jiron are going to take the two horses and follow them.

"But what about the rest of us?" Dave asks.

"You will have to follow as best you can on foot," he explains.

"But…" he begins to protest then falls silent, giving in to the inevitable.

"Fifer," he says, "I want you to be in charge until our return."

"You got it," he says.

Coming close to him and whispering so only he can hear he says, "Don't let anyone kill Dave."

Smiling, he gives him a nod.

He and Jiron mount the horses and then he turns to the others. "With any luck, we'll be back soon. If by the time you've reached the next town and we haven't returned, find an inn and stay there until we do."

"But we haven't any coins," Fifer says. "They took all I have." Glancing to the others, he gets answering nods saying their coins are gone as well.

Moving to the horses, James rummages through the packs still attached there. Not finding anything of value, he goes to the two corpses. He finds two sacks of coins, one on each. One of the sacks is burned badly from when the older man had been torched by James' spell so he transfers the coins from it to the other.

"Hopefully this should be enough," he says as he hands it over to Fifer.

"But what about you?" he asks as he takes the offered pouch.

"We'll get by I'm sure," he replies. Then with a nod to Jiron they return to the horses and mount.

"Good luck," Miko says as they turn to follow the road up the mountain.

"You too," he replies. As he kicks his horse to move, he can hear Dave mumble, "I knew it was a bad idea to let them come with us." Ignoring the remark, he breaks into a gallop and has soon left the others behind.

They don't get far before they find the wagon sitting abandoned in the middle of the road. "What happened?" Jiron asks.

"Perhaps they heard or saw what happened back at the camp and decided to beat a hasty retreat," suggests James.

"I was hoping they would still be on the slow moving wagon," says Jiron.

"Me too," he replies. A cursory look shows very little to have been left behind when the wagon was abandoned. They get moving again and quickly leave the wagon behind. The tracks of all their stolen horses leave a clear trail for them to follow. As long as the sun stays out they should have no trouble in following them.

After riding in silence for awhile, Jiron asks, "Do you suppose the bandits we were warned about might still be in the area?"

James chuckles at that and says, "Jiron, the people who told us about the bandits, were the bandits."

"Oh yeah, right," he says a little embarrassed.

"But in the mood I am right now, no bandit better hope to cross our path," he says in all seriousness.

Jiron gives him a nod and they continue to ride on throughout the rest of the afternoon. Whether they are catching them or not is hard to tell as neither of them are experienced trackers. One thing's for sure though, Kerrin and Gayle have a good head start with lots of fresh horses to change off with to better maintain their speed.

When night finally comes James decides to stop and rest. They're both still feeling the effects of the drug used on them and are in need of some rest. Building a fire and eating what little food they find on the horses, they make camp and take turns standing watch throughout the night.

The following morning they're up early and on the road before the sun crests the mountaintops. Riding hard, they continue to follow the road as it meanders through the mountains until finally reaching the summit. It's not a sharp summit but a gradual one and they're unable to look very far down the other side.

An hour after cresting the summit they come across what appears to be the camp Kerrin and Gayle used the previous night. A fire pit and mounds of fresh horse manure show that they were there. Off to the left of the road lies a lake which is the source of the river they've been following.

"May not be very much further behind them," Jiron says.

"We have been riding hard," agrees James. "Let's take a moment and find out."

Dismounting, he goes over to a free standing pool of water near the side of the road. Kneeling down, he concentrates on Kerrin and an image appears of him and Gayle riding fast trailing a line of horses behind them. The image shows them to still be in the mountains, the road they're on winding among the hills and trees.

Expanding the image, it's hard for him to determine just where or how far away they are. "At least they're still on the run and haven't met up with anyone," announces Jiron.

"That's fortunate," adds James as he cancels the spell. Getting to his feet, he mounts and they continue down the mountain. The wind here in the upper elevation bites with cold as it whips at them. They huddle more into their jackets as they race down the road.

James is feeling fortunate there hasn't been any snow falling yet here in the higher elevations. Though the clouds above have thinned somewhat, they still exhibit the inherent threat of more rain or snow. As cold as the air feels he wouldn't be surprised to see snow begin to fall. Of course the temperature is worsened by their speed, the wind chill making it feel worse than it probably is.

As they continue speeding down the mountain they come to a rocky area where the trees start to thin. This section of the pass looks to have been obliterated by a mammoth rockslide some time in the recent past. A way through has been cleared to enable traffic to continue across, large boulders dot the area. The slide couldn't have happened recently as bushes and small trees have begun to grow among the rubble.

James' horse becomes skittish as they enter the boulder strewn section of the pass. "Easy boy," he says, patting its neck in an attempt to calm it down.

"What's wrong?" Jiron asks.

"I don't know," he replies. "Something's got my horse spooked."

Jiron signals to come to a halt as he scans the area. His horse has begun to exhibit nervousness too.

"Think there's a problem?" James asks.

"Maybe," he replies as he continues scanning the boulders. "I don't see anything out of the ordinary." After searching for another minute he adds, "Would be a good place for an ambush though."

"I was thinking that too," says James. Up ahead of them the road winds its way through large piles of boulders which could very easily hide raiders of one kind or another.

"Kerrin and Gayle made it through," Jiron finally says, "and I don't see anything." He glances to James and continues, "Let's take it slow and keep our eyes open."

Nodding, James nudges his horse to move at a slow walk. Keeping his eyes open, he reaches to his slug belt and removes one, keeping it ready just in case.

Their horses continue to show signs of skittishness and at one point Jiron's stops and refuses to go further. He kicks it a couple times in the sides and finally gets it moving. Glancing to James he sees the worry he feels mirrored in his face. Pulling a knife, he signals for James to wait while he proceeds ahead.

Nodding, James waits.

Taking it slow, he works his way slowly forward, eyes scanning the road and rocks ahead for any indication of what has the horses so spooked. He moves twenty feet from James when a black shadow lurches toward him from out of the cover of the rocks ahead and to the right.

Easily half the size of a horse and running like a dog, it charges with a growl. Jiron's horse rears up and he vaults off the back, landing unbalanced on the ground. Falling to the ground, he rolls and quickly regains his feet. The creature sinks its teeth into the horse's chest, literally ripping a large section out. With a scream the horse collapses in a heap.

James' horse neighs in fear and turns, bolting back down the way they had come. It comes to an abrupt stop when another of the creatures enters the roadway and blocks its path. Eyes rolling white, the horse cries out again and bolts suddenly to the side, causing James to lose his balance and falls off the horse to the ground.

"James!" Jiron cries out. "What the hell are these?" The creature which had killed his horse stands there with a strip of the horse's hide dangling from the corner of its mouth as it stares at him. It looks like a giant wolf or some kind of dog. Long sharp teeth fill its mouth and a malevolent intelligence stares from out of its eyes.

Moving slowly and never taking his eyes from the creature, he backs up to where James is getting himself off the ground. In the pits he never had the opportunity to fight animals. Though confident in his prowess as a fighter, the size and ferocity of this creature gives him more doubts about the outcome than he's had in quite some time. A growl behind him causes him to glance back and see the other creature on the road and James making his way toward him quickly.

A sudden shimmering forms around them as James creates the barrier. As if that was a signal the creatures charge right at them and slam into the barrier. Knocked back for a moment they begin circling.

"Do something," Jiron says as they continue moving around the perimeter of the barrier.

James takes the slug in his hand and launches it at one of them. It strikes the creature directly in the middle of the chest and seems to pass right through without causing any damage. "Damn!" he says in shock as the slug hits the ground behind the creature. It didn't look as if the slug had any affect upon it at all, the creature didn't even slow its pace.

"They're not entirely real!" he says to Jiron.

"What?" he asks.

"The slug went right through them," he explains.

"How is that possible?" he asks.

"I don't know," James replies. "But I doubt if your knives will have any effect either."

The two creatures continue to pace around the edge of the barrier, their eyes never leaving those within. One comes to a stop and turns to face directly at the barrier. Raising one of its forepaws, the creature touches the barrier.

Aaaaaahhhh!

James cries out from the sudden increase in magic being pulled from him to maintain the barrier. Despite the enormity of magic rapidly being taken, he watches in shocked amazement as the creature's paw slowly inches its way through the barrier and touches the ground on the inside. The rest of the creature slowly begins to follow.

Jiron moves to the part of the creature on the inside of the barrier and strikes it with a knife. When the blade comes into contact with the creature, it sends a burning sensation through to his hand. Crying out in pain, he releases the knife and looks to find an angry red burn now upon his hand. The knife which had struck the creature lies on the ground and is glowing red.

He glances back to James who stares with eyes wide in surprise. "Get back here," he tells him.

Jiron nods and returns to his side. "What are you going to do?" The creature's snout has now begun to inch its way through.

James doesn't reply, his mind is working too hard on the problem. He comes to notice the area where the creatures have been pacing along the outside of the barrier has been scorched from their passing. Add to that the reaction when Jiron struck it with his knife and he comes to a disturbing conclusion.

Creatures of fire? Hell hounds maybe? Where did they come from? Sensing the hand of Dmon-Li in this, he tries to come up with an effective attack. Already the creature has managed to get its head in and is starting to move its other foreleg through. It won't be much longer before it'll be completely inside.

Jiron puts his other knife in his belt. He knows it will be useless and there's nothing he can do here. It all rests on James now.

How do you fight a fire creature? Cold? Water? Ice? Glancing above them to the clouds, an idea forms and he staggers slightly as he begins to implement it. Jiron puts an arm around him as he settles to the ground.

The clouds above become denser as they race together from all directions. James is beginning to sweat, the strain from maintaining both the shield and summoning the storm is rapidly draining his strength.

By the time the creature has its other leg and all of its head within the barrier, drops begin to fall from the sky. When they strike the creatures, hissing can be heard as they quickly evaporate.

The rain begins to fall in increasing intensity, but that's not what he's wanting. He hunts through the clouds above until he locates what he wants and pulls it closer. The strain of doing so brings black spots to his eyes and he's not sure how much longer he's going to last. Hopefully long enough.

The temperature begins to drop as he brings the system he wants closer and the rain changes to hail. Where the rain didn't seem to bother the creatures, the hail does. As it strikes them, it almost appears to be causing them pain. Also the creature making its way through the barrier halts its progress. The pull of magic needed to maintain the barrier eases off slightly.

Watching the other creature on the outside, Jiron notices that where the hail is striking, dark patches are beginning to appear. "I think it's working," he says encouragingly. There was also a note of hope in his voice too.

James has his eyes closed and can tell that though this may be working to slow and bother them, he'll have to do more in order to vanquish them. Besides, he'll not be able to keep this up for long. The clouds above are fighting him as the winds in the upper reaches work to pull the storms away.

Maintaining the hail storm, he sends out an additional tendril of magic toward what's already fallen on the ground around them. Ice pellets begin moving along the ground toward the creatures and begin attaching themselves. He also attempts to change the barrier, similar to how he did it another time long ago. Back then he changed it to fire to burn off an acidic ooze, this time he's changing it to extreme cold.

As it begins to change, the temperature within the barrier drops dramatically and the creature caught in the middle of it begins to exhibit panic. It tries to get out but James continues to reduce the temperature of the barrier and it cries out from the pain being inflicted.

The other creature on the outside starts growling and snapping at the barrier but when it comes into contact with it, an audible sizzle sounds. The hailstorm still falls outside, the hail beginning to accumulate around them. The odor of sulfur begins to permeate the air as the creatures are struck by the falling hail.

James and Jiron begin shivering from the temperature within the barrier, it has to be below freezing now, way below freezing. The creature caught in the barrier starts thrashing about from side to side in a panicked attempt to free itself but is unable to extricate itself from the barrier. Finally, with a nightmarish cry, the half within the barrier comes away and falls to the ground. Erupting in a cloud of noxious black smoke, it disappears, leaving a charred area on the ground.

With the destruction of the one caught in the barrier, the strain on James diminishes dramatically and he's able to concentrate on the other one. It's visibly weakened from the ice coating it, steam rising in clouds from where it sticks to its side.

Releasing the clouds above he turns his attention fully on the ice lying upon the ground outside the barrier. He has to use his senses for the barrier now has a layer of ice upon it and nothing on the other side can be seen from within. His mind is beginning to lose its battle with consciousness, he knows it's simply a matter of seconds before he's gone. Using his powers in one last surge, he gathers the hail on the ground outside and creates his last spell before passing out.

Jiron is there by his friend when he feels him slump into unconsciousness. Making sure he's okay, he gets to his feet and goes to the barrier to listen. As he draws near, the ice shrouded barrier shatters as the second creature smashes through.

Covered in ice, acrid steam rising from it in a cloud, the creature bursts through with a growl. Knocked backward by the creature, Jiron hits the ground but rolls quickly back to his feet. The creature swings its head from side to side as it contemplates James and Jiron. Making its choice, it emits a growl which sends shivers of fear through him and launches itself at Jiron.

Moving quickly, he races to a nearby boulder and jumps upward, landing upon it. Not taking the time to look backward, he then takes two steps and jumps again, this time grabbing a tree limb and swinging up just as the creature leaps to grab him. He can feel the heat from the creature as it passes just below him.

Coming to rest on top of the limb, he watches as the creature paces along the ground below. It seems as if the creature is trying to figure out the best way to get him down. Not in immediate danger of dying, he glances back and sees James lying there amid the melting remains of the ice which had coated the exterior of the barrier.

His eyes widen is amazement when he notices two objects lying not three feet from the shattered edge of the barrier. He rubs his eyes to make sure they're not playing tricks on him. Sure enough, lying there in the ice are two knives entirely made of ice. How they came to be there he doesn't know, probably James when he knew he was about to pass out.

With the creature pacing beneath him, he can't just hop down and rush over there. He takes in his surroundings and notices where the ground drops away just to the right side of the tree. Moving from limb to limb, he makes his way over and sees that the drop-off goes down about twenty feet or so. Making up his mind as to his course of action, he makes his way back to the far side of the tree, the creature pacing beneath him the whole time.

Getting into position, he takes a deep calming breath as he takes hold of the branch he's standing upon. He watches the creature in its pacing and waits until it's in a good position for what he plans, then he swings down like a gymnast and sails through the air toward where the drop-off lies.

The creature immediately surges in pursuit as he hits the ground running. Praying this works, he takes several steps and jumps to grab a limb overhanging the edge of the drop-off. Swinging up onto the branch, he just escapes being caught by the creature as it jumps after him and sails over the edge of the drop-off.

Not taking the time to congratulate himself, he immediately drops down to the ground and races for the ice knives lying on the ground over by James. Before he even reaches them he hears a growl behind him and glances back to find the creature has already regained the top and is coming after him.

He redoubles his speed. It's a race to see if he can reach the knives before the creature reaches him. When he draws close he dives for them, takes one in each hand and then rolls back to his feet facing the approaching creature.

No sooner is he back on his feet than the creature is upon him. Lashing out with a paw, the creature tries to connect with his midsection. He deftly deflects the attack with one of the ice knives which elicits a roar of pain from the creature when the knife connects. "You didn't like that did you?" Jiron asks as the creature looks at him with malevolent hate.

The knives are extremely cold but not so as he can't hold onto them. After seeing the reaction the creature had to the touch of the knife, he launches into an attack, his confidence once more restored in his ability to hold his own. Striking out at the creature, he connects with one knife and scores a long sizzling line across one of its forelegs.

Snarling in pain and anger, the creature advances upon him incredibly fast. Jiron concentrates on defense and counters every attack the creature makes. After several passes and scoring numerous hits upon it, he suddenly realizes that his knives are smaller than they had been. *They're melting!* The heat of the creature is causing them to melt with every strike. He needs to finish this soon or he won't have any weapon left with which to fight.

He backs a little to plan his attack and kicks up some of the hail still peppered across the ground. It does little to slow the creature. Suddenly the creature leaps at him and he swerves to the right but not before receiving a long scrape along one arm. Burning pain erupts from the red welts forming along the cut as the heat of the creature burns him.

Taking the fight to it, he launches into a series of blows which the creature deflects but not without receiving wounds from the knives. Finally seeing the opening he's been waiting for, he closes the distance rapidly and plunges one of the knives into the chest of the creature.

Bellowing in pain, it staggers to the side and then he plunges the other knife though where the neck and the shoulders meet. Stepping back, he watches the creature thrash about upon the ground until it finally comes to rest. Then it erupts into a cloud of noxious black smoke just as the other had. When the smoke clears, the two ice knives are gone.

Breathing hard from the fight, he makes his way back to where James is lying. Sitting down next to him, he rests his head on his knees. Glancing to his friend he wonders just how long he'll be out this time.

He closes his eyes for just a moment before a nearby noise brings him suddenly alert. Opening his eyes, he turns to find a man in robes approaching and a dozen soldiers of the Empire behind him. Three have crossbows leveled at him.

"That was quite impressive," the Empire's mage tells him as he continues to draw near. "Don't know how you defeated the Guardian's set against you." Glancing to James lying comatose on the ground beside him, the mage turns to the soldiers and says, "Take them."

Unable to do anything with the crossbowmen there, he does nothing as they tie his arms behind his back.

Chapter Twenty Two

_____

After they tie him securely, he's put into the back of a nearby wagon along with the comatose James. The mage takes a seat in the front of the wagon with one of the soldiers next to him taking the reins. One soldier and crossbowman climb into the back of the wagon with their prisoners, the others mount awaiting horses. Then the soldier driving the wagon flicks the reins and the wagon begins rolling. Moving onto the road, they head down it toward the Madoc side.

Sitting in the back of the wagon as it rolls along, bumps making his position decidedly uncomfortable, Jiron keeps an eye on James. Other than the predicament they're in, he seems okay. The soldiers and mage are silent as they roll along which suits him just fine. He tries to work the knot of his bonds loose but the soldier in the back with him notices and shakes his head. Seeing the implied threat in the man's eyes, he stops.

They roll for another several hours before turning off the road. They follow a path which is little more than a game trail for another twenty minutes before arriving at a clearing where a camp has already been set up.

More soldiers are there as well as many slaves. How they managed to get all this here without being detected is something Jiron isn't likely to find out anytime soon. Several tents dot the clearing as well as three other wagons. As they roll to a stop the mage gets down and says something to one of the soldiers before disappearing inside the largest tent which sits in the center of the clearing.

The soldier comes over to the side of the wagon and says to Jiron, "Come on down."

Doing the best he can with his wrists tied behind him, he rises in the back of the wagon. Putting one foot on the edge he hops over to the ground below. The soldier and crossbowman in the back pick up James.

"This way," the soldier says as he turns and leads him over to another smaller tent to the side. The two carrying James follow.

The other people in the camp pause in what they're doing to stare at the new arrivals. Whispered mutterings can be heard throughout the clearing. As they approach the tent, one soldier holds open the flap as he and James are put inside. Then they proceed to remove all their items but the clothes on their backs.

Shortly after that a civilian and a slave enter and come over to where James is lying on the ground. The man is holding a vial in his hand and with the slave's help, pours the contents into his mouth. After waiting several minutes to make sure it was swallowed, he and the slave leave.

Aside from a guard posted outside, they're left pretty much alone. Jiron works at his bindings and finally gets them undone. He doesn't bother trying to awaken James, he realizes that aside from the fact he probably wouldn't wake up anyway, having again overextended himself with magic, he's likely drugged as well.

Moving close to his friend, he checks to make sure he's still breathing and otherwise okay. Then he sits back and waits for whatever their captors plan to do next. He has a pretty good idea of the layout of the camp and sits near the edge of the tent in order to attempt to keep track of what's going on outside.

Not more than a half hour goes by before footsteps are heard approaching the tent. The flap is pulled aside and the mage enters followed by two soldiers. Once inside, the tent flap is again allowed to close.

The mage glances from the unconscious James to Jiron and notices he's managed to remove his bindings. One soldier pulls his sword to keep Jiron at bay while the mage approaches James.

"Don't touch him!" warns Jiron.

The soldier with the drawn sword comes forward and strikes him across the face with his other hand. "Impertinent dog!" he says derisively.

Kneeling down near James' head, the mage lifts one eyelid and examines his eye for a moment before closing it. Returning to his feet, he glances again to James. "So, this is the mage causing the Empire so much trouble," he says. He looks to Jiron as if for confirmation but Jiron remains silent.

"Doesn't seem like much," he continues, "but you two did defeat two of the Guardians." He stands there, gaze boring into Jiron for a moment. "Now," he finally continues, "tell me where the Fire lies?"

"Fire?" questions Jiron. "What's that?"

A dark expression comes over the mage as he says, "Don't take me for a fool, you know what it is. You and he have been together almost from the beginning."

The beginning of what? Jiron questions to himself silently. He remains quiet and defiant.

"Tell me what I want to know!" he demands with more of an edge to his voice. When Jiron is again uncooperative, he raises his hand and pain flares throughout Jiron's body.

Back arching and muscles contracting painfully, he clenches his teeth together and fights the urge to cry out. He doesn't want to give them the satisfaction.

As quickly as the pain began it quits. "Now, my patience is beginning to wear thin," the mage tells him. "Tell me where it is!"

Jiron raises his head and gazes into the mage's eyes. Sweat beads his forehead and his breath is a little ragged from the excruciating pain he just endured. Giving no indication of compliance, he stares defiantly at the mage.

Raising his hand again, the mage causes pain to once more erupt along every nerve in his body. His muscles again contract painfully, almost to the point where they'll begin breaking the bones they're attached to.

Try as he might, he can't keep a small gasp of pain from escaping. After what seems like an eternity, the pain stops and he flops back to the floor, eyes closed and breath coming in ragged gasps.

"This will only get worse if you do not tell me," warns the mage. "And let me assure you, we have as long as it takes." He then says something to one of the soldiers in their language. The soldier promptly leaves the tent and returns shortly with a chair for the mage. Taking his seat, he gazes down at Jiron who has managed to regain some of his composure. "Shall we begin again?" he asks.

Jiron just spits at him, the spittle managing to land on the hem of his robes.

The soldier closest to him strikes him across the face and begins yelling at him in their language.

"Enough," the mage says and the soldier stops his tirade. Looking back to the mage, he sees him motioning for the soldier to move away from Jiron, which he does.

Holding his arm out, the pain once again flares along Jiron's already flayed nerve endings. Back arching almost to the point of snapping his spine, he gnashes his jaws together to prevent the cry of pain from being torn from him.

"Tell me," the mage says softly. "Tell me where the Fire is hidden and this will all end."

Through an almost insurmountable obstacle of pain, Jiron cries out, "Never!"

Unrelenting, the mage sends wave after wave of pain through Jiron's nervous system, each worse than the one before. Suddenly, one of the guards standing near the mage bumps into the mage and breaks his concentration ending the spell.

"Clumsy oaf!" the mage screams to the man as the backlash of magic burns through him. Pushing the man away, his anger slowly turns to puzzlement as the man staggers a moment and then falls face down. Protruding from his back is the back half of an arrow.

No sooner has the soldier hit the ground than the tent flap is pulled aside and another soldier begins talking rapidly to the mage. From outside the tent screams and the clash of swords can be heard. Then the soldier at the tent flap suddenly jerks upright and falls to the ground, two arrows embedded in his back.

The mage gets to his feet, points to Jiron and James as he says a few words to the remaining guard and then hurries from the tent.

Jiron lays there, the residual pain coursing through him beginning to subside. Outside he hears explosions from magic the mage is wielding against whoever is attacking. The remaining guard is at the tent flap peering out, occasionally glancing back to make sure Jiron isn't trying anything.

As he lays there, strength beginning to return from the torture of the mage, he looks to the soldier peering outside. While his attention is focused on the events unfolding outside the tent, Jiron tries working his muscles to be sure they're okay. From the beating he took from the mage, he wasn't sure if anything permanent had been done. After a few minutes he's sure all is well, the pain must have been more in his mind than physical in nature. Things like that were mentioned in some of the old sagas he used to listen to growing up.

He feigns docility as the soldier turns to glance back toward him. Outside, the clash of arms continues as does the explosions from the mage. Men are screaming and crying battle cries. One battle cry he recognizes is that of Madoc, it must be men from there who are attacking the camp.

At first he thought it might have been Fifer and the others but then realized there would have been no way for them to reach here so fast. They have to be at least a day or two behind, coming on foot as they are.

Once the soldier makes sure that Jiron remains passive on the ground, he turns back to the events unfolding outside.

Moving slowly, Jiron quietly begins getting up off the ground. Just as he's reached a crouched position, James lets out with a groan which draws the attention of the soldier back to the inside of the tent. Gasping at seeing Jiron there ready to attack, he hollers out for help as he draws his sword.

When James groaned, Jiron's heart sank as the man turned to look at him there ready to pounce. Moving quickly, he grabs the chair the mage had used and barely blocks the strike of the soldier. Chips fly as the blade hacks out a section of a leg.

Not giving the man a chance for a second swing. Jiron immediately closes with him, pushing the chair toward him and running him into the side of the tent. The resulting impact brings the tent down and the man's sword becomes entangled in the loose folds of the collapsing tent.

Jiron quickly grabs the soldier's swordarm and rams his knee into the man's middle. The soldier's other fist lashes out and catches Jiron across the jaw but has little effect as he didn't have leverage to put much power behind it.

His knee comes up and catches the soldier in the groin causing him to freeze immobile for a brief moment, which allows Jiron to elbow him across the throat, smashing his windpipe. The man begins gagging in a vain attempt to breathe but his compacted windpipe starts to swell from the blow and he soon passes out from lack of oxygen.

Taking the man's sword, Jiron crawls through the collapsed tent until he reaches James. "James!" he whispers urgently. "Wake up!" His eyes flutter open and he mumbles something incoherently. Whatever they had given him still keeps him from functioning properly.

"Damn!" he curses as he turns onto his back and thrusts the sword upward through the tent material. Sawing with the sword, he quickly cuts a three foot slit and pokes his head out to see how the battle's going on outside.

The men from Madoc have the numbers but the Empire's mage is taking them out readily enough. Arrows fly toward the mage but none reach their mark, he has a barrier surrounding him similar to the one James utilizes. So far no one has taken any notice of the collapsing of the tent, so intent are they on the attackers.

Jiron uses his hands and widens the gap further and slips outside. Reaching back in, he uncovers James and then looks around for an escape route. Over by the main tent are several horses, fortunately still saddled. The Empire's forces are over to the far side where the attackers from Madoc are mostly concentrated.

Hoping that his mistreated muscles will bear the weight he reaches down, lifts James over his shoulder and begins carrying him toward the horses. The sound of swords clashing and the cries of men caught within terrible magic resound throughout the clearing.

The gloom of twilight lends an eerie feel to the proceedings but gives Jiron the shelter he needs to remain unobserved as he crosses over to the awaiting horses. Once he's reached them, he puts James over one and begins to secure him on.

"Jiron," he hears him say as he's tying his hands and feet together with a rope looped under the belly of the horse.

Moving to where his head hangs, he hears James ask, "What happened?"

"Captured by Empire soldiers," he replies. "They took all our stuff and we're getting out of here."

"My crystals?" he asks.

"I don't know," he says as he cinches the last knot tight. Jerking his head toward the main tent they're next to he adds, "Maybe in there. Do you need them?"

Shaking his head, he says, "As we leave, take me closer."

Mounting the horse next to him he asks, "Why?"

"Just do it," he says.

"Alright but we don't have much time to waste," Jiron tells him. Looking around, he can tell the battle is going badly for the men from Madoc. The Empire's mage has all but wiped them out.

"Don't need much," he says.

As he takes the reins of James' horse in hand, a cry arises nearby and he looks to see one of the Empire's soldiers pointing in their direction and shouting. The mage turns and sees them on the horses, then pain suddenly erupts in Jiron's middle and he almost falls off the horse. Bringing them close to the tent he says through the pain, "We're here."

In a voice cracking, speech slightly blurred, he says as loud as he can, "Spoilsport! Act Three! Fifteen!" As he utters the last word he can feel power being drawn from him by the crystal within the tent. Even Jiron notices as what little power he has is being pulled into it as well. To Jiron he says, "We haven't much time."

That's all he needed to hear. Kicking his horse in the sides, he races toward the edge of the clearing, bowling over several soldiers in the process. The pain ripping through his middle increases dramatically and it's all he can do simply to remain in the saddle and hold onto the reins to James' horse.

Bolts start flying as crossbowmen begin taking shot at the fleeing duo but miss as Jiron dodges their horses this way and that to avoid the flying bolts. The Empire's mage turns from the remnants of the Madoc attack force and moves quickly toward them, all the while maintaining the pain wracking Jiron's body.

When he nears the main tent wherein the crystals lay, the effects of his spell on Jiron diminishes as his power begins to be drained as well. That's when he takes note of what's transpiring within the tent.

As the pain begins to ease up, Jiron looks back as he leaves the clearing and sees the mage beginning to enter the tent. From beside him, he can hear James counting, "...thirteen...fourteen...fif..." Before he can finish the word, a massive explosion rips through the tent and engulfs a good portion of the clearing. The concussion from the blast rolls over them and the horses stumble a moment. Jiron fears they may go down but they manage to right themselves and race to leave the destruction behind them.

"What was that?" Dave exclaims from where he and the others are beginning to make camp for the night.

Off to the east thunder rolls as a fiery blast is seen reaching to the sky many miles away. "That had to be James," Miko replies anxiously. "He must be in trouble."

A clatter of wood comes from the side of the camp where Fifer was bringing some back for the evening fire. "No resting tonight," he says as glances around at all the faces. "He needs us."

Not one person gainsays him. The plans to make camp and continue in the morning are set aside as they begin to hustle down the road in the fading light.

Jiron continues riding well into the night. Even though that blast most likely took out the mage and most of the others, he dares not stop. At one point James indicates he can ride and after a short stop to untie him and help him into the saddle, they continue down the road.

"You okay?" he asks him once they've resumed riding.

"Not great," he replies. "Head still spins and doubt if I could do any magic for awhile, but other than that I think I'll live."

"What did you do back at the camp?" Jiron asks.

James glances at him and flashes him a grin. "Set a time bomb."

"A time bomb?" he asks, never having heard the expression before.

"That's right," he replies. "Don't ask me to explain, there are certain things I would rather not introduce to this world."

"Why?" he asks in confusion.

"Let's just say if the wrong people here come to know all that I do, it could lead to some very unpleasant things happening," he explains. When Jiron turns to look at him, he gives his friend a serious look which says there's no point in pursuing this any longer.

"As you wish," he finally says. They ride on in silence for awhile as Jiron's mind mulls over what he just said. He wonders what more James is capable of.

Another hour finds them coming to a river which exits from a break in the mountain and joins the road as it follows it down the side of the mountain to Madoc. James indicates they should pull off the road and make camp.

Moving far enough through the trees so that anyone passing by will unlikely be able to see them, they stop and set about making camp. James is all but exhausted, still not having recovered fully from the fight with the creatures and the effects of whatever was in the vial. Jiron offers to watch while he sleeps and he's in no position to deny him. He no sooner lays his head on his arm than he's out.

Awakening in the morning, he finds Jiron has managed to catch, clean and cook a small animal for their breakfast. "Hungry?" he asks from where he sits at the fire. Next to him is a pile of leaves with James' portion lying upon it.

"Man you know it," he says as he gets to his feet and comes over. Shivering from the cold of the mountains, he readily moves closer to the fire. Jiron hands him the leaves with his food. "Thanks."

"No problem," Jiron replies. "Thought you might need it."

After taking a bite, he sits there a moment chewing before he asks, "Do you think it wise to have a fire? Won't it attract anyone in the area?"

Shrugging, he says, "You need it. Besides, that explosion had to have taken out most if not all the soldiers back there. Anyone else it might attract would probably be from Madoc."

"Perhaps," he replies. Then the memory of those two creatures comes to mind and he's not so sure. He sits there and contemplates them, what they were and so forth. That's when he notices Jiron's knife sheaths are empty. "They took your knives?" he asks.

Nodding, Jiron says, "They took everything. After I killed the last of those creatures they showed up and took us to their camp. Thanks for those ice knives."

James looks at him questioningly, "Ice knives?"

"Yeah," he says. "After you passed out and the remaining creature crashed through the ice which had formed on the barrier, I saw two knives lying there on the ground. Thought you had made them."

Thinking back, he vaguely remembers something about that. "Don't recall doing that, but maybe. My memory is sort of hazy from then."

"Understandable," he says. "But regardless, those ice knives did the trick. Where mine were ineffective, those worked perfectly."

James sits there chewing as he attempts to recall exactly what happened but the memories of that time are still a bit foggy. Perhaps they'll come back later. He does remember what he realized about those creatures, that they were creatures of fire. It stands to reason then that ice knives would have more of an effect upon them.

"You said those creatures weren't entirely real," Jiron says. "What did you mean by that?"

"One of the theories about the universe is that there are many levels," he explains. "According to that theory the plane of existence we live upon is simply one among many. Some hold to the belief that there are planes of existence where fire, air, earth and water rule. This one we live on would be considered a sort of centralized one where each of the four has an equal footing. Each one has an opposite, the creatures of fire for example are hurt most by forces made up of water or ice."

Jiron nods as he begins to understand, though is still having a hard time with the concepts.

"Gods and those associated with them live on yet another plane, one more removed from that of the elements. I'll not even get into the theory of alternate reality and the fourth dimension. Those even stymie many of the great thinkers of my world." *Great thinkers, right! More like a bunch of kids in some backroom role playing.* He smiles at the thought. These were just the sort of discussions he, Dave and the others used to have on a regular basis.

"How many planes are there?" Jiron asks.

Shrugging, James says "Who knows? Now all this still may be only conjecture and not fact. It's just that after seeing those two creatures earlier brought it to mind. We may never learn one way or another." *Of course Igor and Morcyth have to come from somewhere don't they?*

James finishes the last of the roasted animal and gets up to go over to a stream where he takes several deep drinks. After that they put out the fire and remount to continue heading down the mountain.

The next several hours find them coming to the foothills at the base of the mountains and after cresting one such hill can see the plains open up below them. Several miles further ahead, smoke rises from a town nestled in among the hills. The road they're on continues toward it and then through it as it disappears into the horizon to the east. Another road runs along the base of the mountains moving north and south.

"Think Kerrin and Gayle are there?" Jiron asks indicating the town ahead of them.

"They had to pass through in any event," replies James. "We'll ask around when we get there and see if we can discover anything."

"Can you do that mirror thing?" he asks.

"Possibly," he replies. "I'll worry about that when we get there, should we be unable to locate them."

Nodding, Jiron kicks his horse and they hurry along down the road.

Chapter Twenty Three

The town they come to is fairly large, the smell of smoke from many iron smelters permeates the air. "Looks like they do a fair amount of iron smelting here," comments Jiron as they ride past several buildings doing just that.

"It would seem so," agrees James. Past the smelting complex they begin to enter the outskirts of the town itself. Several beggars line the streets with their hands out imploring the passersby to give them a coin. He feels sorry for them but has no coins with which to give, Kerrin and Gayle took all he and Jiron had. The horses they appropriated from the Empire's camp didn't have any on them when they checked earlier.

"How are you going to find out if they're still here?" Jiron asks.

"I don't know," he replies as they continue riding casually through town. Ahead of him he spies the mouth of an alleyway and sitting against the corner of a building near the entrance is an open barrel. He moves his horse toward it and notices it is a barrel full of water, set there to catch the rain as it runs off the roof.

Glancing around he doesn't see anyone in the immediate vicinity so brings his horse to a stop and dismounts. To Jiron he says as he nods to the barrel of water, "I'll use this. Keep an eye out for anyone coming."

"You got it," he replies as he gets down and stands watch.

Moving to the barrel, James releases the magic as he concentrates on Kerrin and Gayle. The surface of the water shimmers momentarily and then he sees them riding along a road. The string of horses they had behind them earlier is nowhere to be found. He expands the image but is unable to tell in which direction they're riding.

Letting the spell go, he then concentrates on the medallion bearing the Star of Morcyth. He wants to see if they got rid of it as well or if it still remains with them. The image shifts and becomes dark.

"Someone's coming," Jiron says quietly.

Canceling the spell, James gradually moves away from the barrel as the shopkeeper whose store they're standing next to comes toward them with an empty bucket.

"Here now," he says when he sees them loitering there. "What are you two up to?"

"Nothing, good sir," James assures him. "Simply getting a little bit of water from your barrel."

"This isn't for everyone," the man says with a grimace. "You two just move along now." He stands there with a stern expression on his face.

"Let's go," James tells Jiron and they take their horses and begin walking away. He glances back after they've moved along a ways and sees the merchant filling his bucket from the barrel and then returns to his store.

"What did you find out?" Jiron asks quietly.

"They're no longer in town," he replies. "They no longer have our horses with them either."

"Think they got rid of them here?" he asks.

"Would think so," replies James. "I don't think my medallion is with them either, though I couldn't find out exactly before that merchant came along."

"If we find the horses, we may find your medallion," suggests Jiron.

"That's what I was thinking too," he replies. Pausing a moment, he then mounts and Jiron follows suit. They ride through town looking for the horses. He thought about doing his bubble seeker spell again but discards the idea. If one mage from the Empire was in the area, then another could be too. The last thing he wants right now is to attract the attention of the wrong sort of people. After all, he's weakened magically speaking and Jiron has no weapons.

Cruising through town, they come to the market square where numerous hawkers are making their pitch.

"Last fruit of the season!" one merchant hollers who's standing out in front of a stand with the saddest lot of fruit James has ever seen. He suddenly has a desire to taste one of the peaches from home one more time. Sighing, he moves on.

"Come get the finest perfumes for your lady," another says. "One of these will bring you closer to her heart."

"Illion's best knives here," one lad says. He stands on a box in front of a store, a long wicked looking knife held in each hand. "Knives for every occasion! Whether for the lady in the kitchen or the warrior on the battlefield, we have them all!"

James glances over to Jiron and sees him longing to go over and examine the knives. If only they had the money they would stop and get him a couple. Then suddenly a memory surfaces, one from early on when he first came to this world.

It was shortly after leaving Trendle that first time, two men were being robbed and he helped fight off the thief. *"Well James, if you're ever in Illion, you're welcome to our hospitality,"* one of the men had said. *"We own and operate an iron mine and smelter. Maybe you've heard of us, Renlon's Iron?"*

Turning to Jiron he says, "I may have an idea." Stopping near a boy on the street he gets his attention and asks, "Could you tell me where I might find Renlon's Iron?"

The boy gazes at him a moment and then points off down to another main street which branches off the one they're on. "Turn down there and you'll find it at the edge of town," he says.

"Thanks," replies James.

Just as he's about to leave, the boy asks, "Don't I get something for telling you?"

"I'm a bit short right now," he says. "Sorry."

"Sorry yourself," the boy says derisively. When Jiron makes to move in his direction the lad runs off into the crowd and is gone.

"You didn't have to scare him," rebukes James.

"I know," replies Jiron as he turns to glance at James. When no further comment is forthcoming, they make their way to the intersection and turn into the lane the boy had indicated. At the edge of town when the street comes to an end, they find a large complex of smelters with smokestacks belching black smoke.

A man is loitering around one of the buildings and James rides over to him. "Where might I find the owners of Renlon's Iron?" he asks.

Indicating a building near the center of the complex, he says, "Most of the time you can find them in there."

James gives him a nod and replies, "Thanks." Leaving the man behind, they work their way through the complex until they come to the indicated building where James dismounts. "You stay here with the horses and I'll see if they're inside," he tells Jiron.

Nodding, Jiron remains on his horse as James enters through the front door.

Inside he finds an office with several tables and many shelves lined with books. Behind one is the older gentleman from before. He looks up from where he was making notations on a piece of paper and sees him walk in. "Can I help you?" he asks. Then suddenly his face lights up as he recognizes him. Coming to his feet, he moves around the desk and asks, "James right?" Holding out his hand, he gives James a vigorous shake.

"That's right," he replies. "I wasn't sure if you were going to remember me."

"After what you did it would be hard to forget you. Here, take a seat," he says as he gestures to one next to the desk. As James takes a seat he props himself on the edge of his desk. "So what brings you around these parts?"

"Actually I was hoping you could help me with something," he says.

"If I can I will," he assures him. "What do you need?"

James explains to him in brief detail the robbery and subsequent chase leaving out the parts concerning the Empire and his magic. Once he's done, he finishes by saying, "So you see, I believe they may have sold our horses somewhere here in Illion along with our other belongings. You wouldn't happen to know of anyone who might deal in stolen goods do you?"

Sitting back on the desk, he contemplates for a moment. Then the rear door opens and his son comes in. Stopping just inside the door when he sees his father talking with James, he breaks into a smile and comes forward. "So, you decided to take advantage of our hospitality after all?" he asks.

"In a way," James replies.

Glancing to his son, his father fills him in on James' plight. Father and son exchange glances for a moment and then the son says, "You might try Orlander."

"Orlander?" he asks. "Who is that and where can I find him?"

Nodding, the father turns to James and says, "He's a bad one, into all the less than honest dealings which go on around here. He runs a tavern on the other side of town. You can't miss it, it looks shoddy and in ill repair."

"If your stuff is with him, you best just leave it be," the son warns. "Those who cross him tend to end up dead."

"We'll see," says James. "I appreciate your help in this. Thank you."

"Isn't there anything else we can do to help?" the father asks as James makes to leave. "We owe you a lot."

Pausing, James glances back to them and says, "Well…"

He finds Jiron still on his horse when he exits the office. The father and son come out with him to bid him goodbye. Walking up to his friend, he hands him a bundle wrapped in cloth.

"What's this?" Jiron asks as he takes the bundle. When James doesn't say anything he unwraps it and finds a belt with two exceptionally fashioned knives. "Oh my!" he says as he pulls one from out of its sheath. Holding it up, he tests it for balance and sights down the blade as he checks for straightness. The craftsmanship is exceptional and the balance is the best he's ever felt.

"Where did you get these?" he asks, replacing the knife in its sheath.

"A present from some friends of his," the father replies. "For services rendered."

"Thank you," he says. Removing his old belt which had held his now lost knives, he discards it and secures the new one around his waist. Once it's secured tightly, he quickly draws both knives and in a blur of speed, they dance around him briefly before being returned to their sheathes. "Excellent," he says glancing to the two men. "Absolutely excellent."

"They were made by a master weapon smith some time ago," the son explains. "They were to be a gift but the person died before we were able to give it to him."

"You may need them where you're going," the father states.

"What?" he asks.

"I'll explain as we ride," James says as he mounts. Turning to the father and son he says, "Thank you for all the help. It's much appreciated."

"You're welcome," the father says.

"Stop by again if you're able," the son says.

"Will do," replies James as he and Jiron turn their horses and begin making their way from the Renlon's complex. After leaving it behind, he glances over to Jiron and pats a bulge in his shirt. "They also gave us some traveling money," he says.

"Oh?" asks Jiron hopefully.

"Don't be getting too excited, it's only about a gold's worth," he explains.

"That should at least last a few days on the road," he says.

Nodding, James returns his attention to the crowded street as they maneuver their way through the people. Making their way across town to where this Orlander's tavern lies, they eventually see a building exactly as the Renlon's had described, rundown and looking about to fall apart at the seams.

Outside are several individuals whom James wouldn't want to meet up with on the wrong side of a knife in some dark alley. They all look like thugs who would just as soon kill you as look at you. When they near, he signals Jiron to continue down the street. After putting some distance between them and the tavern Jiron asks, "Why didn't we stop?"

"I didn't think our horses would still be there when we came out," he explains.

"Good thinking."

Finding a reputable business, a chandler's shop by the look of it, they come to a stop and secure their horses among two others already tied there. "We going back?" asks Jiron.

"You bet," replies James. "If he has our stuff, I mean to recover it."

They begin walking back and Jiron says, "It could get nasty."

Sighing, James asks, "You got a better idea?"

Shaking his head, he replies, "No."

"Hopefully he'll listen to reason," James says wistfully.

"Doubt it," Jiron replies confidently.

One way or another, he has to retrieve that medallion, not to mention the other one he found in the underground temple. Jiron's necklace designating him a Shynti was also taken. If nothing else, those three things must be recovered.

Approaching the thugs outside the dilapidated tavern, they're stopped by one of them before reaching the door. "What do you guys want here?" the thug asks. Standing there blocking their way with a sword on one hip and red hair waving in the slight breeze, James thinks he must really think he's something.

"Want to talk with Orlander," he says coming to a stop.

At that the others edge their way closer to the pair. "What for?" the red haired thug asks.

"That's between me and him," James says with finality. He stares down the man with courage he didn't realize he had. Before coming to this world he would've been a quivering mass of jelly if someone had confronted him like this. Amazed at the backbone he's acquired he takes a step forward.

The thug stops him by placing his hand on his chest and says, "You ain't getting in."

Jiron starts to move to take out this man when James holds up his hand to forestall any violence. Looking into the thug's eyes he says, "Either remove your hand or lose it."

In the face of such calm certainty the thug hesitates a moment and then removes his hand. "Thank you," he says as he begins to move forward.

Shhhhht!

Five swords leave their sheathes as the thugs draw their weapons. "Now I said you ain't gettin' in and I meant it," the red haired thug reiterates as he threatens them with his sword. The other four are close and their swords are less than a foot away.

Frustration and anger begins to get the better of him and he's about to let loose the power when the door to the tavern opens. "What's going on here?" a large balding man says as he steps out. This has to be Orlander. Big, scars covering most of his exposed skin, and an air of command no one can ignore.

"These fellows wanted to see you," the red haired thug says.

"About what?" he asks.

"They wouldn't tell me," the red haired thug replies.

"What is this about?" Orlander asks.

"I'll tell that to you inside when things are less public," replies James.

Orlander considers it a moment and nods. "Very well," he says as he returns inside the tavern.

James takes a step forward and 'Red' has to step aside to prevent from being walked into. Not even looking back at them, he follows Orlander inside.

The inside looks just like every other tavern except the clientele is a little more tougher looking. Seven people are seated at the various tables, four of whom are having a game of cards off to the side. One is seated on a stool by the bar with a loaded crossbow laid across his lap, most likely in case of trouble.

Following Orlander across the barroom, James feels the eyes of everyone in the room upon him. Ahead of him Orlander reaches a door on the far side and opens it. Passing through, he leaves it open for them to follow.

Two men with crossbows and another with two swords strapped to his back are already in the room as he enters and takes his seat behind a desk situated against the far wall. After James and Jiron enter, the man with the swords closes the door and takes position behind them.

"Now," Orlander says, "what is all this about?"

"We're here to recover some items which were stolen from us," he says.

One of the three other men in the room chuckles at that and Orlander gets an amused expression on his face. "What makes you gentlemen think I would have anything to do about that?"

"Word on the street is that you would be the man to see about such things," Jiron states.

"I have been known to expedite the return of certain articles," he tells them, "for a price."

"So you might be able to help us?" James asks.

"First I would need to know of what you are talking about," he says.

"Two people, a man and a woman robbed me and my friends a few days ago," James explains. "They took off with our horses and many of our valuables. We know they passed through Illion and left with less than they arrived with. The only items which we are truly interested in are three necklaces."

Nodding, Orlander says, "It seems I recall such a pair passing through. Don't know as what they may or may not have liquidated here in Illion. If those items were to turn up, say, what would you be willing to pay for their return?"

"What do you mean?" James asks.

"I mean," clarifies Orlander, "how much gold would you be willing to give me to expedite their return?"

"We don't have much on us right now I'm afraid," admits James.

"Then why should I even bother with you?" he asks. Snickers can be heard coming from those around them.

"Because it's the right thing to do," James tells him.

Breaking out into a laugh, he says, "Get them out of here."

"Let's go," the man with the swords says as he lays a hand on Jiron's shoulder.

Spinning around fast, Jiron knocks the man's hand off as the men with the crossbows take aim.

"We should leave," James says to him. Then in a barely audible whisper he says, "Later."

Swallowing his anger, Jiron backs down and the man with the swords gives him a grin and then precedes them from the room.

Following him across the barroom, they move to the door and are escorted outside. "Don't come back unless you have gold," the man says.

'Red' is there looking at them and their eyes lock for just a moment before James turns. Then he and Jiron move off down the street.

Once they're out of earshot, Jiron asks, "Why didn't we do anything?"

"I wasn't sure if he had them or not," he says. "I can't just go around and indiscriminately kill everyone who crosses my path."

"What are you going to do now?" he asks.

"Find out if our stuff is there or not," he replies.

"And if it is?" prompts Jiron.

"We go back tonight and reclaim them," he states.

Nodding, Jiron follows him down the road a ways until James ducks down a deserted side alley. Moving away from the entrance, he comes to a stop. Glancing around quickly to make sure no one is observing them, he creates his translucent seeking bubble which he has used before.

Letting it go, it begins floating through the air as it hunts for the medallion bearing the Star of Morcyth. Moving out of the alley, it's barely perceptible as it drifts along through the people on the street. One young girl does a double-take as she takes notice of it but then her mother pulls her along and she dismisses it.

They follow it from a discreet distance, just far enough to be able to keep it in view. Even though they know exactly what they're looking for they still at times lose it only to pick it up again a second later. It bobs around people as well as over and under wagons and carriages as it continues making its way through the street.

When it begins nearing the thugs outside of Orlander's establishment, James watches it carefully. If it's not in there, the bubble should go around the building. If it is, stop at the door. He made it so as not to go through walls, he was afraid he might lose it if it went through a building.

Sure enough, it floats toward the door to the tavern and comes to a stop. Just as the red haired thug begins to notice something there, James cancels the spell and the bubble disappears. 'Red' squints his eyes and with a shake of his head returns to his conversation with another of the thugs.

"So it is in there," states Jiron.

"It would seem so," replies James. They turn and move back further from the tavern, coming to stop in front of an ironsmith. The sound of the smith's hammering creates quite a din.

"What are we to do?" Jiron asks. The hammering coming from the building next to them drowns out their conversation.

Glancing back down the street in the direction of the tavern he says, "Let's find an inn and get some rest. Tonight we'll pay them a visit."

Grinning, Jiron says, "I like that plan."

They return to collect their horses and then find an inn. Eating a quick bite, they retire to their room for some sleep before the coming of night.

"Doesn't look as if anyone's around," Jiron says as they watch the tavern from across the street.

They waited until well past midnight until only a few hours were left before the dawn. James had thought the place would have some activity even at this hour, it was a tavern after all. But when they got there, the place was dark and no one was about.

The entire area around the tavern was deserted, not even a bum lying in the street. No one passing by or anything, altogether giving off the feel that something wasn't quite right.

"Do you think they are waiting for us?" James asks.

"Maybe," replies Jiron.

They stand near a building across the street for some time and still no one or anything makes an appearance. "Guess we better do this," James whispers.

Sensing more than seeing Jiron's nod in the dark, they begin making their way across the street toward the building. Nestled in James' hand is a stone,

one of many he acquired since his slug belt was stolen. The rest are in his pocket.

Approaching the front door cautiously, Jiron indicates they should go around the side and see if there is a back entrance which may afford them a better entry. James turns to follow him as he begins heading around the side.

As they follow the side of the tavern, no opening presents itself. After turning the corner to the rear of the building, they find another door. Apparently the only other way in besides the door in the front, this must lead to the office where they talked with Orlander earlier.

Jiron motions for James to halt as he puts an ear to the door. After a moment he whispers, "Don't hear anything." He puts his hand to the door handle and attempts to open the door only to find it locked.

Pulling a knife, he begins working on the lock while James keeps an eye out for anyone approaching. A soft 'click' can be heard following several tense moments and Jiron turns the handle and then slowly opens the door.

The other side is dark. The only light being what is filtering in past them through the door. They move inside and Jiron closes the door behind them just as a soft light springs into being on James' hand. Jiron turns to find his glowing orb resting upon his palm.

"We better hurry," James tells him and receives a nod.

They start moving into the room when they come to a quick halt. It is indeed the office in which Orlander had met them but that isn't what stops them. Resting upon the desk in plain view are the three necklaces, situated as if on display.

This can't be good. James glances to Jiron and can see his worries reflected in the eyes of his friend. "Just grab them and let's get out of here," he says.

Jiron nods as he moves to collect the necklaces.

Standing there nervous, he waits while Jiron goes to the desk and picks up the necklace designating him as a Shynti and puts it around his neck. He then picks up the medallion bearing the Star and tosses it over to James who does the same. The necklace with the three dots and lines almost connecting them he puts into his pouch.

"Let's get the hell out of here," James says as he extinguishes the orb and moves to the back door.

As he opens the door, light springs to life outside as the shutters from several lanterns are pulled back.

Chapter Twenty Four

"I thought you might try something like this," Orlander's voice comes from the dark behind the light. The other door leading from the tavern to the office opens behind them and the red haired thug comes in with the rest of his cronies, swords drawn and menacing.

James and Jiron stand there in hesitation as they take in the situation, Jiron has his knives out.

"No one steals from me," Orlander says as he steps into the light. His face is contorted with anger as he advances, sword in hand. The rest of the men out there with him begin advancing as well. "Kill them!" he shouts.

Jiron grabs James and jerks him inside the office, slamming the door shut just as several crossbow bolts thud into the other side. Turning quickly, he moves to engage the half dozen men coming in through the inner door.

"You can't hope to win," boasts Red as he and the others move to intercept.

James pulls himself off the floor and drops the bar to secure the outer door as Jiron's knives clash with that of Red's sword. Turning to the fight, he begins flinging stones and the thugs drop quickly.

Those on the outside start pounding on the door in an attempt to force it open.

The confidence Red felt at the outset is rapidly diminishing when his cohorts begin dropping like flies and the man he's facing with the two knives counters every attack he throws at him.

As the last of the other thugs falls, James asks Jiron, "Need any help?"

Laughing, Jiron replies, "Not with this." Having taken Red's measure, he launches a series of attacks. Red tries to defend himself but winds up leaving himself open and one of Jiron's knives thrusts between two ribs and pierces his heart.

Staggering backward, Red falls to the ground and the light fades from his eyes as Jiron puts his foot against his chest and removes his knife.

Wiping his blade clean on the dead man's shirt, he turns to find James over by the strong box in the corner. "What are you doing?" he asks. "We've got to get out of here!"

Lifting the lid, James reaches in and removes a bulging sack. After a quick glance within it, he tosses it to Jiron. "I was willing to be content with simply retrieving our possessions," he says. Removing another pouch, he puts it into his shirt and says, "But after this, I'm not." Tuning to Jiron he adds, "Consider this recompense for 'pain and suffering'."

The pounding upon the door continues and Jiron moves to the door leading into the main section of the tavern and glances out. Slamming the door shut, he presses his shoulder against it just as someone slams into it from the other side. "Not this way," he says. "What do you plan to do?"

Coming over to the door Jiron is holding, he lays his hand against it and applies a holding spell. When he's sure it is set properly, he has Jiron move away and the door continues to hold against the incessant beating from the other side.

The lantern one of the thugs had upon entering the office lies on the floor tipped to one side. James moves over and grabs it. Glancing to the ceiling, he gets an idea.

Climbing up onto the desk he reaches up and is able to touch the ceiling. With his hand pressed against the ceiling, he casts a spell and then gets down from the desk quickly. "Move back," he warns Jiron who joins him in moving to the other side of the room. After a couple seconds the section of the ceiling he had touched suddenly explodes outward leaving a jagged hole roughly two foot in diameter.

"That's not big enough for us to get through," observes Jiron.

"Don't be dense," says James as he returns to the desk. Brushing aside the debris from the explosion he clears a spot for him to again stand upon the desk. Reaching up to the hole he takes hold of one of the blasted boards and pulls. With a creak and then a crack, the board breaks off, widening the hole.

Glancing back to Jiron he gives him a grin as he repeats the process again. When the hole is wide enough, he motions for Jiron to precede him through.

Climbing onto the desk, Jiron jumps up and manages to wriggle through the opening into the crawlspace above. Reaching down his hand, he says, "Take my hand."

"Just a moment," James says as he gets down from the desk. He glances over from one door to the other and can see they're not about to last much longer. The doors themselves are surviving the impacts well but the walls around them are beginning to show signs of cracking. Taking the lantern he smashes it into the floor, the oil within catches fire as the flame begins to burn the pool of oil. He then removes papers and some of the debris from the desk and piles them on top of the flame.

As he climbs back onto the desk, the fire begins to burn fiercely and is starting to spread. "Do you think that was a good idea?" asks Jiron as he starts to choke from the smoke moving through the hole in the ceiling. It's acting like a chimney and is funneling all the smoke right past them.

"Maybe not," admits James as he takes Jiron's hand and makes his way up into the crawlspace.

The crawlspace isn't very large and they're forced to move along on their hands and knees in order to make their way from the hole. Moving quickly, they traverse the length of the building and reach a vent in the side of the tavern leading outside. Jiron grabs hold of it and manages to pull it loose.

When the vent comes free, the opening accelerates the venting of the smoke which in turn causes the fire to burn hotter.

He glances outside and finds they're in an area currently free of people. "I think we made it," he says as he glances back to James.

Coughing from the effects of the choking smoke, James replies, "Just hurry."

Turning around, Jiron exits through the vent feet first until he's all the way through and hanging by his hands. Then he lets go and lands on the ground outside. Pulling a knife, he rubs his eyes with his other hand in an attempt to clear the tears the smoke had produced.

Glancing up, he sees James' feet coming out and then shortly afterward he drops to the ground beside him.

"There they are!" a cry goes up and they turn to see men coming around the corner of the tavern. One has a crossbow and lets a bolt fly.

In reflex James brings up his barrier and the bolt is deflected. As they race away, light from the fire burning within the tavern silhouettes them as the others give chase.

"I'll kill you both!" Orlander screams as he rounds the corner. Hate and rage radiate from the man as he and his cohorts race after the fleeing pair.

Crumph!

The street behind them erupts and slows their pursuers. Dodging down an alley, Jiron says, "Get to the inn and saddle the horses."

"What are you going to do?" James asks.

"Give you time to do that," he says. "Now get going!" With that he thrusts James further down the alleyway where he breaks into a run.

Jumping up onto a stack of old crates against one wall, he reaches up to the window ledge above. Pulling himself up, he gains the room on the other side of the window just as the mob enters the alley behind them.

They pause there just a moment when one catches sight of James running down the far end. "There they go!" one yells.

Jiron looks down and sees Orlander enter the alley. "Orlander you fat pig!" he shouts from the window. The mob down below pauses as they look up to see him illuminated by the lights from their lanterns. "Your mother was a whore and your father a mule!" he adds as he spits in Orlander's direction. The spittle flies through the air and lands right between Orlander's eyes.

"Get him!" he screams in rage as he points to Jiron in the window.

"What about that other guy?" another of the men below asks.

"I want him!" Orlander says with rage as he points to the smirking Jiron.

The men begin to immediately pound the door below and Jiron hears it crashing in. He turns from the window and comes to an immediate stop when he sees a man standing there in his nightclothes holding a sword at the ready.

"Stay right there," the man says, his voice somewhat shaky.

Drawing his knives, Jiron advances upon him. A woman screams from the nearby bed as the man's sword strikes out at him. Jiron easily deflects the blade and follows through with a punch to the side of the man's face.

As the man stumbles out of the way, he races past and out of the bedroom. From downstairs the sound of many feet can be heard running up the stairs. Running along the hallway away from the stairs, he comes to the last door and smashes into it. The door bursts open and he rushes into the room, quickly closing it behind him.

He looks around for something to bar the way and realizes he's stumbled into a nursery, over to one side of the room is a small child standing in a crib. Couldn't be more than a year old, the child holds onto the side of his crib as he stares at Jiron. The pounding of feet toward him down the hallway tells him he doesn't have much time.

Pulling a dresser over to in front of the door, he braces it with a couple chairs and then heads to the window next to the child. The child just stares at him curiously as he looks out. The street below appears to be empty.

Bam!

The door is hit from the other side as his pursuers attempt to break it in. He glances and finds the dresser and chairs are for the moment keeping them at bay.

"My baby!" can be heard coming from the hallway.

Ripping the sheet off the baby's bed, he ties it to the side of the crib and then puts the excess out the window. At this point the child starts to sob and then lets out with a god awful scream. Jiron glances toward it and sees the child is attempting to reach through the bars for something.

On the floor next to the crib he finds one of Tersa's teddy bears. *Are these things everywhere now?* Picking it up, he hands it to the child who immediately quiets down. It must have been lifted from the crib when he had removed the sheet.

Bam!

The door opens an inch and begins to be pushed further into the room as those in the hallway put their weight into it. Swinging out of the window, Jiron takes hold of the sheet and proceeds to climb down. Unfortunately the sheet only extends several feet and he has to let go and freefall the remaining ten feet.

Landing on his feet, he glances up just as Orlander's head pops out of the window. "He's on the street outside!" he hollers. He leaves the window and a crossbowman takes his place. Taking aim at Jiron he fires just as Jiron begins running away down the street and misses, the bolt strikes the ground where he just vacated.

Coming to the edge of the house, two of Orlander's thugs round the corner and engage him. Not even slowing, he waits until the last possible moment then drops to the ground and rolls into their legs. One hops over him as he rolls and the other fails to move fast enough and is tripped.

Coming to his feet quickly, he turns and goes on the offensive with the one still on his feet. Feinting with one knife, he draws the man's sword into a defensive position. Using his other, he knocks the sword out of the way and ends it with a kick to the man's chest which sends him stumbling backward, tripping over his comrade.

Turning, Jiron resumes racing down the street as more of Orlander's men leave the house and gain the street.

The commotion on the street has begun to draw the attention of those living in the vicinity and many are sticking their heads out the window to see what's going on. When they recognize Orlander and his bunch, they immediately pull their heads back from the window and throw the shade.

Just three streets away is the inn where hopefully James has begun to get the horses ready for a quick getaway. Needing to give him a few more minutes to assure he'll be ready when he gets there, he pauses at a corner at another junction where he's sure the light from the moon overhead will illuminate him. Making sure he's seen by Orlander's bunch, he then races around the corner.

Ping!

A crossbow bolt strikes the building near where he had just stood. The thunder of pursuit remains behind him as he continues to lead the mob through town. At one corner a member of the city watch appears before him.

"Here now…" the man begins to say as Jiron runs right into him without even slowing. Bowling the watchman over, he continues fleeing down the street.

Hoping James has had enough time to get the horses ready by now, he begins to make his way back toward the inn. Shouts from all over begin to be heard as Orlander's group splits up to cover many of the streets. The watchman join the group, seems they're on rather friendly terms with Orlander. He must've bought them off.

Pausing for a moment to catch his breath in a darkened doorway, he holds still as a group of five men race past. He waits there until they turn at the next junction and then continues heading toward the inn.

In the dark of night with nothing but the moon to light the way, he's not entirely sure he's kept his sense of direction until he sees the inn coming up the road ahead.

Crumph!

From the back courtyard of the inn a loud explosion can be heard. Between him and there are three men all running with swords drawn toward the courtyard. Jiron leaves the protection of the shadows and races behind the three men. With knives in both hands, he comes up behind them and stabs two through the back and as the third turns to face this threat, slices him across the throat.

Leaving the dead and dying behind him, he races to the side of the inn and enters the courtyard. He finds James standing by the saddled horses holding off three men. A stone flies from his hand and takes one out as the other two charge.

With a cry, Jiron races to intercept. The men hear his cry and turn as he advances upon them. One moves to intercept him as the other continues toward James. The man heading to James suddenly cries out as he's picked up and thrown across the courtyard where he smashes into the side of the stables.

The cry of his partner distracts the remaining man just enough for Jiron to get inside his defense and slice open his belly. Then he kicks out with his foot and smashes the man's knee. As the man falls to the ground he yells to James, "Get on the horse!"

Closing the distance to the horses, James gets into the saddle just as Jiron catches the pommel of the saddle of his horse and quickly swings himself up. Without a word, they both kick their steeds into quick motion as they race for the way out of the courtyard.

As they near, Orlander and his bunch show up. "Don't stop!" Jiron cries and they both hug their horses' neck as they ride through the group.

Orlander and the others have to dive out of the way in order to avoid being trampled by the charging horses. When he gets to his feet, Orlander yells "I'll kill you both if it's the last thing I do!"

Leaving them behind, the two riders race through town following the western road leading to the mountains. "Let's rejoin the others," James tells him.

"I'm for that," he replies. Behind them the glow which was once Orlander's tavern lights the night.

Once they are again within the beginnings of the pass, they slow their speed. They don't ride very far before Jiron asks, "Do you think the Empire's men are still around?"

"Never know," James replies. "Best if we kept an eye out."

"Next time around should my horse become skittish I'll be more careful," he says, remembering the creatures they fought not too long ago.

Nodding, James says, "You got that right."

As they ride the sky begins to lighten with the coming of the dawn.

Two hours after leaving the town behind, the thunder of approaching riders begins to be heard coming from the pass. Deciding discretion may be the wisest course at this time, they edge off the road and hide within a copse of trees.

Just as they gain the cover of the trees, the horsemen reach them and thunder past.

"Fifer!" James exclaims at the departing riders as he quickly returns to the road.

The rider in the rear turns around to glance back and cries out, "It's James!" Miko stops his horse and turns back, the others following suit.

"What the hell happened?" Uther asks as they come close.

"A lot," Jiron replies. "Sure am glad to see you guys."

"Where did you get the horses?" James asks Fifer as he pulls up next to him.

Nodding back the way they came he says, "Back a ways. We were hurrying to follow you when a couple soldiers from the Empire suddenly appeared in the road ahead of us. Seems they were coming from a hard to see trail and must not have seen us. When they finally saw us, a cry went up and one of them fired a crossbow but fortunately failed to hit."

"Yeah," interjects Uther, "after that we charged and took them out. From the looks of them they had already seen some action, bandaged as they were."

Nodding, Fifer looks to James and says, "Some were even sporting severe burns."

"We saw the explosion," Dave says, not wishing to be left out of the conversation. "What happened?"

"Let's find a spot off the road where we'll not be observed and I'll tell you," he says to them.

Turning off the road, they move through the trees until they find a suitable clearing where they can rest without those passing on the road finding them. Once settled in, James and Jiron take turns in describing all the events which transpired since they left the others.

At the description of the creatures, Dave asks, "Hell hounds?"

"Possibly," answers James. "Water and ice affected them where cold iron didn't."

"That's not good," he says, worried.

"I know. If they have those, what else can they have to throw at us?" James gives his friend a knowing look. Dave nods silently.

"We should stay here and rest," Qyrll states. Everyone looks to him as he continues, "We haven't had rest for two days and you two look dead on your feet. If the Empire should show up again, we'll need to be at our best to survive."

"Orlander's bunch too," adds Jiron.

"Exactly," he agrees.

"It would probably be best to pass through Illion at night anyway," says James. "Orlander may have people watching for us."

Several heads, several tired heads nod in agreement. Breaking out what little rations the Empire's men had on their horses, they have a quick, cold meal. Eating in silence, each ponders the events of the last several days and wonders just what may lie ahead for them.

After they've finished eating and Qyrll is set to take first watch, Miko suddenly asks, "Did you find out about Ironhold?"

"What?" asks James. Then understanding hits and he says, "Damn! I was there and forgot to ask." He glances to Jiron who just shrugs with a slight grin.

"You going back?" Fifer asks.

"We have to know where it is," he replies. "If anyone around here would know, it'll be the Renlon's. I mean they're in the iron business and all."

"True," agrees Jorry.

"Do you think that's wise?" asks Dave. At that, grumbling can be heard and 'coward' is mentioned by more than one. Giving them an annoyed glance, he looks to his friend.

"No," James says, flashing the others a looks saying to knock it off. "But I have to get to Ironhold. Since we don't know where it is, I have to go back and find out."

"I see," Dave replies with a worried expression. To him things seem to be spiraling out of control and he doesn't wish to lose his only friend in this world.

"Let's get some rest while we can," Fifer says and they all settle down for sleep. Qyrll takes first watch and moves closer to the road where he can better keep an eye on those using it.

An hour into his watch, Qyrll hears horses coming up the road from the direction of Illion. Hunkering down lower behind a large bush, he watches as seven horsemen gallop past on their way up to the pass. From his vantage point, they don't look like soldiers from the Empire. He figures they may be part of that bunch with Orlander James had told them about. They're soon out of sight and the sound of their hooves becomes fainter until finally disappearing.

Chapter Twenty Five

Securing their horses near the outskirts of Illion they slowly make their way into town, all the while keeping alert for any who may be looking for them.

James, Miko and Fifer walk at a steady pace in an attempt to avoid attracting attention. The others are waiting further from town along the road to the pass for their return. It had been decided for James to take Miko and Fifer with him instead of Jiron this time. Jiron had complained but Fifer told him that Orlander will be looking for two men, not three. Also, Jiron may be recognized which could only confound the situation.

James pulls the hood of the cloak tighter around his head to keep his face from being seen clearly. Though it's dark he doesn't want to take the chance. Before they left the others, Qyrll had given him his cloak saying it would help him to avoid being spotted.

As they pass through the streets, they take notice of a crowd gathered around a man standing next to a building ahead of them, bathed in the light of a nearby lantern.

"War is coming!" the man cries.

"We know that," one man replies.

James slows as they come near the crowd. The man looks like some crazy guy, like one of those who would stand on the street corner in those old movies and hold signs saying 'Repent!'

The crowd seems more amused by the man than actually taking him seriously. "The Empire isn't moving any further until spring," another says to him. "We have awhile before we need worry about them."

"The Empire is but the finger of the true enemy!" he cries to the crowd. "He shall rain fire down and all will be consumed." Gesticulating wildly, he begins rocking from one foot to the other.

"James," Miko says.

Suddenly coming back to himself, James realizes he stopped in the middle of the street. "Sorry," he says as he resumes his way down the street.

"The ground will burn and dark shadows will walk the night," the man cries. "They will feast upon the living until none survive!"

A chill runs down James' back as the man mentions shadows. A memory comes to him of another place where shadows had walked in a fire blackened forest. Coming to a stop again, he turns toward the crowd.

"We can't stop here," Fifer warns, glancing down both directions. So far, no one seems to be paying their group any attention.

Not heeding his words, James moves closer to the wild man. Miko and Fifer glance to each other in concern and move to follow.

"You're a nut!" one lady exclaims to the laughter of the others.

"Go away and tell your tales of doom elsewhere," another hollers to him.

James reaches the edge of the crowd and begins making his way through to the front.

"We must fight him!" the wild man cries out. "We must drive him back!" He suddenly stills his frantic motion and his voice becomes all but inaudible as he says with quiet intensity, "But it's not by the sword that he will be turned aside."

The crowd guffaws at him and other insults are cast at him as James reaches the leading edge of the crowd. "What are we to do?" he asks the man.

Specks of foam form at the corners of his mouth as the man's eyes turn to him. "The temple must rise," he says, so quietly that James almost can't make out the words.

"What temple?" he asks, heart pounding.

Then madness seems to take him as he cries out, "The temple must fall! Else all will be lost!"

"James!" exclaims Miko as he grabs his shoulder.

The crowd begins to scream as several armed men approach with swords in hand. James turns to find Orlander, along with six other men coming toward him. That's when he realizes his hood had fallen off while he was listening to the wild man.

"You're dead!" Orlander screams as he and the others race forward.

"Come on!" Miko cries as he turns James and propels him away.

Racing away, he turns to glance one more time to the wild man but the man is nowhere in sight. *Must have been scared off by Orlander and his bunch.*

"Which way?" Miko asks as they run down the street.

The wild man forgotten, James is now more concerned about losing their pursuers. "Renlon's are off that way," he says indicating to the far side of town. "But I don't want to involve them." Suddenly, a flash of light bursts into life far above them for a brief moment before disappearing.

"What was that?" asks Fifer.

"Just letting Jiron and the others know we need help," he says as they turn around a corner and race down the main thoroughfare of Illion.

People are on the street and they receive many words of protest as they race through them, at times knocking people over or items out of their hands. Behind them, the crowd parts quickly when they see Orlander's group hot on their tail.

"Blast them James," Miko cries out.

"Too many innocents around," he says. "I dare not."

Ahead of them is an intersection where another main street crosses the one they're on. To the left would lead them to Renlon's Iron so James turns to the right and moves onto the new street.

Suddenly from out of the crowd on the street, a porter carrying several boxes appears before him and he crashes into the man. Boxes flying everywhere, James and the man go crashing down to the street.

Miko and Fifer in their haste move past before they even realize what's happened. When they do, they come to a stop and return to him just as Orlander and his bunch show up.

James pulls out a rock from his pocket as he and the others ready to meet the charge. Then from behind Orlander's group, several horses appear in the intersection they had just left. Another starburst in the sky and the horsemen turn to race their way.

"No tricks are going to save you this time," Orlander says as he readies his sword and advances upon him. He takes three steps forward before he hears the thunder of the hooves approaching from behind. Turning, he sees Jiron and the rest bearing down fast. Lurching to the side, he moves out of their way a split second before they would've run over him.

Jiron reaches down a hand to James who swings up onto the horse behind him. Qyrll grabs Fifer and Uther takes Miko. They fly down the street away from Orlander. Glancing back, James sees him picking himself off the ground and staring at him, hate in his eyes.

At the next intersection, he signals Jiron to come to a stop. "I still need to talk to the Renlon's."

Nodding, he says to the others, "Go back and get their horses, James and I are going back."

"Are you mad?" Dave asks from his position next to them. "They'll kill you!"

"Not now Dave," James tells him. To everyone he says, "Meet us east of town in half an hour or less."

"We'll be there," Fifer tells him.

As the others begin leaving, Dave hesitates. "Go on Dave," James tells him. "Stay with the others, I'll be alright."

Not happy about the situation, Dave turns his horse and gallops after the others.

"Let's make this fast," he tells Jiron.

Turning down a side street, they angle their way quickly around town until the complex of Renlon's Iron appears before them. The whole place looks deserted for the evening save for a single light coming from the window of the office building where he met them the last time.

Coming to a stop before the door, James gets down and says, "Don't go anywhere."

Chuckling, Jiron replies, "That's a dumb thing to say."

James flashes him a grin and nods. Moving to the door, he opens it and passes through to the other side.

The older Renlon is sitting at the desk as he was the last time. Looking up, his eyes widen is surprise when he sees him come in. "James!" he exclaims coming to his feet. "What are you doing back here?"

Dispensing with the pleasantries, he asks, "Ever heard of a place called Ironhold?"

"Ironhold?" he asks. "What makes you ask about that?"

"I need to find it," he explains. "Do you know where it is?"

"Sure," he says. "Just follow the north road out of town and you'll run right into it."

"Thanks," says James as he turns to leave.

"Just a minute," the senior Renlon says.

Pausing, James turns back and says, "I haven't much time."

Nodding, he replies, "I heard about Orlander's tavern, bad business that. You do that?"

"Yeah," he says. "Didn't mean to, things just sort of got out of hand."

"Heard he wants you in a bad way." Looking at him with a worried expression he asks, "He didn't follow you here did he?"

Shaking his head, James says, "I don't think so."

"Good, we don't need that headache," he replies. Returning to his seat behind the desk he motions for James to sit in the chair opposite him. "About Ironhold," he begins. "Just what takes you there?"

"Can't really explain," is all the answer he's willing to give.

He looks at him for a moment before saying, "It's the northern most town in Madoc, situated in the pass leading to the northern kingdoms. Used to be a mining town, been there for as long as I remember. They say it's haunted."

"Haunted?" James asks.

"That's right," he says, nodding. "Over the last century or so there have been those who have tried to bring those mines back in service. But every time something happens and the project fails."

"Like what?" he asks.

"Last time the miners claimed apparitions of those who have died in the mines before appeared. Scared them bad and they left. Other times ore carts are found broken apart, things come up missing. I even heard one time several miners disappeared for several days only to be found wandering around in the forest days later."

"The whole place is cursed," he warns. "You might wish to reconsider going there."

James sits there a moment as he digests what he just heard. Then he says, "Nevertheless, I have to go."

Getting to his feet, the senior Renlon says, "Then be careful."

"I will," replies James as he, too, gets to his feet. "I appreciate the warning."

The door opens and Jiron's head pops in. "James, we've got to go."

"Be right there," he says. Turning back he holds his hand out as he says, "Thanks."

"You're welcome," Renlon says, shaking his hand.

Moving quickly to the door, he joins Jiron outside and they mount. He turns to the sound of the door opening and waves to the senior Renlon standing there as Jiron kicks the horse into motion and they bolt away into the night.

As soon as they leave Renlon's Iron, they turn and ride around the edge of town until they meet up with the others on the eastern side. "Any trouble?" asks Fifer.

Shaking his head, James replies, "No." He dismounts from behind Jiron and moves over to mount his own steed.

"Did you find out what you wanted to know?" Dave asks.

"Yes I did," he says. "If we follow the north road out of town, we'll come right to it."

"Excellent," Uther states. "How far is it?"

James' enthusiasm dampens somewhat when he replies, "I forgot to ask."

"No matter," interjects Jiron. "We know where it lies."

They get their horses in motion and circumvent the town until they reach the north road then turn to follow it. James doesn't inform them about the strange occurrences at the mines. He figures they have enough to worry about right now. Besides, they could be the overactive imagination of miners left too long alone. Somehow that idea doesn't bring him any consolation.

Riding through the night, they decide to put many miles behind them before they stop and rest until morning. The road moves through the foothills for the first couple of hours but then finally leaves them behind as it moves into open plains. No inns in sight, they pull off the road and make a camp some ways from the road.

Bellies grumbling from lack of food, they settle into their blankets. The stars are bright overhead which on the one hand is good as there'll be no rain. But bad on the other as what warmth there is in the air will be gone by morning, escaping back into space.

In the morning as the sun breaks over the horizon, they awaken to find frost covering the grass and their breath fogs in the cold air of a fall morning. Shivering, they break camp and return to the road.

"I'm starving," complains Dave as they make the road and turn to follow it north.

"We all are," assures James. "We'll get something to eat at the next town."

"If there is a next town," he hears his friend grumble under his breath.

Sighing, James rolls his eyes and tries not to worry about his friend. Frankly he has too much on his mind. He worries whether or not Orlander will be coming after him, if the Empire has more forces in the area, not to mention those creatures.

Also on his mind is what that crazy guy back in Illion had said. *The temple must rise.* Then he went and contradicted himself by saying the temple had to fall. He would completely dismiss it if it weren't for the other things the man had said about shadows and fire. He could've been just a crazy man and his ramblings nonsense, but he doesn't think so. And finally ahead of them is a place he's been told strange occurrences have been happening for some time. Altogether too much to worry about.

Dave rides next to him as does Miko, one on either side. Two hours after leaving camp, a farmstead appears off to their right, quite a ways off the road. People are seen working the fields around it, probably bringing in the last of whatever crop they had.

"Fifer," he says coming to a stop. "Take Miko and go over there to see if we can buy some food." He pulls out the pouch he acquired at Orlander's and removes some coins which he hands to Fifer.

"Sure," he says, taking the coins. He and Miko then leave the road and begin making their way to the homestead.

James sits there with the others as they watch them approach. When the farmers notice them approaching, they hurry from the fields to the house. Fifer and Miko come to a stop near the house and look to be talking with the locals. After a few moments, one of them is seen going to the house and returning with several sacks and gives them to Miko. Several more words are exchanged before they turn about and return to the others.

As they approach, he sees Miko giving him a big smile as he holds up one of the sacks the farmers gave him. "We got food!" he exclaims once they're close enough.

"Should be enough for a day or two," Fifer says.

"Good," says Dave coming forward.

Miko begins handing out some bread, cheese and dried beef to the others before they resume their northward trek. Once everyone has their share, James is gratified to see that the sacks still contain quite a bit of food.

They continue on for the rest of the day, the sun doing little to warm them. A cold breeze feels like it's blowing down off the mountain. "Might be an early snow," Uther announces at one point.

"Let's hope it holds off until we get back over the mountains," Jorry says.

"Amen to that," James adds.

The proximity of the mountains probably has a lot to do with the drop in temperature. Of course a cold northern could be on its way down to make life a misery for the travelers. Either way, they pull their jackets closer together and do their best to keep warm.

Throughout the rest of the day, the riders fight off the cold as they steadily progress northwards. By the time night again falls there have been no sign of inns or anything else which would provide them some comfort through the cold of night.

Finding a place near a few lone trees on the plains, they make their camp. At least they're fortunate enough to find enough wood for their campfire to last through the night. They again rotate the watch, the threat of the Empire still very real. With any luck, Orlander has remained back in Illion.

Another cold morning, even colder than the last has them shivering before the fire roars to life. They take just enough time to warm up and eat some of the rations acquired yesterday before they set off again.

The sky is a crystal blue without a hint of clouds. They ride for several hours before the sun has managed to warm the air enough so their breath no longer fogs. James is thankful for what warmth the sun gives them.

Trees begin to appear with more frequency and ahead it looks like the road enters a forest. Close to noon a town appears straddling the road ahead of them. As it turns out, it sits at a crossroads just within the forest.

"Let's get something to eat and find out which way Ironhold lies," James announces when the town first appears.

"I'm for that," agrees Miko enthusiastically.

The town looks to be not very large, mainly servicing the traffic moving along the two roads which converge there. Off to one side sits a large sawmill with piles of stripped logs awaiting their turn.

"Be interesting to see how they do it here," Dave says to his friend.

"Sure would," agrees James.

They approach the town and find an inn sitting on the outskirts. Looking it over, James nods and says, "Let's try this one. Looks clean." Pulling up, they dismount and secure their horses to the rail out front and make their way inside.

Over to one side is a table large enough to accommodate them so they make their way over and take their seats. Shortly a serving girl comes over and takes their order. Instead of regular ale, James and the rest opt for mulled ale with a hint of spice to better warm themselves from the cold of the road.

"Wonder how far Ironhold is from here?" Miko asks.

"I don't know," replies James. Turning to the table next to them where a man and a woman are sitting, he says, "Excuse me."

They both turn to look his way and the man asks, "Yes?"

"Do you know which road to take to reach Ironhold?" he asks.

"Ironhold?" the man asks surprised. He glances to the lady and then turns a serious look back to James. "Why would you want to go there? It's said the place is haunted by spirits."

"What?" asks Miko.

"That's a bunch of hogwash," Uther says. Jorry just snorts.

"What do you mean?" prompts James, trying to ignore the reaction of his comrades.

"I heard that some miners went up there in an attempt to reopen the mines and were never heard from again," the woman says.

"Never?" asks Miko, fear creeping into his voice.

"Now don't exaggerate dear," the man chides her. "Most of them were found." Turning his attention back to James and the others, he continues. "They disappeared for a time and all but two were found lost in the mountains. They claim a spirit came and took them away, leaving them lost in the woods. No mention was ever made of the fate of the remaining two."

James glances back to the others and can see emotions ranging from the fear in Miko's eyes to the disbelief in Uther's. "Has anyone been up there lately?" he asks the man as he turns his attention back to the couple.

Shaking his head, the man replies, "Not that I've heard. None dare even go near there. Those that pass through do so quickly without stopping."

"James," Miko says, "maybe we shouldn't go there."

"Your friend is right," the woman tells him. "It's a bad place."

"Be that as it may," asserts James, "we need to get there."

"Then take the north road out of town through the forest and it will lead you there," explains the man. "The road continues past Ironhold to the northern kingdoms but no traveler dares to spend the night there. Those that have tell of strange sights and sounds."

"We'll keep that in mind, thank you," replies James.

"Just be careful," the woman says, concern in her voice.

"We will," James assures her.

Turning back to the others he says, "Seems an interesting place."

"Interesting?" asks Miko. "Cursed more like it."

"Relax," Uther says with confidence. "Most likely it's simply the wind howling through the trees or something."

"Sure," adds Jorry. "There's no such thing as spirits."

Laughing, Jiron draws every eye to him as he says, "Well let me tell you about..." He then goes into the tale of complex in the swamps which everyone must have already heard a dozen times. He reminds them of the spirits of the dead which they encountered there. "So don't go discounting tales of spirits so easily," he concludes.

Uther and Jorry don't look convinced. Sure, they've heard the story many times but never put much credence in it. After all, some of their tales are just as scary but truth be told, most of them are not altogether true.

"Do you still think it wise to go there?" Dave asks.

"Wise or not, that's where the trail leads," he replies.

Turning back to the couple he asks, "Pardon me, but do you know how far it is from here?"

Over his shoulder, the man says, "Couple days I think. Not for sure though, never had the occasion to travel there."

"Thank you," James says as he turns back to the others with a grin. "Not that much farther."

"Great," mumbles Miko next to him.

Chapter Twenty Six

Leaving the crossroads behind, they take the northern road through the forest where they're told Ironhold will be found. Dave and Miko are dead set against going but follow along as they have no choice since they're unwilling to abandon James.

Following the road through the trees affords them some protection against the bite of the wind. The further north they travel the denser the trees lining the road become and the thicker the canopy of leaves above them.

Their horses' hooves crunch with every step as they ride through the layers of dead leaves the coming of fall has deposited upon the road. A few lone travelers are encountered coming from the north but none are talkative and keep to themselves.

By the end of the day they're still within the forest. When the light begins to fade they find a clearing alongside the road and make camp. At least this night the trees will keep the elements at bay and hopefully James won't freeze again.

Once camp has been set up, James says, "Get a fire going, I'll go find us some food."

"Can I come?" Dave asks.

Nodding, James gives him a grin and says, "Sure." Miko comes along as well. As he enters the forest, he bends over and picks up several stones which will do nicely. Putting all but one in his pocket, he keeps the other one available in his hand.

"Are you going to kill something?" Dave asks.

"Shhh!" James says to his friend. Then he nods and whispers, "Yeah."

"I thought you wouldn't ever kill anything?" he asks.

Shrugging, he replies, "Back home I never would. Here it's a matter of survival. Now be quiet and keep your eyes open."

They slowly creep their way further between the trees until Miko lays his hand on James' shoulder to get his attention. Pointing off to the right, he directs his gaze to a small animal sitting upon a fallen tree.

"Right," breathes James. Cocking his arm back, he lets loose the magic and throws the stone. It flies through the air and strikes the creature in the head knocking it off the tree.

"You got it!" exclaims Dave as he breaks into a run toward the fallen animal. James and Miko follow.

They find the animal with half its head blown away. "Gross," Dave says as he bends over and picks it up by its tail. Blood drips from the opening.

"Take it back to camp," James tells him. "I'll try to get another before it gets too dark."

"Alright," he says and heads back to camp.

Shortly after Dave leaves, James bags another animal. He and Miko then return to camp where the animals are dressed for the fire.

The night passes quickly and in the morning they have a quick breakfast, finishing off the remnants of the roasted animals of the night before. Once done, they mount up and return to the road and continue north.

All day long, the forest alongside the road remains constant. An hour or so after noon, they begin to notice the odor of wood smoke in the air. Shortly after that a cluster of buildings appears along the road out of the forest ahead of them.

"Wish we could've stayed there last night," complains Dave.

"Would have been nice," replies James. The others just give Dave an annoyed glance.

The village ahead of them doesn't have all that much going for it, a few main buildings such as an inn and a chandler's shop and not much else. Scattered amidst the surrounding forest, houses can be seen here and there.

One man is leaving the inn and James rides near and asks, "How much further is Ironhold?"

The man pauses and glances up at him. "About a day and a half," he replies. "When you reach the foothills you'll know you're close."

"Thank you," James says and then continues on through. Glancing back, he sees the man hasn't moved from his spot, merely standing there and staring at them leaving. The way he's acting gives him the creeps.

Jiron notices him as well and says, "Wonder what that's all about?"

Shrugging, James says, "Maybe he just wants to remember the fools going to Ironhold."

Laughing, Jiron nods his head. Jorry and Uther join in.

"What's so funny?" Miko asks.

"Nothing," replies James and breaks into a chuckle as well.

They pass through the village and return to the forest. The rest of the day is pretty much as it has been and they finally make camp as the light begins to fade.

James again takes Dave out into the forest and they manage to bag a large animal similar to a deer back home. It's too encumbering for one to carry so together they bring it back to camp.

Along with the roasted meat from this kill, they also finish the rest of the bread and some of the cheese they had bought from the farmer earlier. Seeing their dwindling supply of food, James wishes he had thought to buy several more day's worth in that small village they passed through earlier.

What can't be helped must be endured. Through the night, they keep the fire going and the one on watch continues roasting the meat so they can take most of it with them when they leave.

Early the next morning they break camp and return to the road. "We should be there before night, I think," James announces.

"I can hardly wait," moans Dave.

"Cheer up," his friend tells him. "Doubt if anything will give us trouble there."

"You know," Dave says as they ride along, "in the horror movies back home, the person who always says things like that is usually the first to die."

"So?" asks James. "Those were just movies."

"I just think you should approach this with a little more gravity than what you are," he says.

"Don't think that just because I am not visibly worried that I am carefree," James tells him. "On the contrary, I'm not. The tales concern me and I intend to use extreme caution and vigilance while there."

"I hope so," says Dave.

They ride throughout the day and sometime after lunch the forest begins to thin out and the terrain turns into rolling hills. "Must be getting close," says James.

Not long after the hills appear they come to a junction. Either they can continue straight or take the road to the left. James continues on straight and from the rear he hears Qyrll say, "We should take the road to the left."

Coming to a stop just past the left hand road, he turns his head back and asks, "Why?"

"We've been gradually turning to the east," he explains. Pointing to the road branching to the left he says, "That one leads almost due north."

"Are you sure?" Dave asks.

"Absolutely," the Parvati replies.

"I think he's right," adds Jorry. Uther nods agreement.

Taking a moment, James looks around and notices the way the shadows are falling and begins nodding his head. "I think you're right," he agrees. "This way it is." Turning his horse around, he returns to the other road and they begin following it.

They're soon to realize this is the right way to go, the trees continue to thin and they catch glimpses through the trees of the mountains ahead of them to the north. Nestled somewhere within them lies the old town of Ironhold.

As they continue through the hills, the trees thin but don't disappear altogether. Steadily, the hills become steeper and the road meanders first one way then the other in an attempt to follow the gentlest way.

Two hours after they left the other road, the hills open into a sort of plateau before the road reenters the mountains further ahead. A caravan is camped off to one side, other travelers are scattered throughout the area.

"Wonder what this is all about?" asks Jiron.

"I don't know," James replies. Giving the area a better scrutiny, he notices many spots which are currently unoccupied which once had been used. Sites of old campfires are seen throughout the plateau area.

Moving along, they come to three men sitting next to a wagon having what looks like stew. They look up as James approaches. "Excuse me," he says to them. "I was wondering why everyone is camped here? I mean it isn't that late."

"Don't want to take the chance of being in Ironhold when night falls," one of the men tells him. "Most travelers who come this way stop here and continue on through in the morning."

"One time," another man adds, "we were coming through Ironhold and our wagon wheel broke. It was just about sunset and by the time we got it repaired, the sun had dropped below the horizon." One of the other men nods his head in affirmation to what he's saying.

"Before we could get all the way through a white shape appeared atop one of the old buildings and began wailing." His eyes widen at the memory as he continues, "The sound seemed as if it was going right through you. We whipped our horse and got out of there fast. We'll never take the chance of being caught in Ironhold when the sun goes down again."

"Thanks," James says.

Nodding, the men return to their meal.

Glancing back to the others, he can see fear and doubt creep into their eyes, even Uther's. "Better find a spot and we'll enter Ironhold in the morning," he says.

"Might not be a bad idea," agrees Jiron.

"Think it was a banshee?" asks Dave as they head over to an unoccupied spot near an old campfire ring.

"Who knows?" responds James. "Just don't let your imagination get the best of you."

"I'll try not to," he says.

They get the horses settled in and set about gathering enough wood to last the night. "I think we should still maintain a watch here," he tells them once the fire is going and they're having their dinner. "Don't necessarily trust everyone here."

"I agree," Miko says.

Several more groups of travelers appear from the road to the south and join with the others in waiting for the coming of dawn. Not one person enters the pass at the other end.

Sleep doesn't come easy for any of them that night. Thoughts of what they may encounter the next day run through their mind. During their turn at watch, each tends to pace nervously in an attempt to work out their anxiety before returning to their blankets when their turn is over and trying to go to sleep.

Another crystal blue day dawns, cold and freezing. They gather around the fire to dispel the chill which has crept into their bones through the night. The plateau is a bustle of activity as the various groups of travelers get underway.

James is in no hurry to be the first, rather he just as soon wait and be the last to leave. They have breakfast while they wait for the last few to get underway. When at last everyone has either left or is in the process of heading for the pass, James decides it's time to go.

Mounting, they ride at a leisurely pace as they allow those few still moving toward the pass a chance to enter it first. The wagons and caravan move slowly, causing James and the rest to proceed at a pace more sluggish than he would like. But if he wishes to be the last into Ironhold then he must endure it.

"What are you planning to do there?" Jiron asks him.

"Not sure," he says. "There has to be a reason Ellinwyrd told me to come here."

"Are you even positive this is the Ironhold he is mentioning?" Uther asks. "It's possible there could be another."

"He's right!" perks up Miko. "Maybe we should go and find out."

Shaking his head, James dashes his hopes by saying, "No. This is the right one. I know it."

They finally crest a hill and below them they see Ironhold, or rather what's left of it. It looks to have once been a sizable town with many buildings. All of which now stand in ill repair, some even having collapsed.

"Oh man," he hears Miko say from beside him when he sees the dilapidated buildings.

"Looks like a ghost town," Dave says.

"It does, doesn't it?" comments James.

"A ghost town?" asks a shaky Miko.

Glancing over to him, James says, "It just means a town where no one is living. There are a lot of them where I come from and not one of them have actual ghosts. So relax."

Coming down off the ridge, they follow the caravan as it approaches Ironhold. All the other travelers have already passed through and disappeared further into the mountains. A breeze blows through bringing the cold air down off the mountains. The peaks all have snow accumulations already and James is hoping it doesn't drop any lower until they leave.

He brings them to a halt about a mile from the outskirts of Ironhold and waits until the caravan has passed through to the other side. When the last wagon rolls out of town, he nudges his horse forward and they make their way down.

It's an eerie feeling riding into a deserted town in the middle of nowhere. He's sure the feeling of unease they are all feeling is being magnified by the memory of what the man told them the night before. Every shadow holds a monster, every noise a creature bent on their destruction.

The first building they come to looks to have been an inn at one time and James brings them to a stop before it. Dismounting, he says, "We should split up in order to cover more ground quicker."

"Split up?" questions Miko. The look on his face says he's not liking this idea at all.

"We want to be out of here by night don't we?" James asks him. When he sees him nod his head, he says, "Alright then. I'll take Dave. Fifer, you go with Qyrll, and Miko, you stay with Jiron." Jorry and Uther look to him questioningly but he returns a gaze telling them he shouldn't have to tell them they're paired. They always are.

The pairs form up as he takes out his medallion. Holding it up before them, he says, "We're looking for anything with this symbol on it. Understand?" He shows it to everyone and receives a nod from each in reply.

Putting it back within his shirt, he says, "Meet back here by the horses in an hour."

"You got it," Jiron says as he grabs Miko and heads deeper into town.

Before Fifer and Qyrll leave, Fifer says, "We're not going to be able to search the whole town before dark."

"I know," he replies. "This could take a couple days."

"Days?" he asks.

"Don't worry, we'll leave town before it gets dark and then return in the morning," James assures him.

"Okay," he says. Then he and Qyrll leave for the center of town.

Turning to Dave, James says, "Shall we?"

"Let's," he replies. He appears more at ease now that it's just him and James, the others always put him on edge.

They move along the outskirts and begin checking the buildings starting with the inn where their horses are tied. The front door has long since fallen off its hinges and lies on the floor within. Dust covers everything, including the fallen door. Other than small animal tracks, there's no sign of anything or anyone having been inside for a long time.

"Check upstairs," he says to Dave as he nods toward the stairs. "I'll check around down here and meet you up there."

"Alright," he says as he heads to the stairs.

While Dave begins searching the rooms on the floor above, James looks through the rooms on the bottom floor. Room after room, he finds nothing out of the ordinary and no indication of Morcyth.

Aaaaaahhhh!

"Miko!" he cries when he hears his scream. He rushes out of the kitchen and enters the common room just as Dave comes to the top of the stairs.

"What was that?" he asks, his voice cracking due to his nervousness.

"I don't know," replies James as he rushes out the door. Turning down the street toward where he heard the cry, he takes out a stone and readies it. He turns the corner and sees Jiron standing there with Miko.

When Jiron sees him running, he rolls his eyes heavenward and nods to Miko.

"What happened?" cries Fifer as he and Qyrll come running from the opposite direction.

Miko turns toward them and holds up a rat's skeleton. "Sorry."

"When he opened the door it fell on him," Jiron explains.

Sighing, James flashes Miko an amused look then turns to return to the inn. He meets Dave on the way back and he explains to him what happened, at which Dave grins.

Back at the inn, they take a quick moment to finish the search and then continue on to the next building. Hours go by and no one finds anything of note. They meet back by the horses periodically to check in, primarily making sure no one comes up missing.

Throughout the day people continue to pass through going either to the north or to the south. Though they take notice of James and the others wandering through Ironhold, they speak not a word to them, simply rush through as if they didn't want to linger any longer there than necessary. Which they probably don't.

During a search of an old tannery, Miko walks into its back room and a door begins to slowly open on its own. He stands there, fear rising as his feet stay frozen in place. Wanting to run but unable to, he's only able to stand there and watch the door open. Suddenly from the other side, Jorry and Uther jump out and yell "Boo!"

Miko yells in fear as he jumps backward three feet, landing awkwardly. Losing his balance he falls to the floor.

Jorry and Uther laugh as they leave the room. Miko gets to his feet just as Jiron enters, the sound of the other's laughter still can be heard from outside. "You okay?" he asks.

Miko glances to him, face red from being scared as he was. "Yeah," he replies.

Jiron glances out a side window and sees the duo passing by. Jorry looks back and sees Jiron staring at him and gives him a grin. Face turning into a frown, he turns back to Miko and says, "How would you like to get them back?"

Brightening at the idea he replies, "Man, would I!"

"Alright then," he says. "Come with me." With Miko in tow he leaves the building through another exit and works his way to a point where he can keep an eye on the pair as they move along the street without being seen.

When they finally enter a building to begin searching, Jiron pauses and turns back to Miko, saying, "Okay, here's what we do..."

"I don't think there's anything here to find," Jorry complains to Uther. Other than the fun they had with Miko, so far Ironhold has just been a rather boring place.

"I know," replies Uther. "Maybe we can get Miko again later." Chuckling at the thought, he makes his way upstairs with Jorry right behind him. The building they find themselves in used to be an inn.

He and Jorry met shortly after the fall of the City of Light when they joined with Miller and his band. Both having gone through hardship and sorrow, they felt a bond between them almost from the beginning.

"It wouldn't be so bad if there was something to find once in a while like coins or something," he says. They have found some, but not nearly enough to satisfy his need for diversion.

Jorry stops at a door while Uther continues on to the next. Opening it, he walks into a room with several beds and over to the side is an upright wardrobe. He gives the room a casual once over and then moves to the wardrobe.

Just before his hand connects with the handle, the doors swing open and two figures leap out at him with a roar. Clothed in tattered remains with faces black as coal, they give him such a fright that he cries out and staggers backward. His leg hits one of the beds and he falls over, his back hitting the floor.

Getting to his feet quickly, he bolts for the door just as Uther comes running to see what the problem is. **Bam!** He runs right into Uther and they both collapse to the floor in a heap.

"What happened?" cries out Uther as he and Jorry quickly untangle themselves and get to their feet.

"Ghosts!" cries Jorry in fright.

Just then laughter can be heard coming from the room he just fled. "Ghosts huh?" Uther says as he draws his sword and approaches the room. Coming to the door, he glances through and there sitting on one of the beds are Jiron and Miko laughing hysterically. Turning back to his friend, he says, "It's just Miko and Jiron."

Jorry comes to stand in the doorway beside Uther and looks on them in anger. Miko sees his expression and doubles over in a more intense spasm of laughter.

"Payback huh?" Uther says, sheathing his sword.

Jiron grins at them with tears in his eyes. "You could say that," he says.

From below the sound of feet running across the floor and then hitting the stairs comes to them. In a second, James appears at the top of the stairs, out of breath. He sees Jorry and Uther standing in the doorway and as he approaches sees Jiron and Miko sitting on the bed. He takes in the way Miko and Jiron are dressed, old tattered clothes and face blackened with what looks like soot. The fact that they're just recovering from laughing tells him all he needs to know.

Putting the stone back into his pocket, he glares at them and says, "If you all are quite through, we have some serious searching to do."

"Sorry James," Jiron says from the room. Uther glances to him and sees he's not sorry in the least.

To Jiron and Miko he says, "Get cleaned up. We still have a while before lunch and I would like to cover at least some of the city by then?"

"Okay," replies Jiron as he gets off the bed.

"But they started it," accuses Miko.

James glances from one pair to the other. Dave comes up the stairs behind him and stops as he takes in the situation. "I don't care who started it," he states. "I want it finished now. Understand?" Four heads nod affirmative. "Good." Turning his back on them, he sees Dave there and rolls his eyes heavenward. With Dave beside him, he leaves the inn.

Once James and Dave are on the stairs and out of sight, Uther gives Miko and Jiron a look saying 'This ain't over yet'.

After another hour of searching, they meet back at the inn where they have lunch before setting out once more. The sun continues its path across the sky and begins to drop toward the mountain peaks to the west. When the sun is close to passing behind the peaks, they decide to go out once more before calling it a night.

"Maybe we should stop now?" suggests Miko. Eyeing the sun's proximity to the top of the mountains he's worried about being within Ironhold when the sun disappears.

"Just a quick search," James tells everyone. "Check two more buildings and then return here. We'll start in a different area tomorrow."

"I don't think you're going to find anything here," Dave grumbles.

Turning to his friend, James says, "There has to be something, Ellinwyrd wouldn't have said to come here if there wasn't."

Fifer pauses on his way into town, turns back and says, "He could be mistaken. Everyone makes mistakes."

"I've considered that," he says and then stalks off. Dave has to hurry to keep from being left behind. Doubt has been creeping in ever since nothing was found right away. Maybe it's just pride or stubbornness, but he feels to the core of his being that this is where he needs to be.

A half hour later after another fruitless search they reconvene by the horses. The sun by this time has dipped behind the peaks. Though the town is now in shadow, the peaks to the east still have the sun's rays upon them.

Mounting, they move out and head to the edge of town. They follow the road for a mile or so before coming to a good spot where they can camp and still keep the town in sight. "Don't you think we're a bit close?" asks a nervous Miko.

Turning his gaze upon him, James puts his hands on his hips and vents the frustrations of the day. "I'm sick and tired of you whining about this and complaining about that! If you don't want to stay here, then by all means you're more than welcome to move further away. I am staying here."

Miko's eyes reveal the hurt he feels from the words his friend just spoke. "Didn't mean that," he says softly. He then turns away and moves across to the other side of the camp where he rolls out his bedroll and lies down.

"Kind of hard on him weren't you?" Jiron asks.

Sighing, James says, "Probably. But there comes a time when a man has to grow up and stop being scared of everything. It was cute when he was younger, but now he needs to start facing his fears."

"How can you say that after all we've been through?" accuses Jiron. James starts to turn away and Jiron takes him by the shoulder and pulls him back. Eyes locking, he says, "Miko has been your stalwart companion from the beginning and he deserves better. From what you both have told me, he's saved your life on numerous occasions when he was scared. He's cautious, yes. But don't you ever confuse that with cowardice!"

Sighing, James nods his head and says, "You're right." He glances over Jiron's shoulder and sees Miko stretched out on the ground turned to face out of camp. "I better go talk with him."

"That would be a good idea," agrees Jiron. "The rest of us will take care of the fire and dinner."

"Thanks," he says as he starts heading toward Miko. He doesn't take two steps when from behind him he hears Jiron say to Dave, "Come on, we're on wood duty." Dave's complaining accompanies him all the way to where Miko lays.

"Uh, Miko," James says as he comes to stop next to him.

"What?" he says, face remaining turned away.

"I'm sorry for what I said." He comes around to the other side. "You're too good a friend for that."

"It's alright," he says. "You're right though, I do complain more than I aught."

"No it's not," James tells him. Sitting down next to him, he glances at him and then says, "I'm just frustrated by not finding anything today. I took it out on you and I shouldn't have."

Giving James a crooked smile he says, "If you can't blow up at your friends once in a while, then what good are they? I'm not mad. I know you have a lot on your mind."

"Glad you feel that way," James says sincerely. He gives him a smile and then glances over across the camp where Dave has just returned with an armful of wood. He's standing there staring at them, emotions running through his face which James is unable to make head or tails of. The only thing he's sure of is that they're not good ones.

Sighing, he says, "I'm going to help the others." Patting Miko on the shoulder, he gets to his feet and comes over to where Dave is standing.

"Need any help?" he asks.

Whatever emotions had been there before are gone now. Giving him a shake of the head, he says good naturedly, "Naw, we got it covered." He puts his load of wood down near the fire and then returns to the trees for another.

He watches his friend for a second before going over to where Fifer is working to get the fire going. Sitting down, he glances around and then asks, "Where's Qyrll?"

Jerking his head in the direction of Ironhold, he replies, "Over there. Said he wanted to see if there were any ghosts walking the streets."

Looking in the direction indicated, he sees him leaning against a tree as he looks out over the town. "Hope he doesn't find any."

"Me too," agrees Fifer.

They get the fire going to dispel the cold of the mountains. If they thought it was cold down on the plains, it's downright frigid here at the base of the mountains. The wind whips the cold air down from the upper elevations and with the setting of the sun, the temperature drops rapidly.

Breaking out the rations, they have their meal while the light continues to fade. Qyrll takes his meal over to his position looking out over the town. The heat from the fire doesn't reach that far but he doesn't seem to mind. His people live in mountains so he most likely can take the cold better than most.

The others come to join him from time to time but the cold always drives them back to the fire. By the time they determine it's time for sleep, no ghosts or spirits have yet to make their appearance.

Chapter Twenty Seven

Throughout the night, those on watch kept a constant vigil on the town below. Though their imaginations played games with them and gave several a brief scare, nothing ever happened.

When the sun is about to crest the peaks to the east, they're already on their horses and heading down to Ironhold. James takes them to another section of town away from where they searched the day before. Another day, maybe two and they'll have this whole town searched.

On the way down, Miko asks, "Why don't you use your magic in the search?"

"For some reason, the thought of doing magic here bothers me," he explains. "Can't really explain it more than that. If after we've thoroughly searched the entire town and come up empty, then maybe I will."

"What about the mines?" Jiron asks. When James glances back at him he clarifies, "Maybe what Ellinwyrd meant were the mines and not the town at all."

"You may be right," James concedes. "We'll begin searching there after we've finished with the town." There is one small road, hardly wide enough for a single wagon which they saw earlier, leading away from town to the west. One of Ironhold's mines could lay down there.

By the time they get to the starting point for the day's search, the traffic from the north and south begins rolling through. At first the quicker riders appear and then shortly after them roll in the caravans, only two it looks like today. One is heading north and the other south. Some of the travelers take note of them dismounting but none stop to offer a greeting, merely shaking their heads as they hurry on their way.

"Just like yesterday," he says. "Comb the town in pairs and stick together. We don't need anyone getting lost or separated." Glancing to the jokesters of the day before he says, "No fooling around today. Got it?"

"Sure," assures Jorry, the others nod their agreement.

"Alright then," James says.

Jorry and Uther give Miko and Jiron a sidelong glance which is returned. James notices and sighs. *Why do I even bother?*

"We'll be okay," offers Fifer. Giving James a nod, he and Qyrll head off as they begin searching the buildings leading into town. Dave and James take the buildings going to the left and Jiron and Miko to the right. Jorry and Uther head further into town past where Fifer and Qyrll are searching.

Building after building, they search but to no avail. No sign indicating Morcyth or anything else is discovered. They continue to check back in by the horses every hour. Jiron suggests they could cover more area if they didn't have to come back all the time but James says he would rather it take longer than have something happen to one of them.

During the last hour before they have to return before noon, Miko and Jiron are leaving a home where it looked as if a large family had lived. Within were many rooms, some still containing the remnants of fine furniture.

"I don't think this town has what James is looking for," grumbles Miko.

"Either do I," agrees Jiron.

"Then why are we here?" he asks.

Sighing, he turns to Miko and says, "Because James says to. He's proved us wrong before when we thought what he was doing didn't make any sense."

"True," he agrees.

At one point Miko asks him if he plans on continuing the jokes on Jorry and Uther but Jiron shakes his head. "James is right, we need to finish this and get out of here." He pauses a moment and says, "Of course if they do something then we should hardly just take it without retaliation."

Miko likes the sound of that. So not only is he looking for signs of Morcyth but is keeping on the lookout for the next prank Jorry and Uther may pull.

Walking back onto the street, Jiron gestures to a rundown building across the street and says, "Should we try this one before heading back?"

"Alright," agrees Miko just before his stomach sounds off with a loud rumble, "but let's not take too long."

Jiron gives him a grin and they cross the street. The door is closed but opens readily enough when Jiron turns the handle. It's a three story residence and Jiron offers to check the upper floors while Miko searches the ground floor.

The one part of this Miko likes is opening all the old chests and boxes lying around. So far he's found quite a number of interesting objects, not to mention the odd coin or two. As Jiron hits the stairs to search above, he leaves the front room and enters the kitchen area.

Opening the various cabinets he finds them all empty. A door is set in the far wall, and he walks over to it. Grasping the handle he pulls it open and finds a walk-in pantry on the other side. Old rotted containers still line the shelves, whatever they had once contained is long gone. He moves inside as he checks for anything which may have been left behind. He's become quite the scavenger.

Not finding anything he turns to leave and takes two steps before coming to stop. A cold chill runs through him and his heart skips a beat at what he sees in the other room. Standing there, looking directly at him is a figure of a man, gaunt and pale. The skin is pulled tight to his bones and his hair is scraggly, looking like it has fallen out in patches. Clutched in one hand is a pickaxe such as a miner would use.

The instant of fright leaves him as he says, "Alright guys, enough is enough. You're not fooling anyone."

When the figure makes no reply and continues to stand there staring at him, his feelings of unease return. Fear begins to take him again as he comes to realize this isn't Uther or Jorry.

Standing there frozen in fear, Miko is speechless as they both gaze upon the other. Then the miner's mouth begins to move but nothing comes out as he turns slightly toward Miko. Taking a step forward, he reaches out his other hand as if to grab him.

The movement of the miner breaks the spell fear had over him and Miko lets out with a god awful inarticulate scream of fear as he backpedals into the pantry. Reaching out in panic, he takes hold of the pantry door and pulls it closed behind him.

Moving as far back as he can, he stands there in the dark, eyes locked to the door afraid the miner will open it and come for him. The darkness of the pantry does nothing to alleviate the terror that continues to rifle through him.

Suddenly, the door swings open and he sees Jiron standing there, knife in hand. "What happened?" he asks. Then he sees the wide eyed, pale expression on Miko's face.

"He was standing there!" Miko says, pointing to the other room.

"Who?" Jiron asks. "Who was standing here?" Looking around the kitchen, he doesn't see anything.

"A miner," he says. "I think he was dead."

Reaching his hand out to him, Jiron asks, "Were they playing another joke on you?"

Shaking his head vehemently, he says, "No, it wasn't them."

"Come on, let's go tell James," he says.

Nodding, Miko takes the hand and leaves the panty. Reentering the kitchen, his eyes dart around for the gaunt miner but other than him and Jiron, the kitchen is empty. Coming to where the miner had stood he says, "He was standing right here!" He takes hold of Jiron's shirt and says, "He was reaching for me."

"Calm down," Jiron says as he leads him out of the building. "He's not here now."

On their way to find James, they run across Fifer and Qyrll who join them. Jiron gives them a brief rundown of what happened as they continue moving toward where James and Dave are hunting. Jorry and Uther are nowhere in sight.

When they reach the area, he calls out "James!"

From an upper window of a nearby building, they hear a "What?"

Looking up, they see James peering down at them. "Miko saw something!"

"It was a miner!" he hollers. "I think he was dead."

"I'll be right down," he says and then ducks back inside. A moment later, he and Dave leave the building and join them in the street. Coming to Miko he asks, "What happened?"

He relates to him his encounter with the dead miner, as now he's sure that's what it was. "He was reaching for me and I panicked," he concludes. "I slammed the door closed as I fled into the panty. When it opened again, Jiron was standing there and the miner was gone."

"And you're sure it wasn't them playing another joke on you?" he asks.

When Miko shakes his head no, he says, "Take me there."

Together they hurry along back to the building where the dead miner had been encountered. When they approach, James says, "You all stay here, Miko you come with me." With Miko right beside him, he goes up to the open door leading into the kitchen and stops before entering.

"Now," he says as he turns to Miko, "just where did this miner appear?"

Pointing to the spot, he replies, "Right there."

Entering through the door, James comes to the spot and examines the floor carefully. If the miner had left footprints they were obliterated by Jiron and Miko walking over them when they left. He stands there a moment with his eyes closed but fails to pick up anything such as coldness or a sense of danger, things he heard always accompanies the supernatural.

Turning back to Miko he says, "Whatever it was, there's nothing here now."

"I tell you I saw it," insists Miko defensively.

"I'm not saying you imagined it," James tells him. "I'm just saying there's nothing here now."

With a tremor of fear in his voice, he asks, "What are we to do?"

"Let's go have lunch while I think on it," he says. "After that we'll see."

"Alright."

They leave the house and rejoin the others. "There's nothing there now," he says when he draws near. "Let's go back to the horses and have lunch. I want to comb this area after we eat." The idea of searching a mine is forgotten after Miko's encounter with the miner.

Moving down the street toward where they left the horses, Qyrll moves next to Miko and asks, "What did it look like?"

Qyrll seems to have a rather keen interest in this sort of thing and practically grills Miko about the subtle details. By the time they've returned to the horses, he brings his questioning to a close, for the moment satisfied he's learned all there is.

Jorry and Uther have returned in the meantime and are filled in on what just happened.

They remove the food for their meal from their horses and take it inside a nearby inn where they sit at a table near a window. James sits there in silence while he eats, the others talking quietly among themselves.

Suddenly from outside, they hear the horses neighing and then see them racing away down the street. "The ghost!" cries out Miko as they all race out of the inn into the street. Weapons at the ready, they find the street deserted except for their fleeing horses.

"Fifer, Miko, you two go after the horses," James says. As they race down the street after them, he says to the others, "Fan out and see if you can find anything. Dave, you stay with me."

Qyrll returns his sword to its scabbard as he moves out quickly, Jiron right behind him. Jorry and Uther go down a side street. James motions for Dave to follow him as he goes over to where the horses were tied to begin their search from there.

Moving quickly, he races down side streets and ducks into buildings only to end up finding nothing. By the time Fifer and Miko return with the horses, they've all returned to the inn.

"Nothing," Jiron says to James when they return. Jorry and Uther have likewise turned up nothing.

"What spooked them?" Fifer asks.

"Ghosts, that's what," replies Miko. Ever since his encounter with the miner, he's been constantly on the lookout, head turning this way and that.

"I think we all need to be extra cautious from this point," James says. "We still need to find what we came here to find."

After securing the horses again, they return to the inn and finish their meal. Once over, they head back to the place where Miko saw the miner to start the afternoon's search from there. "If any of you see anything out of the ordinary, call for me right away," James tells them.

"You can count on that," Miko assures him. Jiron just grins at his enthusiasm at carrying out that command.

"I still want us to meet back here every hour until dusk," he tells them and then they head out to continue their searching.

Miko's miner and the action of the horses have them all spooked, including James. He wouldn't let the others know but he's actually quite worried about the whole thing. Back in his world, these things wouldn't bother him nearly as much. But here where gods are active and magic works, who knows what could happen.

Throughout the rest of the afternoon, several of them think they may have seen the miner out of the corner of their eyes, moving across a window of a nearby building. But each time after they called for James, a closer look revealed nothing.

When the sun at last hits the top of the western peaks, they call it a day and return to the same place they made camp the night before. While the rest get the camp set up and a fire going, James takes Dave and sees if he can't bag something for dinner. Their store of rations is dwindling and he doesn't want to run out before doing something about it.

Shortly after the camp disappears behind them in the trees, movement from up ahead catches his eye. Moving forward, they make their way through the trees until they see a deer-like animal standing still ahead of them. Its head swivels from side to side as if it's trying to find something.

"He may have caught our scent," Dave suggests in a barely heard whisper.

"I think you may be right," replies James just as quietly. Removing a stone from his pocket he slowly gets into position and then cocks his arm back. Taking a deep breath to calm himself, he aims for the deer and releases the magic as he throws the stone.

The deer must have noticed his movement, for at the last second it jumps away. Its hindquarters are thrust to the side when the stone catches it off center, ripping a chunk out.

Dave jumps up and races after the deer, knife in hand. It isn't dead, only injured. James rushes after.

The deer, though faltering in its stride due to its injury, still manages to lead them on a merry chase before finally collapsing from loss of blood and exhaustion. Dave comes up on it first having moved ahead of James during the chase. The deer raises its head off the ground as he approaches, it tries to get to its feet to run away but is too week and stumbles back to the ground.

Reaching its side, Dave strikes out with his knife across its throat and ends its misery. The strike sends a splatter of blood droplets across his face. When James reaches him, he looks a gruesome sight with his face covered in blood as well as part of his clothing.

Dave turns at his approach and says, "Let's get this back to camp."

"Right," agrees James. "Then maybe you need to wash up a little."

Looking down at himself a moment, he then glances to his friend with a grin and asks, "I am a mess aren't I?"

"Oh yeah," affirms James. He takes the hindquarters and Dave takes the fore, together they raise the animal off the ground and that's when James comes to the realization that he doesn't know which way camp is. In all the excitement of chasing the deer, he got turned around. "Do you know which way is the camp?" he asks.

Dave glances around a moment and then says, "Uh, no."

Trees in every direction as well as rolling hills, every direction looks the same. The light is fading fast and if they don't find their way back soon they may not get back until morning.

"Which way?" asks Dave.

"Let's set this down and I'll figure it out," he says. Setting the deer down, he picks up a small stick from the ground and rests it on his palm. Concentrating on Miko, he releases the magic and the stick swivels upon his palm until coming to rest pointing off to his right.

Nodding in that direction, he says, "They're that way." Releasing the magic, he drops the stick back to the ground and then bends over to pick up the deer. Grunting from its weight, he and Dave begin hauling it back to camp.

They slowly work their way through the trees as the light continues to fade, winding their way between two hills. It isn't far before the smell of smoke from the campfire reaches them and they breathe a sigh of relief. Following the direction from which the smoke is originating, they continue around the hill until the light from the campfire comes into view.

He's about ready to call a greeting when he stops in his tracks. Grabbing Dave, he pulls him down against the side of the hill. "That's not our camp," he whispers to his friend.

"Are you sure?" Dave asks.

"Yes. There are more people there than there should be," he explains.

Letting the deer lie on the ground, they make their way to the top of the hill to overlook the camp. Upon reaching the crest, they gaze down and find over a dozen men sitting around a campfire. They're too far away to hear what the men are saying but who they are is apparent. The armor some of them are wearing reveals them to be from the Empire.

He glances to Dave and can see that he's reached the same conclusion. They stay there a few minutes and watch the activities of those in the camp below them. There are fourteen men at arms and two dressed in civilian attire. The men keep their armor on and the horses remain saddled.

The area in which the camp lies is a depression between two hills which would hide them from anyone passing through. Unless of course they stumbled upon them as James and Dave did.

Having seen enough, he indicates with a nod for them to return back down the hill. He and Dave slowly and quietly make their way to the bottom.

"What are they doing here?" Dave whispers.

"Only one thing would draw them this far from the Empire," James replies.

"You?" he asks.

"Can't think of anything else," he states.

"But how would they know you're here?"

"I don't know," he replies. "Magic probably." *This is getting irritating! Going to have to figure a way for them to stop tracking me.* "We better hurry back and tell the others."

Leaving the deer where it lies, they move away from the hill and then circumvent the camp with the Empire's soldiers before continuing to follow the general direction the stick had indicated. About the time the light has completely faded, they see their campfire ahead of them through the trees.

When they emerge from the trees, Jiron is the first to notice them and comes to his feet in alarm. "What happened?" he asks.

James at first isn't sure what elicited that reaction until he glances to Dave and sees that the deer's blood still covers him. "He's fine, just splatter from an animal," he explains. "But we've got real problems." He then tells them of the men camped less than a mile away.

"How in the world could they have tracked us here?" asks Fifer.

"Magic is the only explanation I can come up with," he says. "What I don't understand is, if they know we're here, why haven't they attacked yet?"

"They looked like they were settling in for a wait," adds Dave as he begins cleaning the blood off. He glances at James then continues, "They kept their armor on and their horses remained saddled as well."

Jiron gets a thoughtful look and then shakes his head. "It doesn't make any sense," he says. "They've never hesitated before."

"They could be waiting on something," suggests Qyrll. "Or somebody."

"It's possible," James says.

"What if they were part of the force you encountered by Illion," offers Fifer. "They may have reinforcements on the way."

Remembering the creatures he fought, he doesn't like the sound of more possibly being on the way. "It didn't look like they were going to do anything tonight," he tells them. "Let's get some rest and post a sentry, not only to keep watch here but to keep an eye on the woods between here and there."

"Good idea," Jiron says. "If they move, we need warning."

"Why don't we just leave?" Dave asks. Every eye turns to him. "Hostile forces camped less than a mile away and you all want to just hang out until they attack. I don't get you at all." He glares back at them in turn.

Turning to his friend, James says "What would you have us do? If we leave we would pass right by them, and you can be assured they'll have the pass south watched. It's either here or go into Ironhold."

"Why not attack?" offers Uther. "If they are in fact waiting for reinforcements, then the odds will only get worse the longer we wait."

"You got that right," adds Jorry.

"I don't like attacking without cause," objects James.

"Without cause?" Jiron asks incredulously. "They are the Empire's soldiers and we have had hurt after hurt because of them. I lost my city because of them. Many of those we care for have died and been enslaved because of them. If that isn't cause enough for you I don't know what is."

"James," Miko says. "If these are soldiers of the Empire then we should take them out before they possibly join up with others. Even if they aren't planning on doing that, their destruction is our duty anyway. They are our enemies."

"He's right," agrees Fifer. Qyrll nods in agreement as well which surprises James as he's from the Empire.

"You all are a bunch of bloodthirsty killers," Dave says from where he stands behind James. "All you talk about is death and destruction. You won't be satisfied until we're all dead."

Jiron steps forward with a hand on the pommel of one of his knives, anger building behind his eyes. He opens his mouth to tell Dave off when James holds up his hand forestalling his tirade.

"I see the wisdom in what you are saying," he says. Then adds to include Dave, "What you're all saying." Turning to Jiron and the others, he says "But what you all need to realize is Dave and I come from a world where the arbitrary killing of your enemies is frowned upon, extremely discouraged you might say. It's hard for me to go and seek the death of a group of people that are no immediate threat."

He pauses a moment to let that sink in. Many there who have traveled with him for awhile will understand what he's talking about. Then he says, "I need to know for a fact they plan to come after us." Looking to Qyrll he asks, "Would you be willing to find out?"

Looking surprised, he says, "They will think it odd for me to suddenly appear among them all alone. I don't think they would tell me anything."

"I don't mean that," James clarifies. "Just sneak close and try to overhear what they're saying. Could you do that?"

"Perhaps," he says. "If they're not vigilant and lax in the posting of sentries."

"Good. Then take Jiron with you and see what you can learn," he says.

Smiling at the prospect of having the Shynti with him, he nods his head. "I would be honored to have him accompany me."

James gives them a general idea of where to find the enemy camp. Then when Qyrll and Jiron are about ready to head out, he adds, "Don't take too long."

"We won't," Jiron assures him, then they leave the camp.

The others murmur among themselves, all the while casting glances over to where Dave remains standing near James.

"Come with me," James says to his friend as he leads him away from the fire and into the night. When they leave the proximity of the fire, the cold makes its presence felt. They pull their jackets closer together as they move further away from the others. Once they've reached a spot where they won't be overheard, he comes to a stop.

"I know what you're going to say," Dave begins before James has a chance to start. "I'm sorry, but it's true. All they talk about is killing and death."

"That's not true," counters James. "We are in the middle of a war. Those on the other side are continuously seeking to make our lives difficult in any way they can. Given the world in which these people have grown up, I think their responses are true to form."

"But they're going to get us all killed!" insists Dave.

"We could sit on our butts and that will still happen," says James. "We grew up in a relatively safe environment where conflict to this degree simply was not a factor. If we were in one of our campaigns we used to play in the chess room, what would you be doing?"

Considering the question for a moment, he then says, "Probably arranging an attack to avoid possible future complications."

"Remember," James tells him, "this world is similar to that of our role playing, more so than I would have thought possible. That's probably why the advertisement in the newspaper said role playing a plus."

Nodding, Dave says, "I see your point. But I am still going to caution you against actions which I feel are wrong."

Laying his hand on Dave's shoulder he says, "I wouldn't want you to do otherwise. I need a voice of reason in this chaotic and hostile world."

Giving his friend a grin, he says, "You got it."

"Now, let's go back to the others," suggests James. "And this time, don't go calling them blood thirsty killers."

"I won't, promise," Dave assures his friend.

As they're walking back to the fire, a sound comes to them from the darkened town. A wailing sounds in the night as if a spirit is writhing in torment. They rush to the edge which overlooks the town and see a light atop one of the buildings. From this distance it's hard to make out just what it is, but it looks to be the size of a man and it's moving.

"What the heck is that?" Dave asks.

The others join them as he says, "I don't know."

"It's a ghost!" Miko exclaims.

"Could be," agrees James. *Too bad Qyrll is missing this. He would've loved it.*

The light continues to pace back and forth along the roof as the wailing continues. It lasts for ten minutes before the light and wailing disappear.

A hushed silence falls over the companions as they stand there in the dark and cold a moment. When it doesn't look as if the spirit will be returning, they make their way back to camp.

As James takes his seat and begins warming his freezing hands, he considers the predicament they're in. On the one side they have a hostile force most likely bent on their destruction. On the other is a city with free roaming spirits. At least the spirits mostly come out at night, mostly.

Chapter Twenty Eight

It's been over an hour since they left. Where are they? Pacing around, James is worried about what may have happened to them. To add more to his already worried mind the spirit from Ironhold makes two other appearances in different parts of town, always a lone spirit and always on top of a building.

No one is getting much sleep tonight, not with the racket going on when the spirit appears. It's been twenty minutes or more since the last spectral appearance and a few of the others have fallen asleep. The only one other than himself who's still awake is Miko. Try as he might, he can't bring himself to relax enough to slip away.

James glances in his direction every once in awhile to see if he's managed to fall asleep, and each time he sees his eyes wide open.

The silence of the night is broken by the sound of something moving toward the camp through the trees. Miko hears it too and sits up, his hand on the hilt of his sword which is resting on the ground next to him. He glances to James and begins getting up when Qyrll and Jiron enter the firelight.

"Glad you're back," James says in relief. "I was getting worried."

"Sorry," apologizes Jiron. "It took us some doing to move close enough for Qyrll to be able to understand what they were saying."

By the time they take their seats at the fire, the others have awoken and moved closer to hear. "What did you learn?" he asks Qyrll.

"From what I heard, they are but one band of many situated in the hills surrounding Ironhold," he explains. "They are waiting for something, no one said for sure exactly what. One of the men was complaining about something not being here yet, couldn't tell if it was more men, one man or what."

"So if we attack them," James says, "it would be safe to say the other bands will go on the offensive right away."

Nodding, he replies, "I think so. If they were discovered, their first inclination would be to attack."

Looking around the assembled faces, he summarizes their situation, "Either we attack one band and face what's out there now, or we wait for whatever else may be coming."

"That would seem to be the choices before us," agrees Jiron.

James sits back and thinks on the situation for a minute. The others remain quiet to give him time to think. He glances to Dave but he knows what he'll say, 'Leave'. The others want to attack, he's sure of that. They're men of action and don't like the idea of waiting.

"If what they're waiting for takes another day or two to get here," he says, "we may be finished and on our way home."

"I don't think we should count on that," Fifer states.

"He's right," agrees Jiron, the others nodding in agreement.

James sits and contemplates the various options before him. He can see the logic in an attack, but his inclination is to avoid direct confrontation if at all possible. "Right now, we do nothing," he tells them. Around him he can see them reacting negatively to his decision, all that is but Dave.

"We'll keep an eye on the band near us through the night and tomorrow we find another place to hole up, maybe in one of the mines." He glances to the others a moment before saying, "It would be more defensible should they attack."

"With no way out," Miko warns.

Turning to him, James replies, "I know. But it's still better than sitting out here in the open. If anyone comes up with a better idea, let me know. Now let's get some sleep while we can."

He no sooner says the last word before another wail comes from Ironhold.

"What was that?" Qyrll asks as he gets to his feet and moves to where he can look out over the town.

"The ghost of Ironhold," Fifer says.

"He's been going on that way for some time now," Miko explains.

The others come to stand near him and see the spirit atop another building on the far side of town. Qyrll makes to move toward Ironhold and James puts a restraining hand on his arm. Qyrll glances to him and sees him shake his head.

"Might not be a good idea to go down there," warns James.

Mixed desires war within him but he finally sighs and stays put. The spirit stays active for a few more minutes and then again disappears.

"It's been doing that since shortly after you guys left," Miko says.

"I really didn't think the tales we heard were actually true," admits Jiron. Glancing to James he says, "Think that's the miner Miko saw?"

"Could be," replies James. "Though from what Miko said, it wasn't glowing or making any sound."

"It's possible it will only do that at night," suggests Qyrll.

"Perhaps," nods James.

They stand there a moment longer before the cold drives everyone but Qyrll back to the fire. Since it doesn't look as if he has any intention of going to sleep right away, Jiron hollers for him to wake him when it's his turn at watch. Qyrll nods in reply but never takes his eyes off the darkness concealing Ironhold.

As the night progresses, the visitations of the spirit diminishes until finally coming to a halt sometime after midnight.

Dawn comes, cold and crisp. A high pressure system must be keeping the clouds at bay, the sky is a dazzling crystal blue and frost covers most everything.

When James gets up he sees Miko over near the fire where he's been trying to keep warm during his shift at watch. Glancing around he notices Qyrll is nowhere around. Coming to Miko he asks, "Where's Qyrll?"

"He went down to Ironhold," he replies. "Said something about wanting to investigate where the ghosts appeared."

"What?" he exclaims. "How long ago did he leave?"

"About a half hour or so," Miko tells him. "Said not to wake you, that he would be back shortly."

"Damn!" curses James. He quickly moves around and gets everyone up, telling them that Qyrll has gone into town. "Get up and get ready, we're going after him."

"Why?" asks Dave. "He's a big boy and can take care of himself."

James glares at him and says, "Just get your horse ready."

"Alright, fine," he replies and then gets up to do just that.

It's just a few minutes before they're ready to ride. Moving away from the campsite, they head down the trail to town. As soon as they're upon the main road, they hear coming from behind them several horses as the travelers from the plateau begin making their run through Ironhold.

The first one to reach them gives them an odd look, he knows they didn't come from the area to the south as he and the others have. Not bothering to stop, he races on past in a hurry to get through Ironhold as quickly as possible.

One thing James has noticed is that those traveling through Ironhold don't talk. It's almost as if everyone is afraid to disturb the tranquility of this place. Or of disturbing what may lurk here.

"There he is," Fifer says, pointing to a building not too far away.

James' eyes follow where Fifer is pointing and finds Qyrll atop one of the tall buildings.

"I think that was one the spirit walked last night," suggests Jiron.

Nodding, James says, "You may be right." Moving through the streets toward the building Qyrll is on, he finds his horse tied to the rail before the front door and comes to a stop next to it. Dismounting, he hands his reins to Miko and says, "Hold this."

Taking the reins, Miko says, "Okay."

Jiron and Fifer dismount to accompany him to the roof. They make their way inside and take the stairs up to the third floor where they find a ladder leading to an open hatch. Climbing the ladder, James gains the roof to find Qyrll bending over and examining a section of the roof.

From the ladder he asks, "What do you think you're doing?"

Qyrll glances up and sees him there in the hatch. Getting to his feet, he makes his way over to them. "Wanted to see if the ghost left any evidence of its passing."

"Why?" asks James as he moves down the ladder to allow Qyrll room to descend.

"To know if it was real or not," he replies. As he steps off the ladder and onto the floor of the third floor hallway, he adds, "Didn't find anything though."

"Spirits don't leave footprints," Jiron tells him.

Nodding, Qyrll says, "Now I know for sure."

They make their way back down to where the others are waiting outside. On the way Fifer asks, "Why are you so interested in this anyway?"

Shrugging, Qyrll replies, "I don't know. It fascinates me for some reason."

"I can understand that," says James. "Where I come from there are all manner of people who hunt for ghosts and such things. Why, there're even tours you can take that will bring you to the most haunted areas."

"Really?" asks Qyrll, intrigued. "I'd like to do that."

"Most of them are just shams to get your money," he admits. "Though there are a few that are legitimate I suppose. Never been on one myself."

Returning to the others, they mount their horses and make their way through town to the last section they have yet to search. After a brief warning to be alert, they split off into their pairs again. James gives Jorry and Uther a stern gaze warning them not be up to any shenanigans today. They assure him they'll behave, probably the sight of the spirit the night before had a sobering effect on them.

The morning goes by and still nothing is discovered. James is beginning to become discouraged at the lack of anything to do with Morcyth. Ellinwyrd had to have led him here for a reason and one to do with what he learned at Saragon.

At noon when they return for the noon meal, Fifer says, "I think I saw someone on a hill to the south watching us."

"Probably one of the soldiers," Qyrll says.

"I'm sure they're keeping their eye on us," Jiron replies.

"I hope they don't do anything," wishes Miko as he glances to the surrounding hills.

"Wouldn't think it likely until whatever they are waiting for arrives," says Qyrll. "They seem content to watch us from a distance and as long as we continue as we are, I doubt if they will do anything."

"Let's hope not," says James. "Tomorrow we'll begin checking the mines and then if nothing is found, we'll leave."

From where Dave sits, he can hear him mumble, "Should leave now." He glances over to his friend and only receives a glare in return. All day his mood has steadily deteriorated and James isn't sure why.

When they're done with the noon meal, they once again split into pairs as they search the few remaining buildings. So far, the miner Miko encountered the day before has yet to put in an appearance.

Miko and Jiron head off for a building which looks to have once been a temple of some sort, though now the years of disuse have turned it into a dilapidated building. Slightly askew on its foundations, it sits cocked to one side. The windows which at one time must have been beautiful lie shattered in the street.

Coming to the entrance, they find a pair of double doors. The one on the right sits closed, the one on the left has fallen off its hinges and lies across the front steps. Stepping carefully around the fallen door, they move inside.

It's not a very large building, merely two stories high. The interior actually has a couple plants growing through the floorboards near one of the broken windows. Whatever furnishings it once had, have long been removed, most likely when the town was abandoned.

"Sad," Miko says as they walk across the floor.

"Sad?" questions Jiron. "What makes you say that?"

"Oh, I don't know," he replies. Glancing to him, Miko says, "The place depresses me. Do you think this could have been a church to James' Morcyth?"

"Never know," he says.

At the back of the temple they find two sets of stairs, one going up to the second floor and another leading down into darkness. Jiron glances to Miko and asks, "Up or down?"

"I'll take up," he says.

Jiron nods and turns to descend into the darkness.

On his way up the stairs, Miko is careful to make sure the steps will support him. On several different occasions over the last few days some of the buildings they've searched have been rotted, termites or other such insects having robbed the wood of its integrity.

He places his feet gingerly on each step before moving to the next. One step cracks and he immediately removes his foot. Stepping over the suspect step he continues up until finally reaching the upper rooms.

This area is smaller than the one below as most of the second floor is taken up by the upper reaches of the service area below. There are only three rooms here and he makes his way first into one and then another. The second room looks to have been living quarters of the priests, four beds are spaced evenly about the room. Two chests sit at either end of the room and he moves forward toward the one closest to him.

In the back of his mind he hears James telling him not to open chests as they may be booby trapped. He remembers that one occurrence in the swamp when a trap sent him flying across the room when it exploded in his face.

Disregarding James' voice of caution, he continues toward it. *I can't imagine there would be anything dangerous with a chest here.* Even though he feels that way, when he reaches it he slows down and hesitates a moment before reaching for the lid. Taking hold of it, he flings it open while at the same time jumping backward. The lid flies up, hits the wall behind it and then slams shut again.

Miko waits a moment and when nothing fatal happens, goes back over and opens the lid slowly. The inside of the chest is empty. He reaches in and feels around the sides and bottom but fails to feel anything which might indicate something hidden. Disappointed, he closes the lid and turns to walk over to the other chest.

As he moves across the room to the other chest, he looks at it closely. It looks just as the other had so it's unlikely anything will be wrong with it too.

Three feet from the chest, the floor suddenly breaks open slightly and his foot crashes through. "Aaaaaahhhh!" he cries. Pain erupts from where his foot is wedged in between the broken boards.

"Jiron!" he screams. He tries to pull his foot out but that only increases his pain, the jagged edges of the broken planks are cutting into his skin. He starts to panic when he sees drops of blood begin to well from where the wood is imbedded into him. "Jiron!"

Down below in the basement, Jiron walks with a makeshift torch. He found a chair and broke it apart. Using one of its legs, he tied an old cloth around it and then used flint to strike a spark to light it.

The basement is fairly empty, some old boxes and crates. He rummages around for several minutes before he hears Miko's cry from upstairs. Pulling a knife, he races back up the stairs to the ground floor then takes the steps leading to the second floor.

His foot hits the one step which Miko had bypassed before and it breaks in two beneath him. Losing his balance, his foot sinks through the step and he falls upon the stairs. The torch goes flying out of his hand as he stops himself and comes to land a few steps above him.

"Jiron, help me!" he hears Miko cry out again.

"Coming!" he hollers back. Pulling his foot out of the hole, he finds only a few scrapes on his calf and then gets to his feet. Stepping over the hole in the stairs, he picks up his torch and races the rest of the way to the top.

"Where are you?" he hollers as he reaches the top.

"In here!" Miko yells, a touch of fear in his voice.

Running down the hall, he bolts through the door to the room where Miko is stuck and comes to a stop as he sees him there. "What happened?" he asks as he sheaths his knife.

"The floor gave way and my foot's trapped," he explains. "Help me out of here will you?"

Grinning despite the gravity of the situation Jiron comes over to him. Miko's leg is sunk into the floor to just below the knee and he takes note of the jagged edges biting into him. He puts out his torch so it won't catch the building on fire and then kneels down next to him.

Blood is now flowing from a couple wounds. He tries to pull his leg out but that only drives the wood in deeper and elicits a cry of pain from Miko. "Don't!" he cries.

Next he tries to push the boards away but that hurts just as bad. Not sure just what to do, he looks at Miko and says, "I need to get the others."

A haunted look leaps to Miko's face as he realizes Jiron is suggesting leaving him here alone. "Don't leave me!" he exclaims.

"I don't see that I have a choice," he says. "I could get you out but not sure how much pain and damage I would cause in the process." He gets to his feet, "I won't be long."

"Jiron," Miko says pleadingly.

"I'll be right back," he says as he races from the room.

Taking the steps two and three at a time, he hits the bottom running and is soon out the front door, racing to where James and the others are searching. "James!" he hollers as he runs through the streets.

"James!" he cries again.

"What's wrong?" Fifer asks as he and Qyrll dash around a corner to see what he's yelling about.

"Miko's hurt," he says.

Just then James and Dave enter the street further down and run toward them. Uther and Jorry come running down a side street. "Where's Miko?" James asks.

Turning back the way he came, Jiron says, "He's hurt. His foot broke through the floor and it's wedged in there pretty bad." Breaking into a run, he leads them back to the old temple. "Need help to get him out."

The others follow him as he races back down the street. When the temple appears down the road ahead of them, they see Miko being led out of the front by someone who looks just like the miner he mentioned seeing days before.

"Miko!" James cries.

The miner stops dead in his tracks and glances their way. He begins moaning and wailing as he reaches out toward them with one hand.

Jiron takes in the scene, Miko having his hands tied behind him and a gag in his mouth. "The miner is no ghost!" he exclaims, drawing both knives as he bolts forward.

Miko lurches toward the miner and knocks him down the stairs. Losing his balance, Miko falls as well and lands upon the steps with a thud.

The miner rolls down to the bottom of the stairs and quickly gets to his feet. One glance at Jiron approaching and all pretense of being a ghost disappears. The man turns and runs for his life down the street.

"Get the miner!" James yells to the others. "I'll take care of Miko." As the others take off after the miner, he approaches Miko and helps him to sit up.

With a groan, Miko gets to a sitting position. His leg that had been entrapped in the floor has a blood soaked cloth tied around it, with more blood still oozing through. James removes the gag from his mouth and then uses it to tie around the wound in an attempt to stop the blood loss.

"He came to me up there," Miko says through gritted teeth. "At first I thought he was a ghost but then he gagged me and got me out of the floor." Gasping, he stops talking when James tightens the knot securing the rag in place. "Ripped my leg some doing it."

"I think that will do for now," he says. "When we get you back to the horses we'll do a better job."

"Thanks," he says.

The sound of approaching feet heralds the return of Jiron and the others. Marching in front of them and looking the worse for wear is the miner. His face is reddening slightly on one side and a trickle of blood can be seen from the corner of his mouth.

"Good job," says James.

"He almost lost us by ducking into a building but Fifer was smart enough to run around to the other side and tackled him as he left," Jiron says. Shoving the miner forward toward James he says, "Not much of a ghost."

Shaking his head, James replies, "They usually aren't once you figure out what's really going on." He glances to Dave with a grin and says, "A man in a mask."

At first Dave doesn't know what he's talking about but then cracks a brief grin as he nods. "I get you," he says, remembering Saturday morning cartoons.

"What should we do with him?" Uther asks.

"I say we kill him right here," Jorry threatens.

"No!" the miner cries out. "Don't kill me. I wasn't going to hurt anyone."

"Oh yeah? Then what were you going to do with our friend here?" he asks as he indicated Miko.

Defeated, the man says, "I just wanted to scare you away. I would've let him go after awhile."

"Were you the ghosts we saw last night?" Qyrll suddenly asks.

Glancing at the tattooed visage of Qyrll, the man nods. "Usually that's all it takes before everyone leaves. You guys wouldn't go."

"Have you been doing this long?" James asks him.

"Years and years," the man explains.

"Why?" Jiron asks.

When the man doesn't reply, James says, "There are only two reasons I can think of. One, you like your privacy and I somehow doubt that would be the reason. Or two, you discovered something up here you would rather not share with the rest of the world."

The miner's eyes widen at the last one and James nods. "Thought so. What did you find?" he asks. "Gold? Gems?"

Staring back in silence, the miner refuses to answer.

Taking a knife out, Jiron asks, "Want me to persuade him to talk?" Holding the knife before the miner, he threatens him menacingly.

"No and put that away," James tells him. "We don't need to know that badly." To the miner he says, "You keep your secrets, I really don't care."

"What are you going to do with me?" he asks.

"What should we do with you?" asks James in return.

"I will cause you no more trouble," the man whines. "If you let me go, I'll not bother you again. I swear."

"Very well," says James, seeing the earnestness in his eyes. "I see no benefit in either your death or keeping you with us. Get out of here."

As the miner is about to leave, Dave pipes up. "Ask him," he says.

"What?" asks James.

With the others looking on, Dave explains. "We've come all this way and can't find what you're looking for. Maybe he knows."

The miner stops and glances around at everyone. "I don't know anything." He resumes moving quickly away from them.

"Hang on a minute," James says to the miner.

The miner, having reached the edge of the group, bolts away only to be quickly tackled and returned by Jorry and Uther. "He wanted to ask you a question," Uther tells him.

Standing once more in front of James, the miner looks at him in trepidation.

"I am on sort of a quest," he tells the miner, "and it has led me here. Maybe you would be kind enough to aid me?"

Glancing at the others, he realizes he has no choice. "How?" he asks, feet shifting nervously.

Pulling out the medallion, he holds it before the miner. "Have you ever seen this design before?" James asks.

His eyes widen in recognitions. Nodding he says, "Yes, once."

Getting to his feet, James asks, "Where?"

The miner's lips twitch in agitation as he gazes into James' eyes. Pointing off to northeast, he says, "Deep in the mountains near a small lake are some old ruins." He glances around to see what effect his words are having. "I saw that design on one of the buildings there."

"Can you take us there?" James asks him.

"Why should I?" questions the miner.

"If you do," James tells him, "I promise that we will keep the secret of who and what the ghost inhabiting Ironhold really is to ourselves."

"Otherwise we tell everyone from here to Cardri," Jiron assures him.

Sighing, the miner says, "Alright. I suppose you want to leave now?"

"That's right," replies James.

"Very well," he says. "I need to get my horse and some supplies before we head out."

"Jorry, you and Uther go with him so he won't have a change of heart," Jiron says.

"Don't you trust me?" the miner asks.

At that several of them there break into a short laugh. "Hardly," replies Jiron. To Uther he says, "When he's got his stuff together, bring him back here."

"You got it." To the miner Uther says, "Let's go."

As he and Jorry escort the miner to collect his horse and belongings, the others go to retrieve their own horses.

"Now maybe we can get back home soon," Dave says as he walks next to James back to where the horses are tied.

He said home. Encouraged that his friend may be coming to accept his life here, he feels like a load has been lifted off of him.

They return to the horses, and after doing a proper job on binding Miko's wound, are soon back at the temple. Another ten minutes and they see Jorry and Uther come walking back with the miner, his horse trailing along behind.

Once they're all mounted, Jiron asks, "How far is this place?"

"Couple days," he replies. "It's not really all that far, it's just hard to get to."

"Lead on," James says. The miner nudges his horse into motion and the others follow.

When they've disappeared down the road, two figures leave a nearby building. "Spread the word," one of them says. "They're on the move."

Chapter Twenty Nine

They take the east road out of town and travel for a couple hours. It's much smaller than the main one going north and south. As it turns out, it does in fact lead to one of the abandoned mines in the area. A small ramshackle cluster of buildings sits several hundred feet from the entrance.

"Every mine in the area had a small group of buildings to house the miners while they worked," the miner explains to them when they come into view. "These were little more than barracks, the miners spent their off time in Ironhold."

"How do you know this?" Fifer asks.

"Been here long enough now to piece it together," he explains.

"Ever seen an actual spirit?" inquires Qyrll.

The miner eyes him before replying. "Never actually saw one, no," he admits. "But I've heard things while here that has set my nerves on edge, could've been just the wind."

They make their way through the buildings, several of which are in need of an extreme amount of repair to make them serviceable. One has a roof that's collapsed and another has a big hole in the wall, looks like something at one time ran into it.

Past the buildings they head toward the opening of the mine, but turn off onto a small path before reaching it.

Looking at the dark entrance, Jorry asks, "How many mines are there?"

"Three main ones," the miner replies. "I found several other places where it looked like people had begun a new one but gave up."

"Where do you mine?" Uther asks.

At that the miner becomes quiet and leads them on in silence for awhile.

The path they're following is little more than a game trail and at times are forced to ride in single file. In the lead is the miner with James following right behind. Jiron is behind him with Dave next in line. Jorry and Uther have the thankless duty of bringing up the rear. Winding through the trees, the path makes its way through the hills until finally coming to a place where the trees open up. In the valley below is a large lake.

"Is that the lake you were talking about?" James asks as he gazes at the panoramic view. The lake is a startling blue, nestled in against the backdrop of a mountain range to the north. Altogether a stunning scene.

Glancing back to him, the miner replies, "No. That one lies another day or two to the north. We're going to have to make our way to the left around this lake until we come to a river that flows into it from the lake we're heading for."

"Oh," grunts James.

By the time they get to the shore of the lake, the sun has dipped to the peaks in the distance. "We should stop here and continue in the morning," the miner announces.

"I agree," states James. To the others he says, "We're staying here tonight."

Dismounting they set about making camp and have a fire going in no time. Sitting around the fire, the miner glances to James and asks, "Just what is your interest in this place anyway?"

"A long time ago, there was a god named Morcyth whose followers were fairly wide spread," James explains. "Ever heard of him?"

Shaking his head, the miner says, "No."

"Not surprising, his followers disappeared around five centuries ago." Taking out the medallion, he shows him the design and says, "This was the symbol for their religion. I've been trying to find where the last priests went, you see they disappeared about the same time."

"And you think they went here?" the miner asks.

"Perhaps," he replies. "Won't know until we get there. But it's likely."

The night begins to settle in and the stars appear above them. They've acquired a good store of wood for the evening, already the temperature has dropped significantly. The clear sky above them tells of another cold night to come.

"Do you think they followed us?" Jiron asks after the meal when they're sitting around the fire.

"Who?" asks the miner. "Who followed us?"

"You didn't see them around Ironhold?" asks Fifer.

Shaking his head, the miner says, "The only ones I saw were you."

"Forces from the Empire have been camped in the hills around Ironhold since we showed up, maybe before," James tells him.

"What do they want?" the miner asks.

"Me, us," replies James.

"You going to get me killed!" the miner exclaims.

"Now settle down," Jiron tells him. "They've known of our presence there for days and have done nothing so far."

"So far," he says, none too happy. He scans the woods around them as if expecting an imminent attack at any moment.

"As soon as we get to where you saw the design, you can leave," James tells him.

"Just be careful about running into them on your way back," suggests Fifer. "They may want to talk to you about us."

Scowling, the miner looks at each in turn then stares at the fire, deep in thought.

To Jiron James says, "Better have two on watch at a time tonight, just in case."

Nodding, Jiron replies, "Good idea." He then sets up a watch schedule and those not pulling the first watch lay out their blankets as close to the fire as they can.

The night passes uneventfully and they are up and on their way with the rising of the sun. The miner turns them north and follows the shoreline of the lake. They don't travel very far before coming to a medium sized river flowing from the north.

Before James has a chance to ask, the miner says, "This ain't the one. We have to cross it and continue following the lake until we reach the next river. Then we can follow that one north to where you want to go."

Turning upriver, he leads them to a ford a mile up. After crossing, he backtracks along the other side of the river and returns to the lake. Following its shoreline, he continues along as it curves to follow a more easterly direction.

The going here is slow, as they have to at times forge their way through tangled undergrowth. Several hours pass as they make slow headway. Finally the shoreline becomes inaccessible to them when the side of the mountain rises up against the water's edge.

"We have to leave the lake now and work our way through the mountains," the miner says. "If we're lucky, we'll reach the river before the sun goes down."

"Why would that be lucky?" Uther asks.

"Just a figure of speech," the miner says, annoyed he's being taken too literally.

"Oh," replies Uther.

Picking up another game trail, they leave the shore and move into the forest. The terrain becomes increasingly rugged and as they climb up the side of the mountain, the density of the trees diminishes proportionately.

As they climb, the wind hits them with more biting chill than it had when they were in the protection of the forest. Now that the trees are thinning, the wind is able to get to them more effectively. Pulling their jackets closer, they push on.

At one promontory the miner stops them for a short break. Off to the side they find snow on the ground among the trees. "Man that's not a good sign," Jorry states.

"At least it's clear now," Fifer says hopefully, looking to the sky. "If the clouds move in we can expect snow."

"I agree," says James. "We're definitely above the snowline now."

Qyrll has climbed up above them and is standing on an outcropping of rock. James notices him there peering out over the way they had come. "See anything?" he asks.

The others take note of what he's doing as he looks down to James and shakes his head. "Nothing."

"Maybe they didn't follow us," offers Miko hopefully.

"Oh you can bet they're out there," states Dave. Looking back through the trees, he adds, "I doubt if they'll give up this easily."

"You seem awfully sure of that," Jiron says as he comes to stand before him.

Anger building, Dave replies, "If they followed us to Ironhold, you would think they would have kept an eye on us. Any fool should know that."

"I don't like the tone of your voice," Jiron says, his own anger beginning to rise.

Stepping in between them, James holds a hand up to each and says, "Enough of that!" Staring them both down, he adds, "We have too much to worry about already, we don't need your squabbling adding to it."

Jiron gives Dave a glare then turns to James, "Sorry." Turning his back on Dave, he stalks off.

"You two need to get along," James tells his friend Dave.

"I ain't the one not getting along," he says. "Nothing I do or say will make any difference." He turns aside and walks back to check on his horse.

James just stands there and stares at his two friends walking away. Saddened by how they don't get along, he just shakes his head. Try as he might the rift between them continues to grow, neither of them seems even remotely interested in trying to mend it.

They get underway shortly thereafter and as they proceed, an awkward silence hangs over them. By the time they stop for lunch it hasn't improved any. James sits eating his food and glances from one to the other. Dave has sunk into another depression with anger seeming to be boiling under the surface. Jiron on the other hand appears his regular self, that is until he glances toward Dave. Then James notices a slight tightening around the eyes and a grim expression comes to him.

After their lunch break they once again forge their way along the path through the mountains. Near the midafternoon an enormous mountain to the north comes into view. Snow capped and rising high into the sky, it dominates everything around it.

"Would you look at that!" Miko breathes as they crest a ridge and the mountain comes into view.

"Impressive," agrees James. It easily rises a thousand foot or more over that of any other peak.

The miner glances back to see the reaction the sight of the mountain has brought forth. Giving them a grin he says, "That's Kiliticus, the king of all mountains. They say no mountain is taller in the world."

A shiver runs through James as he looks to the mountain in the distance. "Would where we are going be at the base of that mountain?" he asks, mouth suddenly dry.

"Yes, it would," the miner replies. "A small lake sits at its base and along its shores are the ruins."

His voice catching in his throat, he asks, "Does the lake have a name?"

Shrugging, the miner says, "If it does I never heard it. Why?"

James glances around him and he can see what he's thinking reflecting back in the eyes of the others. *At the foot of the king, bathe in his cup.*

"Ellinwyrd must have been meaning the mountain, not Ironhold," Jiron says.

Nodding, James says, "Yes! That's got to be it." To the miner he asks, "How long until we get there?"

The miner glances from James, to the others and then back again, he can see something is going on. "We'll be there tomorrow," he answers.

"Good," says James, his spirits again high. Not even the tension between Dave and Jiron is able to dampen his mood now. His goal is about to be reached.

Evening finds them winding their way down to the bottom of a deep valley with a river cutting its way through. "That's the river we'll follow to those ruins," the miner announces. "If we leave first thing in the morning, we should be able to get there by late afternoon."

"It doesn't look all that far," Uther says as he gazes to Kiliticus in the distance.

"Don't let its size fool you," he says. "It's further than it looks."

"Damn," mutters Jorry in awe.

Another hour finds them nearing the base of the valley and they hunt for a good place in which to make camp. Once found, they set up camp.

The valley acts like a funnel for the wind coming off the mountain. They build a large roaring fire to ward off the chill and spend a very cold and uncomfortable night. The person on watch never wanders far from the fire and makes sure to keep the blaze going well throughout the night.

As the morning brightens with dawn's approach, they quickly get underway. Everyone is anxious to get there, find what they came here for and then get out. They definitely don't want to be here should snow begin falling. The trip back, over the terrain they just navigated would be most treacherous indeed if covered in snow.

Two hours after dawn, the sun finally rises over the peaks to the east. The sun does little to warm the riders as they make their way along the river. Throughout the day, Kiliticus continues to rise ever higher as they draw nearer.

The river, beside which they're riding, is little more than a glorified stream. There are two places where they have to leave its banks in order to make it around boulders jutting out of the ground. The whole valley is a rugged wilderness, a place James feels sure few people have ever been.

After a brief stop for a bite to eat around noon, they head out again and ride another hour before the lake at the base of Kiliticus comes into view. Sitting as it does at the base of the mammoth mountain, it appears small by comparison. But as they approach, it's revealed as being fairly large.

The miner brings them to a stop and when they've all gathered near says, "If you look on the far shore of the lake, you will see the ruins."

Sure enough, when James looks he can make out several structures. Excited, he urges them onward and they move as quickly as they can. It takes a little over an hour before they reach the southern side of the lake, the area from which the river they've been following issues forth.

James takes the lead in his impatience and hurries around the lake. The ruins grow ever closer and his excitement and anticipation mounts. He glances back to the miner and asks, "Where exactly did you see the symbol?"

He points to the largest structure situated in the middle of the ruins. "It lies within that building."

Kicking the sides of his horse, James bolts forward.

"James, wait!" Jiron hollers but he doesn't pay attention in his excitement. Kicking his horse into a gallop, he and the others race after him.

The ruins are the size of a small village. There's even evidence of a dock which had once extended out upon the water, small pilings protrude from the water. All the buildings are moss covered and overgrown with vegetation. Many of the buildings have plants growing within their interiors, as well as a few trees growing right through what used to be the roofs of two of them.

Jiron scans the area for any dangers, but doesn't find any. The only danger he feels they're likely to find would be some large predator that may have made one of these buildings its own.

James flies around the dilapidated buildings until finally arriving at the large structure in the middle. He brings his horse to a stop near the front entrance and dismounts just as Jiron arrives next to him.

"You shouldn't run headlong into unknown territory like that," chides Jiron as he gets down from his horse. The others arrive and begin dismounting shortly after.

"Sorry," apologizes James. "I just got caught up in the moment."

The building before them has to have been a temple at one time. No statues or other adornment are visible but the feel of the place brings them to that conclusion. The front doors are closed tight and blazoned upon each is the Star of Morcyth.

"This is it," breathes James. Excitement rising like an irresistible tide, he steps forward toward the three steps leading up to the doors. Jiron moves to go around him but he lays a hand on his arm and says, "Not this time."

Jiron nods and allows James to be the first to enter.

James takes the steps to the door with the others following close behind. Hand trembling in anticipation, he reaches out and takes hold of the door handle. Taking a deep breath to calm himself, he turns the handle and opens the door.

The ravages of time have not spared this building either. The door opens several inches before stopping. Turning back to the others, he says, "Feels like there's something blocking it."

"Push harder," Uther suggests just as Jorry asks, "Need any help?"

Turning back to the door, he shoves hard with his shoulder and the door suddenly bursts into the room. Something hits him in the leg, a little sapling is growing before the door and had snapped back after the door was pushed over it. "Just a tree," he says to the others.

Inside the building, one of the large windows has been broken out and a pile of leaves as well as other dead vegetation lie beneath it from where the wind deposited them over the years. The room he walks into is a large central meeting area. It looks nothing like any church or temple he's been in before. This may have served as more than just a meeting place to worship Morcyth.

Tables and chairs are situated about the room, many having fallen prey to insects and lie rotted upon the floor. Off to one side is what has to be the altar. It's made of wood and shows the wear of time as everything else does.

Jiron makes his way toward it and asks, "Doesn't this look familiar?"

James comes over and takes a closer look. It's a roughly four foot high pedestal with a small platform atop it. Upon closer examination, the platform has the Star of Morcyth engraved within it. Glancing back to Jiron he shakes his head, "No, I can't place it."

"It's the same as the one we found back in the City of Light when we first met," he explains.

"Right, under your hideout," he says. Now it comes to him. When he and Jiron first met, they ended up having to flee through an underground secret passage which the medallion had opened. There they found a room with a marble pedestal with a crystal platform on top similar to this one. Only that one, instead of having the Star of Morcyth engraved within it, had an open space within it in the shape of an inverted pyramid.

He reaches up and tries to remove the platform but it is an integral part of the altar and doesn't budge. The one in the City of Light had revealed a secret door when removed. He tries putting the Star diagram of his medallion on the Star of the platform but that fails to yield any results.

The others have spread out to search the building, Fifer and Qyrll take the stairs to the upper level and return shortly. "Nothing up there but a couple rooms filled with moss covered furniture."

"Let me see," says James and he takes the stairs up. Two rooms sit across from each other at the top of the stairs and after a brief examination, turns up nothing.

As he comes back down, Jiron says, "I don't think you'll find anything in here."

"Why not?" James asks.

"Remember the riddle from Saragon?" he replies. "It said 'At the foot of the king, bathe in his cup.' Seems to me the 'cup' would be the lake out there." He then points out the open window to where they can see the lake a short ways away.

He contemplates that for a minute, and after another quick glance around the temple says, "You may be right." He then turns to Fifer and says, "Take the others and see if you can find a building we can use as a headquarters while we search the area. Get the horses settled in and gather wood, we may be here a while."

"You got it," he says. Taking Qyrll, Jorry and Uther with him, he takes care of it.

Leaving the temple, James and the rest move toward the lake. Jiron turns to the miner and asks, "Is there another way out of here?"

"Why?" he asks.

"In the event the Empire's forces show up, we may not have the option of returning the way we came," he explains.

"I'm not sure," he admits. "I only came here once and that was years ago."

Glancing around at the area surrounding them, he hopes there may be another way out. The fact that the Empire's soldiers had been camped around Ironhold makes him nervous. Despite not having seen any evidence of them being followed, he knows they're out there somewhere.

At the water's edge, James comes to a stop and looks around. He mumbles to himself, 'At the foot of the king, bathe in his cup. Pull his beard to make him sit up.' Gazing first one way and then the other, he doesn't see anything which could remotely be considered a beard.

The water doesn't even come to the edge of the mountain. Rather it ends several hundred feet before, most of the buildings sit between the water and where the mountain begins its rise.

"Maybe you have to get into the water," suggests Jiron.

Turning to glance at him he exclaims, "Are you crazy? That water must be at or near freezing. I wouldn't last more than a minute."

"Yeah," adds Dave. "Think next time."

Jiron turns a cold stare toward him which is returned with equal intensity. His hand is flexing upon a hilt of one of his knifes and only the presence of James prevents him from killing Dave on the spot. Getting his anger under control, he returns his attention to James and says, "It did say 'Bathe in his cup'." Gesturing to the water he adds, "That seems to be the only thing around here which could be considered a cup."

James brings his gaze to the water and a shiver runs through him as he contemplates the idea of entering its frigid depths. "Man I don't want to do that," he says. "If we can't come up with another theory, I'll do it tomorrow. Until then, let's try to figure another way."

"As you will," he says.

The sound of someone approaching from the town causes him to turn and see Fifer walking toward them. "We found a building which will suffice," he says. "It has all four walls still intact and most of the ceiling. It's large enough for us as well as the horses, might've been an inn."

"Good," says James. Glancing to where the sun is reaching toward the peaks to the west, he turns to Jiron and says, "We better make sure to post a watch tonight. Don't want the Empire getting the drop on us now, not with us being so close and all."

"I figured as much already," he says. "Two to a watch."

They follow Fifer back to the building he's staked out for their headquarters. It does look like an inn, there are several rooms off the ground floor but they're all planning on staying together in the common room. Better to keep warm that way.

Once there, James tells the miner that he'll no longer hold him should he wish to depart.

"If it's all the same with you guys, I'd just as soon stay," he says. "With all the talk of the Empire being out there, I wouldn't want to head back alone."

"You're more than welcomed to stay," James assures him.

James and Dave have the first watch. They figure Dave will be okay on watch as long as he's with his friend. No one else would have him any way.

Bundling up tight, he and Dave leave the inn after having a quick meal and set about finding a spot from which they can keep an eye on what's going on. A nearby building with an upper story will work out perfectly. One wall has caved in and most of the upper area has as well. From up there they have an unrestricted view of almost the entire settlement.

"Can't we have a fire?" asks Dave after ten minutes of freezing in the cold breeze.

"We dare not risk it," replies James. "Besides ruining our night vision, anyone in the area will know we're up here."

Teeth chattering, Dave says, "I don't care, I'm freezing!"

"Relax, it's only another hour before we go get Jorry and Uther for their watch." The darkness is beginning to settle in and it isn't long before they can't see much more than shadows.

Their watch passes uneventfully and Dave is quite happy when they return to the warmth of the inn and wake Jorry and Uther for their turn at watch. James explains to them where the lookout they found is and they're soon out the door.

Dave settles in by the fire, dropping off to sleep quickly. James on the other hand sits up for awhile as he tries to figure out another way other than getting into the water.

Chapter Thirty

The following morning, the only alternative James could come up with is constructing a raft and floating out upon the surface. If that fails to produce any results then he'll brave the icy water.

It takes them some time to construct a raft large enough to support him safely. Miko suggested for him to use his magic in the effort but he was simply too concerned with there being another mage in the area who might pick up on it. If a mage was with the Empire's force, who knows what he would do should he detect magic being used.

So it took longer than it could have but they finally put one together before lunch. James is more than happy to put off going out there while they take a break and have something to eat.

"What are you looking for out there?" Jorry asks during their meal.

"I don't really know," he replies. "On the face of it, it seems kind of dumb."

"Prophecies are often that way," agrees Uther. "They make no sense until it's time for them to be understood."

"I guess we'll just have to see," he says.

"...a thin, white blanket. You then walk with a lantern underneath and it makes the glowing apparition appear." From across the room James hears the miner, who has yet to tell anyone his name, explain to Qyrll how he produced some of the spectral effects. "You have to make sure you are far enough away so no one will see through the disguise."

Nodding, Qyrll says, "Makes sense.

James just shakes his head at them. Qyrll has been after the miner for his secrets on haunting Ironhold and he's been more than glad to share them. Seems he's been out of contact with people for a long time and Qyrll's keen interest makes him feel good.

When at last the meal is over and James can put it off no longer, they all go down to the lake where the makeshift raft sits. Uther was there securing the last few logs together while the rest finished their lunch. The whole thing looks rather dubious. Having put it together without the aid of an axe has left many branches sticking out at odd angles. To James it looks like a giant porcupine, at least there will be plenty of handholds to keep him atop it.

Jiron plans on coming along and has a long stripped pole which he'll use to move the raft away from shore. Lying in the center of the raft are two wide strips of bark which they'll be able to use as paddles when the pole is no longer effective. Moving to the raft, Jiron boards it first while Jorry and Uther hold it steady.

"Hurry up man," Jorry says from where he stands in the water. "I think my feet are going numb." He makes his way on and then holds onto a protruding branch while James comes forward.

Stepping carefully, he makes his way onto the raft and takes his place in the center. Once he's seated firmly on the logs, he nods to Jorry and Uther who release the raft and hurry out of the water.

Taking his pole, Jiron begins pushing them away from shore. "How far should we go?" he asks after they've moved out a dozen yards or so.

"Middle, if we can," he replies.

"Don't think my pole is going to be able to reach the bottom much longer," he tells him. The depth of the water has steadily increased, especially once they've moved fifty feet from shore. Suddenly, the pole sinks almost to the surface of the water before Jiron brings it to a stop. Pulling it up, he lays it across the raft.

Picking up one of the pieces of bark they'll use for paddles, he hands it to James and says, "Looks like we use these from here."

James takes the 'paddle' and moves to the side opposite Jiron and begins paddling. At first they start to spin as either he or Jiron paddles harder than the other, but then they get a good rhythm down and start moving in a more straight line toward the middle of the lake.

As he paddles, he glances back occasionally to those still on the shore and the mountain behind them. They remain there, staring at their progress across the lake. The sun riding high in the sky keeps the chill at bay. At times water splashes onto him from when he dips his paddle in the water and he realizes just how cold this water is, freezing may be an understatement. They paddle until the raft reaches roughly the center of the lake and then they stop.

"Now what?" asks Jiron.

"I haven't a clue," he says. "For all we know that line may simply be there to throw people off. Nothing ever said that every line of a prophecy has to mean something."

"Can you give it to me one more time?" asks Jiron.

"Sure," he replies.

When the Fire shines Bright,
And the Star walks the Land.
Time for the Lost,
Will soon be at Hand.

At the foot of the King,
Bathe in his Cup.
Pull his Beard,
To make him sit Up.

Seven to Nine,
Six to Four.
Spit in the Wind,
And open the Door.

"Hmmm," muses Jiron as he contemplates the words. "The second verse refers to the king in every line. Seems important." He then turns his attention to the mountain which dominates the entire area. Kiliticus rises immensely behind their comrades on the shore.

"Does a mountain have a beard?" he asks after a few minutes of silence.

"I don't think so," replies James. "Is there an outcropping of rock perhaps that appears like a beard?"

They both stare at the mountain and scrutinize its surface. There are many outcroppings and overhangs, but nothing which even remotely resembles a beard. "I think we may be going about this the wrong way," Jiron says.

"What do you mean?" asks James.

"This isn't accomplishing anything," he says. "Think we should return to shore and see if we can come at this another way?"

The only other way which James can think of is to take the line literally and get into the water. He's simply not willing to do that unless there's no other alternative. "We haven't been out here very long," he says. "Give it a couple more hours and if we're still without a clue, we'll go back."

"Very well," he says. Making himself as comfortable as possible, Jiron waits. At first the view from the center of the lake is enough to keep him distracted, but after awhile he begins nodding off. Not too concerned, he's sure James will wake him should anything happen.

If he didn't have the possible future of going into the water, James would find this a lot more relaxing. Out here in the middle of the lake is very peaceful. The mountains surrounding them give the area a charm he hasn't found for a long time. Snowcapped mountains covered in trees with the blue sky above them, absolutely beautiful.

Over on the shore the others have given up watching him and begun to explore the ruins. He doesn't blame them, he's sure at first they thought something important was going to happen. When it failed to materialize they grew bored and began finding something else to do.

The quiet seems to rejuvenate his spirit, bringing him a peace he hasn't had for some time. What with all the fighting and bickering between the various members of his group and all the attempts made on his life, this is really the first time he's been able to completely relax in weeks. Putting his cares aside for a moment, he tries to enjoy the tranquility.

His mind drifts back to the time he and Meliana spent together on her father's ship just after they came to his rescue. You can bet he was surprised when he saw who it was that rescued him. A smile comes to him at the thought of what his grandparents would say if they knew he was in love. Yes, he is in love. All doubt had been shattered when he looked at her at the railing as he was climbing up from the rescue boat.

Once things settle down he'll return to Corillian and find her, though how long that will be is uncertain. Most likely she'll find another man by then, the thought dampens his mood somewhat. But then the fact that she made the long voyage all the way from Corillian on the off chance he may be in Cardri comes to mind. She wouldn't have done that unless her heart was driving her, and it's unlikely she'll find another unless all hope of their union is gone.

Hours drift by and he realizes nothing is going to happen, but the peace of where he is keeps him there. The gently rolling of the raft as it floats upon the water and the sun beating down on him lulls him into a deep relaxation which brings him to the brink of sleep.

Splash!

"Aaaaaahhhh!" he cries as frigid water drenches him from head to toe.

"What happened?" asks Jiron as he's wrenched from slumber by James' cry.

"Some damn fish just breached and splashed me with water," he says.

Jiron looks over to him and sees where water is running down the side of his face. Laughing, he says, "It must have been some big fish."

"It's not funny, I'm freezing," he complains. His hair is now slightly matted to his face and his clothes are sticking to him.

"Time to return?" asks Jiron.

Nodding, with teeth slightly chattering he replies, "Yes." Picking up one of the crude paddles he begins paddling back to shore. The day is already coming to a close, he had no idea they had been out there that long. Over to west the sun is nearing the peaks and the shadows are beginning to grow long.

One person remains on the shore, looks to be Miko. When he sees them paddling for shore, he gets to his feet and races back to the ruins. Shortly the others gather by the water's edge to greet them on their return.

When they're about halfway to shore, James' eye catches something from the mountain and he glances to its slopes. Not sure at first what caught his eye it takes him a moment to realize just what he's seeing.

Concentrating on his paddling, Jiron doesn't realize James has stopped until the raft begins to turn in a circle instead of forward. Looking to his friend, he sees him staring with mouth slightly open at the mountain. He stops paddling as he turns to look. He's about to ask him what's going on when he sees it too, a shadowy face on the slope of the mountain. And the face has a beard. "How is that possible?" he asks.

Grabbing his paddle, James replies, "I don't know but try to remember where the end of the beard is." Paddling with renewed determination, he and Jiron push for shore.

They continuously glance at the shadowy visage upon the mountain, trying to fix in their minds exactly where the end of the beard lies. It looks to end at a large outcropping of stone jutting out from the side of the mountain.

As they near the beach, James yells, "We found it!"

"Where?" asks Fifer.

Beaching the raft, James and Jiron jump to the sand and break into a run. "Up the mountain!" he cries as he and Jiron race for the spot before the light completely fades. It's a little ways up the mountain from where the ruins sit and as they climb, the sun drops behind the mountains and the shadows disappear.

"What did you see?" asks Miko.

"A face in shadows," replies James.

"A face?" questions Qyrll.

"Yes," he answers.

"But how is that possible?" Uther asks as he follows along behind.

From the front of the group, James' voice comes back to him, "I don't know."

They continue working their way up the slope. Darkness begins to creep into the world as the light slowly fades away. Before it fails altogether, the outcropping of rock which coincided with the shadow's beard comes into view.

The rock around them begins to show signs of having been worked. Right angles, which could never be formed with such precision by nature start to appear. What use they held can no longer be determined.

Forging through the underbrush James suddenly comes into a clearing and before him lies the outcropping. The signs of human workmanship can be seen all over now. Holding out his hand, his orb suddenly springs to life for him to see better as the light has all but faded away.

In the glow of the orb, he approaches the outcropping. "Examine the whole area," he says. "Look for any sign of the Star." Suddenly, several other orbs spring into being and the entire area is flooded with light.

"Won't this attract anyone in the area?" Jiron asks him.

"Damn, forgot about that in my excitement," he says as he looks around at the blazing orbs. Then he glances back to Jiron and shrugs, "Too late now."

"At least we have the high ground," Qyrll says.

"What?" asks Jorry.

"The high ground," he explains. "The fighter upon the high ground has a better tactical advantage."

"Oh," he says.

"You should know that," Uther pipes up. "Remember that time when…" He and Jorry go off together as he begins another of his stories.

Pull his beard to make him sit up. *Should that be taken literally? If so, then how do you pull a shadow?* Questions run through James' mind as he ponders the best course of action. The others are hunting as well, looking over, under and around for any place bearing the Star of Morcyth. He is sure that is what must be found. Down to the center of his being he knows that to be true.

Dave is standing off to the side, not being very helpful. Oh sure, whenever James glances his way he makes it seem that he is actively looking. When he turns back, he goes back to watching the others, a look on his face saying this is dumb.

It was during just such a time when Jiron comes up behind him and asks, "Why aren't you helping?"

Dave turns around to see him there with fists on his hips and a scowl on his face. "What business is it of yours?"

Eyes narrowing, Jiron replies slightly louder than necessary, "You are supposed to be James' friend. Yet when everyone else is trying their best to aid him, you stand around as if you don't care or are just too lazy." After a moment of silence as they stare at each other, he adds in contempt, "You make me sick."

The others pause in their searching while they move closer to where the growing drama is unfolding. From the far side of the clearing, James takes notice of what's transpiring and hurries over.

"Why don't you leave me alone?" Dave says, voice rising in irritation. Glancing around at the others he continues. "You all have done nothing but treat me like dirt ever since we first met. You can all just go to hell!"

"Dave!" exclaims James as he comes to stand near them.

"Sorry to have to say that James," he says, "but it's true. You care more about these butchers than you do about me. And I've been your friend longer."

"Butchers?" Uther retorts his anger getting the best of him. "We ain't the ones going around killing girls!"

At that Dave looks in shock at him and takes a step backward.

Uther turns his attention to James and says, "That's right. He's the one who's been killing all the girls wherever we go."

James looks in horror at Uther then glances to Dave. "Is this true?" he asks, voice barely able to speak the words.

Before he has a chance to reply, Jorry adds, "We saw him with that innkeeper's daughter the evening before she turned up dead."

Looking pleadingly at his friend, Dave says, "I had nothing to do with her death. You've got to believe me."

"You were with her then?" he asks.

Nodding, he says, "For a short time. She was nice and we talked, but that was all. I left her alive!" Glancing at the others standing around him, he sees they don't believe him. "You all are just trying to turn him against me!"

"Is that what you were planning on doing to Tersa?" asks Jiron enraged.

"Everyone settle down!" yells James. "Jiron, back off."

Jiron flashes him a look but holds his ground.

"Now, did anyone see him kill anybody?" he asks. Looking around at them, he sees them all shake their heads negatively. To Uther he asks, "What makes you believe this?"

"Girls have ended up dead wherever we go," he explains. "I think it more than coincidence that he was seen in the company of one before she turns up dead."

"James," Dave whispers, "you've got to believe me."

"He's also been acting odd ever since he's joined us," adds Fifer. "Moody, easily angered."

"What he's been through could explain that easily enough," James replies. He looks to his friend and sees a look of abject pleading. *Could it be?* The thought goes against what he knows of his friend and he refuses to even give it credence by considering it more.

He gazes from one to the other, in everyone's eyes he can see they believe him to be guilty. At last his eyes settle on his friend, his life long friend. So many times Dave's been there for him. He knows what kind of person he is and it isn't a killer. Years of shared experiences, fun, is he to throw all of it away?

The others are waiting for him to make a decision but it's one which can only go one way. "Since no one witnessed the act, I can't bring myself to believe it could happen," he finally says. "Where I come from we believe in the credo 'Innocent until proven guilty'. As no one saw the crime, I cannot simply assume his guilt."

"Then you believe me?" asks Dave. His lower lip trembles as he awaits James' answer.

"Yes Dave," he says, "I believe you."

"Well I don't," Jiron says as he moves toward Dave.

"Jiron!" cries James but he pays no attention.

Before anyone can react, Jiron strikes out with a first and connects with Dave's jaw, sending him flying backward. He stumbles into Fifer who pushes him forward only to be greeted by another roundhouse which lifts him off the ground a foot.

Oof!

His breath is knocked out of him as his back slams to the ground.

"Jiron stop it!" cries James and rushes to protect his friend but Jorry and Uther grab his arms, preventing him from interfering.

Walking toward Dave lying on the ground, Jiron says, "This has needed doing for far too long." Dave tries to scramble backward out of his reach but Jiron reaches him and kicks him hard in the side.

Crying out, Dave rolls over and continues rolling to avoid the next kick which barely misses him.

"You'll kill him!" James yells but Jiron doesn't even flinch.

Dave suddenly rolls right to the side of the outcropping and runs out of space as he rolls against the rock. "You're out of room," Jiron says as he nears.

"No!" cries out James as Jiron pulls back his foot to kick him in the head. Suddenly, a wave of force ripples through the air toward Jiron and throws him through the air where he strikes the outcropping. Falling to the ground, he gets to his feet quickly and turns a face full of rage toward James.

"Let me go!" he yells to Jorry and Uther who promptly let go. He rushes over to his friend lying on the ground, blood oozing from the corner of his mouth where he bit his lip when Jiron struck him.

"Dave!" he cries out and Dave looks up at him just before passing out. Making sure he's okay first, he then turns to the others. Jiron is getting up off the ground and James says, "No one will hurt him. Do you understand?"

Jiron glares at him.

"You are my friend," he says to him. Then to the others he adds, "You all are but this witch hunt will end here," he says. "Dave will not be mistreated in any way. If you have proof, lay it before me otherwise I don't want to hear it."

He stares at each in turn and one by one they give him a nod. When he at last comes to Jiron he waits but no nod is forthcoming. "Jiron, you are to leave him alone," he insists.

Jiron simply stares back at him in defiance. He never thought to be on the receiving end of James' magic and he's not sure how to take it. After another moment, he nods his head almost imperceptibly.

"You okay?" he asks Jiron.

Giving him another slight nod he turns away and walks out of the lighted area into the night. Qyrll and Fifer go with him.

He watches him stalk away, saddened by the fact he used his power on him. Jiron has always been a trusted companion and with any luck this won't come between them. Returning his attention to his friend Dave, he kneels down next to him.

Laying a hand upon his chest, he gives him a little shake and says softly, "Dave." When he receives no reaction, he shakes him more vigorously, "Dave, wake up!"

Eyes flying open, they look around quickly but then finally focus on James' face there before him.

"How are ya doing?" he asks, concern for his friend in his voice.

"Where's Jiron?" he asks in reply.

Nodding off to the side, he says, "Over there somewhere. He won't bother you again."

Sitting up, Dave looks around at the others staring at him, distrust and a little bit of anger is all he sees. "I'm sorry for everything James," he finally says.

"It's alright Dave," assures James. "I understand." Getting up, he holds out a hand.

Taking it, he makes it to his feet. His jaw is sore from where Jiron connected with it but otherwise still serviceable.

James glances around and that's when he notices the outcropping where Jiron hit is cracked. He didn't think Jiron hit all that hard but a one inch crack runs down the side. Intrigued for some reason, he moves toward it and realizes the crack is much too straight and even to be the result of the impact.

Uther comes up behind him and says, "Maybe we should resume the search in the morning when there's more light and everyone has had a chance to calm down."

Not paying him any attention, James reaches out to the crack and inserts his fingers within it. Pulling slightly, the crack widens and then the piece of outcropping suddenly comes loose and falls to the ground with a crash.

"Would you look at that," Jorry says from where he and Uther are standing behind James. Everyone moves closer to look, even Jiron comes out of the dark to see what's going on.

On the face of the outcropping where the other piece detached is engraved the Star of Morcyth. "James," Miko breathes in anticipation, "use your medallion."

Taking it out, he removes it from around his neck and sets it in the diagram. When nothing happens, he tries to turn it and a good portion of the rock surrounding the Star rotates a quarter turn before stopping.

From further up the outcropping, a grinding noise can be heard as a section of the rock face rises. Jiron rushes over and peers inside. He glances to where James and the others are watching, "Stairs and they go down."

"That's it!" exclaims James. Removing the Star from the diagram in the outcropping, he places it around his neck again and hurries over to where Jiron stands next to the opening. The glowing orbs illuminating the clearing suddenly wink out and a single one springs to life on the palm of his hand. "Let's go," he says as he moves through the opening and begins to take the stairs down.

Jiron and Dave both move to be the next to follow, but after a warning glare from Jiron, Dave backs down and is the third through. Even the miner goes with them, intrigued by all the unusual happenings. Of course most likely he didn't want to remain out there all by himself.

Finally, Jorry and Uther bring up the rear and the clearing is once more dark and quiet.

Chapter Thirty One

The first thing James notices after entering the opening is a slight breeze coming from within. It brings the smell of earth and mustiness with it. Twenty steps bring him to a small narrow way carved out of the rock. Barely wide enough to allow one man to walk without scraping his shoulders, it extends further into the mountain.

"Be careful," Jiron says to him.

"Hadn't planned on not being careful," he replies.

He follows the narrow passageway and eventually comes to a natural cavern that's barely large enough for them all to fit. One section of the wall on their right has been smoothed and seven recesses have been carved into the surface.

Six of the recesses sit in two rows, one atop the other. The first and third in each row are of uniform size and each center recess is a third of the size of the others. It goes: large, small, large. The seventh recess is a foot away from the others along the wall and contains many small iron cubes.

Miko moves to the cubes and picks one up. Rust has begun to eat away at it but the cube hasn't deteriorated very much. Holding it up for James to see he says, "Wonder what these are for?"

"I don't know," James replies. Glancing around he realizes the only way for them to leave is the way they came. The breeze he's been feeling is coming through a small narrow fissure in the wall on the opposite side from where the recesses lie.

"Another secret door?" Jiron asks. He remembers all the other times when it looked like there was no way to proceed and each time James had managed to discover a secret door.

"I would think so," he says. "Everybody stand back and give me room." He begins examining the walls with his fingers, checking every nook and cranny. When he gets to the fissure where the breeze is blowing through he brings his orb close to try to look through to the other side but is unable to see anything. Spending extra time there, he fails to find anything and then moves on.

"Going to use your magic?" Jiron asks.

Shrugging he says, "If I have too. But let's see if it can be figured out without that. Might attract unwanted visitors, though they may already know we're here anyway."

"At the foot of the king, bathe in his cup, pull his beard to make him sit up," Fifer says from where he's standing watching James do his thing. "That makes sense now. At the base of Kiliticus, you got on the water and saw a bearded figure made by the shadows cast by the setting sun. At the spot where the shadow's beard lay, we pulled down a piece of the outcropping and with your medallion, a piece rose up."

He glances over to where James had paused in his search to listen to him. "Maybe the next set of lines will aid us here."

Seven to Nine,
Six to Four.
Spit in the wind,
And open the door.

"That's the last of the prophecy," he says.

"Okay then," says Fifer. "There's a breeze coming through here so that could be the wind. But what does seven to nine and six to four have to do with anything?"

"How about these?" suggests Miko. Everyone turns and sees him there with one of the iron cubes in his hand. "These have to be here for a reason."

"Could the numbers mentioned in the prophecy correlate to the two rows of holes in the wall?" Qyrll asks.

Coming to where Miko stands before the iron cubes, James does a quick count and finds there probably could be enough to put the specified numbers in each of the four major recesses. "Let's see," he says as he and Miko begin taking the cubes from their resting place and putting them in the recesses.

On the top row they put seven cubes in the left one and nine in the right. The second row gets six in the first one and four in the last. "There's still some left over," Miko says as he points to the four cubes left.

"That's probably to throw off whoever makes it this far," suggests James. "Without the prophecy they would be trying to use them all and it wouldn't work."

Nodding, he replies, "Makes sense."

They all hold their breath for a moment, expecting something to happen, but the room remains quiescent. "Nothing's happening," Uther says.

"Maybe you should spit into the wind," the miner suggests. When James turns to look at him he shrugs and says, "It is part of the prophecy."

"Very well," he says. To the others he says, "Stand back." As the others move to get out of the way, he turns to face the breeze and lets fly a big wad of spittle. Just then a gust suddenly blows through the opening and causes the spittle to fly back toward him and hits him in the face.

"Hahahaha," Miko breaks into uncontrollable laughter as James begins wiping his face clean with his arm.

"Well that didn't accomplish anything," he says, giving Miko an irritated look. No wall opened or anything.

Jiron moves to where the breeze is coming through and takes hold of the fissure and tries to pull and then push it open. "Maybe it wasn't so much that you had to do it but rather to indicate where the door is." Try as he might he can't budge it.

"We're missing something," he says as he comes over and joins Jiron in attempting to open the door, if door it be.

From where Qyrll is standing, he hears him mumble, "Seven to nine, six to four." Suddenly, the Parvati lets out with a laugh.

"What's so funny?" asks Fifer.

"We're thinking about this wrong," he says. "It's not seven to nine, it's seven, *two*, nine. The four remaining blocks are supposed to go into the middle areas."

"Worth a try," says James. He moves over to where the four remaining cubes lay and picks them up. He puts two in the top center recess first, then the last two into the bottom. As soon as the last cube is placed within, each recess sinks down a quarter of an inch and a click can be heard coming from the wall with the fissure.

Turning back around to face the fissure, Jiron takes hold and pulls hard. On hinges groaning from centuries of accumulated rust, the fissure swings opens and reveals another narrow passage.

"Yes!" exclaims James in jubilation and he moves to enter. As he passes Qyrll he says, "Smart thinking."

The Parvati simply nods in acknowledgement as James passes.

"So the Star is down here?" Dave asks, looking into the dark opening.

"I would think so," replies James. "All the sections of the prophecy have been utilized, but you never know." Taking the lead, James moves into the passage, the orb lighting the way.

The passage leads further into the mountain for another hundred feet or so before opening onto another underground cavern. This one here is reminiscent of the ones they found when working their way beneath the Merchant's Pass. Stalactites and stalagmites, as well as the continuous dripping of water creates an eerie atmosphere. The shadows cast by the orb as James moves through gives an otherworldly feel to the place.

"Just like the Shasta Caverns," whispers Dave.

James grins at the memory of when Dave's family had taken him on their trip north that one year and they stopped at the Caverns. "It is a little," he agrees.

A flow of water runs along the bottom of the cavern. It enters from a hole in the wall on one side and continues to follow the length of the cavern. Though not very deep, James can see how this little stream could have carved out this cavern over the course of a millennium.

The antagonism between Dave and Jiron seems to have been subdued with the discovery of this secret area. They are more interested in what it may hold than the enmity they hold for each other.

They follow the stream through the cavern. The cavern not being very wide, the orb is able to illuminate both sides as they make their way through. So far there has been no other way to go but forward.

After another couple hundred feet of following the stream, the floor of the cavern becomes less smooth and more broken. The sound of the water increases as it flows over the uneven surface.

As they continue through the cavern, the streambed begins sinking further into the floor of the cavern from where the water has eroded the stone away. Finally, they reach the other side of the cavern. A large jagged opening, encompassing part of the cavern wall and floor allows the water to flow from the room. The sound of the water falling over a precipice can be heard coming from somewhere on the other side.

Back a ways from the opening where the water is escaping, a section of the wall has been smoothed. An arched door sits within it. No handle or any other discernable means with which to open the door can be seen.

Next to it is what looks to be a stone scabbard and sticking out of the top is a shiny handle. James comes over to it with the others right behind. He reaches out for the handle and hesitates. Glancing back to the others, he sees Jiron nod his head. Turning back to the handle, he grips it and pulls it out.

It's a foot long knife, the edge is incredibly sharp. Just as he turns back to show Jiron, he feels the tingle of magic and above the door, glowing letters begin to appear.

> **'With the Knife of Maricel you must take the life,**
> **Of the one that fire aged through strife.'**

"What does that mean?" Dave asks in puzzlement. He glances to James and sees a look of horror on his face. "What?"

James knows full well what it means. Miko is the one the Fire aged through strife. When Miko had the Fire, every time he went into battle the Fire aged him until at last his youth was gone. He looks to Miko and can see he's come to the same conclusion. If they are to continue, Miko must die!

James sits against the wall with the Knife of Maricel resting on the ground beside him. He's been sitting here almost a half hour now as he tries to come up with another meaning to the words glowing above the door than Miko's death. *This can't be right!* Morcyth is a god of good, it's inconceivable that a human sacrifice would be asked by a god such as he.

Miko and Jiron, as well as everyone else but Dave, congregate over by the outflow of the stream. They talk in hushed tones, occasionally casting quick glances over to where James sits in contemplation. Dave sits near him but remains quiet.

A memory comes to James, one from long ago when he first met Serenna back in Willimet, before becoming the leader of a cult. *"I see a long road but you are not alone, another walks with you,"* she said to him. *"He will be the key, a lock must be opened."*

Is this the lock which must be opened? It has to be. But taking Miko's life? Even if it means not fulfilling why he's been brought to this world, it's something he's unwilling to do. Coming to his decision, he takes the knife in his hand and stands up.

The others come near when they take notice of him coming to his feet. Miko comes forward and with a haunted look in his eyes says, "James if you must do this…" His voice cracks and he's unable to finish.

Giving him a smile, James lays his hand upon his shoulder. "I will not kill you Miko," he assures his friend. "Even if it means my quest ends here and forever remains unfulfilled."

"But…" Miko says, tears coming to his eyes.

"If Morcyth is such a god as requires the death of a good man, then I want no part of him," James says then turns toward the door. Walking forward, he takes the Knife of Maricel and places it back into the scabbard.

Suddenly, the tingling sensation he's felt since the words first appeared above the door spikes. Backing quickly away from the door, he watches as lines form around the perimeter of the door. Then in a flash, the door vanishes and the way is open.

Qyrll suddenly breaks into a laugh which draws the attention of the others. When all eyes are upon him, he says, "Don't you see? It was a test of morals. Only one who would not take an innocent life would be allowed to pass. Any agent of Dmon-Li who read those words would have killed and killed in an attempt to open that door. Very clever."

"Thank you," James hears Miko say next to him. Turning toward him, he sees him wiping a tear from his eye. "I could never kill you," he assures his friend. Raising the orb he moves to the opened doorway. "Now," he says glancing back over his shoulder, "let's see what's in here."

He steps through the doorway and into a large circular chamber, the cavernous ceiling disappears into the darkness above. A two foot wide ledge runs around the length of the chamber. Sitting in the center of the chamber is an island of rock surrounded by a fifteen foot wide chasm. The only access to it is a narrow stone bridge which arches its way across.

Sitting in the middle of the island is a small, plain wooden chest. Other than that, the island is bare. James makes to step onto the stone bridge leading across the chasm. Jiron puts his hand on his shoulder and says, "Not this time. Better let me take it from here."

Hesitating a moment, he nods when he sees the wisdom in the suggestion. Stepping back, he allows Jiron to cross.

Uther comes to the edge and looks down. "Let's see just how deep this is," he says. Picking up a rock, he drops it into the darkness below. Jiron pauses before crossing and listens with the others. No sound comes back to them.

Jorry looks to Uther and says, "That's pretty deep." Uther nods in agreement.

Jiron then resumes crossing the bridge and reaches where it ends on the island. Stepping hesitantly upon the stone surface he gradually places his entire weight upon the island. When nothing happens he cautiously walks across to where the chest sits.

Before touching it he does a cursory check and finds a round area on the front with the Star of Morcyth engraved upon it. Realizing he'll need James' medallion as a key, he turns back to the others and hollers for him to come across.

"I think it's okay but it looks like your medallion will be the key to open it," he says when James joins him beside the chest. The others have followed as well and stopped several feet away.

Taking the medallion out of his shirt, he sets it into the Star on the chest and then turns it clockwise. The Star on the chest rotates a full turn and then the lid pops open slightly. Replacing the medallion back around his neck, he lifts the lid.

As the lid opens, he finds a large gem resting upon a velvet cushion. It's comparable in size to the Fire and can only be the Star of Morcyth. He turns back to the others and says, "Miko, come here."

As Miko begins crossing the bridge spanning the chasm, a light suddenly flashes from within the chest and James goes rigid. "Jiron!" Miko cries when he sees James start toppling backward.

Moving quickly, Jiron grabs James before he hits the ground. Lowering him the rest of the way, he looks up at the approach of the others and says, "He's stiff."

"Is he alive?" Dave asks.

"I'm not sure," he replies. Placing his ear against James' chest he can hear the slight lubdub of his heart. "His heart's still beating," he says in relief.

"What happened?" Jorry asks.

"I don't know," replies Jiron.

The city is in ruins but the citizens appear jovial. In the background he can hear a band playing a lively tune and from a side street children emerge as they play a game of tag, laughing and giggling.

As he walks down the street, he notices signs of rebuilding all over. Up ahead is a grand building which looks like it's recently been completed. A temple.

He walks toward the structure and before he reaches the entrance, a figure emerges through the two large ornate doors. Bearing a hat and blue vest, the man looks oddly familiar.

"Welcome," the man says.

"Am I late?" he asks.

"No, you're right on time," the man replies as he opens the door wider to allow him to enter.

Suddenly, he's in an octagonal shaped room with a marble pedestal standing in the center. Atop the pedestal is a small raised platform made entirely of crystal. A bright light shines from a large gem resting upon the raised platform, illuminating the room.

"Where are we?" he asks.

"The High Temple of Morcyth," is the reply.

He glances to the man in the vest and asks, "Why are we here?"

"To show you what must be done," the man replies. "The Temple must be rebuilt."

"Where?" he asks.

"Where it stood in ages past," the man explains. "The only place it may be built."

"Is this why I was brought to this world?" he asks. "To build the Temple?"

"Among other things, yes," is the reply. "A war is going on which you humans know nothing about, one which could lead to the end of all you know."

"What kind of war?" he asks.

"One between the gods," the man says. "You've seen the results already, of what can happen to a world when the forces of evil prevail."

"That place with the shadows?" he asks.

"Yes, that world was consumed by those who follow evil," the man explains. "Dmon-Li is simply one of many who strive for dominance, world by world. When Morcyth's priests were decimated and on the verge of extinction, a plan was set in motion to bring about his return. The balance must be maintained."

"Am I the instrument to bring about his return?" he asks.

"It's already begun," the man replies. "His name is once more being spoken, that alone will not be enough however. He needs a focal point for people to direct their energy toward, in that way his priests can work to counter the evil."

"So the Temple must be built," he concludes. "It will be the focal point."

"Yes," the man says.

He turns to look the man in the eyes and asks, "Am I to be the High Priest?"

Shaking his head, the man says, "No, that task lies with another."

Sudden realization strikes him, "The Temple was in the City of Light!"

"That is correct," the man affirms.

"But, the Empire is in control of the City," he says. "They won't allow us to build it!"

"That is true," the man says. Turning to face him, the man adds, "As long as they control the City."

"But that means..."

"You must drive them out," concludes the man.
"But…"
"It's time for you to go," Igor tells him. *"You can stay no longer."*
"But…" begins James but then the world around him fades away.

They are all gathered around him as he lays there unmoving, worried about whether or not he'll come around. Suddenly, his chest heaves as he takes a deep breath and his eyes open.

He at first looks around, not remembering where he is. Then his eyes settle upon Jiron and Miko standing there with the others and the memory returns.

"Man are we glad you're back," Jiron says.

"We were worried about you," Miko tells him.

Sitting up, he asks, "How long was I out?"

"Not too long," Uther says. "Ten minutes or so."

"What happened to you?" Fifer asks.

"It's all fuzzy," he says. "I think it was a vision of some kind."

"A vision?" asks Qyrll, now keenly interested. "What was it?"

James looks around at the others and that's when he realizes Dave isn't among them. "Where's Dave?" he asks.

"Who cares?" Jiron replies. "Probably gone off to be by himself again."

Getting to his feet, he looks around and he's nowhere to be found. "Dave!" he calls but receives no answer.

"Did you guys do something to him?" he asks, his eyes finally settling on Jiron.

"Don't look at me," he says. "If I had done something I would've told you. We've all been here next to you ever since you collapsed."

"Dave!" he calls again, now becoming worried.

To Miko he says, "Get the Star and put it in your pouch."

"Me?" he asks.

"Do you think that's wise?" Jiron asks. "Considering what happened last time that is."

"I don't think you have much to worry about with the Star," he assures them. "Morcyth is a god of learning. The worst that could happen is that you would become smarter."

Looking dubious at the prospect of handling another item of such power, Miko gives in and goes over to the chest.

"Dave!" hollers James again, now becoming visibly agitated with worry. "Where are you?" His voice reverberates throughout the chamber but no reply from Dave is forthcoming.

"It's gone!" cries Miko.

Everyone turns at his exclamation and James rushes forward. "What do you mean it's gone?"

"Look for yourself," Miko says, standing aside.

James comes forward and looks inside the chest only to find the velvet cushion. The Star is gone!

"I'll kill him!" exclaims Jiron. A knife flashes in his hand as he races for the bridge spanning the chasm. He's soon over it and through the door.

James comes to the same unfathomable conclusion as had Jiron. If the Star is missing, and Dave is missing, then Dave took it. But why? "Jiron!" he screams as he races in pursuit. The others run after him.

Increasing the brilliance of the orb, he races through the door and into the cavern. Ahead of him he sees the back of Jiron as he flies around the stalagmites and pools of water.

"No!" he hears Jiron yell as he somehow starts running even faster. In but a few seconds he realizes what made Jiron yell. The other door, the one that was opened by placing the cubes in the recesses is closed.

Jiron hits the hidden door but it withstands the impact and doesn't budge. "Dave I'll kill you!" he screams through the fissure.

James comes up to him and skids to a stop. Shoving Jiron aside he puts his mouth to the fissure and yells, "Dave!"

From the other side he can hear Dave's voice, "Sorry James." His voice is full of sadness and regret. "I...I have to."

"Dave," he says, trying to get his anger and hurt under control, "open the door."

"You don't understand," Dave says. "My master needs this. H...he said I must bring it to him."

"Dave, we've been friends a long time," James says in a clam, soothing voice. "I can't believe you will leave me here to die."

Dave's voice grows fainter as if he's moving away from the door. "I...I gotta go. They'll be here any minute." A moment's silence and then he says almost so quietly James can't make out the words, "Remember, you said you would always be my friend. No matter what."

"Dave!" James cries out. When there's no response he screams for all he's worth, "DAVE!" When only silence comes from the other side, anger boils up inside him and he tells everyone, "Stand back."

Everyone scrambles back, Fifer grabs the miner when he doesn't move fast enough and jerks him away from the door. Summoning the magic, James lashes out at the door and it explodes outward into the other room.

For a brief moment he can see the light emanating from the Star ahead in the narrow passage leading from the room to the stairs. Sobbing can be heard as Dave races up the stairs.

Jiron flies past James and enters the passage in pursuit. Rushing behind, James and the others follow. James no sooner enters the passage than he feels the tingling sensation of someone doing magic. Then it suddenly spikes and the ground begins to tremble.

"Back!" he yells coming to a stop. Turning around, he and the others beat a hasty retreat back to the room with the cubes. Barely able to keep on their feet due to the shaking of the ground, they race out of the passage and cross the rubble strewn room and make their way into the cavern.

"Jiron, get back here!" James cries as he pauses where the secret door had stood for a moment.

Then all hell breaks loose. The ground shakes even more and stones start falling from the ceiling. A loud roar and then a belch of dust explodes outward from the passage. "Jiron!" cries out James as the sound of a massive cave-in reaches them.

The rumbling continues for a few more seconds then all becomes quiet.

Chapter Thirty Two

"Jiron!" cries out Miko once the rumbling subsides.

Coughing, James begins working his way back through the room toward the collapsed passage. "Jiron!" he cries out. "Dave!" He increases the luminosity of his orb and the light manages to cut through the dust.

"Nothing could have survived that," states Uther as the passage leading out is revealed. Choked with rubble and large stones, it doesn't look like they could have survived.

"Maybe they made it through to the other side?" Miko asks hopefully.

"Let's hope so," says Fifer.

James works his way through the room to the passage and is able to move several feet into it before being forced to stop. "Jiron! Dave!" he cries.

From somewhere within the passage, a muffled, "Here!" can be heard.

"Someone's in there!" he cries and begins removing the rubble.

Coming to help him, Miko says, "It must be Jiron."

"He was in the rear," agrees Uther.

As Miko and James remove the rubble, the others take the stones and pile them further back in the room away from the opening. Slowly, the rubble is removed from the passage. Fortunately it's only the smaller blocks of stone which made it this far and so between them, they are able to move them out of the way.

"Are you okay?" asks James.

This time the unmistakable voice of Jiron replies, "My leg's trapped under a block of stone. I think it's broken."

"Sit tight, we'll get you out of there," Miko hollers.

"Is Dave with you?" James asks.

"No," he replies. "Saw him make it out before the ceiling caved in."

Dave on the loose with the Star, and from what he said on the way to the Empire's forces to hand it over. He just can't believe Dave would do such a thing. What did they do to him?

"I see your light," Jiron tells them after another ten minutes of digging.

James quickens his pace and removes several more stones and climbs to the top of the remaining rubble. Holding his light so it shines beyond, he looks down and finds Jiron lying upon the stairs. A massive stone rests just above him and seems to have given him some shelter against the falling rubble. His left leg looks to be wedged under another large stone.

To the others James says, "Hurry up, we're almost there."

Moving back down, they continue to clear away the rest of the smaller stones. They're forced to leave a couple big slabs as they are simply too heavy for them to lift. When at last they have all the loose rubble cleared away, James backs away and lets Fifer and Qyrll through to see about getting that large slab off him.

"Miko, lend us a hand," Fifer hollers out. "Help Jiron get his foot out when we lift the rock.

Moving in close, he says, "Alright." He moves in next to Jiron and takes his leg.

"Take it easy now," Jiron tells him.

Giving him a reassuring grin, Miko says, "Of course."

Qyrll and Fifer get in position to lift the stone. "On three," says Fifer. "One...two...three!" Lifting with all their might, he and Qyrll strain against the weight of the stone. They manage to lift it an inch and Miko quickly pulls Jiron's leg free.

"He's out!" exclaims Miko.

They carefully set the stone back down and then move to help Jiron to his feet. Miko scrambles out of the way as they help him back out of the passage and into the cube room.

"Set him down over here," James tells them, indicating a spot on the far side of the room. He doesn't want a sudden collapse by the rubble in the passage to possibly cause more damage.

They bring him over and set him on the floor. "Easy!" he says as pain courses through his leg. When they finally have him seated comfortably with his back against the wall, he looks to James. "You're friend has left us here to die."

"I know," he replies in anguish. "I'm sorry."

"What do you plan to do now?" he asks.

Fifer rolls up Jiron's pants and inspects the leg. "Looks like it is broken," he says. He glances to Qyrll and says, "Come with me." With Qyrll behind him, they return back to the cavern and the others can hear them walking off into the distance. Before they get too far, the sound of a flint stone making sparks is heard and another of Qyrll's candles springs to life.

James sits there in silence for a moment and Jiron says, "You haven't answered my question."

"I think the first thing we need to do is figure a way out," he says.

"No, I mean about your friend," he clarifies. "He took off with a very important item."

Sighing, James says, "I know. After we get out, we go and get it back."

"And Dave?" he asks.

Turning sad eyes onto Jiron, he opens his mouth and then closes it again without uttering a sound. Finally he just shakes his head and says, "I don't think we'll have to worry about Dave anymore."

"Why?" Jiron asks, surprised by his answer.

"Remember back when we got the Fire?" he asks. When Jiron nods yes, he says, "The guardian spirits said that *'Only a son of this world may touch it. All others must surely perish.'* The Star is similar in nature to the Fire."

"You think he's going to die?" Jorry asks from where he's been listening in.

Nodding he replies, "I don't know what else that could mean."

Smashing sounds can be heard from far off and soon, Fifer and Qyrll come back with several long wooden pieces they broke off from the chest which had contained the Star. Using them for splints, they tear off strips of cloth from their shirts and bind the broken leg tight.

"That should hold for now," Fifer says. "A priest could do a better job, but we're lacking one just now."

"You could do it," Jiron says.

James turns his attention back to Jiron and sees him staring at him. "I'm no priest," he protests.

"Didn't you say that the spirit of the long dead priest of Morcyth called you one?" he asks.

"Well, yes he did," he replies. "But he was mistaken."

"I don't think so," he says. "You're in good with Morcyth, after all you bear the medallion with his Star. And it has sprung to life for you before."

"I know, but I don't understand how that happened," he counters. "I don't even know if I can heal. Frankly it scares me to death. I just don't know enough about cell structure and vein integrity or anything." He looks at Jiron and finally says, "I could wind up doing more harm than good."

"Very well," he says.

"So, how are we to get out of here?" the miner asks. "I don't know much about what you all are mixed up in but I do know we'll never move that stone without more falling down on our heads."

"Any ideas?" asks James as he glances around the assembled group.

"Blast it out," Miko says. "Use your magic and clear it away."

"Even if I could, there's no guarantee that I wouldn't bring down more on top of us," he says. "Remember, we're under a mountain, a really big mountain." When he sees the lack of hope in Miko's face, he adds, "If all else fails, I'll try."

They pick up Jiron and aid him in moving to the large cavern, finally stopping next to the stream. James bends over and takes a long drink as he considers the next step. He doesn't have that long to dink around, the Star is most likely on the move toward the Empire. He's not sure exactly what would happen should it reach Dmon-Li's priests, but it can't be good.

Almost absentmindedly his eyes follow the stream to where it leaves the cavern through the hole in the wall. Sudden realization hits him, the hole is large enough for them to make it through. Coming to his feet, all eyes are drawn to him as he indicates the outflow of the stream and says, "Maybe we could make it through there?"

They turn to see where he's pointing, Uther jumps up and says, "Might work."

"Yeah," adds Jorry, "the lake out there has to be fed from somewhere. There was water flowing out of it so there must be water flowing in as well."

"What about Jiron?" Fifer asks. "His leg is in no condition to be climbing around in caves."

"Fifer," Jiron says. "What other choice do I have other than staying here?"

"We can help him," says James. To Jiron he asks, "Did you bring that rope with you?" The last time they traveled to Saragon, he had brought a coil of thin rope for emergencies.

Lifting his shirt, he grins as he shows them the rope coiled about his waist. "You know it," he says.

"Alright then," announces James. He motions for Jorry and Uther to come over and he hands the orb to Uther. "Take this and try to find a way through. We'll be right behind you."

Taking the orb, Uther is about to ask if he'll need the light when another orb materializes upon his hand. Nodding to Jiron he says, "You just take care of him and we'll find a way out." To Jorry he says, "Come on," and they head toward the hole in the wall.

Fifer and Miko help Jiron to his feet and they make their way to the opening. When James nears he sees the light from the orb Uther holds already yards away. He's hunched over as he works his way along the narrow passageway.

James enters the opening and finds the footing extremely uneven and treacherous, algae covers many of the rocks and most are not stable. Stepping carefully, he works his way along.

"Easy now," he hears Fifer say to Jiron as they begin entering through the opening. The splint on his leg allows him to put some weight upon it but not nearly enough to enable him to walk on his own.

"James!" Uther hollers to him from up ahead.

"What?" he replies. Slipping and almost falling, he catches himself on a small rock protruding from the side. Looking ahead, he sees them stopped.

"We got problems," he says.

Moving as quickly as he can, he makes his way to where Uther is standing with the orb. When he draws close he sees what Uther is talking about. The stream they've been following suddenly goes over a drop-off and flows down a steep, uneven incline further than the light from the orb illuminates.

The sides of the passage end there as well so there's no way to go around. Down is the only way to go. Shortly everyone makes it there and understands what is before them.

"How far down do you think it is?" the miner asks.

"Could be another five feet or five hundred for all we know," Qyrll states.

"This rope is only fifty feet," Jiron says. "Let's hope it isn't much further than that."

"Maybe there's another way?" Fifer asks.

"The only other one I can think of would be the chasm surrounding the area where we found the Star," James explains. "I doubt if we'll have any better luck with that."

Looking over the side, he sees that it's not a sheer vertical drop, rather a steep narrow incline. With luck they could possible make it. Jiron though will have a hard time, but like he said, what choice has he?

Turning to Uther and Jorry he asks, "Think you can make it?"

"Possibly," admits Uther.

Stepping forward, Qyrll says, "Allow me to lead here." Everyone turns his way as he continues. "Back where I come from we have many instances where we must scale cliffs and overhangs such as these. I would have little trouble with this."

Glancing to Uther, he sees him give a nod in agreement and then says, "Alright. Uther, hand him the orb." After Qyrll has the orb and begins to descend over the side he adds, "We'll stay here, let us know if this way is feasible."

"I will, worry not," and with that he begins to descend in earnest.

James comes over to where Jiron is propped up against a rock. "You doing okay?" he asks.

Shrugging he replies, "As best as can be I suppose. I'm alive at least." He shifts his broken leg and grimaces.

"How's he doing?" James hollers over to where Fifer is keeping an eye on Qyrll's progress.

"Better than I would have," answers Uther. "He's moving fast."

They wait there for another five or ten minutes before Fifer turns from the drop-off and says, "He's waving the orb. I think he's reached the bottom."

James gets up from beside Jiron and approaches the edge. Looking over, he sees him way down below. All that can be seen is the orb moving from side to side.

Next to him Miko asks, "Is he saying it's clear or that he's in trouble?"

"Maybe we should have set up a signal but I didn't think it was going to be so far," admits James. He gauges the distance and doesn't figure on Jiron's rope being able to stretch even half that distance. Coming to a decision, he gathers the others around him and says, "We're going to have to help Jiron down in stages. Fifer, you stay with Jiron and it will be your job to aid him from stage to stage."

"The rest of us will position ourselves in increments of fifty feet or so to hold the rope steady while you two make it down. Then once you're past, we'll follow. Understand?" When he gets everyone's nod, he goes to the edge and waves his orb back and forth to tell Qyrll he saw his signal. Once Qyrll has stopped moving his orb, James turns back to the others.

"Okay Miko, you first," he says. One by one they descend down the side of the drop-off and station themselves at points where the surface levels off slightly and they'll be able to maintain balance while holding the rope. James has remained at the top and once everyone is in position turns to Fifer and says, "Alright, let's do this."

Fifer helps Jiron up and they tie the end of the rope to Jiron. Once James has a secure hold upon the rope and is properly braced, Fifer helps him over the edge. Inch by inch, James lets out slack in the rope as Jiron slowly makes it down to where the miner is waiting at the next stage.

As soon as he's made it there, Fifer waves back to him and he releases the rope. Arms tired and aching from the constant pressure of maintaining a tight grip, he's more than glad to send the rope down to the next person. Slipping over the drop-off, he begins working his way down while the miner holds the rope as Fifer and Jiron work their way down to the next person.

Stage by stage, Jiron and Fifer make their way down until at last they make it to Qyrll. The others arrive shortly after. They find themselves next to an underground lake, a shore of sorts runs along the outer edge in both directions. Jiron wets his finger and holds it up.

"What are you doing?" Uther asks him.

"Seeing if there's a breeze," he replies. After remaining motionless for a minute he shakes his head. "If there is one I can't tell." He turns to James and says, "It's up to you." When he hesitates, Jiron adds, "They already know we're here."

"True," he agrees. In front of him a translucent bubble springs into existence.

"What's that going to do?" the miner asks in wonder. Sure he's heard of magic but seeing it up close kind of unnerves him, first the orb and now this.

"It will lead us to the way out," replies James.

As if floating on a breeze, the bubble begins floating to the right around the lake. Fifer and Qyrll help Jiron to stand and they all begin following the bubble. Those helping Jiron along are unable to keep up, so James has Miko stay with them with one of the orbs while he, Jorry and Uther move ahead keep the orb within sight. The miner stays back with Jiron's group.

The cavern is rather large, stalactites and stalagmites decorate the scene with many colors. Small creatures, blind and translucent, scurry out of the way as the light from James' orb reveals them. From several places, other cascades of water flow from crevices and fissures in the walls to the lake.

Continuing its dance upon an unseen wind, the bubble floats on. It comes to an opening to their right, a dark gaping maw which extends further into the mountain. Rather than entering the opening, the bubble continues on past. James pauses but a moment to look within but the light from his orb reveals nothing.

They continue following the bubble for another ten minutes when a noise can be heard coming from up ahead. At first it sounds like the growl of some wild beast but then James realizes it's the sound of water. The water of the lake is no longer placid but ripples as small waves course across its surface.

The further they go, the louder the sound becomes and the movement of the water along the shore becomes more pronounced, the waves coming with more frequency. Suddenly the source of the sound they've been hearing appears before them and James stops in stunned silence.

Illuminated by the light from the orb is a massive vortex at the end of the lake. Swirling and churning, the water is being sucked down as if through a giant funnel. "Oh my god," he says as he realizes the bubble is moving to hover over the center of the maelstrom.

"You can't be serious," Uther says in disbelief next to him. He glances back to the others advancing toward them. "Oh Miko..." he says in voice loud enough to carry over the sound of the water being sucked into the maelstrom.

The others come close and when they can see why they've stopped, various expletives, not all of them polite issue forth.

Jorry glances to see Miko's face frozen in extreme nervousness. "You ready for a bath?" he asks.

He looks at him and stiffens his backbone as he says, "No problem." Then to James he asks, "Is that the way we have to go?"

"It looks like it," he says.

"It must lead to the lake," Qyrll says. "We may not survive it."

"There is no other way," James tells him. Glancing at the others, he says, "The bubble showed us the way out. It wouldn't have led us here if we couldn't survive." He sees the doubts in everyone's eyes, especially Jiron's. How in the world will he be able to make it with his leg the way it is?

"So what do we do?" the miner asks.

"Get in the water and let it suck us down," James tells him. Even though he knows it's the only way, he's not too keen on the idea either.

"But it's freezing," the miner says. "We're not going to last too long in such cold water."

"Anyone have a better idea?" asks James. "This is the way out whether we like it or not." He stands there a moment while everyone digests that.

Jiron hobbles forward and says, "I'll go first."

"I don't think so," Uther says to him. "If anyone is going to be the sacrificial lamb, it better be someone with all their parts working properly." To Jorry he asks, "You game?"

Shrugging in an attempt to appear nonchalant even though fear is one step away from taking over, he replies, "Sure, why not? Time for my bath anyway."

"You got that right," one of the others says, though who he couldn't tell.

"Better space yourselves apart a few minutes so if it gets rough, you won't be thrown against each other," Qyrll suggests.

James steps toward them and says, "Once you're through, I'll check the lake to see if I can find you. Then I'll start sending the rest through starting with Jiron and Fifer. Be ready to help him when he gets there if you can."

Nodding, Uther says, "Alright." He and Jorry begin shedding everything but their weapons and the clothes from their back. When they're in nothing but shirts and pants Uther looks to Jorry and asks, "Odds and evens?"

"I'll take odds," Jorry says.

They face each other and to James it looks like they're going to do a round of paper, rock, scissors. Bringing their hands down onto their other palm, Jorry says, "One." The second time Uther says, "Two."

Then just before they bring their hands down again, Jorry turns and runs toward the swirling maelstrom. With a "Yeehaaw!" he leaps away from the shore and hits the water two yards out. The water immediately grabs him and sucks him toward the center of the swirling water.

"Damn you!" cries out Uther. He had the same idea but Jorry beat him to it.

Around and around the water gradually brings Jorry to the center and then all of a sudden, his head disappears as he's sucked beneath the water. At that, Uther follows and hits the water. A minute later, he too is sucked beneath the surface.

James moves over to the edge of the lake where he and Miko proceed to dig out an area for the water to fill. Then once it's filled, they close it off from the lake and the water within the depression becomes calm.

Giving them a few minutes, he calls forth the magic and an image of the lake appears. He concentrates on Jorry, trying to center the view upon him. The scene shifts and all they can see is the calm surface of the lake. It's hard to see anything in the gloom of night, only the moon above gives any light with which to see.

Suddenly Jorry breaks through the surface of the water and they can see him splash around a bit before he realizes he's broken through. Shortly after that, Uther joins him.

"Alright," James says as he glances to Jiron, "it's your turn."

"Help me up," he says and Miko and Fifer move to comply.

They walk him over to the edge of the maelstrom and ease him into the water. Since he's starting closer to the edge it takes him a little longer before he gets sucked under. After that the others go in two minute intervals until it's only James, Miko and Qyrll left. They've been watching the scene play out on the lake and saw Jiron break the surface. Jorry and Uther immediately moved to help him. It looked like he made it alright.

"You go next," Qyrll says to James. "They'll need you out there if the Empire shows up."

"Good point," he agrees. "Be sure to send Miko next."

Qyrll nods as James moves to the edge of the water. He stands there and looks out over the swirling, churning water. *It's just a big water slide, that's all it is. The others made it through okay, so will you.* With a quick glance back to Miko who gives him an encouraging nod, he backs up two feet and with a running jump, leaps out over the water.

Splash!

He hits the water and the iciness of it takes his breath away. Working to stay afloat, he starts treading water as the current takes him. Moving ever closer to the center of the maelstrom he tries to calm his breathing and just as he feels the current begin to pull him under, takes a deep breath.

Sucked underneath the water by the current, he's suddenly in total blackness. Thrown this way and that, he feels as if he's being dropped down a vertical shaft. Then all of a sudden, the current releases him and he's freefalling. Air surrounds him and he releases the pent up air within and quickly takes another two deep breaths before slamming into more water.

Again he's caught in a whirlpool and sucked underneath. This time he's pulled down and then the flow of water begins turning more horizontal as it picks up speed. He scrapes against the side of the tunnel and feels some of his skin ripped off. Nothing major but enough to cause him pain.

Then when he thinks he can no longer hold his breath, the current quickly reduces speed and he realizes he's no longer in the tunnel but in the lake. Kicking upward, he swims for the surface.

Breaking through, he gasps for air. Teeth chattering from the cold of the water, he tries to calm them but is unable to. The water has sapped all the warmth from him. He's in serious danger of hypothermia and scans for the shore.

"Over here!" he hears someone yell. When he looks, he sees the others in the moonlight, standing on the shore waving him down. Swimming quickly, he makes his way toward them. Reaching the shore next to them, he climbs out onto the beach.

They're all freezing and his teeth aren't the only ones chattering. They've got to get a fire going and soon. "G…gather s…some wood," he stutters.

"Already done," Uther says as he indicates a pile nearby.

Without any warning, James releases the magic and the wood catches fire, roaring to life. Uther staggers backward in shock but then moves closer to bask in the warm glow.

"James!" he hears Miko's panicked cry from the water.

"Over here!" he hollers back.

Miko and then finally Qyrll begin swimming toward the shore and the welcoming fire. Jorry moves to the water to help but neither needs any assistance. Jiron had survived well and his leg didn't suffer any further trauma, much to James' relief.

"Where are the ruins?" he asks.

They all glance around and Qyrll points off to their left and says, "It's over there around the lake."

"We can't stay here long," James tells the others. "We have to go after the Star. It can't be allowed to reach the Empire." He looks around at them, wet and freezing. They're going to need to wait at least until their clothes dry before they attempt the trek around the lake.

Jorry and Uther throw more wood on the fire, building the blaze so they'll dry all the faster. The warmth is luxurious after the bitter chill of the water, it couldn't have been much above freezing.

They stay there by the fire for a little over half an hour before the consensus is that they're sufficiently warm and dry. After tearing apart the fire, they head around the lake to where the ruins lie, and hopefully their horses still remain there. They have extra clothes and blankets there, if the Empire didn't take them.

Surprisingly when they reach the ruins, they find their horses exactly where they left them. When James' gaze falls upon the horse Dave had used, a red hot anger burns within him. Not at Dave, but at the Empire who had taken his life long friend away from him.

As they mount and are about to head out, James turns to the miner and says, "Here's where we part ways. You don't want to be with us when we catch them."

"Are you sure you know the way out?" he asks.

James glances around at the others and sees both Jiron and Qyrll nod, indicating they do. "I think so. I appreciate all the help you've been."

Smiling, the miner replies, "I actually had the time of my life, been too long by myself. Hate to see you all go as a matter of fact."

James brings his horse close to the miner's and holds out his hand. When the miner takes it, he says, "We each have a secret to keep. I think you know what I mean?"

The miner nods, "I'll not say anything."

"Good," says James, releasing his hand. "Neither will we." Turning back to the others he raises his voice and asks, "Will we?"

"No," replies Uther, the others indicating in one form or another they concur.

"Good luck," the miner says.

"You too," James tells him. To the others he says, "Let's ride!" Kicking his horse in the side, he quickly gets into a gallop. Somewhere ahead is the Empire force, Dave and the Star.

Chapter Thirty Three

They leave the ruins behind as they race along the shore of the lake. The sky is beginning to lighten with the coming of dawn and they're able to maintain a quick pace. The mood is electric as each knows they're riding to battle.

"We should be little more than half a day behind them," Jiron says from where he's riding behind James. His broken leg is tied above the knee to the strap securing the saddle onto the horse to prevent it from flopping around. Also, should conflict erupt, he'll be able to maintain his balance while using his knives on those around him.

"I hope we can catch them before they get to Ironhold," replies James. His anger hasn't subsided any, if anything it's increased. The betrayal of his friend, the loss of the Star, all culminating to create a rage biting at the bit to be released.

By the time the sun crests the peaks to the east, they've reached the far shore of the lake and move to follow the small river flowing out of it to the south. At this point Qyrll takes the lead, he's assured them that he remembers the point in which they leave the river to cut through the hills.

Even though they are setting a quicker pace than what they did when they came, it still takes them until almost noon to reach the cutoff point. When they do, Qyrll turns his horse and leads the way up into the mountains.

Eating in the saddle to save time, they only rest when the horses require it. They aren't able to make good time here as the way becomes narrower and the footing less secure. At least they're comforted in the knowledge their prey won't be able to do much better.

Two hours away from the river, Qyrll comes to a halt. He sits there a moment with his head cocked to the side as if listening for something. Further ahead, the trail enters a narrow area of boulders and fallen trees. They will have to ride single file to make it through.

"What's wrong?" James asks as he draws near.

"It's quiet," Qyrll replies.

James listens for a moment and then says, "It's not completely quiet." Birds can be heard in the trees as well as the far off cry of a predator.

Qyrll turns in the saddle and says quietly, "They're waiting for us."

Scanning ahead, James tries to see anyone in the area before him but there's nobody. "I don't see anything."

"Nevertheless, they're there," Qyrll assures him. He turns back to look at the bottleneck the trail winds through. "It's the perfect place to lay an ambush."

"Do they know we're here?" asks Fifer.

"I would think so," replies Qyrll.

"Then they know we know they're there," states James.

Shrugging, he says, "Maybe. I'm sure by stopping here and discussing this, we've put them on guard."

"What should we do?" Uther asks. "If we go forward their crossbowmen will cut us down before we get very far."

"And the longer we wait," adds Jorry, "the further the one with the Star will pull ahead of us."

James looks at Qyrll for a moment and then asks, "You're sure beyond a shadow of a doubt? Because if you're wrong, I'm going to alert them that we're following."

"They're there," he says. "I stake my honor on it." For a Parvati to say that there can be no argument. Their honor is the single most important thing they hold dear, especially Qyrll whose honor has so recently been restored to him.

"Very well," says James. "Let's move back a ways first and then we'll see what we can do."

They turn around and head back down the trail until the bottleneck is no longer visible. Miko is left to keep an eye out in case the soldiers hidden there make a move toward them.

"Find a pool of water," James says as they all dismount, except for Jiron who's still tied to his saddle.

After a short hunt, a pool is located and James comes over to kneel beside it. Letting the magic flow, he concentrates on the bottleneck ahead of them and an image begins to form.

They see the trees and boulders which form the bottleneck and sure enough, spaced in and behind the trees are soldiers of the Empire. A dozen crossbowmen and another two dozen men at arms, as well as one civilian are lying in wait. Further behind them they find the soldier's horses tied in a group.

"That group the Shynti and I saw had fourteen soldiers and two civilians," Qyrll says. "This could be half the force which was sent here."

"And the other half is with whoever has the Star," finishes James. Whoever has it will need to get through Madoc's lines to reach the Empire so would definitely need the others.

"Nice of them to split their forces for us," Uther says in satisfaction. "Will make this all the easier."

Canceling the spell, James gets to his feet. From atop his horse, Jiron asks, "What's the plan?" He thinks for a moment before turning to the others and says, "Okay, here's what we do…"

James steps out on foot by himself and approaches the bottleneck. The shimmer of his shield is barely discernable in the light of day. Once he's covered a hundred feet, the others begin to follow on horseback. Jiron is in the rear leading James' horse.

Maintaining a quick, steady pace James closes the distance to where the trail narrows. As he gets closer, he detects movement among the trees and boulders where the soldiers lay in wait.

Suddenly, a command is given and a dozen bolts fly toward him. Steeling his nerves, he watches as the bolts come straight for him and continues his advance. One by one the bolts strike the shield and are deflected to the side.

Crumph! Crumph! Crumph!

Three massive explosions erupt amidst the soldiers lying in wait, screams of men are heard as they're tossed into the air. Behind him, James hears the others give out with a yell and charge forward.

Jiron comes forward as well and stops when he draws close to James, staying near in case a soldier gets through.

Qyrll is the first to enter the area of destruction and is peppered by falling debris, fortunately none of any size. Both swords out, he vaults from the back of his horse and engages the enemy. Slightly dazed from the concussions of the three explosions, the soldiers put up little resistance at first. But then others from the rear come forward and the battle is joined. Miko and Fifer are the next to arrive with Jorry and Uther right behind.

Facing off against a soldier in a dark uniform, Miko parries a thrust then returns with a slice. The soldier's movements are quick but Miko is able to deflect the attack. Battle rages all around as each faces off with one or more opponents.

Fifer faces two and is having a hard time in breaching their defenses. Both are master swordsmen and just when he thinks he's over matched, a stone flies from behind and takes one through the chest. Hole opening up in his armor from where James' stone hit, the soldier stumbles backward and falls to the ground. Now having just the one, Fifer is able to hold his own.

Jorry and Uther are back to back holding off two each. One of Uther's suffers from a leg injury sustained during the explosions which makes his attacks less precise. "Need any help?" Jorry asks from behind.

"You worry about yourself," Uther says as he feints to the one without injuries and then strikes out toward the other. Striking him across the throat, the man stumbles backward, holding the wound in a vain attempt to prevent his blood from escaping. Finally overcome with loss of blood, he collapses to the ground.

"Ha-ha!" Uther boasts. "One down." Behind the man he's battling, he sees a crossbowman emerge from around one of the trees and begins cocking back his crossbow. Once it's locked into place he turns toward Uther and brings the crossbow to bear.

Uther is distracted by what he's seeing developing behind his opponent and allows his opponent to maneuver through his defenses, sinking his sword into his side. Crying out and abruptly twisting to the side he moves out of the crossbowman's line of fire just as the bolt is released. The bolt flies and barely misses him as he twists. Going over Jorry's shoulder, the bolt strikes one of his opponents right between the eyes and sinks three inches into his skull.

Uther's injury is bad and he's unable to adequately defend himself from the soldier's attacks.

Hack! Hack! Slash!

The soldier beats against his defenses, each time Uther is afraid that he won't be fast enough to bring his sword back for the next attack. The pain in his side flares as he moves first one way and then the other to counter what his opponent is doing. Finally, he brings his sword up to ward off a severe blow and it's knocked out of his hand. Seeing his death coming, he braces himself for the impact.

A shadow suddenly appears and the soldier is bowled over as Miko tackles him to the ground. "Get back to James!" he cries to Uther as he rolls to his feet. Sword at the ready, he prepares for the assault.

The soldier faces Miko and then launches into a series of blinding attacks which he meets and counters. His skill, having been augmented by his time with the Fire, is superior to that of most and this opponent is no exception. He takes the man's measure and after a few passes begins working to bring his sword into just the right angle. When at last the moment is at hand, he feints an attack to his head which causes the soldier to bring his sword up to just the right place, creating a hole. With speed the eye can barely see, Miko brings his sword around and thrusts through the hole, taking the man just to the left of the breastbone and puncturing his heart.

As the man sags to the ground, Miko pulls his sword free and looks around. The crossbowman which had almost killed Uther with his bolt lies dead on the ground, head blown apart by one of James' stones. Glancing around, he sees the battle is over.

Jorry is tending Uther, the wound is serious but not life threatening. Packing the wound with a spare shirt, he rips cloth from another and ties it tight much to the chagrin of his patient.

"Would you be careful!" admonishes Uther.

"Shut up you old woman," Jorry replies back as he ties the last knot.

"Is there anyone alive?" James asks as he and Jiron come forward.

"Over here!" Fifer yells. One soldier who sustained a cut to his sword arm lies on the ground at his feet, Fifer holds his sword threateningly to keep him quiet.

James rushes over and asks, "Do you understand me?"

The soldier glares at him and doesn't reply. James glances to Qyrll who speaks to the man in his own language. The soldier replies back and Qyrll says, "He understands me."

"Ask him what happened to Dave," he says. "I...I need to know."

Qyrll turns back to the man and for several minutes they exchange words. The soldier's face gets a weird look to it as he talks to Qyrll. When at last the soldier finishes speaking, Qyrll turns back to the others.

"Well?" asks James.

The soldier had originally been a part of a mission to hit The Ranch and attempt to capture the rogue mage. But after the incident in the pass, all their plans changed. They had followed James' group until they reached Ironhold and then settled in to wait and watch while he and the others combed the town.

Word was eventually given that they were on the move and so they began the task of following them. He and the others were never given a reason why an attack had not been launched upon the mage and his companions during their time at Ironhold. Some believed it because none wanted to face the magic which has ended some of the most powerful mages of the Empire. Others felt they were waiting for reinforcements.

After reaching the foot of Kiliticus, they were amazed to see two people on a poorly constructed raft paddle out into the middle of the lake and then sit there all day. At first they thought something would happen but were disappointed.

Finally, the two people came to shore and the group climbed up the side of the mountain and lights sprung to life on the darkened slope. It was at that time word was given for all units to converge on the lighted area.

Before they reached the area with the lights, they went out. Using lanterns, they continued the rest of the way and found the opening in the side of the outcropping. The mage in charge of the group, along with two other men began talking about the ramifications of what is happening.

They were there several minutes before the mage starts barking orders and has them make ready to enter. Then suddenly, a blinding white light erupts from the opening and a man stumbles forth.

The ground began to shake as the mage raises his hands and then the mountain caved in. Dust belched forth from the opening and when it cleared, there on the ground lay a man.

The mage and the civilians were next to him, the rest of the soldiers kept their distance. Clutched in the man's hands was the source of the blinding light. In the light, they saw the man's face contorted in some agony, maybe horror, later none could say for sure. An inarticulate cry began to emerge from him as the mage and the other two backed away.

The skin of the man began turning dark and his cries became more feral, less human. Spreading from where his hands gripped the object, the darkness spread quickly. Soon the man's skin where it began had turned black as coal.

The man's cry was cut off when the black spread up his neck. By the time it covered his entire face, the man had stopped moving and lay frozen.

The light from what he clutched in his hands finally diminished completely and the only light left was that coming from the lanterns. The mage glanced to the others for a moment and then picked up a stick. Moving forward, he quickly struck the object and it broke free, as well as the man's hands. They simply broke off at the wrists.

As the gem-like object hit the ground, the man began to crumble in on himself. After a couple minutes, only a pile of dark, fine dust was left. The mage picked up the gem with a cloth and put it into one of his belt pouches. Then they began moving out of there.

Qyrll glances to James as he says, "They discovered we were following them and laid a trap hoping to slow us down. The others are moving with all speed to reach the Empire."

The horror of Dave's fate is almost too much for him to believe. His best friend, life long companion. Good times, bad times, Dave had always been there for him.

The Empire! Anger, the likes of which he's never experienced before erupts. *The Empire took his friend, tortured him and in the end twisted him to their own ends.* **The Empire!**

Looking down at the soldier at their feet, he says with barely controlled rage, "Kill him."

Fifer looks to James who yells, "I said kill him!" He then glances to Jiron who nods. Striking out with his sword, he ends the life of the soldier.

Turning around abruptly, James goes to where Jiron is holding his horse and mounts. The others quickly get on their horses and then he takes off as fast as the terrain will allow him. When they pass by the horses left by dead soldiers, they pause momentarily while Fifer and Qyrll gather them and bring them along. Extra mounts will enable them to cover more ground quickly as they'll be able to trade off from one to another.

James sits impatiently while the horses are being tied in a line and then once they're ready, again bolts away down the trail. He doesn't get too far before Qyrll comes to the fore. "Let me take the lead," he says.

With a glare of irritation, James acquiesces and allows Qyrll to once more lead the way. After all, he knows the way back better than the rest. Also, he picked up on the ambush back there before any of the others.

They ride hard throughout the rest of the day, only pausing once in a while for the call of nature and to swap horses. Jorry has to help Uther down off of his and onto another when the time to change mounts comes. When he does, he takes notice of a growing red stain that's gradually spreading from the point of entry. "You okay man?" he asks, worried. His friend's face is pale and drawn.

Getting up onto the fresh mount, Uther grunts and then says, "You worry too much."

"Be right back," Jorry tells his friend and after receiving a nod, walks over to where James is finishing cinching the saddle on his spare mount. "Uther's not doing too good," he says.

Glancing back, he sees Uther in the saddle sitting quiet and still, which isn't like him. "Anything we can do for him?" he asks.

"I don't think so," Jorry replies. "All this riding is hard on his wound. It isn't going to heal."

"Might be a good idea if you two take it slower," he says.

"But you'll need us," insists Jorry.

"One more sword won't make any difference," he explains. "Besides, Uther couldn't defend himself now even if his life depended on it. And in a little bit, it may. You two follow along behind as best you can and then head back to The Ranch."

Glancing back to his friend who's sitting askew in the saddle, he says, "I hate leaving you."

"I know," James says in understanding. "But at times, circumstances dictate for us to do that which we don't want to."

"You be careful," Jorry tells him.

"We will," he assures him. "You just take care of him."

Jorry nods then returns to the side of his friend.

Once Qyrll has assisted Jiron in mounting another horse, they all mount and get going. When the others notice Jorry and Uther not moving to keep up with them, James explains the situation.

Making good time, they reach the shore of the large lake. The sun is almost down but no one even thinks about stopping. It's going to be another clear night and they would rather travel slow than possibly allow the soldiers to get any further ahead of them. But they've all been up for over twenty four hours now as it is.

James calls for a brief rest so they can all get a little sleep. Catching them quickly will do them little good if they're all so tired they can't take them on effectively. They don't stay very long, merely five hours or so before they're off again.

Another couple hours finds them approaching the first river they encountered after leaving the mine area on their way to the ruins. Qyrll takes them upriver until they reach the ford then crosses over. On the far side, he stops and gets off his horse.

The others come toward him as he bends over and examines a pile of horse manure. Standing up, he says, "Looks like they camped here last night. Might not be more than a couple hours behind them."

"Then what are we waiting for?" Fifer says as Qyrll gets back in the saddle.

Turning his horse to head downriver, Qyrll leads them on.

As he follows behind Qyrll, James continues to ruminate about Dave, their life together and the tragic end of it all. His anger, which at first had burned like a white hot sun, has cooled a little and he can approach this in a more rational manner.

Last night he was all for razing the entire Empire to the ground, destroying all its cities and citizens. But now his need for vengeance is more directed against the ones responsible for this, the leaders behind the Empire. He feels slightly ashamed of himself for wishing harm on the innocents; the women, children, those who are not part of the war machine.

Once they return to the lake, the going becomes steadily easier and they're able to increase their speed. The foothills afford much more gradual terrain than the hilly, forested region they just came from.

"The mine we passed on our way out is just ahead," Qyrll announces after the lake is an hour behind them.

"Good," says James. "If the mine is just ahead then we'll be on roads from this point and may have a chance of catching up with them."

It isn't long after that when through the hills ahead of them the road leading from the mine to Ironhold appears. Qyrll moves onto the road and then breaks into a gallop as he turns in the direction Ironhold lies. The others follow suit.

Riding hard it takes a little over an hour before they crest a hill and Ironhold appears below. "There they are!" Miko cries out.

Just entering the town are over two dozen riders, and they're riding hard.

"Heya!" James says as he kicks his horse and races down toward the town.

"James!" Jiron cries out as the rest gallop to keep up with him.

Not heeding Jiron's cry, James races at breakneck speed down toward the town. All he can think of is Dave and the Empire's role in his demise. Red begins clouding his vision as the pent up rage begins to take control.

The soldiers have disappeared among the buildings before James even closes half the distance. Which way they went is hard to tell but only one road leads out of Ironhold to the south and that's where they've got to be going.

With the others trying to catch up, James lays along his horse's neck in an attempt to decrease wind resistance and increase speed. He closes the distance with the outskirts of town rapidly and finally shoots down the street between the outlying buildings.

Ahead of him is an intersection and when he reaches it, crossbow bolts fly from the street to the right. He becomes aware of his danger too late and one bolt takes him in the leg while four others strike his horse.

The horse stumbles and throws him from the saddle. He flies through the air and slams into the ground ten feet away. Instantly, he erects his shield around him just as another volley of bolts flies at him. They strike the shield and are deflected away.

His nerve endings tingle when he begins detecting the workings of magic. Looking around quickly, he sees the mage emerge from the side street and come toward him. In his hand is the Star. His troops set up a blockade to prevent the others from coming to his aid as bolt after bolt is fired.

Jiron and the others are forced to retreat from the deadly volley. They quickly backtrack to the edge of town and then their group splits, Jiron and Qyrll going to the right and Miko and Fifer going left.

James gets to his feet, his right leg from which the bolt is still protruding barely able to support him. Thankfully it's only embedded in the muscle and didn't hit the bone, although the pain it's inflicting is almost unbearable.

The tingling sensation suddenly spikes as the Star pulses and a wave of force strikes him. His shield is little protection from an attack of this magnitude and he's thrown backward where he strikes the side of a building. His lungs freeze from the impact and it takes him a couple seconds to get his breath back.

The mage's soldiers are keeping guard against the appearance of James' comrades, the crossbowmen and soldiers lining the streets.

Crumph!

A massive explosion rips apart the street upon which the mage is standing, several of the soldiers adjacent to him are thrown into the air. The others stagger from the concussion of the blast.

When the dust clears, the mage is standing unscathed.

Crumph! Crumph! Crumph!

Three more explosions erupt beneath the soldiers this time, James targets them to better enable his friends to come to his aid.

A sudden spike in the tingling and an explosion similar to those he used on the soldiers erupts beneath him. His shield protects him from the brunt of the impact but he's still thrown to the side. Landing on his injured leg, he drives the bolt deeper into his thigh, eliciting a cry of pain.

Using the side of the building for support, he works his way back to his feet as he turns to see the mage approaching. Behind the mage, Qyrll suddenly appears on horseback with Jiron right behind. They begin wading into the men disoriented from the explosions, Qyrll's swords from the vantage of the horse's back are deadly as they fell man after man. Jiron, though only having his knives and tied to his saddle, is just as deadly.

At the sound of combat behind him, the mage turns and sees his men beginning to be cut down. From the other side, Miko and Fifer join the battle as they begin taking out the remaining crossbowmen before they have a chance to unleash their bolts.

James sees the mage turn toward his friends and raises the Star.

Crumph!

He unleashes the magic and the building beside which the mage is standing suddenly explodes outward. A shimmering field immediately encircles the mage as the building sags and then finally collapses on top of him.

The mage taken out of the battle, James turns his attention to the remaining soldiers. Despite the increase in pain, he bends over and picks up stones and begins throwing them, taking out soldier after soldier.

He's takes out his third when the rubble covering the mage suddenly explodes upward and the mage comes to his feet, again unscathed. A large section of stone wall comes flying toward him from the blast and he dodges out of the way to avoid being crushed. The stone smashes into the building right where he had been leaning and creates a large gaping hole.

Fifer is fending off the attack of one soldier when the eruption takes place. He's hit by one of the flying stones in the side of the head. Stunned, he's unable to counter the sideways slice which strikes him just above the knee, severing his leg. Crying out, he topples to the side.

Jiron, momentarily free of attackers, sees him fall. Kicking his horse, he lurches toward the soldier moving to finish off Fifer.

James struggles against the pain the bolt in his leg is inducing as he tries to remain on his feet. Turning to face the mage, he again feels the tingles just before a fireball roars to life over the mage and comes hurtling toward him.

Unable to move fast enough to avoid the impact, his shield flares once again into being. With a roar the fireball impacts with the shield and he's immediately engulfed in intense heat. Every breath is agony as the heat from the fire coating his shield burns his throat with each inhalation. Changing the aspect of the shield, the interior begins to cool as the shield counters the effects of the fire. With a sudden pulse, the shield emits a blast of frigid cold and dispels the fire coating it.

As the flames recede, he sees the mage with the Star ablaze in his hand. A frown crosses his face as his eyes narrow and the tingling once again spikes.

"Fifer!" Jiron exclaims as he rides to his rescue. The soldier stands ready to meet his charge and at the last minute, Jiron throws one of his knives. The soldier dances back to avoid being struck by the knife only to be bowled over by the horse.

As the soldier falls to the ground, Jiron takes his remaining knife and cuts the rope securing his broken leg to the saddle. Swinging off his horse, he lands on his good leg just as the soldier regains his feet.

Smiling, the soldier advances on this man with only one good leg who's only wielding a solitary knife.

Nearby, Fifer groans as the blood is pouring from his severed leg rapidly.

Jiron makes ready to meet the attack, realizing he'll not likely survive it. From behind him, he hears the roar of a Parvati war cry as Qyrll races from where he's just finished off his opponent and is coming to his aid.

The soldier's eyes widen when he sees the Parvati bearing down on him. He slices out at Jiron who manages to deflect the blade and then Qyrll is there.

Lashing out with his small sword, he draws the soldier's sword to the side then follows through with his longsword and the battle is joined.

Leaving Qyrll to finish off the soldier, he hobbles over to Fifer. From the looks of it, he's already lost a lot of blood, a pool has formed on the ground at the base of the stump of his left leg. His face looks ashen as he glances at Jiron's approach.

Kaboom!

A massive explosion erupts from over where James and the mage are battling, the concussion knocking him to the ground. Glancing back, he sees several buildings in the vicinity beginning to collapse. Whatever is going on over there, he hopes James is able to deal with it or they're all dead.

He crawls over the rest of the way to where Fifer lays and removes the belt from around his waist. Securing it around the severed stump, he cinches it as tight as possible to reduce any further blood loss.

"I think it's too late," Fifer says.

"Nonsense," Jiron says. "You'll be fine.

"Liar," he replies with a weak grin.

Jiron glances around the battlefield and as far as the mage's soldiers are concerned, the battle is over but for the one Qyrll is fighting. Miko is nowhere to be seen, he hopes he isn't lying dead among the others in the street.

"Just hang in there," he says to his friend. He and Fifer have known each other many years, both grew up in the fight pits of The City of Light. Reunited shortly after the fall of the City, they've been together ever since. A stalwart companion and one Jiron would hate to lose.

From the battle between the mage and James, a crackle and sizzle can be heard. Then another explosion followed by the collapse of yet another building. Smoke begins issuing from the area as the buildings start to be consumed by flame. He longs to go to James' aid but he knows there's little he can do with his leg the way it is.

A cry rips through the air and Qyrll's opponent falls to the ground. Pulling his longsword from the dead man, Qyrll surveys the battlefield. Seeing Jiron with Fifer he moves toward them.

"Go help James!" yells Jiron as he points to the swathe of destruction the magical duel has produced.

Nodding, he wipes his swords on a dead man's shirt and then puts them in their scabbard. He then races toward the budding inferno to see what he can do to aid against the Empire's mage.

Jiron glances to Fifer and fears he may be dead when he sees his eyes are closed. But the rise and fall of his chest reveals he still lives.

Since this duel with the mage began, James has done little more than be on the defensive. The power of the Star gives the mage incredible power and endurance, by rights he should be all used up. Instead he acts as if throwing all that magic around has had little effect upon him.

Around him several buildings are aflame and the heat is beginning to become unbearable. Through the heat's haze, he sees the mage approaching, the Star raised up before him. So intent on James is he that he fails to notice a figure emerge from a nearby building being consumed by fire.

The figure runs directly toward the mage and strikes out with his sword, only to encounter the shield surrounding him. His sword strikes the shield and rebounds sharply. The unexpected resistance causes the sword to fly backward out of Miko's hand.

Turning to greet this new threat, the mage sends a wave of energy toward his attacker and tosses him backward into the burning inferno. He then turns back to James, the Star in his hand.

The Star's light sparks a memory, one from an earlier time when he met the shade of the long dead priest of Morcyth:

The ghost nods its head and replies in a far off sounding voice, "Greetings, fellow priest of Morcyth."

James glances at the medallion he's holding and replies, "I'm not a priest."

The apparition reaches out, almost touching the medallion he's wearing. "The glow only comes from his priests, it manifests for no others," the ghostly voice says.

And then another:

"That should hold for now," Fifer says. "A priest could do a better job, but we're lacking one just now."

"You could do it," Jiron says.

James turns his attention back to Jiron and sees him staring at him. "I'm no priest," he protests.

"Didn't you say that the spirit of the long dead priest of Morcyth called you one?" he asks.

"Well, yes he did," he replies. "But he was mistaken."

"I don't think so," he says. "You're in good with Morcyth, after all you bear the

Reaching into his shirt, he pulls out the medallion and holds it up. "Morcyth! Lend me your aid!"

Just then the tingling sensation spikes again and a beam of light flares from the medallion. Shooting forth, it impacts with the Star and the spell the mage was about to cast fails to materialize. Keeping the medallion before him, the beam of light remains constant as it goes from the medallion to the Star.

The mage cries out as a glow erupts from the Star in his hand and then begins coursing down his arm. A scream of pain is torn from his throat as the glow continues to advance down his arm and to his torso, just as the darkness had moved down Dave's.

In seconds the mage's entire body is engulfed in the glow. One final scream, a blinding flash and the glow disappears. The Star falls to the ground.

Nothing of the mage remains, no clothes or anything. It's almost as if he vanished.

Getting to his feet, James shuffles over to where the Star lays in the street, making sure to keep his distance. He doesn't want to suffer the same fate as Dave. "Miko!" he cries out when he remembers him being thrown into the burning building. Glancing in that direction, he sees the building suddenly collapse, the fire having destroyed its load bearing beams.

"Miko!" he cries. Leaving the Star where it lays, he moves as best he can toward the raging inferno. Suddenly from around the building, he sees Qyrll emerge with Miko. Hair singed off in two places and covered in soot, he has an arm around Qyrll's shoulder for support and gives James a grin when he sees him standing there.

"Is it over?" he asks.

"Looks like it," James replies.

"James!" Jiron yells.

He turns to see him there by Fifer. They make their way over to them and he asks, "Is he alive?"

Nodding, he replies, "Yes, but not much longer." He looks pleadingly at James.

He knows what he's going to ask but this is something he dares not mess with. Jiron can see the denial in his eyes and grows crestfallen.

"The Star could save him," Miko suddenly announces.

"What?" Jiron asks.

"The Star," he repeats. "It comes from the gods, it should be able to."

Hope rekindled, Jiron looks to James. But James shakes his head, "I dare not touch it."

"But…" he begins then once more becomes quiet. Perking up again, he glances to Miko. "You can do it!"

"Me?" he asks incredulously. "Are you crazy?"

"You've held one of these before," Jiron says. "If any of us can make it work, it's you."

He glances to James who shrugs, "I don't know. If we do nothing, Fifer will die. Healing comes from the gods, at least I think it does. Here on this world anyway. I can't touch it so another must try and Jiron's right in that of everyone here, you have the best chance of making it work."

"But what if it kills me like it did with your friend Dave?" He glances down the street to where the Star sits in the dirt.

"It won't," replies James. "Of that I'm positive."

Just then Fifer gives out with a groan and his chest stops moving. Getting up, James says, "Move!" to Jiron as he makes it to Fifer's side. Hoping he's doing it right, he begins CPR. A series of presses upon the breastbone and then breathe air into his lungs. After breathing into his mouth the first time, he starts pumping his chest again and looks to Miko.

Miko returns the gaze and nods. Getting up, he hurries over to the Star. Before he reaches it he slows down, fear making him hesitate. "Hurry!" he hears Jiron holler. Heart beating fast, he takes the last few steps and then reaches down. His fingers hesitate a moment before grasping the Star.

Frozen in place, he waits for death to take him but nothing happens. Sighing in relief, he turns around and hurries back to Fifer. "What do I do?" he asks as he kneels next to him.

"Grasp the Star, pray that he will live and that his wound will heal," James says. "Be sure to invoke Morcyth's name." Bending over, he grabs Fifer's nose as he breathes air once more into his lungs.

Taking the Star in both hands, he glances around at the others then closes his eyes. In his mind, he beseeches Morcyth to come to the aid of his friend, to return his life and heal his wound.

The others watch as he sits quietly with eyes closed. His lips move silently as he prays for Fifer to live. A gasp from Qyrll brings James' attention to Miko and he stops what he's doing when he sees a shining nimbus surrounding him.

He can feel the magic from the Star, different than that which he feels when mages summon it. The glow from the Star envelopes Fifer and they all move back as they watch what happens.

For a full minute, Miko and Fifer are surrounded by the glow. Finally Fifer's chest begins to rise and fall as he starts to breathe on his own. The wound where his leg was severed begins to close as new skin forms over the wound.

Fifer's eyes flutter open and the glow dissipates.

"You did it!" Jiron says excitedly. To Fifer he asks, "How do you feel?"

"Tired," he replies softly.

"You go ahead and rest then," Jiron tells him and he closes his eyes again.

Miko glances from one to the other. "You okay?" James asks him.

"I…I think so," he says. "I feel good." The patches of singed hair on his head are as new, as are the other scrapes and injuries he had before healing Fifer. The Star healed him too.

James smiles at him and then grimaces as the pain begins throbbing again from where the bolt is sticking out of his thigh. Jiron comes over and asks, "Should we have Miko fix you too?"

Shaking his head, he says, "I wouldn't use that" pointing to the Star, "unless it was a matter of life or death."

"It's got to come out," Jiron tells him.

"I know. Best do it now."

"Qyrll, give me a hand," he says.

The Parvati comes over and braces the leg while Jiron gets into position. "Ready?" he asks.

"No, but go ahead," James tells him, gritting his teeth in anticipation of the pain to come.

Jiron grasps the bolt and after a quick glance to Qyrll, pulls it out which elicits a cry from James. Blood starts to flow and he tears off a strip from his shirt to pack the wound. Then he tears off more to tie it securely.

Around them, the old buildings continue to burn. The wind whips the fire from one to another as more and more become engulfed. "We better move," James says as the smoke begins to thicken.

Qyrll lifts Fifer from the ground and Miko, after placing the Star within his pouch, does his best to help both James and Jiron to follow.

They find a building still in good shape away from the consuming inferno and one unlikely to be in the fire's path. They bring in wood for a fire and decide to wait until Uther and Jorry show up before returning to The Ranch. While James waits for their arrival, he amuses himself by watching those passing through Ironhold as they take in the damage. He can just imagine the wild stories that are going to be circulating about this latest unexplained incident, a third of Ironhold has fallen to the fire.

The morning of the third day since their return to Ironhold, Fifer is doing much better though James and Jiron still are unable to get around very well. Miko seems his same old self, at least having the Star in his possession shouldn't bring about negative consequences such as the Fire had. James wonders what effect having been exposed to two focal points will be to his friend.

Near noon, horses can be heard approaching and before they make it to the door to see who it is, Jorry's voice can be heard. "…had to be here. He's the only one who could level a town this effectively."

"Well, maybe," replies Uther. "But remember that time when we went…" He cuts off just as James comes walking out the door, using a long stick as a crutch. "Thought you might be around," he says as he glances around at the devastation.

"Just waiting on you guys to show," he says.

"Everything taken care of?" Jorry asks.

"You could say that," replies James. "Come on in and we'll fill you in."

Jorry dismounts first and moves to help his friend who's still having trouble despite the days since the injury happened. "…it was way up north when we ran across the Wizard of White Pass…" he continues his story as he enters the building and the door closes.

Epilog

Walking across the snow covered ground, he makes his way to the meeting. Only four of them know of this meeting, secrecy is of the utmost importance. The inn isn't far and he's soon through the door and up to the room where the others are waiting.

"Good," James says as soon as Jiron enters, "we're all here." He waits until Jiron has taken his seat before he begins. He glances around at them one at a time, Jiron, Illan and Delia. "You and I are to be the only ones who know of what transpires here," he says.

They each nod in turn. "Why all the secrecy?" asks Delia. Her caravan is parked in the usual place, that clearing outside of town. When she received word that James had needed to talk to her, she quickly made her way back to Trendle.

"There's something which happened when we found the Star that I have yet to tell anyone," he begins. "I had a vision."

He relates to them the vision in detail. His meeting with Igor, the High Temple of Morcyth and all that was said, including that the temple must be rebuilt in The City of Light.

"But how are we to do that?" Illan asks when he's through. "The Empire now controls not only the City but a good portion of Madoc. And from what intelligence I've been able to gather, they are likely to launch another offensive in the spring in an attempt to break the defenders at Lythylla."

He remains silent for a moment, knowing what effect his words are about to have. "Come spring, when the passes are once more clear, we travel to Madoc."

"And then?" Jiron says in the silence that followed.

"And then," he says glancing from one to next, "we drive them back to the Empire!" The death of his friend still weighs heavily upon him. *They say paybacks are a bitch? Well this is going to be like nothing the Empire has ever seen before!*

The adventure continues in:

<u>Shades of the Past</u>

Book Six of The Morcyth Saga

Check out the epically adventurous worlds of fantasy author

Brian S. Pratt

The Broken Key Trilogy

Four comrades set out to recover the segments of a key which they believe will unlock the King's Hoard, rumored to hold great wealth. Written in the style of an RPG game, with spells, scrolls, potions, Guilds, and dungeon exploration fraught with traps and other dangers.

Dungeon Crawler Adventures

For those who enjoy dungeon exploration
without all the buildup or wrapup.

Fans of his previous works, especially *The Broken Key*, will discover *Underground* to be full of excitement and surprises. First in a series of books written for the pure fun of adventuring, *Underground* takes the reader along as four strangers overcome obstacles such as ingenious traps, perilous encounters, and mysteries to boggle the mind.

Ring of the Or'tux

In many stories you hear how *'The Chosen One'* appeared to save the day. Every wonder what would happen if the one doing the choosing bungled the job?

In *Ring of the Or'tux*, that's exactly what happens. Hunter was on his way to a Three Stooges' marathon when in mid-step, he went from the lobby of a movie theater to a charred tangle of stone and timber that once had been a place of worship. From there it only gets worse for the hapless *Chosen One*. First, an attempt to flee those he initially encounters (who by the way are the ones he was sent there to save), lands him into the merciless clutches of an invading army (those whom he was supposed to defeat).

The Adventurer's Guild

Jaikus and Reneeke are ordinary lads whose dream in life is to become a member of The Adventurer's Guild. But to become a member, one must be able to lay claim to an Adventure, and not just any adventure. To qualify, an Adventure must entail the following:

1-Have some element of risk to life and limb

2-Successfully concluded. If the point of the Adventure was to recover a stolen silver candelabra, then you better have that candelabra in hand when all is said and done.

3-A reward must be given. For what good is an Adventure if you don't get paid for your troubles?

Jaikus and Reneeke soon realize that becoming members in the renowned Guild is harder than they thought. For Adventures posted as Unresolved at the Guild, are usually the ones with the most risk.

However, when they hear of a party of experienced Guild members that are about to set out and are in need of Springers, they quickly volunteer only to discover to their dismay that a Springer's job is to "Spring the trap."

If they survive, membership in the Guild is assured.

CPSIA information can be obtained at www.ICGtesting.com
Printed in the USA
BVOW01s0750240414

351472BV00002B/518/P